PRINCE OF LUST

CHILDREN OF ASMODEUS
BOOK 1

DAME RHO

Prince of Lust

By

Dame Rho

This is a work of fiction, names, characters, places, and incidents either are the product of the author's imagination or are used fictitiously. Any resemblance to actual persons, living or dead, events, or locales is entirely coincidental.

AI STATEMENT

No generative artificial intelligence (AI) was used in the writing of this work. The author expressly prohibits any entity from using this publication for purposes of training AI technologies to generate texts, including without limitation technologies that are capable of generating works in the same style or genre as this publication. The author reserves all rights to license uses of this work for generative AI training and development of machine learning and language models.

DEDICATION

For every single one of you who were taught to feel worthless, those who hurt in silence even though that weight was crushing you, and those who thought they were broken because of it. I'm here to tell you, you're not. You're just as you should be, scars and all. This is for you.

FOREWORD

Thank you for picking up this book. It means so much to me as a debut author. I'm so grateful you're taking a chance on an unknown.

I've included a short glossary at the end. Though I don't think the reader needs it at this point, you may be curious, nonetheless.

You're in for a sexy treat with this book. I hope you enjoy Vale and Oliver's journey. I'm so glad you're here.

TRIGGER WARNINGS

Do read trigger and sexual content warnings. I care for your well-being. I don't want you to be triggered by my book. I love my book, but you may not and that's absolutely okay. Protect yourselves, you know what you can handle. Consent is important!

Trigger Warning

References to child abuse (not on page), torture, physical and emotional abuse (after the fact)

Flashbacks

Profanity

On-page depiction of a panic attack with racing thoughts

Religious trauma, cult

Fictitious religious ideas (cult)

References to alcohol/drug use

Mental illness

Female oppression and loss of identity

Mutual stalking

Sexual Content Warnings

<u>Sexually explicit content!</u> Please, take this seriously, this is **not** a

clean read. Assume nothing happens behind closed doors. You've been warned.

Dub/Con

Sexual threats

Dirty talk

Sexual thrall

Sexual obsession

Questionable morality

Hymen worship, play

Size difference

Bodily fluid exchange

Domination

Primal play

Blood play (Vampirism)

Voyeurism

Exhibitionism

Unsafe sex

Loss of virginity

Painful sex

Biting

Feeding

Lust—because Asmodeus should have a warning label.

Edging the reader with a 40% chance of making up for it. Sorry for the rug burns.

IN DREAMS

Dark shadows coalesce into monstrous creatures whose eyes glow blood-red. Every single face resembles my father. Those intimidating eyes watch me from every angle with hatred and a rage so great it stabs into me like vicious claws. *I'll take it out of you!* The voice is a deafening shriek but strangely, none of them move their lips. *It's in you!* Breath is stolen from my lungs while the shadows bay and slither around me. They wrap around my throat just like his hands do, like snakes tightening their coils around their prey. I fear death. I fear it every time he does this to me. I cry out as best I can, forcing my voice out into the nightmarish hellscape around me, but they won't stop. He never does. No matter what I do, I can't fight the shadows. I can't pull them off me, even as my light starts to fade. I'm going to die.

Another monster appears, dark but different. Instead of a shadowy-like creature, he's solid, tall with broad, muscular shoulders, a severe masculine jaw, and skin as dark as night. He's studying his surroundings with confusion, knotting the space between his brows. This one doesn't belong here, he isn't like the others. When our eyes meet, his are completely black, just like the rest of his skin and the strong wings that sit high upon his back. He narrows his gaze on me, studying my face while his lips perk up in a peculiar smile.

"Would you like me to kill them for you?" the new monster asks.

"Please, help me!"

He beats back the shadows, grabbing ahold of them and shattering them like glass. The remains sparkle like glitter in the air around me. The sun rises in the dreamscape and I run to this new monster. He kneels before I get to him and I wrap my arms around his neck.

"I will protect you, little one."

My cheeks are wet with tears as I look up into his alien-black eyes that look nothing like a human's. I pull away from him, intimidated but still grateful for his help. "Are you a demon? My father says I have a demon inside me. Are you my demon?"

"I am Ashmodai," he says proudly, slamming a fist over his heart. "And you? What is your name now?"

"My name's Vale Granger. I'm six and I live in Atlanta, Georgia."

He stays on his knees for a moment, head tilting, and a frown on his face. "It's always the wrong time, isn't it?" he says, and I want to hold him because deep in his eyes, he looks so sad. I want to wrap my tiny arms around him again and make him feel better. He stands tall, turning to go.

I'm so scared my hero will leave I scream out, "Please don't go. They take my breath. I don't want to die again."

Those words stop him. He turns around with wide, worried eyes focused on me. "Have you died before?"

I nod my head.

"Do you die outside your dreams?" he asks me.

I nod my head and grab my throat. "Thank you for making them go away. I don't like them. They hurt me."

He kneels again in front of me, pressing his thumb into my cheek, lifting the corner of my lips into a silly smile. "Do you know who all monsters fear?"

"I don't, maybe the demon Asmodeus. I don't like monsters, they scare me."

"They're all afraid of the biggest, baddest monster of them all. Me."

I smile up at him. "You're not a monster, you're beautiful. Can I braid your pretty hair?"

My words make him smile, and he turns around, sitting down on the ground while I stand between his wings. I've never seen a man with such long hair. It's longer than mine and a unique color in the sunlight, it shines blue. When I'm finished, a long braid hangs between his shoulder blades, all the way to the base of his ribs.

I sit down beside him, and the dreamscape changes. We sit upon a mountainside in a field of delicate wildflowers in a rainbow of colors. I grab one daisy after another, knotting them together as best I can for a crown. I stand up, reaching out to place it upon his head. "You're a prince."

He reaches out and a mirror appears before him. He smiles at his own reflection. When I see it, there's a stranger there that doesn't match his facade, but the mirror fades quickly, and I forget all about the stranger.

"You are my fiery Princess," he says with a grin.

"I'm not a princess."

"You will be."

INTRODUCTION

Summers spent in Silver Springs were a peaceful escape from the real world, but he showed up like a sudden, violent storm, crashing into me, hellbent on breaking the lock which held all my emotions at bay. So powerful, he could devastate me with a simple, indifferent look. He was the Prince of Lust and an inspiration of dark hungers better left unexplored by innocent young women. Oliver Byron was as beautiful as he was unobtainable, and I wanted to gain every single piece of him. He would be mine, he just didn't know it yet.

1

HAPPINESS IS A HOT GEORGIA SUMMER

VALE

It's late June, the third week into my summer vacation. I'm eighteen years old with all kinds of ideas for what this summer will be, but my Gramps has other ideas of course. "Hard work is what your generation doesn't understand. Someone has to teach you, and since your parents are off saving the souls of nonbelievers, I'm the only one you have. You're going to succeed in life if it's the last thing I do."

Gramps is still mad at my mother. She gave up her dreams to marry the pastor of the Flaming Righteous Church. Gramps doesn't have a problem with religion, he has a problem with how my father forcibly removed his daughter from medical school so she could do God's work. He's mad because my mother was kept away from her family for being deemed nonbelievers. Gramps says that's the hallmark of a cult.

I don't actually believe in my parents' religion, but it affects every aspect of my life outside of Silver Springs, Georgia. It's hard to leave it behind, even harder not to hear my father's words echoing inside my brain every time I do something he'd deem evil, which is almost every-thing because I'm female.

I don't want that life. I don't believe in their uptight beliefs or the way they force those beliefs on others. I'm not an atheist though. I know there's something out there, I just don't know what it is yet. In my opinion, not knowing is just fine, even if I have to hide that fact from my parents.

What I want is freedom from my upbringing, freedom from my parents, and eventually I'll get it. I want to live out fantasies denied me. Most of all, I want to be free, free to make my own decisions, free to do whatever it is I want.

That's why I'm grateful for the summers I've spent with my Gramps in Silver Springs. It's the safest place because my parents aren't here, and they never will be. Not once had they shown up while I was with Gramps. Without the threat of them, I'm able to breathe for a little while, to live in peace. I don't have to worry all day about my simplest actions. Or about my father exorcising my demons with his hands wrapped around my throat, stealing the breath from my lungs. I don't live in constant fear of stepping over some perceived line. Living without that fear is something I hold precious in my heart. I've needed these summer breaks to survive.

Unlike my parents, Gramps wants me to know who I am, what I like, what I don't like. He tries to broaden my horizons. He wants me to experience life and to be happy. During our summers together, he'd play music he didn't like just so I could figure out what I liked. He'd buy records from the flea market and play them in his office. When I'd played punk records for hours on end in his office, he hadn't gotten mad—though he did move the record player to my bedroom where he wouldn't have to hear "Blitzkrieg Bop" one more time.

Then, when I fell in love with the universe as a child, my Gramps had a platform built onto the screened-in sleeping porch connected to the old master suite on the top floor so I could study the stars. Grandma and Gramps had bought me my first telescope after a trip to the U.S. Space & Rocket Center. It wasn't allowed in my parents' house and immediately found its way into the trash when I got home. My time was better spent on my knees, in prayer, not gazing at the stars, my father had told me. So I stopped bringing my telescopes and equipment home. They stayed with Gramps for safekeeping.

I'd learned my lesson. I learned to shut down when I went back to them. I wore a disguise whenever my parents were near. They didn't know me at all. It was safer that way. But every year, I'd look forward to the summer and the freedom of staying up late and staring at the stars from my own little observation deck.

Gramps is the best man I've ever met, and I respect him. He never pushes me too hard or too quickly to be something I'm not. And though he's overprotective in some ways, like with his "no dating policy," he understands my lack of freedom at home. I have very few responsibilities here, and he lets me get away with almost anything as long as I let him shape my moldable mind. Mostly, I'm to read a list of books he advises and do a few chores. Other than that, I'm free. I get to hang out with friends, and I'm even learning to drive.

Gramps has been teaching me for the last three years—four if you count the go-karts we used to zip around the neighborhood in back before his hips started hurting. Even though my parents had told us no when I wanted to get my license the summer I turned sixteen, it was the first thing Gramps asked me about when I got off the plane in Atlanta this summer, "When are you going to take your driving test?"

But my father had warned me before I left, promising no end of punishment if I went against his rules. I have nothing left to take away but my weekly calls to Gramps, and they're what got me through the long weeks locked in my bedroom, so I can't break their rules, not if it means losing him.

There are only two houses left in the historic district on Hudson Street, and they sit right next to each other in a lonely neighborhood at the edge of the "boonies" as my best friend Kat calls it: Gramps's and the house next door. The rest of the neighborhood, where once beautiful Victorian homes used to stand, is now just large, vegetation-covered lots, with tall, spindly pine trees dressed in silvery-green Spanish moss that dances in the breeze.

Those lots always reminded me of some postapocalyptic world, one where most of the humans are gone, and nature is a silent beast, sleeping underground and waiting for its perfect moment of sunlight and dew before bursting to life and taking over once again.

Gramps's house stood like the last bastion of humanity fighting off an intimidating forest with manicured lawns and brightly colored flower beds. It isn't scary for me though. I like the peace, and how it muffles the existence of nearby town.

The other house, however, had once been a grand Queen Anne, but after the previous owner passed, some thirty years ago, it's sat abandoned. With no family, it went up for auction several years back, making my grandfather worry that the neighborhood would be developed, but even after someone bought it, it's still sat empty. The decorative spindles had long been broken and splintered, and part of one cantilever had caved in, leaving pieces hanging morosely. The clapboards had aged to dark brown, and the rot was covered in the green algae that builds up in humid climates. Even with all that damage it was beautiful.

Some of the kids in town said it was haunted, and I found myself staring up at its second-floor windows, at how dark they were, and wondering if the ghost there was friendly or something more sinister. I didn't really believe there were ghosts in there, but I'd seen enough horror movies that it made me anxious, so I stopped looking at those darkened windows for fear that one day there would be something there, looking back.

I'd hoped someone would finally move into the big house, then, last year, Gramps told me about the construction crews from New Orleans that came to restore it. With a little work, it's now the prettiest house in Silver Springs. Grand it is once more, painted in varying shades of bright white, robin's-egg and navy blue. Witch's caps of gray slate with bronze finials at the tips stand tall over the gabled roof. The decorative spindles are back in all their delicate glory. Garlands wrap around the front, and the paintwork is so detailed I can't wait to see it up close.

They had manicured the front lawn in bright green turf grass with flower beds of contrasting deep red roses. The color of the roses pop against the delicate blue of the lacy clapboard. The eye's drawn to the intricate facade, the inviting bay windows. I long to see the interior, knowing it'll be just as spectacular as the painstakingly revived facade.

"I think they're here." I'm jerked away from my childhood memories by an excited Gramps.

I jump off the porch swing and watch as the movers close up their trucks. One by one, they drive onto Hudson Street like good little soldiers in a row, not even offering a wave when Gramps nods his head toward them.

One person stays behind, a man we'd seen before but who hadn't introduced himself. He stands out like a sore thumb. Where the movers wore white coveralls and gauze slippers over their work boots, this man wore dark, fitted suits, no matter the temperature.

Today, the man had parked behind Gramps's old, powder-blue Mustang, so Gramps dons his hat and leaves the porch to greet him. They chat for several minutes while I watch a Carolina wren searching for insects amongst the hydrangeas in the flower bed. I look up just as the stranger hands Gramps a large gold envelope. Just like that, he's gone, turning left onto Hudson Street and heading for the highway in town. Once again, the house next door is empty of life.

"What was that about?" I ask.

"He's a lawyer all the way from New Orleans. He wanted me to pass the key along to the owner. Their flight was delayed, and he couldn't stick around. He didn't want to leave the keys on the porch. Didn't think it was safe. Who would steal it out here?" he says flabbergasted, taking offense to the lawyer's insinuation that the neighborhood isn't safe. It's the safest neighborhood in Georgia—we're the only ones in it.

2

THE NEIGHBOR

VALE

Gramps and I are setting up the grill when a classic convertible speeds down the driveway with an obnoxious roar. It's a silver flash of round yellow headlights, moving faster than anybody should over those new, brown, faux cobblestones in the driveway. Gramps goes inside to get his hat, always the gentleman. He's old-fashioned, always putting on a hat when others are around, unless he's eating a meal of course.

"Excuse me," I hear a deep voice from behind me. I turn toward the driveway as a man steps over the flagstones that join the two properties. I wave him over while I light the gas grill.

I hear his soft footsteps as he makes his way onto the partially covered wooden deck. "One second," I yell out as I close the lid to heat the grates.

One moment, I'm old Vale, a young woman who'd never been moved by the sight of another human being, never felt attraction to a person fueled by hormones, then the next, I'm new Vale, who's barely able to breathe at the sight of the man who's standing in front of me. My teenage hormones aren't ready for the sight of him. Fuck me sideways! He's gorgeous. I suck in air as I study him, my brain needing more oxygen than normal just to function, to process what I'm seeing.

I focus on his fine leather shoes. Then up to his black slacks, up to his thick, muscular thighs, to the junction between his legs, where the outline of his . . . oh no. I force my eyes not to linger as they make their way up to his tailored white dress shirt with bronze buttons stretching over broad shoulders. He looks like some sort of gentleman spy from a movie.

How is he real?

I look up to his pale pink lips. The bottom lip is thicker than the top with a perfectly sculpted Cupid's bow. His lips look so kissably soft and purely sexual. Those lips could convince you to sin with only a whisper. I swallow hard and force the air out of my lungs as my heart races. His face is youthful, unlined by age, yet there's a world weariness in the deep set of his eyes, a haunting look as he stares at me. He can't be more than thirty years old.

Those eyes flash and glow a unique, mossy-green even through the gloom. His eyelashes are long and dark like the thick hair which falls over his forehead in silky waves. Some of the hair is tucked haphazardly behind one ear, the rest is pulled back behind his head at the base of his strong neck.

"Are you okay?" he asks as I memorize each shadow on his face. Then there's the dimple that begins to form as he smirks at me, seeming to know all too well what I'm feeling.

I don't like how he's looking at me with a predator's gaze, so laser focused on my every move, as if at any moment he'll rip me apart. It feels like he can see right through me, into my thoughts, my desires, and I don't like it one bit. I don't like being seen.

I'm ill-prepared for the man before me. I don't know how to act around an attractive man because I've never seen one. That's not an exaggeration. I've never been interested enough in a man to pay attention, but I'm paying attention now. I don't know if I'm capable of looking away.

I shake my head trying to regain control and focus my brain. It doesn't get the memo. Shadows start to slither around him, and I question whether I'm having some kind of stroke, maybe a complete mental collapse. Am I hallucinating? I shake my head again. He's not supposed to look like this, a virile, young man, in the prime of his life. I'd wrongly assumed that the new neighbor would be an old man like Gramps.

"I'm sorry. I just . . . just assumed you were an old man, dude. Not . . . shit. I'm sorry. I'm Vale. My Gramps has your key. Hold on just a second," I tell him as my body chooses flight instead of the fight response. I try to escape, but he steps in front of me, blocking my way.

"I'm Oliver Byron, your new neighbor," he says, then takes my hand, even though I didn't offer it. I'm unable to breathe when he covers my hand with his. His touch is like electricity, sizzling through my nerve endings. It takes all my strength to stand there and let him look at me.

I search for an answer that'll make this entire situation make sense in my head, but I can't find it. I feel his gaze and the touch of his hands, warm over mine. My body jolts to life, as if waking up from a long, deep sleep. My heart pounds in my ears and my breathing becomes even more erratic. He studies me with an intensity that's so raw and overwhelmingly real.

Why is he looking at me like that?

I stare wide-eyed at his seductive mouth when he smiles. I want to touch his lips, feel them against my skin. This is insane. I thought this kind of shit only happened in romance novels. But it's real. It really happens to people, love at first sight. I think I'm in love. My thoughts are racing a million miles a second and it's hard to grab one and roll with it.

I've never had a crush on a boy. The few guys I met in Silver Springs were hardly engaging, most of them flat-out annoying. They never looked like this, like him. I don't know what's happening to me. I don't know why I'm reacting this way.

He lifts one hand from mine and tilts my chin up with his thumb so I'm forced to meet his gaze. This man won't let me hide in my crazy thoughts. "It's nice to meet you, Vale." My name said from his lips is my true demise. It sounds like a prayer, calling to something long buried inside me. I don't know what to do.

"Did I hear *Byron*?" Gramps asks from the kitchen and it's enough to snap me out of my reverie. I pull away quickly, trying to shake off the lust I knew better than to feel.

It hurts to sever the connection between us. My chest aches and burns as I'm torn away from the warmth of this god, torn from the heat of the sun. The cold of darkness envelops me, and tears prick at my eyes. I'm ashamed of the way I've been acting.

His whole demeanor changes as he stands up straight, pulling his shoulders back; I hadn't realized he'd stooped to get closer to me. As Gramps approaches, he turns toward the back door, the look on his face changing unbelievably fast. No longer are his eyes that of a dangerous predator, now they reflect nothing but effortless confidence and ease. I'd never seen anything like it.

"Nicholas Dalton," Gramps introduces himself and holds out his hand while he looks at Oliver.

Oliver grabs his hand and shakes it with a smile. "I'm Oliver Byron, your new neighbor. It's nice to meet you. The solicitor left a note that you would have my key," he says in strangely accented English.

Gramps deflects the inquiry about the key with a question. "Any relation to George Gordon?" His question makes Oliver chuckle, and I roll my eyes.

"I'm not sure actually, but my mother's a huge fan. She named me Oliver George Gordon Byron. I'm fluent in Lord Byron because of her. A true education should be filled equally with that of the pious and the libertines."

Gramps just met his soul mate. They begin talking about books and it turns out Oliver's a fan of the classics. Of course he is, he's perfect. They sit down next to each other, continuing their conversation. I watch, fascinated by the ease in which they befriend one another. How did my grandpa learn to be so confident and well-spoken with others? I'm at best awkward around most people, preferring to fade into the background. I'm quiet and reserved because I've had to be.

I step over and nudge Gramps on the shoulder. I don't want to be rude. "I'm going to cook," I say, my voice like a whisper so not to disturb their conversation too much.

"I'm sorry, Vale. Oliver, this is my granddaughter, Vale Granger. Would you like to join us for dinner?"

Oliver looks up to me and nods in agreement, a smirk on his lips quickly gone by the time Gramps turns back to him. A tingle shoots down my spine, making me more nervous. I rush away to the kitchen to grab the three steaks that've been covered with coarse salt for hours. I'm back at the grill a few minutes later while Gramps rummages around in his office for a good scotch to share with our guest. Oliver lounges on one of the old iron patio chairs, one leg bent at the knee, the other kicked out straight and long while he thumbs through his phone.

"Mr. Byron, how do you like your steak cooked?" I ask, turning away from his long legs and gorgeous face. I need to pay attention to what I'm doing.

"Call me Oliver, and I like it very rare," he says as I jump away from him in fright, not expecting him to be so close when I turn around. My body goes stiff at his nearness. How on earth had he moved so fast, so silently?

"The bloodier the better."

Oliver gets so close I can smell the scent of his skin. It's a heady musk with warm notes of amber, sandalwood, and a subtle sweetness of vanilla. His scent alone makes me feel high. He leans closer near my neck. He's overwhelming all my senses, and I worry I'll faint if he doesn't move away from me. I'm powerless when I hear his audible inhale. We aren't touching, but as he breathes in it's like he's stealing a part of me.

I let out a sigh the moment he stands up straight, then steps away, but I'm not relieved, not in the slightest. My body's on fire and an ache has formed down low. It's a new ache, one that thumps like a heartbeat between my legs, the intensity almost frightening.

"I can hear your heart hammering away in your chest. It's so loud," he whispers so softly I question whether I imagined it or not. He walks away before Gramps returns. I turn back, pretending to focus on what I'm doing.

I grab the plate of steaks and pop them on the grill. It's so hot now I can't leave them on for more than a minute and a half per side for fear that Oliver's steak wouldn't be exactly what he wants. I don't know why I care. I shouldn't, we just met, but Gramps says we should always try to make a good impression on people.

I need a do-over!

I grab the tray and the solid metal tongs which I left beside the grill. I hear my skin sizzle. "Fuck!" I yelp, dropping the tongs with a clatter. I run into the house, turning on the kitchen tap and thrusting my hand under the cold water. My eyes are closed when Gramps and Oliver enter behind me.

"Are you alright?" Gramps asks, and I nod my head.

"The food!" I screech, pointing at the deck and he steps outside, leaving me alone with Oliver who watches me intently.

He glides forward, grabbing my hand from under the water, then inspecting it. The burn starts to sting as the air touches it. I try to pull back, but he holds on tight. "I'm sorry," he whispers, and I wonder why he's apologizing.

Why would he be sorry when I'm the klutz?

My fingers are turning red while he inspects them. The burn is worse than I thought; it's going to blister. "Why are you sorry?"

Oliver looks into my eyes. He looks genuinely apologetic, his eyebrows knitted together and his lips in a thin, worried line. I try to pull my hand away once more, but he doesn't allow it. His fingers tighten around my wrist. I swallow hard, intimidated and not knowing how to get my hand back.

"I distracted you from your duty," he says the last word with extreme enunciation, his accent so thick it makes me wonder where he's from, but I'm too overwhelmed to ask.

My cheeks heat in embarrassment. He knows how I'm feeling. I can see it in his eyes. He's felt it before, but I still have to deny it. Oliver Byron is too old for me, probably. He's a man and I'm a girl. I can't have any sort of relationship with him. Not even if I wanted it.

He lifts my hand to his lips. There's a moment where I think he's going to kiss my wounds like my grandmother used to. Instead, at the last second, he shocks me by pulling my index finger into his mouth. He suckles it into the warm depths, stroking his tongue over my finger.

He does the same to the next finger, then the next until he's staring down at my pinky. That finger receives a gentle kiss.

"I'll leave that one, so you'll remember," Oliver says before turning and walking out the door like nothing happened. But it did happen, and he's shaken my world to its foundations.

I stare after him as I release the breath I'd been holding. What does he mean by remember? How could I ever forget what he did? I take a second to think about it. Does he want me to remember his lips? The warm, wet recess of his mouth maybe? Or does he want me to remember how awkward I am? I'm unsure.

I look down at my hand and see the strangest thing. There's only a single, tiny burn on my pinky. The rest of my fingers are fine. They'd been so red where I'd wrapped my fingers around the metal tongs, I was sure they'd blister. What the hell did he do? Maybe he had magic saliva?

I rub some vitamin E oil on my pinky, then wrap it in a Band-Aid before rejoining them outside. Every few seconds, the stinging from the burn reminds me of his mouth, his tongue, his warm breath against my wrist. The way his lips wrapped around each finger gently as if not to hurt me further.

I eat in silence as Gramps and Oliver chat. I don't listen to them. I can't pay attention. When I can't eat another bite, having eaten my meal but not tasted it at all, I clear the table without a word. I take the dishes into the house as both men thank me for the food.

I stand at the sink, cleaning plates and stacking the dishes. I'm on autopilot, shut off and trapped by the thought of his mouth, his lips that touched me. Did I imagine that whole scene playing out? Had it all been in my head? Have I gone crazy? Surely, no one would ever do something like that.

I'm looking into the darkness through the kitchen window when Gramps stumbles in. "Don't be rude, Vale. Say good night. I'm off to find Oliver's keys."

When I step out, there's a soft breeze blowing, the scent of pine trees and incoming rain on the air. I close my eyes, turning my face into the breeze, feeling it against my heated cheeks.

"Do I frighten you?" Oliver asks, his voice too close. He can't be so close to me. I won't survive.

I open my eyes, but I don't turn around to look at him. "Do you want me to be frightened of you?"

Oliver lets out an audible breath. "It might be better for us both if you were, but no, I don't want you to be afraid of me. I'm sorry about how I've acted around you. You were unexpected, to say the least." He walks around to face me.

His words make me smile. "Well, let's agree on that. I was under the impression you were some old, retired architect who was obsessed with how the walls must be plaster and not drywall," I say, then laugh. "Then you show up and look like this and well, I'm surprised, at the very least."

His smile is so big his bright white and perfectly straight teeth show. He's so beautiful. "Not retired or an old man, but you had me pinned, I'm an architect. There's a lot of plaster in there, admittedly." He chuckles and his cheeks flush as if he's embarrassed by that fact.

Oliver takes my hand in his. He presses his lips against my skin where my knuckles meet the back of my hand. He lingers for a second or two while he watches my reaction. When he lifts his head he asks, "How old are you?" That predatory look is back, and I can feel the fire encasing me. He shouldn't be asking me that. It seems too personal for some reason.

"I'm eighteen, almost nineteen. How old are you?"

He drops my hand as if it's burning him, then closes his eyes and shakes his head. "I'm too old for you, sweetheart, way too old, but one day I'll be just right." I take his words as a seductive promise, that one day the timing would be right for both of us. It's a promise I won't stop thinking about for the rest of the summer, possibly the rest of my life.

What does he want from me?

I'm about to ask when Gramps steps out of the house and I lose my chance. I say good night to Oliver and Gramps before running upstairs to my room. Who knew I could feel so shattered by a person? Oh, how quickly he's stolen my peaceful summer. I think he's broken my brain, maybe on purpose.

3

I LIKE BIG THORNS

VALE

Gramps has been spending a lot of time next door with Oliver. For the last two weeks I've barely seen him. From the time he eats breakfast till dinner, he's at Oliver's house. It's the first week of July, fireworks are still booming off in the distance. Do you know what I've been doing? Not a damn thing! Fuck all, as Kat likes to say. It didn't help that I'd already read the entire book list Gramps gave me.

I may seem a bit bitter, but I'm not upset about Gramps. He needs friends too. Oliver though, he could use less friends. He's had people over there every night since he moved in. They're out there partying till the wee hours of the morning. Sometimes they're so loud I can't sleep. If I do get to sleep, they wake me up.

I'm not spying on him. I'm not! When it's not raining, I'm out looking at the stars from my observation deck. I can't help it, I see it all from there. Then there's the window over the kitchen sink. I watch out of boredom while I do the dishes. People rush in and out all night. I see all the laughter and joy I'm not a part of. I rarely feel a part of anything, but I don't think it used to bother me.

Oliver Byron is the definition of the worst neighbor ever, but I can't seem to get him off my mind. That man turned my world upside down from the minute I saw him—since he kissed my hand and strangely licked my boo-boos better. I can't get over it, his lips, his mouth, that tongue that makes me think of things better left unsaid and unthought. Ah!

I want to hate him. I do!

Three days ago, while I was cleaning my telescope, I saw Oliver carrying what looked like small trees from a delivery truck in front of his house. He's not out often during the day, probably sleeping off hangovers, but there he was, wearing heather-gray exercise pants as if he'd been caught working out when the delivery truck arrived.

Back and forth he went, taking those plants around to the back of the house. He'd stroll back up, a smile on his gorgeous face, and I couldn't look away. I had to watch him because you could see the bulge in the front of his pants. With every step, my eyes were drawn to it. I studied the way that bulge moved and settled. It was fascinating, the way he moved, the way he would glide over the faux cobblestones effortlessly, not a care in the world.

Well, wouldn't you know it, he caught me watching him. The bastard! He saw me staring at his crotch, unable to move my limbs, completely lost in the way his dick bounced with every step. I couldn't look away until he'd stopped moving. God only knows how long I'd been staring, mouth agape, before I noticed he wasn't walking away anymore. He grabbed his dick in his fist and squeezed it like it pained him. I couldn't stop the treacherous gasp that escaped from between my lips.

When I looked up, over his tight white T-shirt that clung to his muscular chest, almost see-through with his sweat, I'd thought I was going to have a heart attack. My heart felt like a battering ram in my chest, trying to escape its bony prison.

He was so hot, literally covered in sweat from the southern Georgia heat. It did nothing, ABSOLUTELY NOTHING to detract from his gorgeousness. I looked up at his face, his eyes covered by black-on-black sunglasses, and he smirked!

The bastard smirked!

I hate him! More than hatred, I want him.

I've never wanted to have sex with anyone before. Sex is more like an idea to me. Sexuality, overall, is an idea. I know how it works between a man and a woman, the logistics of body parts slotting together, which part goes where, but outside of that disassociated, anatomical, textbook-like diagram or the other extreme of emotional, romance novel-like odes to body parts connecting *with love*, it's just a thing I contemplated on occasion. An act that means so much to some and so little to others.

That's not how I feel about Oliver. I want things from him I've never wanted before. I can't stop thinking about him, what his mouth would feel like, his lips, his tongue. Oh, God, help me.

At night, when I'm actually able to fall asleep because his visitors have finally dwindled to a couple carloads, he's there in my dreams, taunting me with his very presence. He's torturing me and he doesn't even know it.

I hate him!

I also want him so badly I'm disgusted with myself. I wish I'd never felt this way. Oliver Byron is too fucking sexy to live next door to my Gramps. Why are they hanging out so much? Surely, they don't have enough in common to actually be friends. Gramps is old, no offense to him. He's earned every single one of those wrinkles, but he can't be friends with Oliver-fucking-Byron of all people.

Oliver's a hedonist! He's a weirdo. I shouldn't want him. I know better. I shouldn't be judging him either, but I can't help it. I might be a tad jealous. My desire sets me up for failure. I'm not supposed to feel things like this. I need to fight it. Is that what my father would say? Or is this just a setup to the pain I'll endure by falling for Oliver's attractiveness? It doesn't matter because suddenly Hell looks like an extremely inviting neighbor.

I've seen all the men and women he invites over, half-dressed or not even, just wearing bathing suits and a smile. I've seen a man kissing Oliver's neck while his head was tilted back against his front door. I've seen the late-night chases through the front garden. Seriously, I've seen Oliver chase full-grown, half-naked men and women through his front yard. I watched with the sole hope that one of them would either step on a thorn or fall into his perfect, blood-red rose bushes so I could smile again.

I can't help imagining what he does to them when he does catch them. As pissed off as I was to hear them laugh while I was reading *Jane Eyre*, I'm curious too. I can't help it. Deep inside, in the place I hide so well, I want to be chased by him too. Who wouldn't? I want him to chase me, catch me, and fuck me against the garden wall. It's as simple as that.

My brain's completely on board for his kind of debauchery and it shocks me beyond belief. I want to deny it. I don't want to feel like this. I swear it's like he has some sort of power over me, although my father would say it's the other way around. And he might be right because the dreams I've had are all my brain's doing, all my fault.

The dreams about him are something else. They're intensely sexual. He does things to me in these dreams I didn't know existed until I wake up and ask the internet. God forbid anyone see my recent browser history. When I wake up it feels like my body's spasming in protest, wanting to be back in that dreamworld, with him. Back where he's mine for just a little while.

Oliver Byron is going to drive me insane or turn me into an alcoholic. More than once, I'd sat in Gramps's office chair, staring at the unlocked liquor cabinet. If I got wasted, maybe I'd have a few hours of being blacked out, a little bit of peace. But I'll be honest, not a touch of liquor has passed my lips. I can't steal booze from Gramps and that's the only way I'd be able to get it.

It doesn't matter how much I despise Oliver. He's so hot, and my desire for him is changing me. I've even started trying to touch myself because my body's in a constant state of absolutely insatiable desire. It doesn't work though. Nothing cools this fire inside me.

I'm going to be miserable for the rest of the summer, especially without Kat here to chat with. I can't tell her all about the new, beautiful asshole who lives next door. I can't tell her how much I want him, even if I already know exactly what her advice would be.

Kat would say, *Vale, get your ass out of bed and go join that party.*

Go make him want you just as much as you want him. Wear that new bikini and make him beg for it.

That's how Kat is—brave.

I can't do it.

Though if Kat was here, I probably would. She'd lead the way, and I'd follow just to experience life through her. Honestly, I'm surprised I've never been arrested or gone to jail for her goofy antics. Maybe I should consider myself lucky for that.

She's gone this summer so she can be with her boyfriend Clark. Funny thing about Clark, the name itself was a joke from his parents as their last name was Kent. I've called him Superman since the day we met, then again so did everyone else. I can't believe Clark talked her into it. Somehow he got her to go hiking, camping, and being in the woods for an extended period of time with no mani-pedis, no makeup, and no plumbing. Had Kat herself not told me her plans, I wouldn't have believed it.

Kat had bagged the perfect man, or so she claims. She swears he's her future husband. Clark isn't perfect, but he has abs, is popular, and plays football. Who could resist him? He's the teenage girl trifecta.

I believe she'll ditch Clark at some point since he's her rebound from her fuck-boy Brandon, who's the inspiration behind our aspirations to go full-blown "hoe-bag" in college. Brandon and Clark had nothing in common. Clark's the golden boy of Silver Springs, nothing like the excitement she's talked about wanting. However, she says she loves him, and I need to support both of my best friend's dreams. The dream of being a future hoe-bag and the future Mrs. Kent. What are friends for if not to support each other's dreams, right?

This summer has been a complete dud without her. I'm being driven mad by a hottie next door while my best friend is off getting eaten by a grizzly bear in the backwoods of Colorado with her boyfriend and his parents. She could be here with me, worrying about my attraction to Oliver and what I'm going to do about it, but no, I have to fend for myself.

My small world has shrunk down to this house and its immediate perimeter. It feels like there's no escape from the boredom that's currently my life, and there's no escape from my desire for Oliver, which just compounds my frustration. This is the first time this has happened, attraction and being alone over the summer. Maybe that's why I can't stop thinking about him. Who knows?

I wish I could regain a little bit of that inner peace from previous summers. I'd accept a tranquilizer at this point. I'm serious when I say I'd do almost anything to have a little peace away from the memory of his lips, his tongue. Fuck, not again! Why me? Why now? What have I done in my life to deserve such a karmic fuckup?

4

THE GREAT RED SPOT

VALE

I can feel him over there, next door, that huge presence like a beacon calling out to my soul. I know he's there and it's driving me insane. Sometimes I wake up covered in sweat, my mouth wide open, calling out his name. "Come to me," my voice cries out. *Help me put the fire out, Oliver, please*. He never comes, and I don't think he should.

It's so bad I almost called my mother for advice on how to stop these devilish thoughts. That's true desperation. I've searched the internet for ways of clearing my mind, such as meditation and staying busy, but nothing helps. He creeps into my thoughts over and over again.

His beautiful face, his warm hands, those long, pianist's fingers flash into my mind. Every thought, every memory makes me yearn for more. I want to be the one he touches. I need to be the one he touches. I need to be touched.

I've gotten intimately acquainted with my own touch because I constantly ache for him. It does no good to try though. It's like I'm trying to put out a fire without having anything to smother it. It burns brighter the more it consumes. Oliver Byron consumes me entirely.

And to make things even more odd, I think Gramps has his first man crush on someone who isn't Winston Churchill. Turns out Oliver has a rare book collection. He has an entire library actually. He's offered Gramps a job cataloguing it. I think that means organizing, but I'm honestly not sure. I knew Gramps would take the job as soon as he told me about it. I think he's been bored in retirement, and he lives for bookish things and the written word. He's inspired by it, and from time to time, he even writes for himself.

Yeah, Gramps is my hero. He understands me, this lust for life, to experience it all before I'm lost to adulthood. He understands there's a person inside me who needs to break out. I hide a lot of my truth from everyone, but Gramps sees me, and he knows what I want to be, the end goal. Unlike my parents and their awful punishments though, he doesn't lock me away when I screw up. He doesn't destroy everything that gives me joy.

Instead, Gramps likes to lecture, he was a professor after all. He'd use those lectures to make me understand my screwups. He'd help me see my errors and turn things around. But I don't get in trouble anymore, and he knows no one's harder on me than me.

Truly, it's my own fault for being bored and alone. I could go into town. I could try to make friends, but I don't. Most people exhaust me. I don't like to pretend that I'm like them because I'm not. My life experience is different from other young people. How am I supposed to explain to people that my father's a cult leader whose hobbies include exorcising demons out of evil women and listening to his own sermons because he likes the sound of his own voice? See? Not normal. I'm lucky to have Kat, I just wish she was here.

Gramps says I can come with him to Oliver's, that I've been invited, but I can't bring myself to go. I'm embarrassed Oliver caught me checking him out. I don't know how Gramps would react if he knew I had a crush on the new neighbor. He might send me back to my parents early. I didn't have many rules but no dating without permission was a big one.

Then I might end up in the middle of nowhere with my parents as they preached to people who were better off without a new religion.

No, I can't lose my place here. I need my summers at Gramps's house. I hope to live in Silver Springs next year. I want to go to school where he taught. I've got plans, you see. I can't mess up now.

It's late, nearing dawn, when I step out onto the sleeping porch in a black tank top and gray shorts—God forbid my parents ever see me in something like this. I open my telescope's lens caps, I'd modified it with dual eyepieces, then look up toward the sky, searching, hoping to get a good view of Jupiter. The sky's clear, and I locate the right area.

The Great Red Spot is visible. I step back and start dancing. "Yes!"

Finally! I've been trying to catch it all summer, but I've never gotten the timing exactly right or there's been too many clouds from the heat and humidity.

I reach out beside me, searching for the stool that normally sits beside my telescope. I step back and look around for it. It was just there. Then I notice the shadows, how they move and slither like smoke. Someone's watching me. I feel the scream sliding up my throat about to burst free and I take off. They grab me and turn me around so fast my head spins.

I look up at my assailant and that's when I realize it's Oliver.

"Shh," he whispers with a smirk.

"What are you doing here? How did you get up here?" I back away from him, trying to calm my racing heart. This man is going to kill me. He's going to give me a heart attack if he keeps showing up . . . if he continues existing so near me is more like it.

Oliver takes a single step back. My heart calms immediately when there's distance between us. This is getting really embarrassing. I can't control my reactions to him anymore than I can control the way my body pumps blood, it's ridiculous.

"You haven't been to the house yet. Nick said you've wanted to see it since I started the remodel. He told me you came out here every night to look at the stars, so I thought maybe if I invited you in person, you'd actually show up."

Oliver leans against one of my bedroom windows. He watches me. He seems so at ease. I grab the stool and make my way back to the telescope. I look through the double eyepiece and let out a loud sigh. "Fuck!" Clouds had rolled in and I hadn't noticed because he was there. I missed it, again.

"Stop saying fuck, Vale," Oliver says. I sit up straight, covering the eyepieces and draping a tarp over the telescope. I feel the temperature drop and I know it's going to rain soon. I can smell it in the air now that the breeze is blowing. The rain would be here within minutes.

I'm angrier than I should be when I face him, but I appreciate the sudden anger over my usual anxiety around him. I press my fists to my hips and close the distance between us to get into his face.

"Don't tell me what to do. I can say and do whatever the fuck I want. I'm not a child. If I were, you still wouldn't be the person who could make demands of me," I explain as my blood boils.

I didn't often let the anger in but when I did, I'd chide myself for screwing up. The rage made me brave, to the point of being stupid. I'd say and do things that were different than my normal self. I became something altogether different. That's exactly why I tried so hard to keep all those emotions at bay. I don't want to be crazed by emotions. It's better to keep them under lock and key, especially around my parents. To hide it is to survive it. And I've relentlessly trained myself not to react, but Oliver brings it out of me.

I don't know what I expect, maybe an apology from my hot as sin neighbor, but I didn't expect the way his eyes light up in challenge or the way he starts to circle me. I follow him with my eyes, turning as he steps around me. Then he's there, in my face, taking all my oxygen and pushing me up against the house. His body is flush against mine, his warmth seeping through the thin fabric of my clothes.

I suck in a breath, desperate for air as he leans in. I feel his hot breath against my face, his eyes alight and inhuman but so completely, utterly fascinating. He's so beautiful he doesn't seem real, he can't be. Men like him don't exist and yet, he's right here.

Am I ready for this man, this beautiful fucking demon that's haunted me? The man who's wound my body up tight, making my heart speed with fear and lust. I wish I understood why I reacted like this toward him. I'd never been a lust-filled girl. I'd been curious about sex of course, but it hadn't filled my every waking hour like it did with Kat. I could see beauty in others, but it had never hit me so hard, not like this. I coveted this man. My body ached, on fire for the first time with absolute hunger.

"I can see very well that you're not a child. I see the way your body reacts to me. I can see your nipples poking through that thin top right now," he says and I want to hide. I try to fold my arms over my breasts, but he stops me. "Don't cover yourself. I want to see."

Oliver looks down at my breasts. He's right. I'm not wearing a bra, and my nipples seem to be trying to bust through the thin fabric. Heat rises in my cheeks as he studies my body. He's too close. My nipples ache, my breasts feel heavy. It's like two nerves coming alive for the first time, leading directly between my legs, pulsating with each beat of my racing heart.

Oliver doesn't touch me, but his breath is warm against my flesh, even through the cotton. A strangled sound escapes my throat, and my body trembles with the adrenaline pumping through my veins.

"You're so sensitive to me. Your arousal is like wine, and I'm a thirsty drunk ready to suck up every . . . single . . . drop," he says, his eyes locked on mine. He leans his cheek against my breast as he kneels in front of me.

What the fuck is happening?

I take in a stuttering breath. "What are you doing?"

He smiles like a predator, his canines a bit overpronounced like a sexy vampire from a romance novel. He looks sinful there in the dark, kneeling in front of me as if he worships me and me alone. This isn't a normal situation. It's too much. This man isn't normal, not in the slightest and sadly neither am I.

"When you touch yourself, do you come quickly?"

My cheeks redden with embarrassment and my body shrinks away, put off by the inquiry. "I don't do that," I lie.

I've done it a lot lately. Every time I think about this man my panties get wet and I touch myself worrying if I should be so wound up over a man I barely know, who's way too old for me and way too hot to ever be interested. Though his presence right now proves me wrong. I think Oliver wants me. Is that even possible?

His smile gets bigger. It's a hungry smile, his eyes hooded with lust.

"There's no shame in it. I fantasized about you the night we met. I stroked myself with thoughts of that long, copper hair wrapped around my fist as I kissed you. I thought about how your eyes would light up when I make you come for the first time. I thought about how your fingers tasted in my mouth, about what the rest of you would taste like."

I try to move away because of the fire in his eyes, the desperation in his words. The truth is it scares me. I fall onto my ass with a wince, unable to hold myself up as he chuckles and sprawls out across the wooden slats. He looks up at the sky. I lay back and join him in his gaze, though I turn back to watch him after only a few seconds.

He's quiet now, and close, but nowhere near as close as he was when he was kneeling in front of me. I'm so embarrassed, and a part of me wants to run away. There's more of me that hopes he'll continue his dirty talk. I want those filthy words whispered in the dark.

Oliver faces me and our eyes meet, but this time it's different. His face is calm, less amused by my reactions. His look is serene as he soaks up the darkness around us. It's as if he really wants to disappear into it. He flickers in and out of the shadows as if he's one with them. He revels in the tendrils that wrap around him like a lover.

"I'm sad because you didn't think about me after I left. I can't get you out of my head. I've thought of little else. You haunt me."

I know the feeling.

I look away, swallowing hard. It's probably a trick, but his words make me feel like I'm not so alone in all this desire. I try to make out Antares flashing behind the churning clouds. I can't look at him when I say it. I can't.

"I've thought about you. I've fantasized as well. I've touched myself thinking about you more than once, but it's embarrassing to admit it. I can't believe I'm telling you now. This whole situation is crazy. You're a man and men don't look at me the way you do. No one has ever looked at me the way you do."

There it is—the truth. I knew he'd never let me hide.

I hear him move, and I turn to face him. His body is facing mine and, like a mirror, I change my position mimicking his. He reaches his fingers out to pull a loose strand of my hair away from my face. His fingers a whisper light touch over my cheek.

"You're wrong. I bet many men look at you the same way. They want you. I want you," he struggles to admit it. He pulls back when I wish he'd get closer.

I reach out, pressing my hand over his heart. He stiffens at my touch, narrowing his gaze on my hand and I question what I'm doing. I worry my bottom lip with my teeth. He looks almost like my touch hurts him.

"I want you," I admit and his eyes grow bright in the darkness. Those beautiful swirling eyes.

I take my chances, and I climb over him. I'm straddling his waist as he stares up at me. He doesn't move. He looks pained, jaw tight as I wiggle my hips over his. His palms are flat against the wooden slats, fingertips digging in as if he has to hold on to something or he'll be tempted to touch me.

I'm nervous when I press both hands to his chest and shift my hips. He groans as I move against him, our bodies barely separated by fabric. I feel him grow and thicken below me. It's exhilarating, knowing that it's a reaction to me, to my body, to the way I roll my hips against him.

"Vale, stop."

I'm hurting him. I must be. I stop moving, even though I'm filled with such desperation for him. My hips jerk against his before I can stand, it's my body's last ditch effort to find some sort of release.

I'm going to stand up, but I'm thrown onto my back, hitting so hard that I'll have bruises tomorrow. As he settles between my thighs, the Oliver from five minutes ago is gone. His eyes have gone dark, black veining out from his pupils, bleeding into the whites of his eyes. He looks like an angel damned to Hell, falling as I watch, unable to stop his descent into madness. He's moving on instinct not intellect, an animal, a beast. He presses his hips against mine, grinding down hard between my legs.

His movements are like the purest oxygen, breathing new life into me as I moan and squirm below him. I become a different person, unable to ever be that innocent girl again as I fail my parents and embrace this sin. This is who Oliver truly is, a demon tempter. Just like the demon Asmodeus. Just like me.

I'm shaking below him, my body high on adrenaline that's telling me to escape, but I can't because I'm completely entranced by him. He leans in, his fingers running through my hair, grabbing hold, and pulling my head back, forcing my body to arch to his will. I can't breathe. I can't move. I feel so much. The bulge in his jeans presses against my wet shorts, stimulating my clit. He feels so good.

He presses his nose into my collarbone. I can hear his sharp intake of air as he breathes me in. That's exactly what it is, he's breathing me in, taking part of my soul with him, into him, stealing it away. When he grinds himself against me, I cry out for more, aching, almost at that pinnacle, almost dying from pleasure as he takes and takes, big gulps that consume my soul with each deafening inhale.

His tongue darts out, licking a hot path up my neck, over my chin, and to my lips. His lips are gentle, his hip movements monstrous. His eyes are closed tight as he kisses me. I've never been kissed before. The most beautiful man I've ever seen is hovering over me, grinding against my body as his hot lips press against mine.

I'm alive. I feel everything. I lick at the seam of his lips, opening for him, tasting him for the first time, sweet like chocolate, spicy like sin. His eyes open and they're still dark, his pupils overcoming the deep green; they're almost entirely black now. He leans back almost as if to stop, but I follow. I press my lips against his. Our lips move together as if in a dance.

"Please," I whisper against his mouth. "Don't stop."

He changes his mind and opens his mouth, pressing his tongue into mine, curling it against my own as I gasp. One of his hands is running down the length of my body to the junction of my thighs. His hips move and he grabs those tiny shorts by the crotch and rips them apart. It's prophetic because I get the feeling he's going to tear me apart too.

I smile against his lips as I raise my hand, thrusting it into his hair and pulling out the band. His long hair falls around his face. It's much longer than I realized. As I reach to move it back, his finger thrusts up inside me so hard I scream. All the air in my lungs escapes as I stare up at him with wide eyes. His finger is long and it feels so deep, pumping in and out. He watches my face, lost in lust and hunger maybe, I'm not entirely sure. He studies me as he adds another finger. I cry out as he stretches me more.

"Are you sure you'd want to take a monster inside you?" he asks with a sadistic grin.

I can't imagine wanting anything else. I'll die if he stops now. My lips are dry as I try to speak. I arch my hips forward when he curls his fingers inside me. "Yes, I want you."

It takes all my concentration to move my hand from his hair. I reach toward the button on his jeans. I've never done this before, and I'm clumsy. I claw at the button, barely able to get it through the hole, but all my dreams center around what's inside his pants right now. How he'll use it to take this bone deep ache away.

I need him inside me. I have to have him.

I free the button and pull the zipper down, which is much faster in comparison. I reach my hand inside his pants and curl my fist around his hot length. I pull him out as gently as I can. He's bigger than I could've ever imagined, my hand barely wraps around his thickness. I feel the moisture seeping out of me where he's still pumping his fingers.

"Will you fit?" I ask innocently. I look into his eyes as I begin to explore the bulbous head of his cock. It's wet just like me.

"I'll make it fit. No one will ever make you come like I can. I'll make sure of it. Now spread your legs for me," he demands. I comply, getting hot over his words.

Oliver steals his cock from my hands. He strokes down, then back up, pumping it in a tight fist, then wiping the wetness all over the tip. He can't take his eyes off the spot between my legs.

I'm quaking with excitement. I can't look away. I can't stop the reaction I'm having to him as he jacks himself off in front of me. It may be the hottest thing I've ever seen. This is what he did when he was alone, wanting me.

He braces himself on one hand and rubs the tip against my slit, getting it soaked in my juices. I'm ready to explode. I need him. Right now. I tilt my hips up to greet him. "Please, I'll do anything," I beg like a slave to his whims.

He doesn't warn me. He forces his hips forward and spears me on his cock. It's tearing me in two. He pulls out once, that wide crown holding me open, then he thrusts again and his hips finally meet mine. I scream into the night as the rain comes, light at first, a few drops against my overly heated skin. It hurts where he's torn me open. It hurts and stings so bad, like salt in an open wound. The pain opens the floodgates for my tears.

Tears fall down the sides of my cheeks as he stares at me from above. He wears a monstrous grin, a smile I should hate. The smile of someone who enjoys my pain, who revels in it. It's a smile that should scare me, at the very least it should intimidate me, but it does nothing of the sort.

"You're mine now," he says. And with those words he tastes my tears, licking up my pain, feeding on it like a devil.

I nod my head in agreement as he starts to move. I feel every thick, painful inch of him. I wince every time he bottoms out inside me. It's excruciating how hard he fucks into me. But no matter how bad it hurts, no matter how helpless I feel in those moments, I can't break free from the pleasure that floods me. Somehow, he feels so good. I hope he never stops.

Oliver licks his lips as he pumps in and out of me, grinding when his hips meet mine as if he's trying to make more room inside me. His violent thrusts are all it takes, and I explode around him, tiny stars bursting into my vision as I cry out his name, arching my spine so my body can get closer. Then he's moving fast, inhumanly fast.

"Remember I'm your monster, Vale. I'll fill your dreams full of sexual devotion and loving, beautiful words, but one day you'll understand there's a price for this, this gentleness. This barely whispered pleasure. You'll understand at some point how you've attracted a monster, someone who could just as easily kill you as fuck you till you pass out.

"I'm all wrong for you, but you don't want what's right. I see it in your eyes every time you look at me. I see it in those innocent smiles. I won't be able to stay out of that tight, little cunt now. I want to live inside it and tear it apart. I'll make it hurt so good, baby."

I cry as he abandons all masks of lovemaking and fucks into me like the monster he claims to be. I feel pain and pleasure swirling, becoming one, new. I feel shame and lust. I feel so much with him plunging inside me that I can't take it anymore. I'm over the edge again, making him laugh and rejoice in my pain, my pleasure. He knows I like it. I love it so much.

Then he's kissing me again, lifting my hips up as he pounds inside me, awkwardly stumbling now as if he's lost to a new rhythm. Deeper and deeper he goes, punishing my body for the pleasure he's given. He's lost in it, just like me. He's fucking my mouth with his tongue in the same rhythm as he rams into my hips, then he rears back with a roar, and I see the truth. He's a monster.

His skin turns dark and his fangs lengthen, looking as sharp as knives. Growling, he plunges deep, pressing me harder into the platform. All the veins in his neck stick out as wings lift up and out from his back.

I know this beast. I know him! But he's different, he's never touched me like this.

Then he's over me and I can't think about anything else but how he feels. I wrap my arms around him, holding him to my body, wanting him to stay. He strikes, his fangs tearing into my skin the way his cock tore into my body. He's drinking me down, huge gulps of blood. The world tilts as the rain plunges down against us so hard it stings my skin.

I sigh in love and fear. I let go. I'm free.

"I love you," I whisper. "I'm yours."

The world spins and nothing makes sense. My vision swims, unfocused as the pounding of my heart drowns out all the sound in the world. It beats in my temples, taking my breath with it. I'm dying. I have before.

I can't take in one breath, not one.

This is the end.

I die.

5

THE TRUTH IN THE WINDOW

VALE

I jerk awake, sitting upright in bed, breathing hard. Sweat coats my brow, my neck, and my heart's pounding in my chest. I grab my own neck, searching for a wound but there's nothing there. My vision won't focus through my confusion. I rip the sheets off me as if there are snakes slithering around my body. The feel of the material is too coarse against my overly sensitive skin.

I jump out of bed, running to the sleeping porch, making my way out to the platform and into the pouring rain. The cold rain soothes my heated skin. I search in the darkness for him, but he isn't there. Why isn't he there?

I'm breathing hard as I search, eyes blinking at every rain drop. There's no sign I've been out here tonight. The telescope is covered and the stool is inside the sleeping porch. I don't understand what just happened. It felt so real.

My skin prickles with awareness when my clothing becomes water-logged and heavy with the rain. I glance at Oliver's house. The lights are on. Several nice cars are parked out front in the circle. I'm close enough to see into one set of bay windows. That must be his bedroom up on the second floor because he's there with someone.

Oliver has a woman's back plastered against the wall. I can't look away as he thrusts his hips up into hers. Her legs wrap tighter around his waist, desperately trying to hold on. His pants are slowly falling while he dips his tight ass between her legs, his muscles clenching with each thrust. She's moaning, but I barely hear it over the rain. I see her head tilt back in what I think is pleasure. I'm so glad I can't see her face through her veil of messy blond hair.

He drags her to the window, bending her over and thrusting inside her again. Her hands hold on to the window casing, and her tangled hair hangs over her bent head, reminding me of a rag doll as he slams inside her, just like in my dream. Her body jerks forward, her head slumps farther every time he thrusts his hips.

I take in his chest, barely covered by an unbuttoned dress shirt, his muscles cut like chiseled stone. With every forward thrust the muscles of his abdomen work, clench and release. He's using his entire body to force himself inside her. I trace the outline of a tattoo on his chest as he moves. Though I can't see the entirety of the art, the shape vaguely reminds me of the red dragon on a Welsh flag.

Then I look at his face and he's smiling. He's at ease in this sexual act. His eyes are closed, his head tilted back on a long, graceful neck, and his thick black lashes create dark shadows under his eyes. His face is achingly beautiful, his pale cheeks flushed pink, unaware of my intruding gaze. Is this what it would be like to be with Oliver? Would he look so content if he were inside me instead?

Is the woman enjoying herself as he almost violently plows into her? With her head tilted down, I can't tell. But I don't want to see her. I never want to see her face. This is all wrong. I don't want to know who she is, yet I admire that she gets to experience this—Oliver's attention, his lust. I wish it was mine. I wish he was mine.

He grasps her hips and it looks painful, his fingernails digging into the flesh where her dress is rucked up around her waist. They create a brutal rhythm with one another. He jerks her backward with every savage forward thrust. It looks like she's barely able to hold on.

Her moans are louder now, almost screaming. I hear her cries and somehow that sound, her voice, it breaks my heart. It hurts. There's an intense physical pain in my chest, a burn searing me from the inside. Oliver is a fantasy and nothing more. He's just a dream. He'll never want me. I'm just a girl, no matter how much I want to be a woman.

My hand is over my heart as I take one last look at his beautiful face. It's as if I need to hold my heart inside my chest or all those tiny pieces will seep out into the world, then be lost on the barest wind. I'll never find them again. It'll never be put back together.

Before I can turn away, his eyes open and he looks right at me. I can't move when our eyes connect. He watches me while he fucks her. He licks his lips, then his eyes soften sweetly, like he understands how bad it hurts for me to see this. His head tilts to the side, his jaw tensing, his face pained with something I don't understand.

Oliver leans forward and places the palm of his hand onto the glass. He's asking me something. My body understands the request, and I lift my right hand from my heart. I hold it up as if we could touch through the windowpane.

Then he tilts his head back quickly, baring the long line of his neck again. I hear his groans. I'm so hyperfocused on that beautiful sound it drowns out her moaning. An audible gasp escapes my lips and my thighs clench together.

This is what he looks like when he comes. This is what I'll never know with him. Seeing him like this is a gift as much as it's a curse. I'll remember this beautiful moment forever, be tortured forever. Tears form in my eyes as I watch him pull out of her, pulling his pants up quickly to cover his cock before I can see it.

She staggers away as she straightens her dress to cover her breasts, jerking the skirt down. He saw me watching him. He knows. He looked right at me.

This is so wrong.

What the hell is wrong with me? Why didn't I walk away? Why did I watch?

I'm soaking wet by the time I run inside. I get to my bedroom and lock the doors. I strip out of my wet clothes and dry off as quickly as I can before putting on some pajamas that cover most of my skin. I feel dirty, guilty. I'm ashamed of my lack of control. My heart is pounding in my chest as I wipe the tears from my face. Why did he have to look up at me?

My phone starts ringing. I race out of the bathroom to grab it, worried it'll wake up Gramps. I say hello in a breathy voice unable to hide how shaken I am.

"Did you enjoy watching me," he says with amusement in his voice, and my cheeks flare with heat.

"I didn't mean to. I'm sorry," I explain. And it's the truth. I never wanted to see him like that. Not with another woman. It should have been me.

"Don't worry, I forgive you. I won't tell Nick, but you need to do something for me," he says in a smug tone.

I can't imagine what he'll ask of me.

"Next time you watch me with a friend, I want you to touch yourself. I want to watch you come."

Surely he isn't serious. Is he making fun of me? What a dick!

Anger boils inside me. The flames burst free and I swear I'm taken over by a rage so great I feel like I'm going to explode with it. "You're a sick pervert, do you know that?" I say, stronger than I really am. I'm putting on a false bravado, but it's not for him, it's for me.

"Pervert I may be, but you like it. The way it is between us. I know you watch me. Don't be afraid. I won't touch you, baby. I'll just watch." The way he says he'll *just watch*, makes my thighs clench and my heart beat in double time.

I can't stop the tears that suddenly spill over onto my heated cheeks. I'm sitting on the side of my bed, holding the phone to my ear as I listen to his soft breathing and think about how to reply. "I don't want to watch you with another woman," I whisper. I don't want to tell him what I really think, how I wish it'd been me.

"A man, then? Would you like to see me fuck another man? Do you want to see me get fucked maybe?" he asks, and my mouth gapes open, my cheeks burning. It's the last thing I expect him to say.

"No! Oliver, I don't want to watch you fuck someone else. That's not what I want," I lie, my wheels turning. I wonder what it'd be like to watch, knowing he knows, knowing he likes my eyes on him. I'm a sick person. I didn't agree with my father the first hundred times he told me, but I agree with my father now. I *am* some sort of demon, lost to my desires. Now I know I'm bad, and it hurts.

"You could've fooled me, Vale. What's the fantasy then? What do you want from me?" he asks, frustrated. "I'm waiting."

This sick son of a bitch actually wants me to tell him my fantasy. He's curious, interested in my desires. Though I doubt it. He's probably just messing with me. "I don't think we should talk about this."

"Because you're oh so young and impressionable," he says, then laughs with a callousness I hate. "I think you know better, but you don't care. There's a saying, stop me if you've heard it, that goes, 'You're old enough to know better and too young to care.' Vale, you don't give a fuck and you know it."

If he'd said it any other time, just in a chat, I probably would have laughed and agreed. I did know better, but I didn't care. Oliver sees me so clearly, I feel exposed. I don't know how to hide from him. If he came here right now and spread my legs . . . well, you understand, I'd let him. I wouldn't care if her perfume was on his skin. I'd gladly let him ruin me.

I think that makes me fucked up.

"If I came into your bedroom right now you wouldn't protest. If I ripped your clothes off and pushed you down into those obnoxious pink sheets, you wouldn't tell me no. You'd beg me to touch you," he says, somehow voicing my own naughty thoughts, as if he knew exactly what I'd been thinking.

"If I kneeled next to the bed and spread your legs, opening those creamy thighs. If I licked your slit till you came in my mouth, your sweet nectar on my tongue, you'd let me. All the while you'd beg for more. Do you want to know why?" He pauses for me to answer the question, but I can't say anything, he's fried my brain with those dirty words.

"I'm your fantasy breathed into existence. You want me. You want me to teach you every naughty, filthy, disgusting thing I can do to a woman. You ache for me to do those things to you, and if you'd just dip your fingers into your panties right now, you'd find yourself wet and ready for me. There's no shame in your desire. Whoever taught you that, they're wrong."

"I don't know what to say to you. I can't," I whisper, the tears still coming. My breath hitches, and I'm sure he knows I'm upset.

There's a knock at my window and I look up in fright. He's standing there in the rain. My eyes are huge when he enters through the sleeping porch, through the door I swear I locked. He removes his boots by the door, then he takes off his jacket and drapes it over an old kitchen chair. He steps closer and grabs the towel from the end of my bed, drying his long, dark hair as it falls around his face.

"Why are you here?" I ask, more in shock than anything else. I sit the phone down on the end table, then stare at him. He's soaked and gorgeous, his long hair curling around his jaw and neck. He's so beautiful it hurts to look at him. Why is he here? I don't understand, and I doubt he's going to explain it anytime soon. He's going to destroy me. He's right, I'd let him. Who wouldn't?

6

CURIOSITY OF THE DAMNED AND DEADLY

OLIVER

Vale is beautiful. So innocent, with tears shining in her eyes like she's lost something. She thinks she's lost me. She thinks the way I touched another woman means something more than it actually does. It was just a means to an end, but I can't explain that to her. This girl is different, though I'm not sure why. Yet. It's not just her innocence or her youth. There's this gentle, coaxing tug, a unique pull urging me toward her. In my long life, it's unlike anything I've ever experienced with a mortal. I've never craved another like this.

I hunger for her.

Every bit of this girl calls to me. I watch her whenever I feel her close by. Sometimes she sees me, but most of the time she doesn't. I'm an obsessed stalker, and so is she. The worst part is I can't do anything about it. I can't tempt her the way I've done countless others. This girl is going to survive me. She'll change me forever. I feel it in my gut, but I can't seem to stay away. The temptation is too great, too powerful.

She's standing there looking at me with ruddy, tearstained cheeks. She looks like a lost little girl whose heart has been broken for the first time. I wish I understood that pain. I want to understand how she can feel so much in this moment. The fact that I care to understand her at all is unusual. What's more surprising is that I wish I could take all the pain away, make her smile.

Oh God, how I want to make her smile right now. I've watched her from the shadows and when she smiles, she lights up the whole damn room. Her joy is infectious. She becomes a different creature entirely.

She asked me why I came, and it was the sound of her tears that drew me. I've hurt her somehow, though I don't know how. I don't do feelings, and I usually don't care if I hurt people, yet I very much care about her feelings right now. I want to erase her pain. I'll call it what it is, curiosity. We've all heard the saying, and I'm afraid I'm the dead cat in that scenario.

"I want to know why you've been crying."

I stand there, waiting for her to talk. She rubs her eyes, wiping the tears away. There's fire inside her. Her heart rattles in her chest, a fast pitter-patter of a beat, but her face looks so sad, so lost. She's an enigma. I wish she'd let that fire free. I want to see her burn for me.

"It's none of your business. Don't you get that? I don't have to tell you anything," she says, defensive, trying to hide.

The way she stares at me, her anger burning bright, it's sexy. Her anger is even sexier than her smile because it doesn't appear as often. It's there, smoldering under the surface, waiting for the moment to escape and burn everyone around her.

As I've stalked her from the shadows, I've seen who she is. She has such a sad acquiescence about her, accepting things she doesn't want, doing things she doesn't want to do without so much as a whisper of protest. But that fire inside her burns so hot, I can't understand why she just goes along with it all.

Who broke her?

I would kill them all if it would make her smile.

She straightens her spine as though she's readying herself for a fight. That's when I notice her clothes are different, she's changed. She'd stood on the platform outside wearing tiny shorts and a tight tank top that left little to the imagination. I mean nothing, I saw all of her. I swear it's what made me come. Now she's wearing a long sleeve

NASA T-shirt and fuzzy fleece pants as if it were winter. She's hiding her body.

Vale's been taught that desire is wrong. I can see the guilt, the shame. She thinks it's wrong to want to get fucked by me. I get it, at one time I might have become a pious man. I might have understood why she worries for her soul. Lust is a sin to her, yet here she is, wanting me. I want to push her further, even if I can't have her.

I step forward and grab her chin in my fingers. "Tell me now, Vale. I want to know why you're so sad. Maybe that's my demand so I won't tell Nick."

Vale jerks her head back, out of my grasp, narrowing her gaze in anger. "You wouldn't," she says, venom in her tone as she grabs my wrist and pushes my hand away from her. "You've got just as much to lose."

"Have I fucked you?" I ask, my tone more harsh than I meant it to be.

"No, that's not my point and you know it," she says so flustered, her cheeks getting hotter.

I smile like the asshole I am. "You know how I'd tell him. I'd say I left the curtains open because I hadn't expected to meet, hmm, let's call her Jeniffer. She looked like a Jeniffer, right?"

Her eyes go wide and it takes a miracle for me not to laugh.

"You don't know her name?"

It's funny how it shocks her. I love it.

I find her righteous indignation adorable. I smile brightly. She's definitely untried. I bet she's so tight. When I make her come it'll feel like her muscles are trying to rip my dick off. The thought of the dirty things I'd do to her . . . oh man, it could be so good. I'm salivating, starving for her already.

"Why would I care what her name is? She got what she wanted, and so did I. We both went our separate ways better for the experience. I don't lie to the people I fuck. They know the score. All I'm saying is I could tell Nick it was an accident, expect him to have a talk with you. *The* talk." I'm trying so hard not to laugh at this entire conversation.

What the fuck am I doing here? Why was I in this girl's bedroom?

Why was I surrounded by obnoxious pink sheets and scary Victorian dolls that probably held the souls of serial killers? Why was I demanding her truth? I had no right to any of her secrets.

"I see," she says. She looks worried now. She's afraid of what'll happen if Nick finds out what she did.

"All I'm asking is why are you crying? I thought you enjoyed what you saw. I offered for it to happen again. So why are you so sad? Why don't you want to see me fuck someone else? It could be our own sexy game. You could tell me what you want to see. You could tell me who with. I'd do it for you, sweetheart."

She shakes her head as if she's fighting some kind of internal battle. I wish I could read her mind, but it's unusually hard to catch her thoughts. Random pictures fall through my grasp like sand through a sieve before I can ever translate what I'm seeing. Mortals are usually easy to read.

Vale looks at the floor and stares at the antique rug. She's so nervous talking about this. Over and over, she twists the bottom of her shirt in her fingers. Her anxiety is genuine. I almost feel bad as I watch her struggle, but not bad enough to stop.

"I don't want to see you fucking someone else," Vale blurts out. "I want you to fuck me. I want to be the reason that look is on your face. I want you to make love to me," she explains, her honesty surprising. Most people don't have the balls to tell their true feelings to others.

I reach for her, placing my arms around her. Her cheeks are hot against my chest. I don't want her to feel alone. She's young, maybe this really is all new to her. It's okay that she feels like this; however, I need to set her straight, even if it bursts her innocent little bubble.

"I hate to break it to you, but what I did to that woman, it wasn't making love. It was fucking. I don't even remember what her face looks like. Once I saw you standing there, you were all I could focus on, all I could see. She didn't matter in the slightest. Why would she when you were right there?"

She wraps her arms around me, giving in to the comfort I'm trying to offer her. I'm surprised she touches me at all. I hold her for a moment, giving her what she needs even as some part of me wants to get away, to escape her clutches. I don't have a lot of experience with how to act in this situation.

I learned a long time ago not to get close to people romantically, especially mortals. They break too easily. If my ardor is strong enough to take an immortal life, then what hope would a mortal have at surviving it. No, that's why I can't have romantic relationships. I can't.

"Is any of this normal?" she asks looking up at me with curiosity, her eyes still swimming with tears.

"Nothing in my life has ever been normal. What about yours? Is your life normal?" I ask as I walk her backward toward the bed, forcing the back of her legs against the mattress. I lay her down, then kneel at her side. She jerks away, pulling the sheets up around her chin. She's not ready for me. She never will be. Who could be ready for a monster?

"I won't hurt you, I promise. I want to be here with you. I can stay till you fall asleep. We can talk and you can tell me about your life."

Why the fuck are these words coming out of my mouth?

I'm curious about her, another rare occurrence. Mortals all seem to blend in together after a while, and there's no reason to make friends with them when you know you'll lose them so soon.

I feel Vale's presence next door even when I don't see her. I know she's right there. Her being there is like a light, drawing me into it, coaxing me forward to damn myself further. Because that's what would happen when I killed her. But I'm unable to walk away, so I offer her more than I do most.

Nick told me about her parents and her strict upbringing. What I didn't expect him to say was Vale's father is the leader of a cult. What monsters they were for taking her out of school and locking her away from the world. Nick was worried they'd force her to marry young and Vale, not understanding her own freedom, would obey to be a good daughter. Her parents might not abuse her in the way the world pays attention, but they'd trapped her nonetheless. They've scarred her confidence by removing her from the sun. Just like her grandfather, I don't want to see her lose that spark that's inside her. I feel protective over her.

Vale scoots away from the edge, unraveling herself from the sheets, then patting the bed next to her. "No funny business," she says. The way heat rises to the top of her high cheekbones when she says it, it's the cutest damn thing I've ever seen.

"I swear, no funny business," I say, and it's the truth. I will reel myself in for the rest of the night if it makes her feel better. It might be hard to believe, but I used to be a gentleman.

Would it be so bad to be her friend? I'm not sure if I'm asking myself or wondering how she'd answer that question. Vale's alone, she may need a friend. I could be what she needs. Maybe she could teach me something. Maybe I could teach her. Then again, did I really want to know anything about the youth in this world?

What could she teach me that I haven't already learned myself? Outside of working to get this library situation under control with Nick, I haven't done much more than hang out in clubs and bars since I got to Silver Springs. So maybe my interest in Vale is just small-town boredom and not real interest. Then again, I'm a professional at denial.

I get into the bed beside her, brushing my wet hair away from my face. I should have pulled it back before I came over here.

"I wouldn't say my life is exactly normal, no," she says with a cute yawn.

I feel the slightest bit of guilt for keeping her awake. It's probably three in the morning by now. I'd check my watch, but she's scooted closer. Her warmth seeps into my side as we lie next to each other. It feels better than nice, it feels right.

"My parents are missionaries spreading the good word around the world. I've never really fit into their life. I get left behind a lot. I don't want to go with them, but I guess it would be nice to live in the same city for more than a few months at a time and be allowed to attend a normal school, to be a normal girl. I'm not a very good Christian. I don't know what I believe in yet. I don't like being forced into a box that suffocates me more than saves me." I hear the frustration in her voice and it makes sense. Her parents sound like assholes.

I nod as I look up at her ceiling. I find familiar constellations like

Orion, Sagittarius, and Scorpius in green plastic stars. *That must have taken forever.*

I turn the lamp off and they glow brighter in the gloom. I smirk up at them. She yearns for the stars. Does she want to escape this world?

Vale's collage of stars makes me want to show her mine. I wonder if she would like the dome and how it mimics her bedroom ceiling. I've been working on it for weeks. Something inspired by a dream, a way to pass those long nights when I can't sleep and there's no real reason to go on.

Now, I want to find some reason, some excuse to get her into my house. I'd take her into the library and have her look up. Would she understand what she was seeing?

"I understand being trapped in a tiny box you don't fit in. My mother wanted me to take over my father's business even though I had no desire to. I tried so hard to be what he wanted, but all I did was fuck up. I haven't spoken to him since. I suppose what I'm trying to say is fuck them for trying to force you into that box in the first place. One day, you won't have to pretend to be what they want. One day, you'll be free to just be Vale."

Honestly, I don't think my mother wanted me to turn out like my father. He's not a good man. But he was a king then, and I was his first-born son. As his heir, it's my duty to rule when he's gone. But I can never be who he wants me to be. I can never be Asher.

I used to pretend with my family. I used to actually try to get along with them, socialize with them. I love my siblings, my mother, but they're still involved with Asher, a fact I can't handle. I'll never be one of Asher's sycophants. I hope I never see him again. In fact, I wish he were dead most days. It's a fantasy of mine, and if it wasn't for my mother's love for the asshole, he'd have been dead a long, long time ago. But I can't destroy her mate, even if he's truly evil. I could never hurt her like that.

Vale sighs and I turn to face her. She's lying there, her knees together, studying my face. Her red hair is damp, tangled from the shower, and her cheeks are still flushed from crying. She doesn't look as sad anymore. Maybe sharing my past, however cryptic, helped her not feel so alone. No, it's definitely not sadness I see as a slow smile creeps up on her face.

"Does everyone fall madly in love with you?" she asks. She traps me with her dazzling aqua eyes. Even in the darkness, I can see them, my eyes capable of tuning to see full color even at night. I wonder what she sees. Does she see the predator or the man?

"Just the ladies," I groan as I reach for her hand. Changing course halfway, I grab her wrist instead. I have no right to hold her hand even if the urge takes me. Vale isn't mine. When was the last time I held someone's hand anyway?

"This isn't normal. Why do I feel such a pull toward you? It's like being in orbit around the sun. I'm unable to get away and soon I'll fall to my doom, burning up within your fire. I've never given a shit about most men, then I see you standing there in the shadows that first night and now—" She lets out a puff of air and I lean closer, unable to stop myself. She's getting frustrated trying to find the words.

"Tell me," I whisper close to her lips. If only I could kiss her. If only I wouldn't destroy her. "I won't judge you, promise."

Her eyes meet mine. She's thinking about it. She's so nervous around me. It makes some part of me sing with pleasure. She's so intimidated by the attraction she feels. *Be brave, my beautiful girl. I can take it.*

"I can't stop thinking about you. My every second awake, or asleep, you're there. I was outside in the rain because I had a dream about you. It felt so real that I could've sworn it actually happened. I thought you were out there, waiting." She's confused, but now I'm intrigued. What were her dreams like? I wish I could slip in and see them for myself.

"Tell me about your dream," I whisper, and her thighs clench as she remembers, her body reacting to the memory.

I smile down at her. She opens her eyes wide, then her hand comes up slowly, touching the angled bone of my jaw with a single fingertip. The moment she touches my skin, I know what she sees. She sees the predator, my eyes changing. But it's dark in here, and her mortal mind will explain it away as a trick of the light.

She brushes her thumb against my bottom lip and it's enough to make her heart race and her eyes soften. I shouldn't let this go on, but I like her innocent touches, so rare in my world. I like how her heart beats a rapid tattoo every time she looks at me, every time we touch. There's truth in her naïveté. In a world full of darkened lies, she is bright, lit up in the truth she's not yet learned to hide.

"You came to invite me to your house because I never come over with Gramps. Then the dream got dark. You touched me," she says before I interrupt.

"Where did I touch you?" I ask, wincing at my own question.

Her cheeks are bright red now. She doesn't want me to know. It's either that good or that bad. Maybe I'm pushing her too hard, but fuck, the way she's biting her lip right now, her secrets are all I want. "Please," I beg her. I need to hear her truth.

"At first you got close, pushing me against the house. You said a bunch of dirty stuff. You made me tell you that I touched myself when I thought about you," she says, whispering the last part.

"And do you touch yourself while you think about me?" I know I'm going to hell as soon as my cock twitches in my pants.

"I'm not answering that. You admitted that you did it while you were thinking about me. I fell for it. I told you what I did. I don't want to tell you the rest. It's embarrassing."

I'm enjoying her sweet humiliation. How cute she is, so flustered. I offer her something I know is bad. I shouldn't, but I can't help myself. This girl makes me desperate. "Tell me what happened and I'll give you anything. Okay, maybe not anything . . . how about a kiss?" My words make her laugh.

"I'm dying here, Vale. Give me your secrets," I demand with mock urgency, even as a smile forms on my lips.

"Has anyone ever told you that you're a pervert? Seriously, how old are you?" she asks, a worry line forming between her brows.

I'm a lot older than she can imagine, but I'm not going to tell her that. "I'm twenty-five. Seven years isn't so bad, is it? Am I such an old man?"

She rolls her eyes. "Fine, I'll tell you, but you don't have to kiss me."

I'm giddy like a mortal who's had too much champagne, the taste of her acquiescence sweet on my tongue. *I've won!*

I know where this is going already. I made love to her under the stars. It's so her. Just like this room with the explosion of rainbow colors that would normally hurt my sensitive eyes and the telescope outside, her escape from the world. I can't wait to hear her fantasies of sweet lovemaking.

"Don't laugh, okay?"

I immediately cross my fingertip over my heart. She continues as she stares at my hand near my heart. She can't look at me or she won't be able to tell me.

"We were lying on the platform. I jumped on top of you. I was rocking my body against yours. You told me we shouldn't. I thought I hurt you at one point, so I stopped. Then something happened. You went dark, your eyes turned black. You flipped me over and started to grind against me. I almost got off when you were on top of me."

Damn. I imagine the picture she's painting. I'd make her come. I wouldn't make her wait, like dream-Oliver would. I'm not a selfish lover. Then again, this isn't exactly the sweet lovemaking I thought she'd tell me about. Dry humping on the porch isn't my thing. Or is it?

"You overwhelmed me. You ripped my shorts off and you kissed me. You had one hand on my body, one fisted in my hair, jerking my head back. I was trapped and under your control. I was in pain, but I liked it. I liked how your beast took over and that's the only way I can describe it. You referred to yourself as a monster and asked me if I was sure about wanting you.

"I couldn't think about the repercussions or if you were really a monster. I begged for more. I needed you. Nothing else existed outside of the bubble we were in. There were no worries about the future, and I didn't care that you were older. I desperately needed you inside me.'

"I haven't had sex. Not yet at least, so I can't believe I dreamed this. I didn't know my mind was capable of such filth. And that's what it was. The things you did to me—” Vale stops talking, getting lost in her memory.

She's overwhelmed by the dream now. Just reminiscing about it is making her body heat climb. Oh, little does she know that in the right hands she'd destroy worlds just to have her desires met. It's a simple equation, but she's too young, too sheltered to know it.

“Go on. It's just getting good.” I wrap one arm around her tense shoulders, pulling her closer. Vale lowers her head to my chest, her hand resting on my abdomen. I don't think she realizes it, but she rubs it lightly over my damp shirt. Still nervous, still fidgeting.

“You warned me about being a monster while you touched your-self. I think that was my favorite part of the dream actually.”

“I didn't do a very good job in your dream if watching me jack off was the highlight,” I say. I'm mad at dream-Oliver, he needs to fuck her better. I want to make it up to her one day. I need to show her what it would be like to be with someone like me.

Vale slaps my stomach and I fake a wince. “I didn't say it wasn't good, but the way you kneeled between my legs, watching me while you touched yourself . . . it was unbelievable being the sole focus of your lust. I've never seen anything so beautiful,” she sighs.

Before she can hide her face again, I tilt her head back so she's forced to face me. Our eyes connect and it makes her body tremble. She bites her lower lip, tugging at it nervously. “So that's the fantasy, you want to see me in the window, alone and touching myself. I see. I'm surprised you didn't ask me to touch you.” I didn't know if I was talking about her dream anymore.

She turns away quickly. I'm worried she won't continue. “Maybe I want to see that, but if you continue talking about it, I won't be able to finish my story and I won't get to kiss you good night.” *Nicely played, beautiful girl.*

“Go on, then.” I pet her hair and shoulders, hoping she won't stop. I need to know how it ends.

Vale's back to caressing my stomach. I wonder if she realizes her hand has gotten quite a bit lower, nearing the top of my jeans, inching under my shirt. I don't stop her because I know she's trying to gather the courage to continue.

"You warned me, one last time, then you pushed into me so hard it hurt and I screamed. I begged for more. You did this thing with your hips when you pushed back inside. It was like you were grinding against some special part of me that doesn't exist in the real world. It drove me insane when you moved like that. I lost myself in it, like I was high on drugs. High on Oliver, I guess.

"When you got rough, I begged for more. I enjoyed it, how you hurt me. I wonder what it says about my brain that I enjoyed it so much. I wanted my first time to be special, but I knew it probably wouldn't be. It surprises me that my brain created this scene for my first time."

"I get it, it's not the rose petals over the bed, candles, and easy lovemaking most girls think they want their first time to be. But I like it. It's raw. I like the way your mind works," I say, and it's the truth. Through this whole tale, I've been calm. I've listened intently. If this is what her fantasies are like before she's ever lost her virginity, then I'm on board to experience her lust firsthand.

She's going to be unstoppable one day. I can see it now. She'll make a man beg for it. I might want to beg for it. Images of her forcing me to my knees to service her float through my mind.

"I guess I'm not most girls," she says, and it's sad, like I confirmed her worst nightmare.

"You're not. If you were, I wouldn't be here, now would I?"

Vale tilts her head back into the crook of my arm, watching me. There's a flash of something in her eyes while she studies me. "You didn't come right away in my dream. You were lost in a baser nature, claiming that I was yours. You told me you owned me. I liked it when you said that. I mean, look at you and look at me. It's not just our ages, Oliver. You look like a rock star and well, I'm this.

"That's why the fantasy was so sexy. You chose me. You wanted me back. Then you freed the monster. I died in your arms as you stole the blood from my veins. You were a vampire in my dream and that's how you came. You bit me while we were fucking, there was no making love. It was dirty, ripped shorts, on the ground, under the stars. I died while you were still inside me. Then I woke up.

"I could feel your touch still when I opened my eyes. I was so hot and confused. I ran outside to cool off, to see if it actually happened, but nothing was the same. Then I saw you through the window, with her, and I couldn't look away. I'm sorry, I shouldn't have told you all that."

We'd come full circle with her retelling, and it was shocking how correct she was. She might not have an idea of what kind of monster I am, but she obviously sensed it inside me. Some mortals know instinctively when they meet me, that I hide away some sort of darkness. They just know, like they have some kind of sixth sense that evil is real and it walks among us. But for some reason, Vale doesn't seem to care and that part, that was unique.

Lots of mortals would go crazy, knowing but unable to prove it. Feeling a fear they just can't understand. How it'd create such a paranoid disposition in them. Vale seems to have made peace with it or just ignored it. She doesn't seem scared at all, which I'm profoundly grateful for. I don't want to have to move away, I'd just gotten here after all.

"I'm honored you dreamed of me, Vale. Honestly, I wasn't mad you watched earlier. I enjoyed knowing you were there, reaching out for me. Had I known you'd just woken up from a wet dream about me, I might've been a little easier on you afterward. Truce?"

Vale smiles up at me. "Truce. Thank you for not freaking out about it or making fun of me. I'm getting really tired though. I need to sleep."

She pulls away, but I grab her wrist. She looks back at me over her shoulder. A vision superimposes itself over the real world, and it almost knocks the breath from my lungs. She's naked, looking at me over her shoulder while she bites her bottom lip. She's got a sexy smirk on her lips. The sheen of sweat across her brow, that flush of her cheeks, the deep wine color of her swollen lips tells me it's the afterglow. It tells me she's been fucked real good and deep. The scene is heady and I want it.

I try hard to blink the vision away. I don't know if it's our future or if it's some sort of déjà vu, but the vision lights a fire inside me. "Have you ever been kissed?" I ask, even though the answer is obvious.

She's awake now, her eyes going wide. She doesn't use words to reply, just shakes her head. I smile at her devilishly. I love how innocent she is.

"Did you kiss her?" she whispers, her eyes screaming some intrinsic truth about who my lips belong to. She wants them to be hers and hers alone. *Greedy girl.* I want her greedy for me.

I shake my head. "Do you want me to be your first?" I ask, and she rolls her eyes before lying back on her pillow with an audible huff. She must think I'm trying to tease her. I'm not. For once, I'm dead serious.

I smile. She's so overwhelmed by desire I believe it that she's never been attracted to another man. She's so torn up about it. I love it. I should be all her firsts, maybe not tonight, but one day. I could fulfill all those fantasies, her deepest, darkest desires.

I'm on top of her before she has a chance to squeak. Her thighs spread to accept me, her body recognizing me before her brain has a chance to catch up.

"Tell me, Vale. Do you want me to kiss you? Do you want me to be your first?"

She swallows hard as her temperature rises. I can hear those wheels turning in her head. I'm almost offended it's taking her so long to reply. I wait for her decision as I settle between her thighs, my hips heavy against her hot core. This is so fucking wrong. I shouldn't be doing this, but I can't stop. I'm moving on impulse.

I'll have to put more effort into controlling these urges in the future. I could destroy this girl. But I don't want to. I want to see her thrive, to live, to dream. I want her to burn bright, and I want to witness her fire.

"I want you to be my first kiss, Oliver, but I don't want to have sex yet. I don't know if I'm ready," she explains so sweetly.

She could never truly be ready for me. She can never be mine. That's what stings the most. I could never ask her on a date or get to know her the way she deserves. I'd get one chance at making love to her. I'm a one-night kind of man, love 'em and leave 'em. It'd never bothered me till recently.

"Trust me, Vale. I'd never force myself on you. I swear it." I would never do something like that. I could do a lot of damage, but I'd never do that. What I get from sex cannot be taken, only given. Rape is a thing I despise. It's the worst type of being who takes something so beautiful and destroys it for another.

"I won't take anything from you that you aren't willing to give. Only a kiss and only if you want it." It's a promise I truly believe I can keep.

Her hand is at my cheek, her warmth seeping into my skin. She searches my face for an answer and once she has it, she whispers, "Kiss me." Her breathy whisper may be the two most beautiful words I've ever heard put together.

I revel in her desire for a moment. It's thick in the air, pressing against me, calling to my soul, my hunger awakening even though I'd fed recently. Then I get an idea, and I wonder how she'll react. I gather her long hair in my fist, the way she talked about in her dream, and I wrap the red strands around it. I pull, not enough to hurt her, but just to tilt her head back.

"Is this how I did it in your dream?" I ask softly, so close to her face I know she feels the warmth of my breath against her lips.

Vale's breath quickens, her pulse visible underneath the pale skin of her throat. The scent of her arousal is stronger, like honey, sweet against my tongue. Her scent is intoxicating. I wonder if it's because she's untouched or if it's uniquely her. I should know the answers to all these questions, I've been around long enough. I just haven't witnessed a goddess being born. That's what she is, a goddess coming to life in my hands.

"Yes," she sighs, and she tilts her head back, baring her neck for me in surrender. I've never seen a more beautiful woman in all my life.

"Are you ready, Vale?"

She can't speak, but I take her slight nod as an answer. I lean down, making our bodies flush against each other, and her legs wrap around my hips. This is it. My lips press softly against her neck where her scent is so strong, so pleasing. I drag my lips along her throat, needing the taste of her skin, as her body twitches against mine. Her chest heaves as if she can't take in enough air.

When our lips finally meet, I'm all softness, just a slight pressure as I look into her aqua eyes. Below me, her body heats to a fever pitch and her thighs tremble around my hips. I've barely touched her, yet her entire body reacts to mine. It pleases me to no end to feel how sensitive she is to me.

I groan against her lips, letting her know she isn't alone in this. I'm with her every step of the way. She opens for me as I lick at the seam of her lips, tasting her sweetness for the first time. In that moment, I know I'll never be able to let her go the way I should. There's nothing she can do to get away from me. I mourn this bright star before me as it pulses with beauty and desire. She's lit up for me. I don't want to snuff out her flames, but I fear it's the road we're heading down.

I tangle my tongue with hers. She licks, sucks, and bites at my lips as I rock gently against her thighs, unable to stop myself. This is heaven. This feels like everything I've ever been denied. She offers me a moment of peace, warming the desperate, icy coldness within my soul. I don't feel so lonely when she wraps her arms around my neck, holding my head closer so I can't escape. She doesn't want to let me go. Little does she know that I want to be trapped in her innocent embrace. I like being there so, so much.

Vale closes her eyes. I don't want to lose that intimacy, but she can't take anymore. I allow it because I don't want to scare her away. I don't want to lose this moment. I want it to go on and on. I want to see everything, feel everything.

"Oliver," she gasps against my lips as her arms falter around my neck. Instead of letting both arms drop, one fist grips inside my shirt, against my abdomen. Her touch is like fire, branding me. She's burning up. I realize something too late, but I smile anyway. She is perfection.

"Look at me, Vale. Please look at me," I whisper against her lips.

Vale opens her lovely, jewel-like eyes. Mine have gone black as I feel the beast rise inside me, ready to feed. She meets my monster with a smile instead of cowering in fear, and her embrace tightens around me. I'm moved by the honor she's bestowing upon me. She digs her heels into my ass, pulling me closer. Her entire body quakes as if she can't contain it, even though she's desperately trying to.

I have to swallow her moans as she comes undone. She's coming so hard against me, her spine arching, her hips jerking against mine. Her breathing is rapid and uneven against my lips.

I feed, not because I can take it, but because she's giving it to me, forcing her essence deep inside me. She's making me take her pleasure. I don't know how she's doing it or if she understands what she's doing. I taste her honeyed essence on my tongue as I gulp it down like ambrosia, swallowing a little part of her.

The beast inside me growls, *She's mine!*

When she stops shaking and her hips are still, I pull back. I'm inches from her, looking down into her wide eyes, studying her beautiful face as she tries to steady her breath. I'm amazed by her. *What is she thinking?* I'm about to say something when she stops me.

"That's exactly what I'm talking about. The way my body reacts to you. The way I—" She can't finish the sentence, her cheeks so red. I know what she's trying to say.

I reverently cup her cheeks in my palms. I know she's right. This thing between us is unique. This is something else entirely. Mortals don't share their essence. I don't know how she did it. Somehow she fed me, purposely. Is she one of us? I don't know if any immortal can do what she did.

"You mean, no one ever comes from a kiss. Are you so sure about that?"

"Does that usually happen when you kiss someone? I mean, it just happened, but I don't understand. I thought . . . I don't know what I thought," she says as she shakes her head and pulls me down against her. She isn't trying to kiss me, she wants a cuddle and to hide her face against my chest again.

"It's not something I've ever experienced, to be honest. But I'm pleased," I say. And again, it's the truth. It was beautiful. I knew I was good at fucking, but I'd never made a woman come from my kiss alone. It was hot. I'm tempted to see if she'll do it again.

Instead of kissing her again though, I roll off her. I can't be thinking about wanting things to happen again. I can't get trapped with those thoughts. This is my m.o.: Leave them when it's over. It's time I left her to sleep and stew over what happened. She grabs my wrist before I can flee.

"Stay with me," she insists, her words whispered, yet brimming with desperation. The need in her eyes is a profound hunger that makes my chest ache. She needs me. She needs my support after I shook her world and turned it upside down. If I walk away right now, it'll hurt her. I'll prove how worthless I really am. It's what I should do, what I need to do.

But I've opened Pandora's box for her. She needs me to get through this. I'm not prepared for the aftermath, but I stay for her because I don't want her to know a single second of pain, especially not caused by me. She's too precious to break.

"Alright, but only until dawn. If Nick catches me here, he'll kill me. Then he'll ship you off to Sierra Leone so your parents can deal with you," I tell her before slipping my arms around her and pulling her against me.

Vale kisses my lips nervously, looking into my eyes, then she quickly turns away. We align, my body spooning against hers. She fits against me so well, and I feel at peace. I want to sleep like this beside her, but it's not possible. It's strange wanting these things for the first time.

She falls asleep quickly, which surprises me. She seemed so nervous only minutes ago, but now she's trusting. I close my eyes, thinking about our kiss. All the passion within her burned so hot while she was in my arms. She's going to make men fall to their knees and beg for her attention. In one way, I want to be around to see it; in another, it seems like my worst nightmares come to life. She doesn't realize it yet, but there are men much better than me out there, who would give their balls to have someone half as beautiful as her.

For the first time in a long time, I look forward to the future and what it will bring. My one hope is that it will bring her back to me, one day, when she's ready. When she's more experienced. Her innocence and youth are intimidating. Still, I want to have my one night with her. I'll only get one chance and fuck if that doesn't hurt my heart for some reason. The heart I didn't realize I had anymore.

7

OBSESSION

OLIVER

I'm being an absolute idiot right now. I drop a note and a single, fragrant, blood-red rose from my garden on her side table. I'm unable to leave her without a word, afraid she'll be unhappy when she wakes up alone. Her happiness is suddenly very important to me. I stand beside her bed watching her sleep like some sort of stalker, obsessing over each fine feature.

Vale Granger is a beautiful girl. While she sleeps, her breathy sighs call to me as she dreams. I've never wanted someone so much in my life. Somehow she's destroyed my hard-fought control and it's pissing me off like nothing else. It scares me. This borderline obsessive need for her since the night we met, it's taken a toll on me. Just the knowledge that she's nearby torments me.

It feels like I'm starving because I don't get to feed from the one thing I want. I've had to feed more often. I've had so many mortals lately. In and out the door, servicing them because I starve for another. I need to feed so things don't get out of hand with the beast, he seems triggered by Vale. He's also been more active over the last few weeks, growling and purring at the sight of her.

I've hurt people before, so many. I don't want to hurt her. I want to see her smile. She's so beautiful when she smiles.

I'm not human. I'm a hybrid vampire-Lilu, something very rare, even in the supernatural community. Vale knows it, at least her unconscious mind does if her dream is anything to go by. She sees the monster inside me, the one clawing to escape, to get to her. By some miracle though, she isn't frightened. She desires me anyway, and maybe that's what confuses her the most. Vale wants what she knows is bad.

She's perfection, even in her rumpled, sleep-swollen state. Her long hair falls chaotically around her head, spreading out over the pillow, a crimson and gold halo. My fingers ache in longing to touch that hair again, to wrap it around my fist the way I'd done during the night. The way she'd dreamed I had.

Her pale skin is flushed in sleep. Her lips kiss-swollen and berry-red from pressing against my own. She's the loveliest sight I've ever seen.

I watch her like the pervert she claimed I was. I study every feature of her face, memorizing every inch. I don't want to forget anything about her. I want to brand this vision into my mind, so I have it a hundred years from now, when she's long gone.

She has the cutest nose, slightly turned up at the tip, with a dusting of golden freckles splashed across it, spreading across her high cheekbones like butterfly wings. Her ears, usually hidden beneath her long hair are pointed slightly, like the fae who once visited our world. Her delicate bone structure looks as if it's been molded by the hands of the goddesses of old. Her slender neck is bare of any freckles with only a slight dip where her clavicles join below it. I want to lick that delicate skin, and the beast inside me wants to mar it with the imprint of my teeth. My knee creeps onto the mattress. Oh, how that little dip draws me.

Vale is exquisite now at eighteen. God have mercy on the men she'd leave in her wake one day. She has no idea the power she'll yield against them. I've glimpsed the woman she really is, the fire in her soul. It shines through when she gets angry, when she smiles, when she laughs, and when she cries.

The way her mind works, the dream she shared with me, it's lovely.

I have a feeling Vale would like my claws. She'd enjoy my bite, and she would fight me for every needy inch. I imagine what it'd be like pumping into her lithe body, her nails raking down my spine as she convulsed in pleasure, and it shakes me. I can see it all so clearly.

Mine! the beast roars inside my head, aching to get out, to get to her.

Her head tilts back while her legs spread. When she moans, a gasping, desperate declaration, I know exactly what she's doing in that dream. I know she's fucking me and it exhilarates me. God forgive me for how desperately I want her.

Vale cries out my name while her hand reaches to one breast, rubbing herself gently. When she moans again and the syrupy and sweet smell of her desire thickens in the air, I stop moving. I can't breathe through it. The scent envelopes me, snaking around my body like a physical thing.

Her scent changes me, thickening my cock as I press closer to her. Lost in her little moans and wrapped in her scent, I almost lose myself. I have to get away. I need to escape because I wouldn't be able to stop and poor, sweet Vale, she'd let me ruin her. It would be so easy. She wants me just as much as I want her.

So I leave her there, running as if the angel of death is chasing me. I run back to my home, up the stairs to my room, slamming the door behind me, but her honeyed scent still clings to my skin, taunting me.

I rip my pants apart, not caring one bit as the button goes flying downward, hitting the floor with a loud *thwack*. I drop to my knees, leaning against the door, and stroke myself like some lost youth. I throw my head back and howl as her image fills me with powerful lust. I bang my head back against the door trying to get a grip, but the pain does nothing.

When I come, it's with her name on my lips and a stuttered prayer of worshipful images of being buried deep inside her while she screams my name echoes in my head. I want her so badly, it's like a sick sort of need with zero innocence. I'm shaken to say the least, and I want to know what it is about Vale that draws me. Is she a witch, perhaps another type of Lilu.

My orgasm was so dramatic I continue to kneel on the floor against the door, gasping as I catch my breath. My eyes are wide, almost frightened by the intensity of it. *What's happening to me?*

Want her, the beast purrs inside my head, prodding at my consciousness. *Need her to survive. Need her light. Need her body.*

His words make the shell of my body feel too tight. It's how I know he's trying to get out, but I can't let him. So I ignore his words, even as his voice grows louder, his roars inside my head turning desperate.

She's the one! Mate! he screams, and it feels like there's power in the voice that hasn't been there in a while. He's stronger when I'm hungry, triggered by the memory of starvation, a hunger so great it tears at your belly, at your mind, while your muscles decay and your lips bust and bleed. The kind of hunger that makes monsters because we can't die from it. It's a type of torture no one should live through, and most wouldn't.

I grab my head, shaking it, begging him to stop. "Don't do this! She's innocent."

She's ours. His voice is a deep growl, but at the very least, the power of it recedes just a bit, as if he's willingly going to take a nap and leave me with a few minutes of peace.

"Fuck," I groan as I clean up the mess I'd made on my floor. I grab a towel and get into the shower. I'm too shaken to sleep today. I might as well get ready.

Girl Problems

My phone's ringing when I get out of the shower, a towel precariously wrapped around my hips as I rush to grab it. I know exactly who it is. She always reaches out whenever something's bothering me, like she has some sort of motherly superpower. She claims our connection is different, not like what she has with her other children. Some part of me doesn't believe her and yet, in the old world, before phones and reliable post, she always seemed to know exactly where I was.

"Hello, Mother." She was past due for a phone call anyway.

"How is my beautiful boy?"

It occurs to me she might be exactly who I need to speak with. She might know what's happening to me. "I'm glad you called actually," I say, and my words make her laugh.

"What a rare sentiment," she says, her sarcasm biting through the line. She's right though, it's rare when I want to talk to her, even rarer when I answer the phone.

"I have a problem." I hear her shifting and feel her worry through our bond. It isn't always so clear.

"I think something's wrong with me. I met a girl who I'm having trouble with." I try my best to come up with the words to explain Vale Granger. "I'm having some difficulty controlling myself with her. The beast inside needles at me relentlessly because he wants her. I've had to feed every day." It's not entirely true, he's not the only one who wants her.

"You haven't had her yet?" she asks, confused. She thinks I'm talking about a normal woman.

"I can't. She's only eighteen. She's innocent."

"What does her age have to do with anything? It's not like we meet any mortals near our own age."

I take a deep breath. "If it was only age, that would be different. I don't want to kill her. I care about her well-being." My cheeks flush as I say it, as if I'm embarrassed about caring for another. Am I so far removed from caring about anyone other than my family that it embarrasses me to speak it?

"I don't want to hurt her. I want to see the woman she becomes, with or without me, and it's driving me crazy." I take a breath before continuing. "There's something different about her, Mother. She feeds me without sex. She controls her essence somehow. I've never met the like or equal of her. I want her more than my next breath."

Mortals might think I'm crazy to talk to my mother about these things, but we've lived for centuries, and we feed on sexual energy. We're beyond being prudes with one another.

I hear an audible inhale. "Is she one of us?" she asks, her tone changing from sarcasm to genuine curiosity.

"No, she isn't. There's no way. She's mortal, human, I think."

"Have you tasted her blood?" The question ignites a longing in my teeth, a pain in my gums I've denied for so long. I don't feed like my father, even though I can. The blood is stronger than sex, but I despise that part of myself. I embraced the Lilu instead of the vampire long ago.

"Of course not," I tell her.

"Then you can't be sure she isn't one of us. You know our people have bred with mortals. She could have dormant genes that are activated by the presence of other Lilu. Happens to the vampires all the time." The word Lilu is one of the oldest for Incubi, while Lilitu means Succubus. However, every supernatural calls our species Lilu as a whole, favoring the male form.

"Is it possible you've found your mate? She must be special to have captured your attention in such an all-consuming way." No longer worried, she now sounds amused by my predicament.

"She's special," I whisper, thinking about her smile, her tears, and my own strange reaction to them.

"You're in love," she says, and I can feel the smile in her tone.

"Of course not. It's more of an obsession. I think." The truth is its denial. Just because I've never been in love doesn't mean I couldn't one day love Vale. It's just unlikely. I don't love, or that's what I tell myself at any rate.

"Don't act like your father. He denies his own nature, always. He continues to deny his love for me. He fights it because he believes love breeds weakness. Maybe it did then, but he's no longer the warlord. This world is different, Ash. Love isn't a weakness in this time. It's strength. So if you love this girl, don't deny it. Embrace it."

"I can't. If I embrace this thing between us, it could change her. I could hurt her. I could take her will, her freedom, a freedom she's yet to experience. She needs to live first," I explain and my chest aches. I don't want to repeat my father's mistakes of course, but I also know myself, the hunger that burrows through my resolve. "I have to let her go for now."

"Then you're a fool. If you give her up, if you let her go, you may sever the cord tied between your hearts. Son, you can't mess with the fates. They get pissed off and they change your destiny. You don't understand how bad it is when your mate won't accept you. It feels like your father is systematically removing my organs without anesthetic, slow torture over years and years. You don't know the hell she'll go through if you deny her."

"She's not my mate! It's impossible," I yell into the phone, my breathing harsh and uneven. *She can't be.*

Mother laughs and it angers me. "I realize she's young and you don't want to taint her. I understand you're worried, but if you cut ties with her, her heart may harden, and you could lose a mate forever. The timing is unfortunate, I admit that. But children are coddled too long in this age, if you ask me. Don't give up on her. Believe me when I say it's unendurable pain to be denied the bond."

I don't want to hurt Vale, but there's something inside me, some part that tells me to break her so she'll leave me behind, but then the beast screams in pain needing her light, her touch. It needs her love.

"I'll be there soon, son. I need to meet this girl. I need to know who's gotten your heart fluttering for the first time. I'm surprised you've been able to protect your heart this long."

I roll my eyes. "Speaking of Vale, her grandfather is cataloguing your library. He wants to meet you. He has a lot to say about the Byron manuscripts. Did you have any idea that when we came back here Nicholas Dalton would be our neighbor?"

Silver Springs isn't large, and I don't understand why this library has to be in this specific town. The library had been my mother and Asmodeus's bright idea. They thought knowledge would be the only thing that brought all supernatural people together, so they'd collected our histories over the years. Vampires, Lilu, Witches, and even more species would be able to benefit from it. The collection had been protected in Hell for thousands of years, but now I'm its keeper. It's my responsibility to protect it.

She lets out a huff of laughter. "Yeah, I'm sure he has a lot to say. I'm surprised you showed them to him. I don't think he'd enjoy learning that his theories were a whole bunch of bullshit and Byron was in love with a lust demon. Don't give away all our secrets because you're in love with his granddaughter. Not all mortals can handle knowing us."

"He found them himself. The collection's too large. I need help, and he knew exactly what we needed. Nick zoned in on those papers. My name didn't help things, Mother."

If ever my mother had loved a mortal, it had been George Gordon. He'd come, all swagger like a Lilu, unashamed of his perversions. He'd been one of her greatest friends, and she'd been one of his many muses. He'd known our secrets. They spent the rest of his very human life together.

I was there when he was on his deathbed, still with so much faith that Mother would find a vampire capable of turning him. There aren't a ton of vampires capable of transforming a mortal, it's a gift only provided to the ancients, closer to Lilith's original line. In the end, she'd found a vampire to turn him, but he was gone by the time she returned.

That's when she left the old world for the new, unable to face a future that George wasn't a part of. I think she mourned his loss, even now. Though I will say, she'd driven him half mad by the time he passed over into Hell, for surely that's where the infamous Lord Byron is now. Probably hanging out with Grandad.

"Oliver, you're my child most like George." Her words make me scoff. "It was time for you to wear his name. Also, I don't like having mortals in the library," she explains. She doesn't trust them with our histories, and she especially doesn't want them to turn on me when I'm here alone.

"I believe Nick and Vale can be trusted with our secrets. You know how it is, mortals explain away what we are. I'm afraid Nicholas Dalton will never believe in Lilu, but he'll still be fascinated with our history."

"That's too bad. I'll be there within the week. I need to tie up some loose ends in France before I come to the US." I know why she's going to France. My father lives there with my sister Gabby and her spouse, a young, idealistic vampire named Frederick, who are expecting their first child after two hundred years of marriage. They aren't mated but forever is a long time to be alone.

My egotistical father thinks of himself as the rightful king of vampires. He's an extremely old vampire who should have been happy to be mated to the first and most powerful Lilu, but he's fought it, convinced Lilu are weak. But there's nothing weak about my mother. She could bring a thousand men to their knees with a bat of her eyelashes. She's the daughter of the demon king, Asmodeus, and therefore more powerful than Asher.

In thousands of years, Asher had never marked my mother as his or completed their mating bond. He's refused to share blood with her, which is only one part of how vampires seal the bond. Even though they'd had children and been together off and on, he still wouldn't give her the one thing she needed—the thing they both needed—the completion of that bond.

Asher is an angry, vile being who admires strength above all. He's fought. He's destroyed whole cities. He's conquered because he could. He's fought for more and more power. But he's also struggled in the modern world. He can no longer fight in secrecy and being a warlord is his entire identity. It's who he is; he's a vampire who wants to rule all the others. On the other hand, my mother has blended in seamlessly, accepting that time changes all.

Vampires and Lilu don't breed like mortals. The births are rare and, in vampiric society, the females are often protected, even after turning. It doesn't matter that Gabby was half Lilu and half vampire, Asher would guard her till their child was born, then guard that child till its turning. He would kill any who came near the child, whether friend or foe. Mother would go to France, if she wasn't already there, to calm Asher for Gabby's sake, then she'd escape and flee across the Atlantic before he could trap her, which he still tried to do on occasion.

As much as Mother loved him, she couldn't stay with him. His stubbornness—denying himself, denying her peace—hurt her too much. I couldn't imagine hurting Vale like that, and I didn't even know if she could be my mate.

Could Vale be my mate?

8

HISTORY

OLIVER

Sometimes I wonder what my life would have been like if I'd never known who my father was. The beast inside me, the one who clawed at my insides trying to escape, that was his fault. I don't mean in a psychological, blame-your-parents-for-all-your-problems sort of way. I mean he actually did this to me. I despise what he made me. I hate him more than any being that exists in the world. Had it not been for him, I doubt I'd be capable of hatred at all.

My mother almost died while she was pregnant with me. She was starving, unable to feed after being trapped with Asher for thousands of years. Her father, Asmodeus, took her in. A demon king in Hell had more empathy for us than my father ever would. I wouldn't be here today without my grandfather's help. You'd think I'd have a better relationship with him now, but I don't. I haven't seen him in years.

My mother escaped Asher because nothing and no one could hold her down. I'd never admit it to her, but I've always admired that about her, that inner strength that's urged her on, no matter what. But I also still hold a lot of anger and resentment inside for how she left me with a monster. How long can an immortal hold a grudge? Only time can tell.

I was twelve years old when she took me to Asher with the bright idea that he could teach me how to be a man. Though that was probably just an excuse; it was more likely it was about her yearning for him, her need to be near him. At first, I was so excited to meet him. I had such love in my heart, fostered by the Hetairai, Aphrodite's famous temple prostitutes, who helped raise me. I had so much love to give that bastard. I felt lucky that he saw himself within me, and lucky that he'd kept me when my mother left him again a year later.

As if being his son wasn't bad enough, when I went through the change, he fed me his own blood, burdening me with more of his sickness. The change created the second form, but it only came out when I needed more strength or if I was starving. After seeing the beast, he didn't see his son anymore, he saw a weapon to be used. I was his blade. At the time, I'd thought, *This is how I become a man.* I did it out of loyalty, duty, and even love. I desperately wanted to make him proud.

Does love make one do horrifying things?

I destroyed entire villages at his command. I murdered the innocent. I burned the world down at a point of a finger. I took lives without argument, without justice because he told me to. He didn't even have to tell me because I wanted that sick smile on his face. I wanted him to praise his little monster. How ignorant was I in my youth?

When the weight of death and destruction became too hard to bear, and the faces of my victims haunted me, I stopped fighting. I let an innocent live. Asher wouldn't accept this kind of weakness. As his heir, I wasn't allowed to be weak. Not once did he ever treat me as if I was his son.

The first time my beast didn't listen to Asher's demands, he beat me in the hall as his men watched. I didn't fight back or make a noise. I deserved every punishment. I deserved that pain. The silence, above all, drove him crazy. More than anything, he hated that he couldn't break me. He hated me more when his men got quiet after they'd been cheering him on in the beginning. He feared their sudden respect for his son.

He had beaten me till he was exhausted, which is an impressive feat for any vampire. I was bloody, my skin flayed off around my ribs where it hurt the worst. I was unable to lift my head, unable to fight back when he dragged me down into the darkness. He left me in a dungeon-like hole where I was left to starve and rot. It was a place to keep those who didn't deserve a blade. It was there where he cut off my wings and demanded I kneel to him, to call him king.

But I wouldn't. I wouldn't kneel to a monster. I would never kneel again to a selfish, wicked king who cared only for destruction.

Had I not been immortal and able to heal from his abuses, things would have been much worse. I thank the Light for small mercies that I didn't bear those scars on the outside. It's bad enough to carry the scars that didn't leave marks, the ones that haunt you forever. The ones that cause eternal pain and are impossible to conquer.

Asher would visit that dark and dank prison. He'd beat me, demanding the same thing, to kneel, to submit to his will. I was so dehumanized I could no longer take my human form. I became the beast all the time. That's when it gained a voice. We split in that prison. He took the brunt of the pain, of the hunger, and I watched, detached from our shared eyes.

To this day I don't actually know how long I was down there before Asher needed me back to fight on his side. Of course he'd made another enemy, he always did. So he'd brought women into the dungeon to entice me, knowing I hadn't fed in God knew how long.

I'll never forget the worst one, a young girl, the one I allowed to live and the reason for my punishment. Shoshana, a name, a face, a memory I wish I could forget.

She couldn't have been more than sixteen or seventeen years old when he brought her to me. Even though I'd been the reason her entire family was slaughtered, she still became a kind of friend during my imprisonment. She would sneak down the ladders and sing to me to try to calm the beast.

But Asher used her to break me further, teaching me a valuable lesson: Love makes you weak. When you care for someone, a target appears on their back.

They'd entered together as big fat tears streamed down her face.

She begged me not to kill her and, under other circumstances, I would have never touched an innocent. She was so innocent even the beast hadn't wanted to harm her. I think he might have refused the blood had Asher not hurt her in front of us.

Asher slit her throat. She died there on the cold, earthen floor. Her blood stirred the hunger inside us, made the beast roar at the smell. Asher demanded submission. He demanded that I kneel. He promised I could have the blood, that he would bring more and free me.

And the beast gave up. He kneeled for the bastard. Right then and there, I hated him. I hated the monster I'd become. I hated the fact that he kneeled to Asher. But I hated Asher most of all. I had so fully become the monster that he took my will, locking me inside my own mind.

I was released from the dungeon after I killed three more women. I was given a day to heal my injuries, then the next day I was fed again and released. Asher leashed me like a dog, then took me to that hall where I'd been beaten. Sitting on his throne, he looked around at his men, then petted my head like a dog as I knelt in front of him. I became the evidence of his power.

See what will happen if you defy me. See what will happen to all of you. Words of warning from a stolen throne, which echoed inside my head.

I thrashed and cried inside, trying to escape, to take control, but I was leashed by the beast, who was leashed by Asher. I needed to stop the madness, but the beast was stronger and wouldn't release me. For a while my memories faded, my existence wiped. I have no idea what we did, who we killed, or how we lived. I ceased living.

Some of the vampires say Asher is an ancient king of Sumer, one who's watched over his people up until the modern age, as if he's some sort of hero. I've heard he was Sargon of Akkad or even the Gilgamesh, but I don't believe any of it. Asher could never love mortals enough to protect them. He never loved anyone enough to protect them. Not my mother and definitely not me.

Asher kept me as his pet, his weapon, only letting me out to reap destruction upon the land he claimed to rule. He kept me in that dungeon and beat me, starved me, over and over again so I couldn't escape. I became the "man" he wanted me to be, a feral beast because there's no doubt that's what we became to please him.

I'd murdered many for Asher's need for power. I'd gifted him an army of poisonous allegiance from men who only bowed because they feared the beast only Asher could control. In return, he'd taken my freedom, my soul, shoving it down so deep that when my mother finally came back, she didn't know who I was. I was trapped so fully inside that beast we could no longer speak or communicate with language. I slept for long periods of time inside my mind, losing myself a little more. When the beast slept, I felt ashamed of what I'd become.

I remembered seeing my mother for the first time through the eyes of the beast as he roared and swiped at her. I was screaming in my own mind, begging her to help me, but she couldn't hear it, she didn't know me. In that form, my body is larger and my skin matches the blackness of my eyes. I'm stronger, faster, and even more lethal as I disappear into the shadows. It's what makes me such a good killer, the ultimate predator.

Even though she was afraid of the beast at first, she came back day in and day out. She came to the dungeon to study me, even at one point asking me what I was. I continued to cry out for her, hoping she'd be able to help me.

A part of her had to know I was her son because she brought Asmodeus there. I wanted to believe he'd known who I was the moment he saw me. I looked like the archdemon when I was the beast. My grandfather made me sleep as my mother cried, then they took me from Babylon back to where I was born, back to Hell.

No one knew the children of a Lilu and vampire would have a second form because Lilu and vampires had never bred with one another. I was a unique specimen to say the least. Asmodeus was fascinated by how different I was to all the other supernatural beings.

He helped my mind heal. They didn't leave my side as I learned to speak again, to change back into my human form. They healed me in a way, but I was forever changed by that abuse, forever stuck with a monster inside me. Unlike my siblings who could control it, I couldn't. It had a mind of its own while their other forms were only extensions of themselves.

It turned out my beast was triggered by blood feedings. I struggled to hold my human form while feeding until we found out I could also feed like a Lilu. I'd never fed like that before, so Asmodeus taught me how. When I could control my hunger again, they brought me back into the human world. I was finally able to leave Hell.

Mother and I traveled around the Mediterranean at first, then into Egypt, staying on the borders of Asher's realm, hoping he'd never come after us. After seeing the new temple in Jerusalem, I realized how much the world had changed while I was in that dungeon, while I was in Hell. Nothing seemed the same.

We fought constantly during our travels. At some point she thought we should go back to Babylon, to face Asher together, but I couldn't. I'd promised his death if I were to ever see him again, and I knew she loved him. So I told her if she wanted her mate to live, Asher and I would need to keep as far away from each other as possible. I didn't feel the need to confront his abuse or start a war when I had no way to fight him. I just never wanted to see him again.

Because I couldn't face Asher and a part of her always longed to be near him, we had to separate. Out of love and respect for her, I had to let her go. If I could help it, I wouldn't be the reason for her broken soul. I wandered some more, always alone, until my travels brought me back to Greece. I went back to where my life had once been happy. Back to Corinth and the temple of Aphrodite.

I'd been gone so long all the women who'd loved me, who I'd called family as a child, were gone, long dead. It may have been the first time I truly understood what it meant to be an immortal. Things can never be the same because the world changes even though immortals do not. I'd come full circle, realizing how painful it was to care about others.

Corinth was buzzing with talk of rebellion and, as always, war. Why did men constantly wage war? I was tired of it. I wished to escape the never-ending fight around me, so I kept to myself near the temple. I stalked the night, selling myself and giving half of my earnings to the goddess, like my mother had when I was a child. I tried to find some peace in the only place I'd ever felt it.

I hid well amongst the humans, most of the time, but the beast was ever present, trying to consume me. I'd barely learned how to keep him under my skin, and it took very little provocation to bring him forth to destroy any perceived enemy. It took years to learn all the big and little things that triggered him.

It was during this time that I met another Lilu, another traveler visiting the temple. She thought I was only a Lilu and bade me to join her. I was lonely, so I did. Junia brought me inside the temple and fed on me.

Lost in lust, we fed on each other over several days and nights. I earned part of my soul back with her. I felt renewed, in control for the first time in my life. But it came at a steep cost. I watched her wither like a faded bloom. Junia became addicted. Minutes after our coupling, she'd beg for more and, by the end of the week, she'd gone from a beautiful youth to a wrinkled husk. Junia, though immortal, wasn't immune to my deadly ardor. She died in my arms. I took her life away. I took everything. And the beast took me again.

No longer able to control the beast, I ran from Corinth. Every place I went there was war and destruction, and sometimes I was the cause. It took a while to understand what was happening. I'm different from other immortals. There's not another being like me in this world. Other Lilu have mortal companions for years, my siblings do. They can control it, but I can't. It's why I can't bed someone more than once. It's my number one rule. It's why I can't love anyone. It's why I want to protect Vale so much. I could kill her. I could turn her into a thing that craves only me, unable to care about her own needs —one who wouldn't eat or sleep, and one who could only be eased by death.

"Don't think about it, son," Mother says, drawing me out of my memories. *Thank goodness.* It isn't safe for anyone nearby when I get stuck in the past.

"It's hard not to," I reply. "I can never be with her because she's not safe. Even if we were both immortal and mates, I'd kill her eventually. I'm a monster."

"No, you wouldn't. You'd rather die than see the light snuffed out in your other half. You wouldn't hurt her, you couldn't."

"Just like Father doesn't hurt you," I say, trying to breathe through the pain in my chest. She stays on the line even with my anger. "Why am I like this? Why is this thing inside me? I don't understand. It didn't happen to my siblings. Why did it happen to me?" I feel helpless, like a lost child all over again.

"I don't know. I wish I knew what to do. It's all I want, to see you happily mated to someone you love. I didn't know you'd be so frightened by it. I thought it would heal you." I know she's crying, hurting for my sake. She still cares, although I would deny it.

I wish she didn't care. I don't want to care about her feelings. I want to stay apathetic or angry. Anger is always so easy. Love is the hardest thing to comprehend. It hurts more than any other emotion. Love is disappointment. It's pain and it's suffering. Monsters aren't scary, love is.

9

HAPPINESS IS A KISS AND A DANCING GIRL

VALE

When I wake up, Oliver's gone. There's a single blood-red rose, carefully stripped of its thorns, and a note on my bedside table. I jump out of bed, then dance around my bedroom, stomping my feet like a crazy person. Fist bumping into the air like everything's finally right in the world, I pretend-scream out to the world, *I kissed Oliver Byron!* I grab the note and hold it to my chest, smiling like an idiot.

Vale,

I hope you dreamed about me last night. I wonder what kind of story it'll be next. Do tell. Please come for dinner tomorrow night with Nick. I'm cooking this time.

Yours,

Oliver

I focus on the word "yours." What did he mean? Was Oliver Byron mine? No way, that's impossible. He's twenty-five. I can't stake my claim to a man like that. Not yet. But I definitely want to. I want his kisses. I want his touch. I want him to be my first in more ways than one. Who wouldn't?

Oliver's tall with broad shoulders and a body I can only imagine is perfect under those fancy tailored clothes. His overly long ebony hair is beautiful, especially when he leaves it down in those gorgeous waves that curl around his face. He has pouty lips that lie like the devil and kiss like the divine. He's everything. I'm right to have a crush on him. I feel justified after that kiss. It was spectacular.

I start to think about my past, my Pre-Oliver era as it would now be known, when I hadn't been interested in guys. I'd been curious but never drawn to anyone. Kat and I used to sit out on the sleeping porch and chat about her crushes or how this or that guy had a future in her bed. Then I'd pretend her crush was hot, and we'd giggle. But really, I never felt it. I didn't think I'd ever feel the way she did.

Katherine Ingram was popular. She never had to ask for a date, and she always seemed to have a boyfriend, even when we were thirteen. Her life seemed so much better than mine, so exciting. Her stories were so outlandish and interesting to someone as sheltered as I was. I wanted my life to be just as interesting.

I wish she was here now so we could talk about Oliver. I want to tell her about him and get her opinion and the advice I so desperately need. Kat's the only person I can talk to about him; she's had the life experiences I haven't. It's not like I can ask Gramps what to do when you have a crush on someone. He'd know who I was talking about.

More than once, I've thought about snapping a picture of him just to show her how gorgeous he is. I want to show her I'm capable of meeting a guy on my own. There's also a little part of me that wants to show him off, to say, *Oh girl, you have no idea how hot he is* and *He's going to be mine.*

I wish he was mine.

I grab my phone from the nightstand, then find the number he called me from last night. I add it to my contacts. I think long and hard about what I'll say to him, writing, then deleting the text a hundred times. Finally, I leave it simple and press Send.

Vale: *I'll come for dinner. What's the dress code?*

I'm in the shower by the time he replies. I rush through my morning routine and still have my toothbrush in my mouth when I check for his reply.

Oliver*: Ripped jeans and band T-shirts. What dress code? This isn't the 1800s. How old do you think I am?*

Vale*: I thought you were so old it'd be appropriate to ask first. Just in case I needed to air out my petticoats and pantaloons.*

Oliver*: No petticoats or pantaloons. They get in the way. ;)*

I'm startled by how quickly I receive a second text from him.

Oliver*: How are you? Did you wake up smiling?*

Vale*: :) I just woke up. Someone kept me up late. It was great. Thank you.*

I send the text and as soon as I sit the phone down, it's ringing. I pick it up quickly, knowing it's him as my heart speeds up, jumping with joy.

"Hi," I say nervously as I sit my toothbrush down, a smile permanently set into my face.

"Hello, Vale. You're so very welcome." His voice sounds low, rumbly, and sexy. "I'm sorry. I'm old-fashioned and can't stand texting for more than a few messages. I don't understand why some people prefer that kind of communication. Anyway, I'm serving pasta tomorrow, come prepared to eat because I always make too much."

I'm surprised he knows how to cook. I don't know why I think that, but he does seem like the kind of man who'd have someone cook for him. Some kind of full staff situation. Maybe all the ladies who are in love with him take care of him. Sex slaves, of course. I'm shocked with where my mind goes when it comes to him. The stuff I think about . . . insanity.

"Can I help?"

"God no. What kind of host would I be? Come over, around seven. I imagine Nick will already be there. He'll be going through the library, you know, the usual."

"I'll be there. Thank you for the invitation. I'll see you tomorrow, Oliver." I try my best to stay calm, though I'm not at all, not one bit.

"Hey, before you go, bring a swimsuit. I've got a pool, and Nick mentioned you enjoy swimming. Have fun being home alone." With that he hangs up without a goodbye. Honestly, I don't know how to take it.

I play music from my phone, then run down the stairs, dancing as I go. I dodge around the house to the kitchen like a silly kid. I jump up when I get to the hallway that enters the kitchen from the backside. There's a big, golden-framed photograph of Grandma at the bottom of the stairs. I blow her a kiss as I pass by.

"Love you, Grandma," I yell as I enter the kitchen.

"Gramps made pancakes! Yes!" I'm so excited I'm near bursting with sunshine, as Grandma used to say.

I heat up the pancakes in the microwave, then grab the butter and the maple syrup from the fridge. When the microwave beeps, I load up my plate. I eat quickly, drinking the leftover coffee from the carafe. I'm surprised it's still warm. Gramps must have gotten out late today.

When I finish eating, I clean the kitchen. Then I move from room to room, dusting, vacuuming, and tidying up the mess I've left throughout the house. I'm kind of a slob when I'm at Gramps's house, but that's okay. I clean it up . . . eventually. Gramps doesn't seem to care unless I make a mess in his office, which I wouldn't do because I love him.

I'm so full of energy today I can't stop moving. Every step is a dance, like I'm walking on air. I feel graceful for the first time in my life as I pirouette dramatically, then giggle. Music is blaring from the speakers as I belt out the lyrics to "Take Me Out." I'm still smiling like a loon while I fold laundry for Gramps.

I'm happy, filled with such splendid joy it feels like it's going to burst from my chest. I've never felt so happy in my life. Not even the one time Gramps let me drive the Mustang without a license.

I got to kiss Oliver last night!

That's the excitement. That's the joy. It was perfect. He made a dream come true I didn't know I had. I'm glad it was him. I know he was with another person before, but I can accept that, even though it hurt to see it. But she didn't sleep in his arms last night, I did. He didn't kiss her, he kissed me.

I told him the truth, that I wanted him. It'd been scary being that vulnerable, but there was a part of me that needed to be. I hadn't wanted to tell him anything at first. I was worried it would scare him away, and I'd be humiliated. But he didn't laugh at my dream; he'd enjoyed it. Then there was the kiss. I don't think anyone in the world could have made me feel the way he did with just a kiss. It was amazing.

I've read the phrase, "He took my breath away," so many times and always thought it was such an alien description because it never made sense. But I understand those words now, in the depths of my soul, I get it. As soon as his lips touched mine, I was lost. I was unable to breathe by the endorphins shooting into my brain. The touch of his lips was all I needed to survive. I felt free in his embrace, floating amongst the stars in the sky.

I would remember that kiss for the rest of my life.

Today, I float on those memories, filled by the joy it created inside my heart. I feed from the memories, hungry for more. Hours pass by like minutes as I do everything I can to make this house sparkle and shine. When I'm done, it's time to make something for dinner, so I make a sandwich and grab a copy of Bram Stoker's *Dracula* from Gramps's office.

10

JOYRIDES AND JEALOUSY

VALE

Gramps walks in around eight o'clock and gives me a grin. I'm still sitting at the island, reading, my sandwich long demolished. He beams at me when he sees the book I have in my hand. "How many times are you going to read that one?" he asks me before popping me on the shoulder.

"I love *Dracula*! Anyway, you're not supposed to judge my books as long as I read your list. You've been busy, and I finished the list already. Don't tell me you've forgotten your own rules, old man?" I ask, my smile growing as I give him side-eye and scrunch my nose up.

Gramps puts his arms over his head and stretches. "Alright," he says. "Point made. I won't judge. I can't believe you finished the list already. Answer me this, do you think Mr. Rochester's deception was justified?" Gramps's left eyebrow jumps up as he waits.

I roll my eyes at him. I've been waiting for the third degree. "Oh please, it isn't about him or his deception. It's about Jane's truth, her hunger to be seen as a woman worth knowing, and to be loved just as she is. Rochester does love her. I think they're soulmates." I take a deep inhale, trying to stop the tears that want to come over that damned book.

"I didn't want to finish it at first. That part when he asked her to be his mistress pissed me off. I questioned whether he loved her at all. It broke my heart, Gramps," I pout, slumping over as I sit my book down.

When I finally look up at Gramps, he's smiling at me. It's such a big smile that it makes the wrinkles around his eyes deepen. "You're a romantic, like Grandma. I didn't think you were till that spiel. Good answer."

I'm surprised there's no rebuttal, there usually is. He must be tired. His comparison of me being a romantic like Grandma fills me with pride though. He goes to the sink like he's going to wash the dishes, but there aren't any. He turns to study the den, searching for something.

"Okay, who are you and what have you done with my granddaughter? You cleaned the house?" he asks in shock.

"I think the words you're looking for are, 'Thank you, Vale.'" I laugh and jump up, running around the counter. I give him a big hug and smile against his barrel chest. I've missed him being around the house with me. It's been lonely, but I don't want to mention it because I don't want him to feel bad. I'm glad he's got something to do and a friend to talk to.

"Thank you, Vale," he says, mimicking my tone. "What are your plans this evening?"

I let go of him and shrug my shoulders innocently. "I was thinking about stealing the car and going for a joyride, maybe to the bluffs so I can see the Aquariids shower. Any chance I can get the keys?" I grin sweetly up at him.

He shakes his head, then reaches in his pocket. My eyes get big, and I hold my hand out excitedly. He drops a key fob in my hand and my smile changes to a pout so fast.

"Really, Gramps," I whine. "I wanna drive the Mustang. Is it worth the jail time if I get caught in a Prius? I'm better than that. Come on."

Gramps laughs so hard his cheeks turn red. I see the tears in his eyes and his belly shakes with the laughter. "You're lucky I'm offering the keys. I wish your mother would let me take you to get your license already. If you get caught, we'll both be in trouble," he explains. "Anyway, the headlights are awful on the Mustang. This is the safer option."

I frown as I drop the key fob into my pocket. "Thank you," I reply because I'm grateful. Gramps is only worried about my safety.

He nods his head. "Okay, you know the rules. No speeding. No talking on the phone while you're driving. I don't care that there's hands-free. Make sure you use the emergency brake up there. No drinking. Nobody else in the car. Also, I've heard a bunch of kids have been up there having parties, if they are, please come back. It's not worth it, Vale."

I raise my right hand to my brow in a pretend salute. "Yes, sir."

It's a Monday night. I doubt anyone will be having a party at the bluffs. In fact, the only person I know who'd be having a party tonight is Oliver. Monday night parties, that seems like it's his kind of thing.

"If you get pulled over, don't snitch. I did *not* give you those keys," he says seriously.

He cracks me up and I laugh, then turn on my heels and run up the stairs. "Thanks, Gramps. Have a good night! Promise I won't tell the cops you're in on it," I yell from the stairs.

He grumbles a "Yeah, yeah."

In my room, I open the closet and grab my travel telescope with the single eyepiece. It's not the greatest, but I'm too lazy to break down the good one and drag it down the stairs. Sitting it on the bed, I open it up to check that everything's in the case, all the extra parts and tools to attach the tripod. I make sure my sky-tracking app is up-to-date on my phone, then grab a clean blanket.

Back at my closet, I stare at my lack of clothes. It would've helped if I'd done my own laundry today. I grab a pair of skinny jeans that are a half-size too small with rips across the thighs, even though I should have donated them a while ago. I clip my hair up in a high ponytail, then switch my baggy T-shirt to a tank top with a colorful zombie grasping a daisy. It's too short and ends a bit lower than my rib cage, but it works. I put some comfy shoes on, then grab all my stuff, including a purse that has my cash and state ID.

I make my way downstairs to tell Gramps bye, but he's on the phone in his office, so I peek inside and wave. When he waves back, I know that's the signal to go on. On my way out, I hear him say something about Lord Byron. He must be chatting with a student.

I put the telescope case in the back seat and stuff the blanket around it, then hook the seat belt around that—it's precious cargo. I toss a bag with snacks, a water bottle, a flashlight, and various odds and ends onto the floorboard.

When I shut the back door, I hear people laughing and a car revving up. We share a driveway with Oliver, but it's not exactly a single driveway. It's two lanes that merge before it meets the road. Gramps's driveway is a pale gray concrete, while Oliver has a terra-cotta-colored, faux cobblestone.

I look over at his house, my heart speeding up. Oliver is hopping down the steps two at a time, laughing, with a pretty blond girl on his heels. She's wearing a flirty, short, floral skirt, that shows off her toned and tanned legs. Her hair is down, and it's long, shiny, and perfect, as if she had a professional blowout for the occasion. Just like all the women who come around, she looks besotted with him. I understand that look.

There are a couple guys, one is standing beside a tricked-out, vintage Cadillac, and another is in the driver's seat. Both look young and boyish with cocky smiles. The kind of guy you might be attracted to if you didn't know any better.

"To the bar!" the guy with auburn hair standing outside of the car yells. He bangs on the rooftop. Monday night fun, yep, that's Oliver's brand of fun.

I start to giggle as I watch Oliver. Our eyes meet and I wave before getting into the car. I connect my phone to a USB cord, so I can listen to music, then start the engine as quickly as I can. When I'm trying to back up, the rear camera starts beeping a warning, and I slam on the brakes. There he is, in the camera. He's bent over, waving with a knowing grin on his face. I shift the car into Park. Shaking my head, I release the seat belt. I blow out a frustrated breath, then exit the car.

"Hey, Oliver," I say with what I'm hoping is friendliness in my voice and not annoyance.

"Are you stealing Nick's car? I know for a fact you don't have a license." He places his hands on his hips as he studies me with a pinched look. Is he trying to act like a state trooper? All he needs is the wide-brimmed hat and a badge.

I roll my eyes. "Free country," I say with a big smile, playing the game he started. Why would he care anyway?

"Not if you're in jail," he responds, tilting his head to the side as if he doesn't understand the stupidity of my actions.

His hair is in a messy man bun of all things, with little tendrils falling down his neck. It's adorable and youthful, unlike the vibe I normally get from him, which is intense, older, and knowledgeable. I'm struggling to hold in a laugh. It seems like he shouldn't look so boyish and carefree out in the open.

"I'm not allowed to tell you the truth. Sorry. Gotta go, see ya later, Oliver," I dismiss him because I don't want to continue this conversation. I don't have to placate this man like I do the other people in my life.

I get back into the car. Just as I start to close the door, Oliver grabs it. I grind my teeth, my jaw tightening in annoyance. *Don't do this, man! Please don't.*

"Vale, wait!" He raises his voice, but there's no need, I'm paying attention already. I haven't been able to stop paying attention for the past two weeks.

"Listen, I have to go, Southern Delta Aquariids," I explain as though he should understand my urgency. It's not the truth exactly, they won't start till much later, but he doesn't strike me as someone who would know that. I'm not saying he's stupid; on the contrary, Gramps said his knowledge is formidable, and I trust Gramps on the matter of intelligence.

I look up at him as he bends at the waist, leaning through the open car door. God, he's gorgeous. The collar of his shirt is open, with several buttons undone. The way he's leaning forward makes it gape, and I'm treated to a peek of his defined pecs. I bite my lip.

When I look back up at his face, my cheeks feel like they'll melt because I checked him out and of course he noticed. He always knows, and that cocky grin proves it. He continues to stand there, waiting for an explanation. I can't tell if he's angry or annoyed, and I don't remember what we're even talking about. I have to shake it off again to think.

"Meteor shower," is all I can say.

"Oh, and this meteor shower is important enough Nick let you borrow the car without a license. Is that correct?" He doesn't think Gramps would let me borrow the car. Oh, ye of little faith.

"I'm not allowed to tell you. He'll call me a snitch," I explain with a giggle. This whole situation is suddenly very amusing.

"Oliver, let's go!" the woman yells.

She joins us as Oliver stands up straight. I watch her come closer, her hips swaying. She grabs his arm and gives me a snarky look. The way she stares at my shoes, my ripped-up jeans, and shirt makes me think she doesn't like how I look. His date is judging me. I wish I could read her mind. I've had people look at me funny a lot over the years. I never cared, but I'm dying to know what her problem is. I don't know if she thinks I look like trash or a rival.

She lifts onto her tiptoes as she grabs his bicep with her manicured fingers. She's so short that at five foot, eight inches I could probably see the top of her blond head. She can't reach his cheek, and he doesn't bend lower for her to do so. When she gives up, she kisses the side of his arm like she's marking her territory.

You know what Blondie reminds me of? One of those purse dogs, a Chihuahua. She's yipping at me with her eyes, like, *Stay away from my man!* She's so tiny, I swear I can see her bouncing up and down with a squeaky toy in her mouth next to his leg. I have to cough through the laugh that bubbles up uninvited.

It's funny until she looks back at me, sizing me up again. Her fingers are digging into his bicep, and I can see how it makes dents in the fabric of his pressed shirt. All her body language yells out, *He's mine, bitch.*

Suddenly, it's not funny anymore. I get very uncomfortable watching her touch him so easily. He's not hers. He doesn't keep any of them. They never come back to his house. Yet her intimidation tactics have worked. I look away, letting her win, and I don't know why.

"Can I go now?" I ask, getting more frustrated by the second as reality sinks in—she's the one he'll fuck tonight, not me.

"Who's the kid?" Blondie asks, and her voice is so nasally, so annoyingly accented that I don't know why he's into her.

My cheeks flush because she called me a kid. It's the worst way she could cut me down without calling me names. I don't want Oliver to think of me as a kid. I don't want him to treat me like that either. He didn't last night.

"Don't you know who that is?" he asks her with a smirk. He makes it sound like I'm some sort of famous actress or something, and I honestly don't know where he's going with it.

The woman bends down to study my face again, then stands back up and shakes her head. Her nose scrunches up like she's disgusted by me. What the fuck did I do to her?

"Nope, don't know the kid," she says, dismissing me completely.

"That's Vale Granger. She's the most impressive woman I know. In fact, I forgot we had a date tonight. I'm going to have to take a rain check," he says as he tugs her hand off his bicep. My heart feels like it's doing somersaults against my ribcage.

What is he doing?

I turn toward the passenger door to hide the shock on my face and the heat in my cheeks. I don't know what to say. He's blowing her off for me. Why?

"Oh no, Olly, that sucks. I was hoping we'd get to hang out just the two of us later." The whiny tone she uses with him is unbearable, I want to gag. And Olly, really? I bet he loves that name.

I want to get out of here, but now I have to wait till these people leave because he said we had a date. Shit! Gramps is going to get mad if Oliver goes with me. I can't have anyone in the car. Shit! Shit! Shit! Gramps is never going to let me borrow the car again.

11

PRICK

OLIVER

Vale's hiding her face because she doesn't want me to see her blush. She doesn't realize that I can hear her heart rate quicken. I can feel the heat radiating off her and see the way she's shifting her thighs—I see how uncomfortable she is. Though I can read the minds of most mortals, I rarely need to. They tend to broadcast their feelings with body language.

Shae is pulling at my arm like a child begging for candy. She's annoying, but I need to be able to feed, which means I need to have a social life. The kind of social life that'll bring me into the fold, make me one of them. Make me a proper man in Silver Springs. And Shae has those connections. She's a real estate agent and thinks we should do business together, but I know what she really wants, especially when her inner voice continues to call me her "future husband." She thinks she has a chance with me even after I told her the truth that I don't date.

I don't need Shae's business, I have enough money to last many lifetimes, but it's about being accepted when you're obviously not like the others. I don't necessarily get close to mortals, but I don't want to be the person they gossip about either. Speculation is a bad thing when you're an immortal, it leads to paranoia. And paranoia leads to torches and pitchforks.

So in the end, I play nice, to blend in as much as possible. I can't have them question why I'm unmarried and alone. I'm in the South, so the moment casseroles start showing up with daughters on arms, that's when I need to get the fuck out of there. I'm the affable playboy in their story, carefully curated for the least amount of attention and drama. Just a fun-loving libertine. That's all I'll ever be in their memories.

I grab her arm gently and lead Shae away from Vale. I don't like how she's looking at her, how she talked to her. I escort her to the car with the rowdy boys. "Can you make sure Shae has a good night tonight, boys? Maybe next week we can get together."

They both wink. "Oh yeah, we can show her a good time, right, Shae?" Vinny says with a knowing smile.

"Who's the hottie?" Brian asks from the driver's side. "She can come too. Wouldn't mind getting a piece of that tonight."

I grind my teeth. My fists clench. *She's mine*, I want to scream. The monster inside me lifts its head and I struggle to keep him down. "She's off-limits."

Brian looks at me with brown eyes gone wide with fear. He feels it, he's on thin ice. "Yeah man, I got you," he says, then turns away, unable to look me in the eye.

Shae giggles and jumps in the car. "Call me," she chirps out the window before they take off. Brian almost shreds his tires trying to get out of here. Good, I hope he's scared.

I turn back to Vale, but she's putting the car into reverse again, trying to escape me. I step behind the car again, hoping she has fast reflexes. I don't want to get run over tonight. She slams the brakes again. It's like a dance with this one, a game. I want to play.

"What the fuck, Oliver?" Vale yells. She shuts down the engine and jumps out of the car. "What's wrong with you?"

I love it when that fire is in her eyes. She's so beautiful when she's angry. I wonder how far I can push her. How angry can I get Vale

Granger this evening? Then again, why would I want to? Gosh, what's wrong with me? This girl fucks with my head.

"Nothing's wrong with me. You don't have a license, Vale. Nick told me," I try to explain innocently, like I'm watching out for her and not actually being a prick. I know I'm a prick. Vale knows it too.

Speaking of Nick, he's coming out the back door right now to see what's going on. The rowdy boys had peeled out of my driveway like a bunch of idiots. Why do I have to socialize with people like that? Oh yeah, because I don't want to starve to death.

"What's going on, Vale?" Nick asks as he takes in the situation.

"Oliver won't let me leave because he knows I don't have a license."

Nick chuckles, his cheeks a bit more pink now as if he's embarrassed. "I told you not to tell anyone, Vale. You're gonna get me in trouble."

He let her borrow the car. I have to say I'm surprised. He doesn't seem the type to let her go out driving at night without a license, alone. This is what he means by letting Vale "get away with murder." He lets her do just about anything she wants so she can break out of that shell she's locked herself up in.

"I can drive her. I want to see this meteor shower she's talking about."

"Thought you were going out tonight with those hooligans." Nick studies me for a moment, then smirks.

"I've decided a meteor shower sounds more interesting than darts and a pint," I explain. But it's a lie. I'm more interested in Vale.

"That's not necessary," Vale counters, trying to stop me. She wanted me last night, but now she doesn't. Why not? I want her to want me.

"I think that's a great idea actually. Then you won't get arrested or have to lie about stealing the car and get a felony."

"I can drive. I'll be fine." She's trying to talk him into it again, but I can tell he's not going to budge.

"I'd feel so much better if you went with Oliver. Come on, he wants to see the meteor shower. It works out for everyone. You might be able to teach him something." He might be talking to her, but he's smiling at me. What's he trying to do right now? If I didn't know better, I'd think he was trying to set me up with Vale.

She slumps her shoulders and gives in without a fight. Her whole demeanor changes. I don't like it, how easily she gives up. She gets back into the car, grabbing her bag. Then she grabs her stuff from the back seat. That fire dies to embers, sputtering out like there's no fight left inside her. She gives in so quickly, and now I can see what Nick was talking about.

Vale makes her way up the deck and hands Nick the key fob. When she faces me, Nick holds his hands together and whispers, *Thank you*, so she doesn't see it. I nod my head in reply.

"I'll take you driving soon," Nick promises her, but Vale doesn't say anything back, just waves goodbye. She looks defeated, broken. I hate it.

"Come on," I tell her, motioning her to follow me. It's going to be an interesting night.

"Alright, Olly."

I hope she's just being snarky.

12

IT'S OKAY TO BE ANGRY

VALE

I'm so mad at Oliver right now. I wanted to drive. I wanted a little bit of freedom. It feels like he stole that from me. I climb into his jet-black Jeep and buckle up. I cross my arms in annoyance and refuse to look at him when he gets into the car.

"Where to?" he asks as he puts the car in gear and we roll forward.

"The bluffs."

The Jeep smells like him. That amber and spice scent that seems to permeate the air around him. My sheets smelled like him this morning. Will they still smell like him when I go to sleep tonight? I hope so.

"Is that the old quarry?"

I nod, unhappy with this whole situation. "Yeah, up the hill, last turn to the left."

I watch out the window, heaving out a sigh as the moss-covered beech trees disappear and pine trees pop up on both sides of Hudson Street. The road gets lonelier the farther we get from Silver Springs proper. There's very few streetlights out here and the farther we get away, the more complete the darkness is around us.

"Talk to me, Vale. Tell me what's going on in that pretty head of yours."

95

"It's nothing," I say without looking at him. I don't want to talk to him right now.

Oliver starts laughing. I turn to glare at him. The touch screen and the cluster are the only sources of light in the car and they illuminate his face. It casts shadows on his high cheekbones and that kissable dimple that only appears when he's amused.

"Nothing, huh?" He laughs. "You could've fooled me."

His words are condescending, and it pisses me off even more. I frown at him as I tighten my arms over my chest. "What about me amuses you so? Is that why you butted into my big night out?"

If he looks at me right now, he'll know how angry I am. He sees everything. I don't like it. I feel like I can't hide and hiding is all I've ever known. I hide aspects of my life from Gramps, even from Kat. No one knows what my life is like, not really. I don't want them to. That's the only way I can cope.

I'd gone along with this whole scenario with Gramps because I knew there was no reason to argue. I knew when it was a lost cause. I'm young and Gramps wants to protect me. Oliver offering me a ride solved all his problems: me driving without a license, me being alone out in the middle of nowhere. But I was eighteen. I didn't need a keeper.

Oliver turns his head for a moment. That carefree smile he usually has is gone. He watches me for a second before turning back to the road.

"Yeah, Vale, you do amuse me. You hide what you want instead of telling me or your grandfather the truth. You need to speak up. Stop acting like a child," he says, and I swear my blood pressure must rise twenty points.

I turn to face the old road in front of us. "You didn't think I was a child last night," I say. I know the moment the words leave my mouth that I'm going to piss him off. One part of me regrets it immediately, but there's another part of me, the hidden, raging female flame that smiles brightly at the thought of starting trouble. That part is unafraid, unapologetic and enjoys pissing him off right back.

I watch his jaw clench in my peripheral. I wish I had a convincing sinister smile and the confidence to use it. Instead, my lips twitch in a poorly hidden smile. *Checkmate asshole!*

I'm surprised when he pulls off onto the side of the road and slams on the brakes. I reach out to grab the oh shit bar as we come to a quick stop, dust flying in the headlights.

"What the fuck is wrong with you tonight?" I yell as I turn to fully face him.

He's facing me and the blue light coming from the touch screen makes his chiseled jaw look menacing. His eyes shine with anger too. I want to roll around in his fire. I want those flames licking at my skin. Why his anger turns me on, I'll never know.

"What the fuck's wrong with you, Vale? If you didn't want me to go, you should have told me. If you wanted to be alone, I wouldn't have blown off Shae. Tell me what it is you want instead of hiding. I don't like these childish games. Tell me what you want."

I take my seat belt off and lean closer, looking into his eyes. He looks down at my chest for a moment, and I almost get flustered. I should have worn a bra, but I didn't think I'd be anywhere near him. I shake my head as I glare at him. I take a deep breath, trying to release my anger, to calm my heart.

"Don't do that," he growls. "Don't calm yourself down. Don't breathe through it. You don't have to hide what you want. Rage at me! Tell me why you're so pissed off. Yell at me, fight me. Just let it out. Don't hide it. I can handle you," he says, leaning in, his lips close enough to kiss me if he wanted to.

"I don't like being called a child. I'm eighteen. I can do whatever the fuck I want. I don't like not having a choice in things. I don't like being looked down on because of my age. I may not have as much life experience as you, but that doesn't make me stupid," I yell at him, releasing some of that rage and building up more in the process.

"First of all, I didn't ask you to come because I didn't need you to drive me. I can drive myself. I like driving. I'm fine on my own. You swoop in to control things, and I don't need it. I'm not an idiot! Don't act like my parents."

The anger in Oliver's eyes fades a bit as he backs away. The anger is still there, but he isn't as fired up. "I don't think you're an idiot. I think you're too scared to tell me what you want. Your fear annoys me." Those words make my heart prick with pain, and it's enough to make my anger fly again as I hide the truth, the hurt.

"I annoy you? You could've fooled me," I growl at him, my eyes narrowing on his face. He knows exactly what I'm talking about.

"I'm already regretting this." He slaps his palm against the steering wheel. It hurts, knowing he regrets being with me.

"Then take me home. Better yet—" My eyes go wide as I grab the door handle. "I'll walk."

I jump out of the car before he can stop me, then slam the door. I leave my telescope in his car. I can get Gramps to get it back from him tomorrow.

"Wait, Vale!" Oliver calls, but I keep walking. "Just wait!" he calls again, and I hear the door slam.

Oliver is too fast on his feet and his long legs catch up with me. He turns me around in the red glow of his taillights. He looks so pissed off and on edge. *Welcome to the club, buddy.* I'm mad too. I'm hurt that he's suddenly treating me like a kid. I'm hurt that he's annoyed with me. Why does he drive me so crazy?

He grabs me by the shoulders and holds me out in front of him. His touch isn't angry, and it doesn't hurt, but it's clear he's not letting me go either. The Jeep idles about ten feet away. I can smell the fumes from the exhaust mixed with the smell of pine trees and old, musty, rotting things in the woods.

"Tell me what you want."

There's a moment when all I want to do is yell out, *You!* I want to call him an idiot and say, *All I want is you.* Instead of having the courage to say that though, I dump it all on him. I want him to regret ever telling me he can handle me and my anger.

"I want to be able to get my license without my parents losing their minds. I want to be able to go out in the middle of the night and drive, alone, if I want to. I want to look up at the stars and dance under the moon like no one's watching. I want people to stop treating me like a child. I want people to stop protecting me. I won't break. I want to be free."

I hold my hands out, pushing him away. Oliver steps back, removing his hands from my skin.

"I don't want you to treat me like I don't know what I'm doing. You of all people shouldn't treat me like a kid, Oliver. You didn't last night and now you're acting just like your friend. You act like I'm a little girl with no mind of my own. Just because I don't speak up doesn't mean I don't know what I want. I know when to fight and when not to."

Oliver's eyes soften. "Then talk to me. I can't read your mind, but I know when you're not telling me something. I don't like it. Last night you told me your secrets. Now I don't want any between us," he explains and I appreciate the sentiment. I do, but it's not the truth.

He acts like he cares, but I know he doesn't. He has an entire life and I'm just some sideshow attraction. The innocent girl next door with the infamous cult leader father. Nicholas Dalton's granddaughter. I'm the girl that'll be gone in a few weeks and he knows it. I'm no better than the men and women he brings to his house to fuck. I'm temporary. If I don't share my secrets with Gramps and Kat, why do I feel this urge to spew it all out for Oliver?

Breath rushes out of me. I shouldn't be so hard on him. We barely know each other. Gramps may have told him a bit about my situation with my parents, but he can't know the whole truth. No one does. No one knows what they've done because I don't think I can bear the look of pity. I'm not a victim. I just need to get through this until I'm free.

"Listen, it's not that I don't want to tell you what I want. It's just that no one *cares* what I want. Expressing my needs doesn't get me anywhere usually. It's what I've been taught my whole life, that what I want doesn't matter. It's why being here is so special. Gramps lets me do whatever I want most of the time, but I don't ask for too much, I don't overreach. I don't want to disappoint him or put him out.

"There's a lot of fear built up inside me. There's a lot of disappointment too. So, if I'm not Chatty Cathy, it's not because I'm a child, it's because I don't want to give up any more power. I need all I have left."

He's waiting for me to continue. He looks curious and apologetic at the same time. His hand tightens into a fist at his hip. Why does he care if I hide away? It's not like I'll be around much longer. It's not like anything I do will matter to him in the end.

"Gramps rarely lets me drive alone. He gave in tonight because of the meteor shower. I don't think he wanted to, but for some reason he was willing to take a chance on me, to trust me. I desperately want someone to have trust in me, to believe I'm capable of something. I wanted to drive. You took that away by offering me a ride. Now I can't even prove I'm responsible enough to drive a car by myself.

"I know I'm quiet and I don't join in with others. I push them away in fact. All I have at my disposal is the ability to prove myself through my own actions. I don't mind proving myself capable, but I'm rarely given a chance to do so."

Oliver grabs my hand without a word and leads me back to the Jeep. He opens the door to the driver's side and holds his hand out in invitation. "All you had to do was ask me to let you drive. Trust works both ways. You want me to give you the benefit of the doubt, you want me to trust you, show me the same courtesy." He turns on his heel and walks around to the passenger door, leaving me there dumbfounded.

Was it really that simple? Could I ask Oliver for what I wanted? Would he give it to me? There are some things I doubt he'd give me, but maybe I'll have the courage to ask him for them one day.

He jumps up into the passenger seat, sliding the seat back and stretching his legs out in front of him before I can even think about getting in. He puts his seat belt on and has his phone out before I can move. I stare at him for a moment in awe.

Is Oliver a good man? Can I trust him? I desperately want to.

"You coming?" he asks but doesn't look up at me. Instead, he starts playing some music.

The Jeep is pretty high off the ground, so I have to prop my foot on the step bar to get inside. I make it into the driver's seat with very little grace but no mishaps.

The Jeep still idles as I adjust the seat. Oliver is so tall it had to be all the way back. When my feet finally reach the petals and the seat sits comfortably, I adjust the mirrors. I fasten the seat belt over my lap. This is huge. He's letting me drive his car. He's choosing to trust me. It makes my heart skip a beat. I probably shouldn't tell him that I've never driven an SUV. I'll keep that little secret to myself.

Why am I so worried about him knowing me? I told him the truth last night and it turned out well. It turned out better than I could have imagined. Why do I fight it now?

"Thank you," I say as I take a moment to look at him.

He looks up from his phone. I can hear bluesy music, barely audible through the speakers. He turns the phone over in his lap and the screen goes dark. "You're welcome," he says with a slight tilt of his lips, not exactly a smile. "You break it, you buy it though."

I chuckle and turn back to the road ahead of me. For some reason it makes me aware of my future. Our future, Oliver's and mine. Do we have a future together? He seems too bright, too beautiful to stay in Silver Springs for long.

I shake my head as I drop the emergency brake. I shift into Drive, and we take off a little too fast. When I spin the tires, he doesn't say anything. This Jeep is faster than the Prius and the Mustang, which sometimes sputters to life like it's half dead already and can't be bothered.

Oliver's seat is farther back now, so I can't see him out of the corner of my eye. I place my hand on the shifter even though it's not a manual. I keep wondering if he's going to correct my hand position on the steering wheel, but he doesn't.

He's quiet when the song, "La Grange," starts playing. I know they're singing about a place in Texas, but I always pretend it's Georgia. I love this song. I turn the music up without taking my left hand off the steering wheel. My left foot starts tapping. I forget about the world around me.

I start to sing the words here and there. For a moment, I'm worry free. I don't think about Oliver sitting beside me. I don't think about going home at the end of summer. I just exist in that suddenly peaceful bubble between us.

I turn into the entrance of the old quarry about ten minutes later. I don't slow down as I tap my foot, still singing familiar songs. I've been there a hundred times. I know exactly where I'm going. I finally press the brake when I see the turnoff to the left to go up the hill. It levels off about two hundred feet before the drop-off, and that's where I park. I pull the emergency brake since it's not completely level until you get to the top of the hill. I press the button to shut off the engine, and the interior lights start to glow and the music stops.

The headlights light up the drop-off. The bluffs are made of stone, exposed by whoever ran the quarry fifty years ago. When they shut it down, they flooded it and took off. There are very few trees out here and at the top of the hill there's a huge clearing.

Kids come up here to party. Gramps acts like it's a new development, but it's been going on for years. I've been with Kat to several parties here. I usually drive her home after, when she's too drunk to drive, but we don't tell him that.

"We're here!" I say excitedly and look up through the windshield at the sky.

When the headlights turn off, the sky is dark. There's been a slight breeze and the clouds have cleared. There's very little light pollution out here. The houses nearby are at least a few miles away. They tend to be farms and not lit up, so this spot is absolutely perfect for stargazing.

13

SATURN LOOKS LIKE . . . WHAT !?

OLIVER

Give Vale a little freedom and her whole demeanor changes. I watch her, studying the way her body moves. She dances around in the driver's seat, belting out lyrics to half the songs I play. She's so worked up around me normally that she fidgets constantly, vibrating with nervous energy. I don't say a word because I want a chance to admire her. I want to see if she's able to forget I'm there, and she does. I'm proud of her, but I don't tell her. I have a feeling she wouldn't appreciate it.

I like watching her when she doesn't know I'm there. Today, I watched her dance around her living room. She was wearing these tiny shorts and a baggy T-shirt with a gray kitten in the center that floated around her when she danced in a circle.

I'd intended to ask her if she wanted to use the pool today, that was why I went there in the first place, but when I saw her dancing, I couldn't stop myself from observing her every move. Her body was taken over by the beat.

When no one's watching, Vale moves gracefully, with confidence. It's a sight to behold. I want her to be like that when I'm there, no modesty, no hiding, and no reservations. I want all she has to give.

When she parks the Jeep, I sit there watching her from the shadows, my arm propped behind my head.

Vale's neck is long and graceful. I can see her cute fairy-like ears because her hair is up in a clip. She's wearing a tight tank top with some sort of zombie on the front that stretches against her perfectly round tits. She doesn't seem to wear makeup or put on any pretense when it comes to the way she dresses. She doesn't have to. There's nothing that can make her more beautiful. Well, that's not exactly true, when she's angry or she comes, she's even more breathtaking.

She's unapologetically herself, but only when she's alone. I want her open and demanding. I want her to stand up for what she wants, even if she has to learn it by fighting with me. I'd willingly be her scratching post. So many times, I've seen the way she disappears into her thoughts as if they're the only place she's safe. I want her to stop hiding.

"We're here," she says in a singsong voice, then looks up through the windshield at the sky. The headlights dim and darkness surrounds us. There's a moment when she smiles so genuinely, it's like I'm not here. She looks so content in the gloom.

Vale turns to look at me. I know she sees the shadows wrapping around me, trying to hide me, protect me. I can't stop the way the darkness embraces me. I'm a predator built from the chaos of the heavens. But by some miracle, she's not afraid.

Her body tenses when she notices me watching her. She doesn't mind the shadows, but I make her nervous. I make her heart race. Honestly, I think she likes my darkness. I think she wants to experience it wrapped around her.

"What can I do?" I ask since she might need help setting something up.

She doesn't answer, only bites her bottom lip nervously as if she's lost in what she sees. I wish I could touch her right now, but I don't want to move in case she frightens easily. Those shadows that embrace me have a tendency to hide my movements until I'm suddenly too close. I don't want to scare her.

The dome light switches off and she jumps. I chuckle. "Are you afraid of the dark?" I ask, knowing she isn't. She wouldn't want me if she was.

"You know I'm not. I didn't expect it, I guess." She rolls her eyes before turning to reach for the door, embarrassment heating up her cheeks.

Vale jumps out of the car, and I take the chance to rearrange my cock. It's suddenly hard and throbbing because I can't seem to help myself around her. She's waiting by the back door when I hop out. After she fishes out her stuff, I hold out my arms, but she gives me this look like she's surprised I want to help, like she doesn't trust it.

"I got it. Show me the way."

She hands me the blanket and a canvas tote bag, but she doesn't trust me with the hard case in her hands. I don't know if I should be offended that she doesn't trust me with her telescope or not. She shuts the door and leads me up the hill a bit.

"You can lay the blanket out there. I need a minute." She points at the ground, while she looks up at the sky.

She pulls her phone out, looking at some sort of map while I lay out the blanket that smells like her. One minute she's looking at the phone, the next she's studying the sky. She takes so long I decide to sit down and get comfortable. I lie back with my forearm under my head. It's been a long time since I've been stargazing. I don't remember the last time I did.

Is it strange that I don't often look up at the sky? Mortals and immortals are similar in this. I think most of us are short-sighted, only seeing what's right in front of us. But here I am, watching the night sky and it's so clear, the stars so bright. Directly above me, I see a meteor chase across the sky. "Vale, look up," I blurt out. "It's started." My eyes are wide with excitement as another darts across the sky.

She drops down to the blanket, then lies back beside me. Chin tilted, she looks up at the sky as she brings the case closer, like it's some precious thing she wants to protect.

"That's not the Aquariids. It's the Perseids starting up. You can see them all summer, all you have to do is look up. It's early right now. They'll be more soon, but we're looking that way." She points to the southern horizon. "It's still a little early. It should start in the next couple of hours," she says as she checks her phone again.

A couple of hours? How long does she normally do this? I know I've caught her out there at all hours of the night, looking down into the dual eyepieces of a telescope. Sometimes she's out there till dawn.

When the screen goes dark, she sits up and opens the case. She turns toward the quarry, looking up every now and again. She's doing something in the case with a tiny screwdriver, and I wonder if she can see anything or if she's done this so many times she remembers the steps. The equipment breaks into two parts, and she holds a cylindrical piece in her hands for a moment.

Vale holds the small telescope up to the sky, and I think she's trying to focus it, but it's not the same kind as what she uses on the platform, it's much smaller. She's quiet as she searches. When she finds whatever it is she's looking for, she stops and reaches for me, tapping me on the shoulder to get my attention.

"Come here," she whispers, waving me forward.

I sit up and scoot to her side. Her heart has sped up, but I don't think it's because of me. "Look through there," she says as she hands me the telescope. "I'll line you up. You won't be able to see anything for a minute because of the light."

I look through the eyepiece, but I don't see anything, not even a star because it's all green. I turn my head and watch her on her phone. She holds her palm out, cupping the underside of the telescope. "Are you looking?" she asks, annoyed.

I smile. "I was watching you."

Our eyes meet and her cheeks heat. "Yeah, well, you want to get your eye on that because I'm turning the screen off. Just look." I like her secretive smile.

I put my right eye back onto the eyepiece and close my left. The color changes as my eye adjusts.

"Do you see it?"

I'm trying to focus my overly sensitive eye because it's wanting to focus on a single speck of dust instead of the sky, but eventually I see it.

"Is that—" I start, but then she focuses it even more. "Is that Saturn?"

I turn toward her excitedly. She nods her head, a huge grin on her face. She's beaming like a beacon in the darkness, her smile genuinely happy.

I look back into the eyepiece. "Wow, it's Saturn. That's another planet. It looks so small," I tell her because it's a tiny reddish dot in the sky, you can barely see the rings around it. It almost looks like an eye actually. There's not much detail, not anything like what *Hubble* sent back years ago. There isn't much to notice, but I can see a protrusion through another circle.

"It should look small, it's almost a billion miles away from earth. We're lucky to see it like this. It gets hazy here in the summer and it's much harder to see anything."

How have I lived so long and not seen through a telescope? Why am I only seeing this for the first time now? This girl makes the world new again. She makes it brighter. I smile so big my cheeks hurt. I take one last look through the telescope, examining the ruddy color and the tiny indent of the rings.

So this is what she does all night. I think she's searching for new worlds. I hope she finds them one day.

I sit back and catch her watching me. I like it when her eyes are on me, especially when it makes her blush. "Thank you," I tell her. I reach for her other hand and squeeze it. "Vale, thank you, truly, for showing me. It's amazing."

Her smile gets bigger. Praise makes her light up like she's never heard it before. She starts laughing.

"What is it? Tell me," I demand.

"My friend Kat says it looks like a clitoris." She cracks up, sitting the telescope back into the case while she laughs. "I'm sure you'll meet her one of these days."

I grab the telescope and find the planet quickly now that I know which direction it's in. I see all sorts of things in the telescope that I could look at, but I want to compare notes about Saturn. "I think Kat's right. Though someone isn't doing a very good job." I laugh out loud at my own joke, but I notice Vale's not laughing. I gently sit the telescope back into the case, and she starts the process of putting it back together.

"What do you mean by that?" she asks when she's finished. No, she's not laughing.

I narrow my eyes on her before shaking my head. "You don't know?"

I can't believe it. She doesn't. I swallow hard, and Vale looks away, embarrassed.

"Are you really so innocent?" Surely she's touched herself before. She must understand how her own body works.

She starts to fidget with her phone, flipping it over and over in her hands. Shit. I want to be the one who teaches her everything. I want to show her what her body is capable of. I hate myself for it, but I wish I could show her right now.

"I'm sorry. I didn't mean to embarrass you. I can explain if you want me to," I offer like an idiot. We should be chatting about the stars, planets, and whether there's life out there. Vale should be looking through that telescope, smiling like before.

"I'm not embarrassed. I just wish—" She stops, and I can see her wheels turning like she's trying to find the right words. "Will you show me?" she asks.

I'm unprepared for the question. Now my wheels are turning, thinking about how I'd show her. I want to touch her. I want to make her come. I want to make her come so fucking hard that she sees stars. Stars she wouldn't need a telescope to see.

"I'm sorry," she backtracks. "You don't have to. It's okay. Forget I asked."

I get up on my knees and sit behind her. I wrap my arms around her shoulders from behind. She stiffens in my hold like she doesn't understand why I'm touching her. "Relax," I tell her. I spread my legs around hers, then pull her back against my chest. I don't want her to look at me when I explain. I don't want her to get any ideas about what we're here to do. I can't even if it's what I want.

Vale leans back, her head resting on my left shoulder. Her hair tickles my neck. She doesn't look up at me, but she does get less tense, relaxing against my chest. "Tell me you know how an erection works," I blurt out. Not in a million years did I think I'd have to explain this to anyone. "You know, how a man has to be hard to have sex with a woman?"

Vale doesn't say a word, only nods her head.

"I'm not trying to embarrass you, but I'm hoping you've at least touched yourself before. You know what your clit feels like, the shape." She nods again. I want her words. I want her to tell me what she's done, every dirty little thing. I want to know how she touches herself.

"It's not so different from a cock actually. When a woman gets turned on, it grows, gets erect, whatever you want to call it. There's a hood that covers it when you're not aroused, but when you get really hot and bothered, the whole thing gets engorged with blood and grows. If you have a good partner, they'll do everything they can to get you turned on before they ever touch your clit. It'll be so sensitive that it'll push through that little hood and be exposed. It makes it easier for a woman to orgasm."

Vale takes a deep breath. "Okay, so you're saying women have lady boners. I've heard that before, but it didn't make much sense. W-well . . ." She stutters this time and tries to straighten in my arms. I hold her to me, not letting her wiggle away. "I guess I didn't know that."

"I find it hard to believe you didn't know that's what was going on when you touch yourself. Though it's not necessarily a drastic differ- ence. You didn't feel it change?" I ask even though I know it's going way too far in this little anatomy lesson.

She doesn't say anything. She struggles to stay still in my arms. "Let me go, Oliver," she whispers as if she's upset. "I need a minute, please."

I drop my arms, but not before I feel her shaking. I want to hold her again. I want to calm the storm inside her. Why did she get upset? I told her to tell me what's going on. I wish she'd trust me.

"Vale, talk to me. I won't judge you, but I don't know what upset you." I reach out for her, but she jumps up and walks closer to the quarry edge. She's trying to get away from me.

14

BROKEN

VALE

I jump up so quickly I surprise Oliver. I hear his footsteps start forward, but I hold my hand out behind me and shake my head. I'm struggling to breathe because he just explained what was wrong with me. My body doesn't do that. I've tried to masturbate, but it doesn't work. I can't have an orgasm.

"Let me help you. Don't run away. Please." He's pleading with me and all it does is make it worse.

I'm broken. I've been broken my whole life. Tears rush into my eyes, and I hold them open wide in hopes the tears won't fall. I don't want him to see me like this. I'm having a panic attack. I try to get my breathing under control. I raise my hands above my head and pretend to stretch, then bend over with my elbows on my knees. My chest feels painfully tight. The world around me spins. I feel like I can't breathe even though I know I am. I hate it when this happens.

"Vale, baby, what's wrong?"

"I shouldn't have asked you. I shouldn't have asked you anything," I blurt out. "Why are you here with me? You're not supposed to be here with me. You're supposed to be out drinking with that woman, Shae." I want him to stop thinking about what I'm freaking out about and worry about his own shit. I want to distract him from what's happening to me.

I gulp down air. I'm trying so hard to breathe, but I feel dizzy. *I can't do this*. My heart is racing, and I feel this deep need to escape and hide. I wish I had the ability to disappear into the darkness the way he can.

"Let me touch you. Let me hold you." His voice is closer. He's worried about me, but I don't want him to be.

I turn around and he's so close. If I wanted him to, he'd hold me. He'd try to make me feel better. It won't make it better though. In the end, he'll never be mine, and he's the only one who can make it better. He's perfect and I'm this thing, this broken thing. Tears start spilling over when I see the worry in his eyes. I shouldn't have looked at him. I don't want to see the pity in his eyes.

"I'm sorry," I tell him. I'm sorry for trying to have any kind of relationship with him. I'm sorry for having a crush. I'm sorry for kissing him because it showed me everything I was missing. I won't ever have that moment back and that's what hurts most of all. I'll never feel that way again.

"Come to me, Vale. Give me a chance. I can make it better." I almost believe him. I want to believe him and that's terrifying.

"All you've shown me is everything I'll never have. I'm broken. I'm glad you told me. I'm happy I finally know what's wrong with me."

"You're not broken," he says it so simply, sweetly, like he actually believes it, but I know. I've always known something wasn't quite right about me.

"Why aren't you with Shae right now?" I ask, trying to refocus his attention on anything else other than me. He reaches for me, but I take another step back. If he touches me, I won't be able to handle it. I'll lose my mind.

"I wanted to be with you. I didn't like how she looked at you. I didn't like how she spoke to you or how she grabbed me like I belonged to her."

"It doesn't matter how she treats me. I wish you were there with her right now, fucking her, making her feel good. You can't do that to me. You know that right." Words fly out of my mouth, but they don't make sense.

"I know," he says sadly, looking down at his shoes. Then he clenches his jaw. "I know I can't have you, Vale. I get it. That's perfectly clear to me. It doesn't mean we can't be friends. I like you."

I laugh like a maniac, taking a step forward in anger. "Friends don't kiss how you kissed me last night. This is so fucked up!" I yell, overwhelmed by the very thought. My hands fly out in front of me to keep him back and my shoulders tighten up.

Why is this happening to me? I push him away, but I wish he was closer. I don't want to give in because I know he'll hurt me. It's not worth it. The pain is never worth it. Break the rules and you get punished. Fall for a fuck-boy and you punish yourself.

He surprises me by getting on his knees. "I'm sorry. You're right. I was wrong. If you didn't want me to kiss you, I'm sorry. I didn't want to hurt you. Please forgive me. Tell me what to do to make it right."

My arms fall to my sides, fists clenching, and my fingernails dig into the palms of my hands so hard it stings. I look up at the sky, blinking the tears away that morph the stars into strange, wavy, glowing lines that crisscross through my vision. When I look at him on his knees in front of me, something snaps.

"Don't apologize for kissing me. Please don't. I wanted you to. I just . . . I . . . fuck!" I can't get it out.

"Tell me, baby. Tell me what happened." His eyes are so sincere, and it makes me want to spill my guts. Just like last night.

"My body doesn't work," I whisper. "It didn't matter before I met you. The first time I had an orgasm was last night when you kissed me. I've tried, but I can't make myself come. I'm broken. My body doesn't do what you said." I can't look at him when the words tumble out. He must think I'm an absolute lunatic, or he pities me, which is worse. I close my eyes and breathe deeply, trying to calm myself. It doesn't work.

"Why do I answer your questions? You want to take my secrets.

You want to steal them all, but I'm the idiot who keeps giving them to you. I can't seem to stop myself."

I feel his arm wrap around me. I jump, trying to get away. I look up at him with my arms up defensively between our bodies. Oliver grips my jaw in his hand, then leans in as if he's going to kiss me but stops. I feel his breath against my face. I wish we could go back to last night when he was in my arms, when I felt whole for the first time in my life.

"I'll be a thief of your secrets. Here's one of mine in return. I'm not sorry for kissing you." When he speaks his lips rasp against mine, barely touching my own. "You know what else? I don't want your forgiveness because it's likely I'm going to do it again."

I'm completely overwhelmed by his proximity, the wild look in his eyes, the heat from his body. I lean in closer.

"You can't! You can't touch me like that. It's not fair to me."

It's the truth. He could show me everything, and it could be amazing, but the problem is I'll never have him. I'll be like all those other people who never return. I don't know if I can handle that. I don't want to be nothing to Oliver. I want to be more to him.

"I want to know you. I want you to tell me your secrets because deep down I know I'm supposed to be here, in this moment, to hear them. Maybe I'm the person who proves you're not broken." He looks at my mouth, getting stuck there for a fraction of a second too long, then back into my eyes.

"Maybe you're the one who tells me the truth finally and proves I'm just as broken as I thought," I reply sadly. "Why does it feel like I'll never feel that way again? The way I felt with you last night."

Oliver turns me and wraps his arms low on my waist. I'm about to ask what he's doing, but he stops me with a finger pressed against my lips. "Lean back against me," he says softly against my ear.

The words make me shiver. I step back, pressing my back against his chest. I lower my hands to his where they sit above my hips. My tank top has ridden up higher, and I have the urge to pull it down, to cover myself, to hide.

He spreads his fingers against the skin of my belly and I gasp. His touch is a shock to my system. My chest starts to rise as my skin absorbs the heat of his hands. I lean my head back on his left shoulder. I try to turn my head toward his, but he stops me.

"Don't look at me. This is to show you that you're not broken. I'm going to guide you. I'm going to show you how, but I don't want to be the reason. So close your eyes if you have to, alright?"

I swallow and nod my head. "Show me," the words fall from my lips. I feel like I don't have any control again.

Oliver flattens my left palm against my stomach. With very little pressure, he slides my hand up my stomach and under the tank top. The shirt jerks up, exposing my breast. I feel the air hit my skin. I hiss when he cups my hand around my breast. Breath sputters from my lungs. I open my eyes, but they're unfocused, unseeing.

I want him to kiss me. I start to turn my head again, but he makes a *tsking* sound that stops me. He takes my right hand in his and slides it up the other side, inching his way up my body to my other breast. With our hands cupping both breasts, my tank rides up to my collarbone, exposing me. He releases a harsh breath against the top of my head.

"Does that feel good?"

I sigh because I can't speak.

His fingers guide my own, and he swirls them around my nipples. I feel so sensitive. "Oliver," I moan.

"Keep touching yourself, Vale. Don't take those fingers off your nipples. Stroke them for me."

When he removes his hands from mine, I want to stop. I don't want to continue without him. But I feel his hands back at my hips where he grabs the waist of my jeans tightly. His thumbs brush inside the waist band, against my skin. "If you stop, I stop. Do you understand?"

"Yeah, I understand. I won't stop." I'm shaking, either with fear or excitement, I can't tell.

"Good girl," he whispers and leans over to kiss my temple. It's an innocent kiss, nothing like the man I know. It's not even a fraction of the devastation he's capable of, and that makes it worse somehow.

I press my hands harder into my breasts. They feel so heavy, aching. My nipples grow stiff against my own touch. There's a sudden line that tugs inside me, working its way down to my core, where my muscles flutter like butterfly wings. The sensation is unnerving.

He pops the button of my jeans and lowers the zipper all the way down. I start panting as I pinch my own nipples. He reaches for my right hand. His breath comes faster when his hand comes in contact with mine. "When we get to your pants, I want you to put your hand inside your panties." His voice has gone raspy.

My right hand is led on a journey down over my ribs and over my belly. My heart is racing as I feel the lace at the top of my panties.

"Now, under the lace, Vale," he whispers, and his breath is against my ear. There's something about hearing him breathe so close, feeling the heat, that makes my heart pound faster. I lick my dry lips. I slip my own hand under the lace, while Oliver's hand follows mine on the outside of my panties. I feel a slight pressure as his hand stops me from going any farther. Each one of his fingers press against each of mine.

I tense when his index finger presses down. I'm so wet my cheeks flush in embarrassment. His touch gets firmer until my hips jerk forward. "I think we've found it."

For the longest time he presses against my finger, putting pressure against my clit. I can feel his breath move against my ear, my neck. I'm burning inside, the flames licking between my thighs that start to twitch and jerk.

"That's right, just feel it. Tell me what it feels like against your fingertip."

I have to think about it for a moment. "It's warm," I say as I stretch my neck back.

"Yeah? What else does it feel like?"

"Really wet." When I say it, he groans against my neck like he's the one affected by this not me. Then his jaw tenses on my shoulder.

"I bet it is. What else?" His voice becomes this guttural sound that makes chills run up my spine. He presses each side of my finger, moving it from left to right.

"It feels like—" He makes my finger slide around it, and I can't speak. I suction in air like I'm having a panic attack again. His mouth is pressed against my neck now. I can feel his lips when he smiles.

"Help me, Vale. Circle it with your fingertip, then I want you to press it like a button. I want you to keep doing that, okay?"

My thighs spasm. "I can't," I cry. "Oliver, I can't. I'm going to fall."

"You can, baby. I won't let you fall, I promise. Trust me to hold you up," he pleads with me, urging me on.

"You won't let me fall?"

"As long as I'm around, I'll never let you fall. I won't, Vale. You can trust me," he says, and it makes me want to. I want to believe he'll hold me up. I want to know that he's worth all the anguish.

"But you make me want to do things I've never wanted before. What if I want to fall, with you?" I ask, surprised by my own words. He presses his finger against mine, and it distracts me from my confession. "Oliver!"

"That's it. Let it take you."

I shake my head against his shoulder as I circle my clit, his hand against my own. Muscles tighten and clamp down inside me, then release. I can't stop them, and my hips start to rock with every slick circle of my finger.

"I can't!" I scream, shaking my head, intimidated by what I'm feeling. I stomp my foot to try to gain some control and contort bending my back forward. My mouth is open as I hang there, those muscles still contracting. I open my eyes as he holds me tighter.

"Faster, Vale," Oliver demands, and I try. I really do.

I'm strumming my fingers against my nipple and against my clit, but it's like I'm hovering over a precipice. I can't fall. I'm being held there, and it's torture. Tears fall from my eyes, and I'm unable to see through the watery waves.

Oliver lets go of my left hand at my breast and I cry out. He reaches across my chest and pulls me back up so I'm standing straight, my head tilted forward as I gasp. His arm brackets across both my breasts, and it's like the touch of his hot skin revs me up. My body vibrates with it. I think I'm going to break apart. I believe for a moment it's going to happen.

He holds me so tight, I feel safe.

"Vale, lift your head." I do as he says, but I can't help myself. I turn my head to look at his face.

Our eyes meet, and I wince. "Sorry," I gasp and look away.

My mind is all over the place now. I can't concentrate. I'm faltering. I'm losing steam. I stop moving my hands, and I slump against Oliver, defeated.

"I told you I can't."

15

PLEASE PROVE ME WRONG

VALE

Silent sobs wrack my body as I stand there. I can feel Oliver's heat at my back, his breath against my neck. I want him to turn me around and kiss me, hold me, anything! But he doesn't move. I failed, again. "Say something," I beg him. When he doesn't reply, I pull out of his hold. I feel his hand pulled from my jeans and his arm drops. I try to pull my shirt back down, but he stops me.

"Just wait," he says. "Let me look at you."

I swallow hard and stop trying to pull my top down. My nipples are covered now, but the bottom of each breast shows under the bunched-up fabric. I awkwardly turn toward him, but I can't look at him.

"You're not broken, Vale."

I shake my head. "I think you proved me right."

When I finally look at him, his eyes are completely black. He looks monstrous as he takes in my appearance. "I've proved nothing, sweet-heart. I've not even started," he says in a deep purr that sends shivers down my spine and causes my heart to pitter-patter uphill and out of my chest. At any second my heart is going to burst and bleed.

His hair is falling out of the bun on top of his head. I've never seen him so disheveled. He looks like he'll pounce on me at any moment.

"What do you mean you haven't started? It feels like we've been doing this for a while, and it didn't work. This isn't why I wanted to come here."

He steps forward. "Oh, we're far from done. I don't give up easily, never have. I don't plan on giving up on you either."

I walk away from him because I can't keep looking at him. I go to the blanket and start packing up the telescope. *So much for meteor showers.* I want to go home and hide. I'm bent over the case when he comes up behind me.

"Don't walk away from me," he growls low like an animal and a shiver drops down my body. I don't acknowledge him. "Keep it up. Go ahead and stay on your hands and knees, see what it gets you."

What the fuck does that mean? When I turn, he grabs me, then drops me into his lap. I push my fists against his chest, but he keeps me there with an arm at my back. "Stop fighting and look at me," he says, but I can't. I don't want to do this anymore. It's embarrassing and it hurts.

I continue to push against him, trying to get my legs under me so I can get up, but it only manages to move me closer to his body. Oliver grabs my hair and jerks my head back. It doesn't hurt, but it does shock me enough to stop squirming. I'm forced to look at him or rip my own hair out.

"Tell me to make you come," he says so close to my lips. "Tell me that's what you need, baby. Tell me that's what you want."

I swallow. He said he wouldn't touch me. He said he'd show me. He leans in and runs the tip of his tongue over my lips and my hips jerk against his. I grab his head by the sloppy bun that's slowly unraveling. Two can play this game. I'm sick of him pushing me.

"Oliver, will you please"—I pause dramatically—"get over it. I failed, okay. It's not the end of the world."

"You're sexy when you're angry, do you know that?" he asks, and the words surprise me.

"Sometimes I wonder why I like you at all."

A sly smile creeps up on his lips. "I know why you like me. I'm tall, dark, and handsome with a big dick and a tongue that rarely gets tired. I was built for this. I was built to make you come. You feel it.

Your body knows it. You didn't come because I wasn't the one touching you. Admit it, that's what you really want. You'd rather get off on me than your own fingers. You need my hands on you. You need me to make you let go."

My jaw drops and I stare at this smirking, exhausting man. "You might be right. Then again, I don't know how big your dick is." I snicker.

He grabs my hips and jerks me across his lap. I feel the ridge of him the same way I felt him last night. It feels so thick, but I don't know if that's a good thing. It's intimidating actually. But it doesn't matter, my body takes over, and I jerk my hips against his. It's like my dream. My hips are moving, and I swear I'm not controlling my muscles. It's like I'm possessed by a demon or controlled by instinct. I don't know how to stop this madness.

"Oliver," I plea as I rock against him.

"Do you like how I feel against you?"

He tilts my head back and I'm looking up at the stars. He touches the base of my neck with his tongue. He licks and nips at my neck till my hips are grinding against him, harder and harder.

"I need more."

"What do you need, baby? Tell me, and I'll give it to you."

"Kiss me," I gasp as his tongue gets to my chin, but he lingers there.

"Dammit, Oliver!" I yell. I yank him forward and slam my lips against his. I don't care if he rips all my hair out. I can't stop.

"That's right, Vale. Take it from me. Take what you need, what you want," he growls out before he fucks his tongue into my mouth.

He's holding me while I jerk my hips against the ridge of his cock. His lips are on mine and I can see how much he likes it when I lose control. This isn't my life, this isn't me, but this is who I am with him. I lose control. I don't want to lose control. I can't.

It's too soon when my body trembles against his. I nip at his lips with my teeth. He rocks my hips back and forth because I tighten up, unable to move myself. I open my mouth and close my eyes as I pant.

Breath is sputtering from my lungs, and I swear I'm going to explode. Oliver Byron is going to break me.

"Just let it happen. I want it. Give it to me." He gets in close. I can feel his breath against my lips. I open my eyes to see he's watching me intently. "You feel so good," he says reverently with hooded eyes that tell me he really does like how I feel against him. "You gonna come for me?"

I nod my head, like I know it's going to happen. My muscles clench and the moment they release, he smiles as if he knows. How can he know?

"That's it. Come for me." I swear his words are what spark my release. They're absorbed through my skin and burst like fireworks inside.

My head flies back as I feel all this energy sink inside me and ball up. It's so much, so hot inside I force it outside of myself with the hope that it's given to him. With my mouth open wide, I scream up to the heavens. I explode outward so hard my hips crash against his. I'm losing it. I see the stars dart across the sky. I see how they flash while I scream and tears fill my eyes once more. This moment is so beautiful it hurts and feels spectacular all at the same time.

"It's beautiful," I cry.

"Yeah, it is. So beautiful. I don't know if I'll ever get enough."

He tilts my head forward and watches me as my body cools. He cradles my cheek in his hand, making me feel precious. I wonder if I'm going to fall in love with him. It would be so easy to fall.

16

COULD IT BE?

OLIVER

Vale is radiant. I knew when she locked up in my arms I'd have to touch her. She was wound up so tight I knew she'd go over the edge if I gave in. As much as I want to deny this living, breathing thing between us, I can't. I'm drawn to her, obsessed. I want it all even though I know it's not a good idea.

I've never wanted a virgin before. What could I offer them? One night of pleasure, then I'd be gone. So I left the virgins to better men. She's different though, drawing me in, forcing me to see all that wild, untamed beauty. I'm not capable of looking away. I have very little control with her because I want to give in. Of course I want to push her away too. I want to keep her safe. It's that duality that made me offer to teach her. I know she isn't broken. I know she can do it. I also know her mind was racing and she struggles to stay in the moment.

I want to press her down into that blanket, to shove my cock so deep inside her that she'll lose herself and scream like a banshee. I want to drop her at her door, her voice so hoarse she can barely speak.

When Vale lets go, she becomes her true self. She's a goddess upon wings of fire. She burns everything around her. Now that I've been burned in that fire, nothing feels as good, nothing tastes as sweet. No amount of feeding has calmed the hunger since meeting her, not until last night when she gave me her essence. She got off by forcing her energy into me. It was so powerful I almost came as she filled me to the brim. It's the first time I've felt full in a long time.

Does she understand what she's doing? There's no evidence she even realizes what she's doing. The way she forces it inside me is unlike anything I've ever experienced. It's warm, like the flames that flash in her eyes. It vibrates with her release, bursting inside me. What is she? Could she be a witch? Maybe a hybrid like me. I recognize vampires, witches, and Lilu by their aura energy. We recognize each other, but Vale doesn't have that. She feels like a mortal.

I'm forcing her to watch me now as her body calms. At this point I wonder if her cunt is so wet it's soaking through those tight jeans. I want all that slippery wetness. It's mine.

"What if I told you I wasn't done with you yet? What if I told you I need to make you come again?" The fact is I need more. I want to gorge on her pleasure again and again. Is this what it feels like to be addicted to a Lilu?

Vale smiles and drops back onto the blanket. She stares up at the sky, her legs spread, with one propped up on my thigh. She huffs out a breath as she watches the heavens. I keep touching her, stroking up her calf to her knee, then back down.

She tugs her tank top down to cover her breasts, but she doesn't pull it all the way down. I can still see her abdomen with that little dip above her navel—I hunger to taste it with my tongue—and her pants are still open, revealing the top of those white lace panties. The sight makes my cock twitch.

Does she understand how beautiful she is? My heart feels like it's being crushed when I look at her. I ache for her. I want to do dirty, unspeakable, fucked up things to her. Dammit! I wish she was mine.

She breaks the silence with a soft whisper. "I don't think you proved me wrong. If it weren't with you, I wouldn't have been able to. I don't want to need you like this, but I do and that scares me, so much."

I lift her leg and lay it down gently on the blanket. I lie beside her on my back. It's not long before I see a meteor burst across the sky.

They burn so hot, so bright for such a short period of time, then they're gone, their light snuffed out. Just like mortals. Gone. My worst nightmare is witnessing Vale's light burn out.

I grab her right hand in my left, then slide my fingers between hers. I hear her quick intake of breath. Why has no one ever held her hand? "I know you don't believe me, but I swear you're not broken. You don't need me, not really. You're just as you should be," I say to reassure her, but she doesn't look at me.

"Thank you."

I rub my thumb over the joint of her thumb. Her fingers are so delicate against my own. She squeezes my hand in hers.

"Are there so many meteors every night?" I ask as I run the tip of my finger up and down her arm, then back to her wrist.

"No." Her voice is a whisper at first, then she clears her throat. "I've never seen so many on the same night. It's beautiful."

I press my palm over her right hip, feeling her hip bone protruding slightly. I inch my hand closer to her navel, then run my thumb over that beautiful dip. Her stomach muscles clench.

"Vale," I say and let her name hover in the air for a moment. "Thank you for bringing me tonight." My hand moves closer to her ribs, and I feel each rung. Her body is a masterpiece, her skin like silk. I want to touch and taste every single inch.

She turns away from me and tries to catch her breath. It's what she always does, she tries to calm any emotion instead of just letting it happen. It's like everything feels too much for her. I wish she didn't feel that way with me.

"You're welcome."

I slide closer and wrap my arms around her, pulling her into me. God forgive me, but she feels perfect in my arms. She fits so well, as if she was built only for me. I spread my hand out against her stomach and pull her closer still.

"You're not close enough," I whisper into her hair.

"It's never enough. Never close enough. I always want more. I know I shouldn't want you like this. It's not right to want anyone like this. I'm sorry. I didn't mean for this to happen." I hate it that she feels the need to apologize for wanting me.

I burrow my face into her long hair, taking deep breaths of her scent. She smells like fragrant gardenias and springtime. I steal her into my lungs. "Don't apologize for wanting me. I'm not sorry for wanting you. I'm not sorry for touching you. I'm only afraid I'll go too far." I nuzzle into her neck. "Never apologize for wanting me. You must know I want you just as much. I need you just as much. I ache for you just as much."

I grind my hips against her ass so she can feel how hard I am for her. I'm a bastard because I want to tempt her. She needs to run away and forget me. I still my hips before I get carried away. I don't know if I'd be able to stop myself. My monster is so close to the surface, stealing my resolve to leave her alone.

"Why do you think it's wrong to want me?"

"I'm a demon," she whispers, and it's the last thing I could imagine coming from her lips.

"What do you mean?" I tense up beside her. Is she like me? Is it possible?

She takes a moment to think before she explains. I wish she didn't. I'm losing my mind, needing to know if we're the same. By the time she starts talking, I want to rip out my own hair.

"Women are the downfall of man. I am capable of monstrous things. I hold the seed of original sin inside me. I am ungodly for my desires. I am vile for my pride. I am built to attract men to their own destruction, to lose their immortal soul. My joy is darkness. I should turn away, to deny myself any earthly pleasures. I am the fire of destruction. I am a devil, a demon, a muse to sin.

"Every thought about you is a sin. Lust is a sin. The way I want you is monstrous because it inspires you to get farther from the light of God. My flesh is to tempt you. My body a vessel of evil because I am a woman."

I don't know what to say when she finishes. I don't know if she believes it or if it's something she's parroting back to me. "Who told you that?" I ask, but I know exactly who told her this bullshit.

"It was a week before my sixth birthday, the first time he tried to take the demon out. He told me a story about innocent Adam and the darkness of Eve. How women were soulless creatures, created to inspire darkness, jealousy, and pain. So he took everything away, even my breath for a time. He took the stars in the skies. He took my mother when she disagreed. He broke her, so she'd stand there silently at his side while he spewed such hatred toward me, toward other women.

"'You must be silent. You must not desire. Joy is evidence of your sin. You must not touch a man until he has made you his wife. You must not look at a man who is not your husband. You must not leave the house unchaperoned. You must force all those feelings down because it is the devil tempting you. It is the fires of Hell that burn you trying to escape. If you feel that joy, the fires escape. You will destroy the world if I don't take it out of you.'"

She sounds so lost it's as if she's not here with me. I know what trauma is like, the memories, and how one moment you're present and the next it feels like you're there in the past, experiencing it all over again. Right now, she's seeing him preaching this bullshit to her, feeling the weight of every sinner on her shoulders. I hate it.

"I am the flame which engulfs the world."

When she finishes, my heart breaks for her. What kind of father could tell their child such horror? To make them believe they're a demon because of what's between their legs. No wonder she searches the stars. She's searching for a way out, to escape.

I hold her tightly in my arms as her spine arches back into me. Her hips press harder against mine.

"You feel so good, Oliver. You feel a lot like joy, and you know what that means, right? It must be wrong. It must be sinful to want you. The things I want are definitely sinful."

"I'd willingly burn in Hell for a moment inside you." The words escape my mouth before I can stop myself. It's the truth. She thinks I crave her secrets, but I just gave her mine. I shouldn't have said it.

Vale turns to look at me, her eyes sad. She's scared of something and for a moment she presses two fingers to her throat. "I don't want to send you to Hell." The way she says it, like I'm precious to her already, touches something in my heart that's been long dead.

I press my lips against hers. "Does this feel like a sin?"

She shakes her head. Her eyes are unable to hide every ounce of pain, every bit of suffering she's gone through. I want to protect her. I want to take the pain away.

"You feel like the only heaven I've ever known." She turns in my arms so she faces me fully. I run the palm of my right hand up over her spine under her shirt. She stares at me, then giggles so suddenly it surprises me. I raise my brow in question.

"I can't take you seriously with your hair like that."

I grab the elastic band in my hair and tug it out. "Don't like a man bun?" I ask with a smile of my own.

She reaches up and runs her hands through my hair, and I lean into her touch like a cat. Her fingers are so gentle though she can't break me. "That's better," she murmurs as she checks her work.

"It's too long."

She looks at me with worry in her eyes. "It's perfect. Don't change it."

I grab the clip in her hair and take it out, tossing it to her bag. I run one hand through the lovely copper strands. She leans back into my touch and closes her eyes in pleasure. Such simple things give the greatest pleasure.

"I brought you here to watch the stars," she says, even as she tilts her head back farther, arching her neck. The long column of her pale throat is sensual. I lean in to kiss it, to taste it. I run kisses down until my lips touch her collarbone. I tug on the fabric of her top so it exposes the tops of her perfect breasts, then I flatten my tongue and lick across each one.

The way she trembles at each touch makes me smile against her skin. I love those honest reactions. I overwhelm her defenses completely. She can't hide when I'm touching her.

"I like the stars," I whisper against her skin. "The stars are nice but no offense, the stars aren't you."

Vale grabs my head and pulls it up so we can look at each other.

I'm not sure what's about to happen, her wheels are turning again. I place my palm on her cheek, and she turns into my hand and kisses each of my fingers. Then she presses her hand against mine and forces it down her body the way I'd done earlier. She watches me with heated eyes as my hand reaches the top of her panties.

I screwed up.

"You told me to tell you what I want, what I need. So I'm telling you. I'll do anything for you if you touch me." There's a need so great in her voice, I can't say no. I don't think I'm capable of denying her.

I dip my hand into her panties and her breathing ratchets up. She's soaked and it only takes me a moment to find her slit. She's on fire. "Are you ready for me?" I ask, my lips tilted up in a cavalier smile.

"Yes," she whispers. "I need you so much."

My fingers make contact with her clit. I've never seen a mortal jump so fast in my life. Her thighs immediately close and clamp down on my hand as though I'm prey stuck in her honeyed trap. She cries out as though she's in pain, closing her eyes tightly. She's about to levitate off the ground. Her essence vibrates in the air, a quivering heat that scorches even as it soothes a deep ache inside me.

I feel the little bud of her desire, feel her blood rush under her skin as it swells at my touch. I smile down at her, devilishly. "Not broken, baby. You feel perfect."

Vale opens her eyes. She looks as if she'll cry at any moment, but I don't want her to. I need to distract her from that sadness. I move my middle finger against her gently. Her hips lift into my hand like she can't get enough.

"Fuck!"

I bend over her breast. "Watch me," I say against her tits. Her nipples are sticking straight up, pushing through the thin fabric. I open my mouth and bite one. She moans as I tease her with my teeth.

She's tugging at my shirt, reaching underneath. The moment she touches my skin, I groan. All of Vale's touches are gentle now, but one day she's going to claw at my back while she screams my name. I can see it in my mind so clearly. She'll draw blood when she comes. The beast suddenly hums in delight.

I want to be her man for a little while. I need to heal that heart. I need to make her feel good and praise every beautiful inch of her. I need to make her understand that she's not bad. She isn't a demon. She's a gorgeous woman who has needs and her needs are okay.

I growl against her skin. "You're so wet. Is that for me?"

Vale grabs my face in both her hands, forcing me to look at her. She's looking into my eyes with a feral type of desperation. "It's only ever been for you. Don't you understand that. Only for you."

I growl like the monster I am. There's some sort of sick pride that I'm the only man who's ever made her wet. My beast revels in it. I revel in it. I kiss her so hard our teeth clang together. Her lips tremble against mine as she pulls me closer.

Vale moans into my mouth, squeezing me to her so tightly, as one of her hands holds my head, and the other moves up my shirt against my ribs, making its way to my shoulder. I feel her sucking in breath after breath, like oxygen isn't enough to feed her fire anymore. She's trembling, and there's a buzz in the air like electricity. That's when I feel it. Her whole body is vibrating with it.

"Don't stop," she cries out.

I circle her clit with two fingers now and press down harder. "I'll never stop," I growl.

"Good, you shouldn't." She moans and her hand starts to roam down my body.

She wants to touch me, but I can't let her. I'm on edge. When she makes it to my pants I shake my head. "Not tonight, not yet," I tell her. "Tonight's about you, baby."

"I want to touch you," she pleads against my mouth. "I want you so much."

"So impatient," I say, trying to ease her.

"Impatient for you."

I swirl my fingers over her, pressing harder over her clit. Vale closes her eyes and tightens her grasp on me. "Come for me," I groan. "I need it. Come on my fingers, baby."

Vale lies back on the blanket, then grabs my hand that's down her pants and holds it to her. She presses my fingers against her harder. She bends her knees and starts to lift her hips, grinding herself against my fingers. It's such a wondrous sight I'll never be able to unsee it. She's losing her inhibitions, not caring what she looks like. She's not worrying that she's broken or evil. She's existing for the pleasure she takes so readily. She's letting go.

Vale's losing herself in my touch. She presses her other hand against her breast and squeezes.

"I like that," I groan. "Does it feel good touching those perfect tits?"

My words make her hips start to jerk harder and I smile, delighted. Vale likes dirty talk. "Are you imagining what it's going to be like when I fuck you? I'll be so deep inside you that you'll never want me out. Do you ache for it?" I ask but never get an answer.

"I'm going to come!" she screams out so loud I'm thankful for the quarry's seclusion.

I lean over her, smiling down. "That's right, come all over my hand. Come for me."

She digs her hips into the ground as her back arches. She opens her mouth and the sweetest, sharp intake of breath cuts through the night. I gorge on her energy, and this time it's so intense I come. My hand shakes under hers while she cries out through the rest of her release.

Vale collapses, spent. She's breathing hard, her eyes still closed. I don't think I've ever seen such a beautiful sight. I want to etch this moment into my memory so I never forget what she gave me. When she's gone one day, I'll still remember how I got to touch the most beautiful woman in the world. That I got to see her let go in the sweetest of surrenders.

17

THERE'S A MONSTER INSIDE

VALE

When I open my eyes, he's the first thing I see. His chest rises and falls with deep breaths. His eyes are dark, clouded by the shadows inside him, but I've never seen a man so gorgeous. "Do you see everything?" I ask. As much as I hate it that I can't hide from him, there's also a small part of me that wants him to see the real me.

Oliver doesn't move. He doesn't speak. Only watches me with those lascivious, black eyes. I want him to tell me what's happening between us because I know this isn't just a crush. This has to be something else. He can make excuses and keep denying it if he wants, but I know the truth, he's the man who's going to take my virginity. It has to be him. I feel it in my soul. All this time, I've had an Oliver-size gap inside me and the only time I've ever felt close to being whole has been in his arms. He's mine.

"Vale," he growls. "I will remember this night always. I want to keep it."

I smile at his strange words. "I want you to keep it. I want you to remember me." It's sad, this feeling of knowing he's mine, yet knowing he can't be. Every moment with him is bittersweet because I know it might be the last.

I stretch my legs, and he looks down where his hand is still in my panties. Then he does one of the strangest things I've ever seen, he leans down and presses his nose against the seam of my jeans, between my legs. His eyes flutter closed as he inhales deeply, a growl escaping that makes me even more wet.

Then he looks up at me with those alien-black eyes. He places a kiss at the seam, and it makes goosebumps break out across my skin. He opens his mouth, flashing those overly pronounced canines, and looks every bit of a sexy vampire. His tongue appears, and he flattens it against my jeans, licking up over the seam. He makes it to where his hand is still sitting inside my panties.

I hold my breath when he pulls his fingers out. I see a sheen of wetness over his fingers, shining in the starlight, before he takes them into his mouth. A sound flees from his throat, a devastating whimper, and I reach for him.

"Oliver," I whisper as we stare into each other's eyes, neither of us able to look away. He's still sucking on his fingers, getting every single drop of me off him. Why is that so hot?

When he removes his fingers from his mouth, he rushes up my body. He moves like a supernatural stalker, so fast I can't keep up with him. He presses his hips against mine, grinding his body against me and reminding me of my dream.

He's losing himself. "Oliver," I say his name, hoping he wakes up. I die in that dream. I don't want to die yet.

He's at my throat a moment later as his hips continue to grind against me, over and over. I'm going to lose my mind if he doesn't stop. I'm going to tell him to fuck me, and he will. But he'd told me this isn't the night. Oliver bites my bottom lip, his eyes like something out of a horror movie. He doesn't look human right now. Why is he so different?

I wrap my arms around him as he growls deep in his throat. My hips jerk against his. I'm so wet, so empty that it's hard to let him continue thrusting against me without begging him to fill me up. I'm dying.

"Oliver, please," I moan. "Tell me what you're feeling."

His breath stutters from his lungs. "Need to make you mine."

I smile against his teeth. "No need to make me yours when I already am."

"Tell me again. Tell me you're mine," he demands against my mouth.

"Oliver, I'm yours. My body, my virginity, it's yours if you want it, only yours."

My words make him gasp, and he jerks away, disappearing into the shadows. I understand. I've felt like hiding from him so many times since I've met him. I lose him in the darkness, so I stand up and button my pants, then pull my shirt down. This doesn't feel right. It feels like a trap, yet I can't let him go. He won't let me hide, and I refuse to let him.

I make it back to the Jeep when I feel him at my back. He pushes me up against the driver's side door.

"I'm sorry, Vale. Give me a moment. I'm not in control right now."

"You don't scare me." It's the truth. The only fear I have is of him breaking my heart when it's over.

"You should be scared." His palms slide up over my ribs and he cups my breasts in both large hands. "If you knew the things I wanted to do to this body of yours, you'd run away from me." His hands squeeze tighter, to the point of pain, and I try my best not to react.

"Tell me. I want to know." I grab his hands in mine, pressing them harder into my sensitive flesh.

He frees one of my breasts, then grabs my hair, pulling my head back. "I want to rip your clothes off. I want to throw you down into the dirt. I want to bend you over on your hands and knees. Then I want to force my cock into that too tight, virginal cunt. I want to make it hurt, make that pussy bleed for me. I want you to remember every single second of the pain before I make you come.

"You won't be able to tell where you start and I end. I'll be inside you so long, you'll beg me to pull out, but I won't. Do you understand that? I won't. I'll take you over and over again. This body is too innocent, too unused for me to do these things to you. I'll hurt you so fucking bad. I'll revel in those screams. I'll make you enjoy it. Don't you get it, I'll ruin you."

He paints a sensual picture of pain and yet my heart beats faster with desire. I get dizzy with it. I don't care if it hurts. It's going to hurt anyway because he's going to break my heart after.

"Don't have anything to say to that?"

I can tell he's smirking. He thinks he won by scaring me away. *Shows how little he knows.*

I shake my head as his grasp in my hair grows tighter. "I think you want to scare me away because you don't trust yourself to leave me the way you found me. Well, guess what? From the moment I met you, I was changed. It's too late. I'll never be that girl you first met, never again."

Oliver jerks away at my words, letting my hair go. I don't turn back to look at him. I think we both know what's going to happen between us. "We need to go," he says, his voice so deep and menacing. "Don't argue with me."

For some reason, I don't argue. I don't speak a word as he walks away. He packs up my telescope while I stand there like an idiot, unable to move one foot in front of the other. I'm forever changed, no matter what he thinks.

He feels like fate. I don't think either one of us has a choice. I stay quiet as I get into the passenger side after he brings my stuff back to the car, sitting it in the back seat behind me. I don't say a word when he gets in. I don't say a word when he starts the car. I don't say anything because I'm done talking and so is Oliver.

18

AFTERMATH

VALE

You know, it's strange when you have your first sexual experience with another person. There's this explosion of longing that makes you ache beforehand. It's all you think about. Then after, you feel bereft, needing it back, only wishing for the return of that pleasurable completeness, the very act that brought the confusion and longing in the first place. Oliver makes me feel a lot of things, and it's been a constant reminder of how I'm failing to hide my emotions. I can't slip into bad habits, even if I'm in Silver Springs.

Oliver drives us back, and it's much quicker and much more silent. I wish I could read his mind because whatever he's turning over in his head creates an impenetrable wall between us. He hasn't spoken to me since he started packing up my stuff. I don't know if he will.

The first streetlight lights up the night. I feel like I'm running out of time. I struggle to keep still. "Hey, um—" I start, then roll my eyes. "I . . . " *Vale, wake up. Say something, anything!*

"Oliver," I say, but he doesn't turn to look at me. He doesn't answer. I groan in frustration. I don't know what to do. I count down the miles left. Three, two, then sadly one. Time is running out. I'm on edge, afraid to let him go after what happened tonight. Like some thief in the night who'll disappear the moment I close my eyes. Had it all been a dream?

When I see his house, I know it's too late. We're here, and I feel like I've failed him somehow. He seemed to shut down earlier. I was willing to accept it, so I went with it, but now I wish I'd done more, anything to make him feel better. I care that he's upset.

At our driveway, he circles the loop in front of his house, then stops beside Gramps house, near the cut-through path. Shifting the Jeep into Park, he then just sits there, looking ahead. He's tapping his fingers nervously on the steering wheel, and I wish I knew what to say.

"Thanks for tonight. I enjoyed showing you the stars. I enjoyed—" He holds his hand up, effectively stopping me.

"Please, Vale, don't. I'm struggling right now. I can't explain it to you. I don't know if I'll ever be able to. Just know that I don't regret anything we did. Don't think I'm running away for any other reason than protecting you from myself. I'm not a good man," he explains, but there's something left unsaid and it echoes in my head as if it were his thoughts bleeding into mine. *I'm not a man at all.*

I take my seat belt off as I watch him. He's still staring through the windshield, jaw clenched tight and seemingly lost. I don't think he ever shows this part of himself to anyone. It's a secret, one of many, I'm sure.

I get up on my knees and lean over the console. Then I grab his jaw and turn his face toward mine. I press my lips against his. The kiss is quick; I don't linger. It's to show him I still care. With both of my hands on his cheeks, I force him to face me—the same way he forces my secrets to escape—then I pull away.

"Tonight meant the world to me, whether you realize that or not. Thank you." He doesn't reply. I realize I'm being dismissed, so I hop out. I open the back door and grab my stuff, making sure my phone is in my hand.

When I walk around the car, I'm startled to see him standing there. I give him a slight smile, then ask, "Can I ask you to do a dumb thing?"

"Depends on what it is," he answers.

I feel so silly, but I continue, "Can I take a picture of you?"

Oliver surprises me when my question makes him laugh. "That's all. I thought it was going to be something like let's do a seance together."

I scrunch my nose. "No way! I don't need to chat with dead people. Do you know the whole town thinks your house is haunted? I can't tell you how many nights I've sat on the platform, laughing my ass off while I watched drunk teenagers try to build up enough courage to walk through the front door of your house. Kat said it was a rite of passage. I wonder what they'll do now? Doesn't look like a haunted house anymore, so they've lost interest."

I hold my phone up when he smiles, a moment before he starts laughing, and take the picture. I'm sure he's perfect in it, so I don't look at it.

"Sneaky girl," he says with a chuckle. "Do you think it's haunted?"

I think about his question. "I don't think it's haunted, but you're the only one who knows that real answer. So, is it haunted?"

Oliver smirks at me. "You'll have to find out for yourself. That is, if you're brave enough to step through my door."

I roll my eyes at him. "Right." I start walking, leaving him by his car.

I make it to the path before he stops me. "Wait," he says, grabbing my phone out of my hand. "Don't send Kat that picture of me. Send her this one," he says. Oliver holds the phone up and pulls me closer. He kisses my cheek and holds it while I smile. He snaps the picture.

"That one is for Kat," he says, keeping the phone held up.

He leans his head back on my shoulder and snaps another one. "That one is for you."

Then he grabs my jaw in his left hand, forcing me to face him, and looks into my eyes. "This one is for us."

My mouth drops open when his eyes fill with heat. His tongue licks at my lips, and I hear the camera shutter go off. "Send that one to me as soon as you get inside," he demands with a wink.

"Okay, I will. How did you know I wanted to send a picture of you to Kat?"

"I thought you would want to tell her about tonight. Girl talk," he says with a smirk.

"I'd never tell her about tonight."

"Why not, ashamed of me?" he asks, and I laugh. How could I ever be ashamed of him? Impossible.

"Of course not. What happened tonight was flat-out tame compared to the shit she tells me." I yawn. "When you give me something juicy to tell her, then I will."

That makes him laugh again. "Yeah, I didn't think dry humping under the stars could be so hot. You've proven me wrong." He smiles at me, trying to school his face. "Good night, Vale, sweet dreams." He winks at me before kissing me on the lips quickly.

"Good night, Oliver," I say in a breathy voice.

He escorts me to the back door, then I watch him walk away. I wave when he looks back. *I can't wait to see those pictures.*

"Hey, Vale," he calls out. "Remember dinner at seven at my house. Tomorrow night. If you're brave enough."

I hold my thumb up in agreement, rolling my eyes, then he takes off into the night. I wonder where he's going, but he's not mine and I've no right to ask.

I close the door behind me. The only light on is a small lamp beside the back door. It fills the kitchen with a warm orange glow. It's not so late, maybe midnight. I haven't looked at the time because when I'm near him, I forget everything else. Nothing else matters.

I sit my stuff down on the kitchen island and step over to the sink. I'm looking for evidence of Gramps's dinner, but all that's in the sink is a crystal tumbler. He's gotten into the scotch. Good for him. He rarely drinks.

I wash the tumbler out and sit it in the dish rack on the countertop. I'll put it back in the office tomorrow. I don't want to take the chance of waking him up.

After I chug a glass of ice water, I grab my stuff, and turn the lamp off. I'm enveloped in a darkness that's surprisingly complete, but it doesn't scare me. I feel at ease in the darkness, always have.

I make my way up the rear staircase to my room. As I sit everything down on the bed, my phone chimes. I know it's Oliver and it makes me smile. I guess he's okay now.

I unlock the phone and pull up the pictures, opening the first one. I knew it would be perfect. He's standing there, leaning against the Jeep, his shirt untucked and unbuttoned at the collar. His long hair is tucked behind one ear and falling in long, wavy strands on the other side. He has this secretive smile, his mouth opening right before he's going to laugh. One of his arms is bent at the elbow, his hand in his pocket, and his long legs stretch out in front of him.

Oliver is so beautiful, but this picture is everything. He's right, I shouldn't send it to Kat. That moment is ours, between him and me. That smile belongs to me and no one else.

I swipe the screen for the next picture. This is the one he told me to send. He's making me the center of it, and he looks like a man in love, a man who wants me if only I'd give him the time of day. I look so carefree, like I'm not intimidated by the gorgeous man who's kissing me on the cheek. I look confident. Somehow he knew I would.

I swipe again, and in this picture he looks relaxed. His head is tilted back on my shoulder, his face close to mine. His eyes are so green they glow. My cheeks are pink, and I look at him from the corner of my eye. It looks like I'm imagining what he'd be like in bed. Like I'm dreaming of our future together. It looks like he's mine.

I swipe again. The breath that rushes out of me is complete shock. From one picture to the next, we both change. Now his hand is cupping my jaw, his thumb on my swollen bottom lip. His head is tilted to the side with his long hair curling against his neck. My mouth is slightly parted in surprise, my eyes full of arousal. His eyes are so dark, so shadowed, the green has all but faded.

Oliver looks at me as if he covets my lips, my soul. He didn't catch the moment he licked my lips, but it looks like we're about to kiss. We look like two stars that are about to collide and explode in bright flames, destroying us both. It's prophetic. This is our truth. I can't help to think he did this on purpose to show me.

Is he trying to tell me something?

My phone chimes again and I jump. I shake my head, trying to clear my thoughts. *He calls me impatient.* I check the text.

Oliver*: Where are my pictures?*

I smile at the message, then skip to the second one.

Oliver*: I know you're there. I see the light on in your bedroom. So why aren't you replying?*

Vale*: You call me impatient?*

I go back to my photos and, just to be silly, I send him the one of him by the Jeep. Then the one for Kat. I make my way down through the photographs until I get to the one of us about to collide.

Vale*: Not what I expected.*

I add the picture to the message and press Send, then I strip my clothes off and grab a sleep shirt and a couple of towels. In the bathroom, I turn the shower on. I'm burning up inside, so I make the water cool. Before I get in, I run back to text him.

Vale*: I need a cold shower after that picture. ;)*

I sit my phone down and jump into the shower. I'm lost as the water washes over me, chilling my skin. When I try to wash my body, my skin is so sensitive I can't use the loofah and end up having to rub the floral shower gel into my skin.

I finish quickly, throwing my hair up in a special hair towel to dry it, though it'll be a mess in the morning, then I wrap a towel around my body.

I look in the mirror.

Do I look different? I feel different. I feel like every time he touches me, I change just a little bit. It's not obvious what changes, but I know it's there. I see the pink in my cheeks and my skin looks a little brighter, healthier.

In bed, amongst my pink sheets, I'm a bit embarrassed. I can't believe Oliver has seen this room. I look around me and cringe. It looks like a little girl's room, complete with a few creepy porcelain dolls on a shelf over my desk.

I laugh. Admittedly, they weren't mine. They were actually my grandmother's dolls, but I kept them after she died. Then there's the dirty laundry strewn over half the flat surfaces, even though Gramps got me a clothes hamper.

There are stacks of books and band posters taped up haphazardly. Plastic bead jewelry hangs on the dresser mirror from when Kat and I made them when we were preteens. A huge purple teddy bear sits on a trunk at the foot of my bed, while a stuffed monkey named Armstrong with Velcro hands and a NASA shirt hangs from my iron headboard. Armstrong's a cute little guy; I won him from a claw machine when I was ten.

I have a toy rocket ship, pictures of Kat and I hanging on the walls, and a cartoon character light switch cover that's so old, you can't make out the pink princess anymore. I don't know why I installed it up here. It occurs to me that I do look like a kid to Oliver. No wonder he's scared to touch me.

But this room is a reflection of summers spent with Gramps. It's a reflection of all the things I can't take with me when I go home to my parents. I don't get rid of anything, with the exception of clothing that doesn't fit, so it all accumulates, a natural progression over time.

Each thing I've kept means something though. They're memories I wouldn't have unless I was here. Memories of the good times, and the silly times too. They're precious.

My phone rings, and I jerk out of my reverie.

"Hello," I answer, but lose my footing. I squeak like a mouse as I drop my phone. I fall to the floor giggling. "Hold on," I say aloud, hoping he hears me. Because I know it's Oliver. No one else would be calling me so late.

I hold on to the side table and pull myself up, wincing. Once I'm back on the bed, I grab the phone and hold it up to my ear.

"Hey," I say. "Sorry about that. I'm back."

"Are you alright?" he asks. "You didn't check your messages. I got worried."

I laugh again. "I told you, I needed a cold shower."

Oliver's silent for a moment, as if he doesn't know what to say. "If I were you, and you've achieved some sort of calm, I wouldn't check those texts tonight then. In fact, don't look at them. Just delete them, okay?"

"Why?"

"Just do what I tell you," he demands, then hangs up.

What's wrong with him? He must have sent me something bad if he doesn't want me to look at it. So, of course, that's the first thing I do. He's sent pictures, but I scroll up to the last message I sent him about the cold shower.

Oliver: *All the glacial water in Norway wouldn't help put out the fire you started.*

I smile at the text. Does he burn for me? I certainly hope so. I hope it hurts as bad for him as it does for me. It's only fair. He's unlocked something inside me that has a mind of its own.

Oliver: *That picture is boner inducing.*

I giggle. Why did he want me to delete these? They're great. He's supposed to be this older, sophisticated person, yet here he is, his words devolving. I love it. I have to read the rest of them.

Oliver: *I keep seeing this image of you in my head. You're in your bed, staring at that picture of us and it makes you come.*

The first picture pops up, and it's of him in a bed. Where is he? That's not the bed I saw in the window. It had a navy-blue duvet on it. I remember because the woman's dress was the same color.

He's not undressed in the picture, but his shirt is unbuttoned and his sculpted chest is partially on display. Oliver works out. He's got a strong, muscled chest. *Oh boy, that he does.* I wish there was more in the picture, but it only leads to where his abs start below his sternum. I wonder if he has that cut *V*, you know, the one that points like an arrow towards his cock. My thighs clench together.

His eyes are dark, and he looks like he's turned on. In the pictures we took, you can't always make out the green. I don't think it's because it was dark outside. I think it's because they change somehow.

I move on to the next message.

Oliver: *I don't like it when you don't answer me. It's torture. Are you trying to play hard to get?*

Hard to get? Is he serious? I might have been nervous last night, but I wasn't tonight. I flung myself at him. How on earth could he think I'm playing hard to get? I need to make it clear that I want him.

The next picture is only of his face. His eyes are closed, head tilted back, while he bites his bottom lip with those perfectly straight teeth. Is he doing what I think he's doing. I don't study that picture because I need answers.

Oliver: *Tell me you want me. Tell me you want me the way I want you.*

There's another picture and it makes my heart race. He's looking into the camera, his fingers in his mouth. The fingers that had touched me. The ones I'd watched him lick. The look in his eyes is bewitching. Those eyes may be the definition of bedroom eyes, the definition of smoldering.

"Oh, my God," I whisper.

So much for the shower I had. My legs tremble and I feel the wetness leak out of me. It spreads between my clenched thighs. I'm shaking when I move on to the next text message.

Oliver: *I'm sorry I'm like this. Your innocence is like some sort of sweet nectar on my tongue. I want to drown in it.*

So maybe he's not devolving, maybe he's more than he's ever been. He just needs some space to let it go, to let those thoughts fly. The separation in these text messages is safe because he's afraid of losing control with me. We're free to tell the truth in these messages. He's showing me his truth.

Those desires slide around my head, and it feels like a powder keg ready to blow sky-high. If this is all we have, then maybe I can give it to him. I think of what I'll say as I open the next text.

Oliver: *Don't hide from me.*

Oliver: *I'm so hard, I'm aching, Vale. I'm dying here. Answer me. Tell me everything. Give me your secrets.*

The next picture shows more of him. His arm covers his chest somewhat, and his hand must be between his legs. His head is tilted back, eyes closed, lips parted, and his cheeks are flushed. Is he about to come? He looks like he's about to explode. *I certainly am.* He wields his beauty like a weapon, and I'm over here dying to be his victim.

I lie back in bed, my pussy throbbing and definitely not calm. I reach down, spreading the towel. When I touch my slit, I'm so wet and sensitive my entire body jerks with one touch. The towel falls off my hair as I lift my head up and open the camera app on my phone.

I probably look like a disheveled mess right now, but I mimic what he's doing. The towel is open, showing the space between my breasts. I'm not on display exactly, my nipples are covered by the towel.

I don't think about it as my eyes close, and I strum my finger over my clit. I press the button to take the picture. I want him to see what he does to me. I open my eyes and immediately set up the picture to send. I add a message:

Vale*: You know my secrets. I want you. You're all I want.*

I rub my fingers against my clit while I eye the pictures he's sent me. When it rings, I jerk and drop it. It hits my sternum, and I rush to catch it. I answer rudely, "What?"

"You're magnificent," he replies, his voice deep and seductive.

"Where are you?" I ask. "You left."

"I drove a few miles, then turned back. I'm at home," he says and something in his tone has changed. He doesn't seem so on edge.

"I thought you may have went to be with Shae since I left you all hot and bothered." I regret it the moment I say it. I'm lying. I wasn't worried about him going to her tonight. I doubt he'd be sending me pictures of himself from her bed, or calling me.

"Jealous?" he taunts, and I can hear the playfulness in that single word.

"What if I am? Would it matter? You can be with her, but you can't be with me."

"That's not fair," he says, and it's true. "You know why we can't be together."

Unfortunately, I'm the one who said he couldn't touch me, that it wouldn't be fair to me. That might be why he said what he did, but I can't possibly fathom the reason he has for not wanting to fuck me. I can't.

"Actually, I don't know why. I'm of legal age. I'm not in a relationship. I've told you I want you, so there's consent. You've already touched me, Oliver. So no, I don't understand why you can't fuck me. Why you can't give me one night like you did with that woman."

I hear his deep inhale, but I stop him before he says anything else. "I'm not asking you for forever. I understand you're not interested in a relationship. I'm asking you for one night, no strings attached. I know you can't promise me anything. You don't have to. I can accept that."

"That's not what you want," he says and there's anger in his voice. It surprises me. "I think you want everything, Vale. I think you want long nights of passion. You want an ecstasy that only exists between lovers who know each other completely. You want loving, whispered words of ownership. You want us to fall in love."

My breath stutters and I know he hears it. That's pretty specific. I contemplate denying it, but I don't.

"Do I paint a pretty picture, sweetheart? You have to know that's not who I am. You say stuff about that woman, but you don't get it. You don't understand that I used her. I fucked her and felt nothing. I didn't know her name. It wasn't worth the brain capacity it took to remember. But I know you. I know myself. I have no illusions about what I want to do to you. I couldn't do it all in one night. I couldn't do it in a hundred nights.

"You're so innocent and sweet. You deserve more than a quick fuck and a man who ignores you after. I wouldn't want that for you. So when I tell you no, it's because I want to protect you. I don't want to be the asshole who breaks your heart, Vale, but that's exactly what I'll do. That's who I am."

I take in a deep breath trying to calm myself. At least he admits it. I knew he'd break my heart. I should be happy he's admitted what he is, what he'd do if we slept together, but it doesn't change the fact that I want him.

"Don't you think I know we can't be together? I knew it from the beginning, but it doesn't matter. I still want you. I knew someone like you would never be with me. You're too good for me, but for some reason you keep showing up."

He growls and it makes me shiver. "I'm not better than you, and you shouldn't accept that. You should fight, rage, and demand what you want. You need to find the words to fight, even if you lose. You have to, Vale. Don't give your power to a man like me. I don't deserve it."

He says don't do it, but it's too late. It's way too late. I don't say it, but I think we both know it. He's the only one in denial here. I don't know why we're going around in circles with each other. It doesn't make sense.

"Alright," I say, giving in. "I won't give you my power. I thought this would go a lot differently when I sent my picture. I can't believe I did that. I shouldn't expect anything from you, you're right. Good night, Oliver."

"Stop, Vale. Just hear me out. I like you. I don't want things to be bad between us. I want to know you. I want to be your friend. The experiences we've shared don't look like friendship necessarily, but I don't want to lose you either. Can we try to be friends? I'll stop flirting with you. I'll try to be good. I'm sorry I've sent mixed signals."

His words hurt, but I won't admit it. They're not what I want to hear. They aren't the sexy words I'd hoped for when I answered the phone. I caused this. I did this when I asked about Shae. I pushed him away.

"I wish we could go back to the beginning of this call and start over."

"Then let's start over. We can wipe the slate clean. I can do that, for you." I know it's a genuine offer but wiping the slate clean means I'll have to forget about his kisses and his touch. I can't forget because they'll be burned into my brain until the end of time.

I sniffle. I don't want to forget. I don't want to lose him. Why is this so hard? Why does it feel like he's already ripping my heart out? I feel the panic rising. I can't breathe.

"I gotta go."

"Vale, wait!"

"I gotta go," I say, the words stuttering out of my mouth, then I hang up. I can't continue doing this with him. It already hurts.

I'll never forget his lips. I'll never forget his touch. I can't wipe the slate clean because I'll never forget any of it. I'll never forget because without him I'll never feel that way again.

19

IS THIS LOVE?

OLIVER

I throw my phone on the bed. "Goddammit!" I yell. She's over there in her bed half naked, crying because of me. I hurt her. Again. Why do I do this? I take what she offers, then I pull back. She's offering me everything, even a way out. She says she doesn't need strings. She says she'll accept one night. I'm beginning to think it's me who can't accept one night. I don't know what to do. I want her so much.

My beast overwhelmed me tonight, taking control and saying those things to her. I couldn't believe it. I couldn't stop it, and I got scared. When I was finally able to take control, it was too late. She knew those depraved thoughts because the monster in me doesn't want to hold back with her. He wants to take her for himself. He wants to own her. *Mine,* he growls in the back of my mind.

I shake my head and take a breath. Think! I can't leave her broken. She deserves so much more than that. She deserves more than I can give her.

I grab my phone, then run out my bedroom door. I speed down the stairs and through the house trying to get to her. I need to make this better. I need to fix this.

Why can't I fix this?

I find myself on the platform outside her bedroom, watching through the window as she pulls a shirt over her head. Her hair is damp, a dark auburn, curling down her back when she pulls it up through the neck of her T-shirt. She isn't facing the window. I can't see her face, but I want to.

Her shoulders are shaking as she bends forward and puts her face in her hands. She's crying. She hurts and in turn it hurts me. Pain stabs through my chest, making me gasp. I did this. I fucked up.

I open the screen door and step through into the sleeping porch not making a sound. I walk the five steps to her bedroom door on autopilot. Silently, I open the door to her bedroom and cross the threshold. I knew it would be unlocked. She wanted me to come. She wanted me to be able to get to her. Oh, if she only knew such flimsy locks can't keep me out. Nothing can keep me away from her.

Her shoulders tense as the little latch connects when the door closes. Vale doesn't turn to look at me though; she doesn't want me to see her face. So I go to her, kneeling beside her on the antique rug. I pull her hands from her face. Before she can speak, I put my finger up to her swollen lips and shake my head. I don't want to talk right now. I don't want to argue or deny either one of us comfort. I lift her into my arms and lay her on her back, covering her with the multicolored quilts from the end of her bed. I take my shirt off and toss it onto her dresser.

She watches me with heartbroken eyes, her cheeks streaked with tears, her eyes shimmering with more of them. I did that to her. In my desire to protect her, I hurt her. I can't stand it.

I lift the quilts, getting in beside her. Her body is tense. She needs to say something. She opens her mouth to start so many times. I turn to her, wrapping one arm under her neck, the other at her back, pulling her against me. Why does this feel right?

Vale doesn't fight it; she comes willingly. How can she let go so fast? I lift her leg and place it across my hips. I want to be cradled with her body, her arms wrapped around me. I want her so wrapped around me I can't escape. I don't want to run anymore.

She looks up at me with teary, hope-filled eyes, and I bend and press my lips against hers. The kiss is brief, innocent and beautiful like her.

"I don't want to wipe the slate clean," she whispers to me. "I don't want to forget you, what we did. That's the only way I could wipe it clean."

"I don't want to forget you either."

We get lost in each other, but eventually we have to face facts. I wish I could forget why we can't be together. I want to break my own rules for the first time in my very long life.

"We can't undo anything we've already done, Oliver. We can be friends but if it does become something else, if we can't stop, maybe that's okay too. We just expand our definition of friendship."

Vale puts it so simply, like anything between us is simple. Yet I can't fight her logic either. The more we build it up in our heads, the more we fuck up. Perhaps we need to give this thing between us a chance.

The truth is I can't live so close and not touch her. We only have a few weeks before she leaves, and neither one of us has to be miserable leading up to her departure. The thought of her leaving hurts, but I have to let her go. It's not safe for her to stay here, near me.

"I'd like that, Vale. No pressure on either of us. We can try," I whisper back. "Just be who we are with each other."

When she looks up at me, I can see she's still hurting and it's all my fault. I wish I could make it better. I wish I could be the man she needs. But I am who I am, and wishes don't fix anything. Wishes won't stop me from killing her when I make her into a helpless addict who can't even feed herself.

Her leg tightens on my hip as she pulls me closer against her. Her cheeks are flushed, her lips red. She's a siren calling me to my death, but I don't want this to go much farther tonight. I want to slow this moment down and revel in the feel of her arms wrapped around me. I've never let a woman hold me.

I pull her into my chest, holding her tight. This feels a lot like fate, like she was meant to be in my arms if only for a little while. We were meant to meet. We were meant to touch.

Her lips are over my heart as she kisses me. Those sweet lips against the dragon tattoo, whose epitaph is only a reminder to guard my heart, not to let anyone in ever again. It's the sweetest kiss I've ever experienced. It makes my heart flutter the way it did when I was young, back when the world seemed new and exciting.

I reach out to turn off the lamp beside her bed. I intend to hold her, to ease her loneliness, her pain. She cups my cheek, and I kiss her delicate fingertips. I move her shirt aside and press my palm against the skin of her back. Her skin is so velvety soft, so warm, so perfect.

Vale breathes deep against my chest as she runs her palms over my skin, exploring me. I do the same. I'm out of my depth right now but touching her feels right.

I've never taken my time to learn each and every nuance of another's skin. I've never needed to. I've never wanted to be gentle with someone the way I am with her. I could touch her like this all night. I could kiss and taste her skin. I could touch every inch and maybe it's not about sex. Maybe it's about loving her.

My eyes widen at the thought. I can't love. Most of the other supernatural beings believe Lilu are incapable of love. They distrust us because of what we feed on, as if we were built wrong and shouldn't exist. We don't deserve love in their eyes. There are days I question whether that's true. My mother is in love with a monster, one deemed perfect for her by the Light.

Of all the Lilu I know, which admittedly have not been many, we are the smallest group of immortals, and none of them are mated. I've been in lust, but I've never loved someone romantically. Is that what I feel for Vale? Is this love? No, it can't be. It's not possible.

I hear her breathe in deep, then a sigh slips out. I pull her closer and the scent of her arousal nearly suffocates me. That cloyingly sweet, intoxicating scent of her arousal. I don't understand this woman. It wasn't that strong when my hand was down her pants, but now she's turned on by a touch. She's glowing with it.

I can't stop touching her. I lean down and pull her face to mine. I kiss her gently, nipping at her lips as I stare into her eyes. I don't push her. I give her the time to kiss me back the way she wants it. Her lips open and she presses her tongue into my mouth, sliding it against mine. She's so shy and gentle. My Vale is so sweet.

Our mouths dance in the darkness as we explore each other. We don't go farther than that. It turns out, that's all Vale needs, my lips on hers, our bodies molding against each other, her hands on my chest. If I were a good, human man, I'd marry her. I'd drag her to a priest, a pastor, the fucking courthouse even, and we'd sign our love and promises to one another. Then I'd take her home and love her like this. I'd be patient as she took me for the first time. I wouldn't stop telling her how much I love her, how beautiful she is. I'd worship every single inch of her.

But I'm not a good man, and I'm definitely not human.

I roll her under me, pressing her into the mattress. My breathing ratchets up like hers. I'm high on her scent, the feel of her restless, lithe body sliding against mine. When I look down at her, those jewel-like, aqua eyes are open, staring up at me. She sees me through the darkness I embrace and still there's a desperate longing in her eyes.

Vale wraps her legs around my hips, pulling me closer. I fall onto my elbows, one at each side of her head. We're so close I feel her chest rising with each sputtering breath against my lips. Her heart speeds up, thrumming inside her.

"I swear, I didn't come here for this, but I get lost in you, Vale. I can't stop," I whisper, admitting my failure. There's such a profound ache inside, an ache only she can soothe.

"Then don't stop."

She lifts up and kisses me once against my throat, then places one hand on my chest, over my heart. I'm filled with a light I can't comprehend, and it's because of her. All this is because of her.

"Don't ever stop," she begs me. "Please, Oliver, don't stop."

I don't want to fuck her like a beast. I can't. However, the need to be closer is calling, consuming me. I unbutton my pants, then pull them down just enough that I'm barely encased in my boxer briefs. I arrange myself, then press against her slit.

Vale is so wet that she soaks my underwear in seconds. I roll my hips against her slowly, letting her feel every inch of me. I wish we were closer. I wish nothing separated us, but it does and this has to be enough for now.

Dammit, this has to be enough! It has to.

Vale's head leans back against the pillows, and she moans softly with each exhale from her lungs. She's on fire, the heat between her legs burning me, scarring me, marking me as hers. I watch her when she comes undone, holding on to me with her entire body. And I swear her skin glows. She can't be entirely human, not when her soul is shining through her skin, trying to burst free. I need her to be free.

When she cries out, pushing her fiery essence into me, I can't help myself. I lean forward, my breath becoming uncontrolled against her open mouth. I come with her name on my lips. I come and drink her essence down. I don't know if I've ever fed so much in one night.

I can barely hold myself up as I take in huge gulps of air. My head is bowed against hers, and I'm breathing hard, like I've run a race. I'm shaken to my very soul—what's left of it anyway. I press my lips to her heart, the same way she did to me earlier. The monster in my head, growls, *Mine*. He's gently tugging at my mind, content but wanting more from her. I don't blame him. I do too.

"Vale—" I whisper, ready to ask her what she is, but I get lost in her eyes.

We're silent as we stare into one another's eyes. I don't have the words to express that moment with her. When I roll to her side, she wraps her arm across my stomach, lifting her leg across my hips. She lays her head on my chest, and a contented sigh escapes her lips. I hold her against me as my gaze gets stuck on those glowing green stars that decorate her ceiling. I feel calm. The monster is awake, but he's not clawing to get out, he just feels.

"Did I make you come?" she whispers.

I smile in the darkness. "Yeah, baby, you did."

Her heartbeat gets faster as she smiles against my chest. It feels good knowing I made her happy. It feels more than good, it feels right. Most things feel right with Vale.

"Good," she says matter-of-factly.

I laugh and she joins in. "That's twice tonight. Wanna go for round three?"

"What?" She doesn't believe me.

"I got off with my hand down your pants," I tell her. "It's so hot when you come. I couldn't help myself."

She lifts up on her elbow and looks at me. "I didn't know. I'm sorry."

"Why do you think I was in such a rush to go? I needed to change," I lie.

"Does that mean you're leaving now?" She lies her head on my chest again.

She's worried I'm going to leave her, so I squeeze her tighter against me. "I'll stay for a while longer, but I have to leave before Nick wakes up. I'll watch over you, sweet Vale," I tell her, lifting her head up so I can give her a quick kiss.

Her head falls again, but she's smiling when she closes her eyes. She falls asleep in my arms once again. I wish, not for the first time, that I could sleep beside her. I wish I could wake up in her arms. I wonder if she'd smile at me with those beautiful eyes when she wakes?

One day, this won't be so hard. One day, I'll make her mine if only for a little while. If only to show her what I can do. So she knows what she needs and she knows it well. She deserves nothing less than a man who can give her everything, their entire being, their soul. Vale deserves the world laid at her feet. She's a queen.

My fiery Queen, the beast purrs.

20

A PICTURE'S WORTH A THOUSAND WORDS

VALE

I stretch out on the bed as I wake up. If I get to spend time with him every night, I'll always wake up smiling. I think we finally figured out things between us. We're not a couple, but that wasn't my expectation. We're going to let things happen naturally, organically. That's the right call, honestly. As much as I can picture a future with him, I'm leaving at the end of the summer. Even though it hurts to think about it, I'm going back home, wherever that may be. I'm not going to be here and he will, so I can't put any more pressure on him than I already have.

I grab my phone from the nightstand and check my messages. I'm surprised to see one from Kat. I open it and see she's freaking out about the pictures I sent her. But I hadn't sent her the picture yet; I was going to do it this morning. I see the messages sent from my phone at 7 A.M., two actually. The first one has the picture Oliver took of us, where he's kissing my cheek.

Vale*: Gramps new neighbor is super HOT! What do you think? I've got a crush!!!*

I start laughing hysterically. I'm going to have to set up a passcode to protect my phone if Oliver's going to do things like this. As funny as it is, I can't imagine the trouble he's going to get me into. I need to

155

check if he sent stuff to other people . . . not that I know many other people.

I scroll down the messages. The next one Oliver sent says:

Vale*: I kissed him last night. I think I'm in love. He's so fucking HOT! KAT HELP ME!!!*

I snicker at that one. He's telling her the truth, though I don't know if I'm in love or lust with him, probably both. He really is so hot. He added a picture we didn't take together. He's sitting on my bed, his shirt off, his head in his palm, his back bent like he'd just woken up, and his long hair coming down in dark waves. The sunlight is barely coming through the blinds. How did he take that? He's not holding my phone. I look in the direction where the camera would be and figure he must have propped it up on my dresser.

I close the text messages, not looking at Kat's replies. I check my pictures. *Oh, my God.* There are at least twenty new pictures of us from last night. I'm asleep on his chest in a few, my cheek down, my palm over his heart. In some, he looks asleep with me, while in the others he's smiling while he kisses my forehead or stares at my face.

There are some where he's standing in front of the phone, his shirt in his hand, his pants slung low on his hips like he's about to leave. Oliver does have that sexy *V* I've only ever read about in dirty romance novels from the local library.

There's a picture where his hand looks like it's about to go down the front of his pants, where there's a bulge. He's smiling at the camera like he knows I'm looking. He winks in another one, and it makes my heart pound because his hand is down over his cock. It makes my entire body flush. *Holy shit!*

Oliver looks like a damn supermodel who's gracing the shoddy room behind him. In every picture he's either with me, next to me, or in front of my bed where I'm sleeping. It's like he left proof he was here with me, that he stayed while I slept soundly beside him. So I'd know it wasn't a dream. That it was real.

The last one was taken outside in the early morning light, and I can't help myself, I go outside. He's being cute as he smiles with those perfectly straight white teeth, though somehow his canines aren't showing. But that little dimple is. He's in front of the window that overlooks my bed. I'm asleep in the bed behind him, my legs spread. My shirt had ridden up and I could see my black panties. I don't remember putting them on. Did he put them on me?

As I study the picture, I think he was sending me a message. He'd had to leave because my clothes rode up, and he wanted to do more than watch me sleep. *Oh, my God, what if he took pictures of me on his phone?* Did he have his phone last night? I don't know. But it doesn't really matter, I wouldn't care if he did.

I race back into my bedroom when I hear my phone chime. I've completely ignored Kat's messages, but I don't have a chance to answer as my phone starts ringing.

"Hello," I say with a yawn. I look at the black cat clock on my nightstand, and it reads half past eleven. I can't believe I slept so long.

"Who's that guy?" Kat asks, demanding information.

"Gramps's new neighbor, Oliver. He's so hot, right?" I giggle as I jump onto the end of my bed and lay back with my legs propped up on the giant purple teddy bear.

"Is he the one who bought the house? Is he, like, living there, next to you, all the time?" She sounds a bit in awe of me at the moment, which is a rare sentiment from her.

"Yes, he's the guy who owns it."

"He's rich too? You better snap him up Vale because if you don't, I'm coming back and I'm going to steal him from you." She sounds like she's joking, but my hackles rise anyway.

"Off limits," I demand, way too loud. "Not yours, Kat. You're the one who went away on an adventure. You could've called dibs if you were here, but he's mine now." I'm drawing the line in the sand. She better respect this girl code I'm putting down.

"Okay, okay, don't get your panties in a twist. He's yours. You can tell he's into you in those pics. But aren't you leaving again in August?"

"Don't remind me."

I hear her tell someone she'll be right back and there's a second when she's silent. I hear something rubbing against the speaker and wonder if she put the phone in her pocket. When she comes back to the phone she asks, "So you kissed him already? How was it?"

I smile, understanding why she stepped away to chat. She probably didn't want to talk about this in front of Clark's parents.

"Yeah, I did. It was wonderful. I'm glad I waited." The memory from two nights ago is now playing through my head. How he'd held me as we talked about that dream.

"He did a number on you, didn't he. What is it? I can tell you're not telling me something, woman." She's dying to know what we did.

"It's kind of embarrassing actually. I had an orgasm when he kissed me. I don't know how. It was amazing, wonderful, sexy. It was all the things. Perfect."

"Aw! My best bud's in love! If you're impressed, then he sounds like a keeper. How did he make you come when you kissed him? Was he doing more than kissing you? Did you fuck him, Vale? I was wondering because that last pic was in your bedroom." She seems so excited by it all, and I wonder if she's jumping up and down.

She's always been a supporter of female pleasure. She's tried to find guys for me to lose my virginity with, so we could compare notes. Sometimes I don't think she has any other female friends. Not real ones anyway. She's popular, so she knows a lot of people, but I don't think they really know her. I'd like to think that I know her though.

"We didn't, I promise. We haven't had sex. Yet. He kissed me so good, I got off. That's the ongoing theory at least. He's perfect, Kat. He's making dinner for me and Gramps tonight. He's so different. I can't wait to introduce you."

"Gramps knows you two are dating? I never thought he'd let you date, like, ever. Not in a million years. Especially not an older man. How old is he?"

I let out a long breath. "Oliver's twenty-five and no, Gramps doesn't know. We aren't dating. But if he asked me, I'd say yes. We're just hanging out, feeling this whole thing out between us."

"You sound like you're quoting directly from the fuck-boy play-book. I think Brandon said that exact same thing to me, 'We're feeling it out, babe,'" she says in a snarky tone. Kat hates Brandon, and rightfully so. "Don't set yourself up for heartache or get attached to someone who isn't gonna be there in the end. Please. I did it, it sucks. You deserve better. Learn from my mistakes, sister."

Kat thought she was in love with Brandon, but he basically fake-dated her to get in her pants, and she fell for it. She told him she loved him and thought they were together, but he was only using her. She lost her virginity to him, then he never spoke to her again. Well, that's not exactly true. She threw a lab chair through his windshield at school. I'm not saying she was right—the stool should have been aimed at his dick, obviously. No wonder she's worried about me.

I can't tell Kat what happened before we kissed, how I'd seen him with another woman. And if I tell her he didn't want to deflower me because he'd ignore me afterward, she'd think he's just like Brandon and therefore hate him. I don't think he'd do that to me, yet I'm afraid he'll break my heart.

"Listen, I'll admit it, I want him to be my first, but I don't know if he does. We don't have to be together to have sex though. I'm okay with that. If we're meant to be, we will be, if we're not, I'm going to have the best time with him that I can. He's a good guy, Kat. He didn't make me promises. We're just going to hang out with each other for a while. I can't make him any promises either, you know."

"I know you don't have experience with guys and how stupid they act sometimes. I don't want to see you get hurt. You need to make him understand that if he hurts you, I'll kill him."

There's a pause in the conversation when we're both quiet. I wish she hadn't gone out west for the summer. "Kat, I really miss you. I wish you were here. If I leave before you get back, it's going to suck so much," I tell her. "I need my best friend."

"I miss you too. Colorado sucks. It smells like weed, even in public. I don't like it. We gave up hiking the mountains. Now we've got a yurt near Estes Park. It's camping in style. There's a toilet!" she screams excitedly, like a toilet means more to her than anything in the world right now.

I laugh so hard tears fill my eyes. "You seem a little too happy about the toilet. Has it been that bad?"

"Well," she says, drawing out the word, and I can tell she's about to let it fly. I'm glad she walked away from the group. "Camping sucks ass. For a few days it's fine. Then you don't shower and your boyfriend doesn't shower. You're so tired by the end of the day. And there's no sex. But you don't want to anyway because you both smell like swamp muck.

"During the day the packs are so heavy. It feels like you're carrying a full-grown man on your back. And it's so hot by day, and by the time night falls it's so cold you think your nipples will break off with the barest wind."

I make a face she can't see and say, "Ick."

But she's not done. "Everyone got fed up. Clark's parents were done, his brothers were done, we were done by the end of week one. No joke, I think this whole trip has ruined our relationship. I have a feeling we're not going to stay together when we get out of here. Currently that's the least of my worries."

"I'm sorry it's not going well." I feel bad it's not working out with Clark. He should have known camping with her for an extended period of time wasn't a good idea. She's high maintenance. Not the kind of girl who wants to rough it.

"Why did you want to go? Honestly, it doesn't seem like something you'd want to do."

Kat sighs. "I was worried Clark would find a new girl out here. One he'd be willing to break up with me for. I was scared not to go after he asked me."

"Maybe it's for the best. He's going to school in Ohio to play football. I know you, Kat. You weren't going to keep it in your pants with a bunch of hot college guys around. You're the one who told me that," I say. You see, Kat's a deep thinker trapped in the body of a bouncy blonde with no impulse control.

"I know. Anyway, I'm trying to get my dad to argue with the airline so I can switch tickets and go home early. I don't want to stay out here. I feel the walls closing in on me like that dude in *The Shining*. I'm so desperate, Vale, that I'm reading! Fun fact, I'm right down the road from the hotel that inspired that book. I think they have ghost tours. Sounds awesome!"

I laugh so hard, I snort. "I'll let Gramps know you read a book. A ghost tour sounds like fun, let me know if you see any. I hope your dad can get you out of there. If not, let me know and I'll get you a ticket." I'd been saving every penny I had for half my life to buy a car.

"You're sweet, but I can't let you break into your hot rod fund. I'll figure it out. You be patient and, if things go right, I'll be back early, and you can tell me all about wild nights with hot neighbors." We laugh, but I still hope nothing dramatic happens between them, especially when she's two thousand miles from her best friend and family. I don't like the thought of her being alone out there.

"You're leaving," I hear Clark say in the background. Kat is silent for a moment, and I wonder what she's going to do.

"Vale, I better go. I love you, girl! My phone has better service here. So call me."

"Love you too," I tell her sadly. "Be safe. Don't get into too much trouble."

"I won't. Bye," she says, and the line goes dead.

I've just witnessed the end of Kat and Clark, but I don't know how I feel about it. I'd known it would come to an end eventually since Kat and I had plans for debauched college fun, and Clark hadn't been mentioned in any of those.

Right now, college feels like a lifetime away. It'd always been my plan to go to Silver Springs University, but unfortunately, my parents put me in a religious homeschool program and because I didn't start in kindergarten, I'm behind. I was so frustrated by the entire situation that I'd secretly taken my high school equivalent test the first week I was back in Georgia. Gramps didn't know about it, but I imagine he'll find out soon when a letter comes in my name.

I was tired of waiting to start my life. I'm confident I passed the test, but not as much about staying here. I didn't know what would happen when I told my parents I was moving out. It would be harder to tell my father I was going to college. My father forbade it outright.

Perhaps it was time I asked Gramps if I could move in, but I'm scared. As horrible as it is living with my parents, a part of me still wants them to love me. I want them to accept me. The refusal to get a driver's license is because I'm afraid to disappoint them. I'm terrified of how my father might punish me. I've spent so much time being punished in my life, being locked up like a prisoner in my bedroom, the idea of going back worries me. For some reason it feels different this time.

I'm an adult now, so why would I want to go back? Why did any part of me want their approval or their love? The things my father did to me when I was little would have landed him in prison. If he hurt me the way he used to, I don't know if I could handle it. I don't want to think about it. I can feel the panic, that tightness in my chest, but luckily my phone chirps a message pulling me out of those memories before they can take hold.

Kat: *Find out if Oliver has a brother . . . or sister. I'm coming home early if it takes me hitchhiking across the Midwest.*

I smile down at the message. I take a screenshot of the text and send it to Oliver with the words, *This is your fault,* included. It's not long before he replies.

Oliver: *I've got a couple siblings. None who I'd bring here because you'd likely want to trade me for a younger, better model.*

I laugh because there's no way I'd trade Oliver Byron for anyone else. You can't get better than perfection. But it gives me an idea. With an evil smile on my lips, I stare down at his message. This is going to be fun.

21

SHE'S A MYSTERY TO ME

OLIVER

I spend the early morning sleeping for a change. I'd been pleasantly tired after spending the night beside Vale. I snuck out of her bedroom early in the morning after I heard Nick starting to move around. She looked so peaceful there, I couldn't wake her up.

I usually sleep a few hours a day, but I don't need much. I sleep out of boredom most of the time, a need to dream and let go. She needs sleep much more than I do. I think she might be different, not completely human, but I don't want to exhaust her. She keeps feeding me when we're together. It worries me even though she hasn't shown any signs of it hurting her. In fact, the way she danced around Nick's house yesterday, it made me think she had more energy than normal. She wasn't as docile as she'd been the last couple of weeks.

I'd spent part of my day talking to Nick about Vale. I asked him to help me get all the information she'd need to take her driving test. Nick said Vale clams up about it whenever he brings it up, but with her turning nineteen in a week, she's old enough to get her license whether her parents allow it or not. The plan is for me to take her to the DDS office, though I won't mention it until we get there, so it'll be like a surprise present.

I get the feeling Vale's mother Shannon gave Nick all her vital records when Phillip Granger decided his child was a demon. It still makes me cringe when I think about what Vale told me. Maybe Shannon isn't all bad if she'd tried to protect her daughter in some small way.

How awful was Vale's childhood? How did she survive it and stay so bright? I didn't want her to go back to them, but what right did I have to ask her to stay? I have no rights when it comes to Vale.

"I've been hoping that girl would come live with me since she was six years old. Phyllis and I saw how her soul seemed dimmer every time she'd stay with us. Vale didn't say anything about being treated badly, but I knew something was going on. Phyllis said we couldn't push her too hard because Vale could shut down. Phyllis was right, and that's why I let her get away with almost anything, in the hope that if she feels safe, she'll speak out one day.

"You know, when she's home with them, she's not even allowed her phone. She gets a weekly phone call as if she's in prison. They even took her out of school. She was on this swim team for home-school students, and they took her out of that as well. She wasn't allowed to keep the telescope we got her either. They tossed it in the garbage. Can you imagine?

"They make sure she's completely cut off from the world. We only got to talk to her because of those weekly calls. I'm all she has, Oliver. I'm glad you're trying to help because, one day, I won't be here and I want to know someone'll be there for her," Nick tells me while we sit in the office on the first floor. I've never seen Nick so on edge, but I understand why he's getting more worried by the day, Vale will be leaving soon.

We chat in the library most days when I come to join him. I've been doing all the translating for him. It's a lot of work, yet we find time to chat throughout the day. He's opened up a lot over the last couple weeks. We're running out of time. Every day is closer to Vale going back to people who hurt her. She may not admit it, but I know she's been hurt. I feel it in my fucking soul that her father hurt her and not just with his sexist, controlling beliefs.

It makes sense now, why Nick started sharing things about Vale. He knows I'll be right next door from her. He wants to make sure she has a protector when he isn't around. I don't blame him for wanting her to be taken care of.

"I'll watch over her. Don't ever worry about that. If she ever needs me, I'll be there," I say, but the words are sour on my tongue. I don't like making promises to mortals. It doesn't feel right. When you don't age, it means you can't stay in the same place for long. I'm lucky if I can get twenty years in one place, but I rarely stay that long anywhere.

I haven't been close with any mortal in a long time. I have acquaintances, but I don't have true relationships with them. Had I never met Vale, I'd have still wanted to be friends with Nicholas Dalton. He's a good man. One with a strength of character that's rare in this day and age. I find myself wanting Nick's approval, which is a pretty strange feeling. I hadn't wanted anyone's approval in a long time.

I'd need to make sure my family knows he's off limits. They can't feed on him, and they definitely can't treat him badly. I would especially have to warn my mother because I knew they'd argue. She's a very strong, opinionated woman, and completely unafraid to express it. I can see it now . . . oh, how they'll fight over Byron's work in this house. For the first time in my life, I want to play protector to someone outside my family. I want to protect Vale for Nick. And I want to protect Nick from my mother.

"Vale's something else. When she's not so nervous, she's something to behold," I say, unable to stop the words that escape my lips.

"That she is. She can argue with the most patient and knowledgeable people. She just holds so much inside," he says with a smile as he grabs the clipboard from my desk. He's been keeping insanely detailed notes on every book, every scroll, even when he needs me to translate their titles and author.

"Did she argue with you?" He gives me a look like he's studying my every move. I feel like he's seeing something he hadn't before.

My cheeks flush at the thought of how we argued. *Get it under control man, or Nick might kill you.* He knows something's up. "Yeah. We've argued a lot actually. I was surprised because she usually seems so timid," I try to explain without giving anything away.

"It's hard to tell her no when she finds something she's passionate about. You should've seen her when we built those go-karts a few years ago. She wanted bigger and bigger engines, always wanting to go faster. Finally, I taught her how to drive a car. Just learn to let her roll with it. If she didn't trust you, then she wouldn't have argued. I'm surprised to be honest. I think someone has a crush." Nick chuckles when he stands up, stretching, his spine popping.

"I do not," I gasp like he said something completely preposterous.

Nick's full-on laughing now. He holds the clipboard to his belly and shakes his head. "I didn't mean you, Oliver. I meant Vale. She's been reading *Dracula* again. That's the third time this summer. I think she's in one of those romantic moods that teenagers have. Be nice if she tells you. Let her down easy because I don't know how to heal a young person's broken heart," he says, then he makes his way out the door. His head pops back in. "I'll see you at dinner."

Oh, if Nick only knew what kind of mood his granddaughter was in, he'd find a way to murder me. He doesn't want Vale to give her dreams up for a man. Oh no, he wants to guard her and push her to achieve all she's ever wanted.

Would he be any easier on me if he knew I want the same thing? That it's one of the reasons I turned her down. I don't want her to lose herself when her life is just beginning. I don't want to destroy her dreams, her future.

If I could have Vale, I wouldn't let her give up anything. I'd push her to work harder to get it. I'd make sure she had everything she needed. I'd fight for her, support her. Alas, Vale isn't mine, and all I can do is make empty promises to Nick so he won't worry about her. Nick has more faith in me than I do. I can't stop thinking about her. I can't stop pondering what I'd do to make her smile. I want to make her happy. I need her to be happy.

The notification sounds from my phone. It's turned over, screen down, so I lift it and see that Vale has replied to my message. I smile as I unlock my phone, then almost choke on my tongue. Fuck me!

There's a picture of Vale, her long copper hair in a single, thick braid that falls over one shoulder between her perfectly round tits.

She's topless in the mirror, her phone in one hand. Her head is cocked to the side, cheeks flushed, as one delicate finger is sliding between her smiling lips.

Vale*: Can't get better than perfection.*

The message couldn't be more true, but it shouldn't be me she's talking about. It's her. I'll never be able to get this out of my head. I'm grateful for her picture, her bravery in showing me, but I know every inch of her I see is an inch I need to touch, to taste. And these teasing pictures make me want her more.

I try to think of anything I can say back, anything I can add that would mean something. In the end, what I have to say is the absolute truth. I can't deny it this time.

Oliver*: No arguments with perfection. I'm looking at it right now.*

All I get in reply is a blushing, smiling cartoony face. I hate text messages!

22

PAINFUL BEAUTY

VALE

I take my time getting ready for dinner. I took a long shower, exfoliated, and shaved my legs. I blow-dried my hair and curled the ends. If we have the chance tonight, I hope he'll touch me again. It's why I'm going through all the trouble. I even did my laundry today so I'd have something decent to wear.

I'd ruined one of my skirts trying to iron it—so much for wrinkle free—and it now had a burned imprint of the iron right on the ass. So instead, I opted for a yellow sundress that could get wet without ruining it and a pair of chunky, cork-heeled sandals with braided straps.

Oliver had told me to bring a bathing suit, so I pack a bag with my new black bikini that I'd yet to wear and clothes to change into that are actually comfortable. Gramps and I haven't gone swimming yet this summer. And with Kat gone, I didn't think I'd get to wear the bikini at all. So, when Oliver offered I was super excited.

I love swimming. I missed it so much. I used to love to compete with the other kids at the gym. I'd swim faster and jump off the high dive when none of the others were brave enough. It was a way to discharge all the energy that left me anxious. If I was exhausted, I didn't get in as much trouble. But that outlet ended pretty quickly once my father learned boys were allowed to swim with the girls.

Hoping to look more sophisticated, I decide to clip half my hair up at the side so it shows the length of my neck. When I look at the floor-length mirror in my bedroom, I feel like an imposter. I feel like an intimidated, little girl, not a woman.

I don't have a speck of makeup on—*Women wear makeup, right?*—so, I grab a tube of tinted lip gloss and slather it across my lips. But I still feel like a fool as I stand there staring at myself, wondering if I'll ever feel like a woman.

I'm about to leave my room but worry stops me. What's going to happen at Oliver's house? Now that my mind has slowed down, I don't know if I can hide what we did from Gramps. Will he know I kissed him? Will I be able to hide it? Should I go? I don't know what to do, but I told them both I'd come, and I'm sure he told Gramps I'd be there by now. I have to go.

I force myself to walk down the rear staircase. This time guilt is slowing me down a bit. Oliver is friends with Gramps; I'm putting him in an impossible position. What will happen if Gramps finds out about what we've been doing behind his back? He'd be very mad at us.

I make my way out the back door, then cross the partially covered wooden deck in the back where I first met Oliver. I step onto the big gray flagstones which connect our yard to his. Gramps and I have always wondered who built the stone pathway. It was one of the many mysteries about these houses. I wonder if Oliver knows. I bet it was someone in love. They must have built the path together to make it easier to get to one another . . . I obviously have love on the brain.

The sun doesn't go down till late in the summer, so there's still sunlight. Though I think a meteorologist would call it twilight. You know, the time of day when the sound of crickets and cicadas singing has just started up. The incessant buzz of a southern, summer-night symphony. I miss that song so much whenever I leave Silver Springs.

What little light is left paints parts of the sky in shades of orange to peach, then to a rich salmon-pink. I stare up at Oliver's house in awe. It looks so much larger now.

I can't help my own curiosity and search for his bedroom window. The light is off. I know he's inside somewhere, probably still cooking in the kitchen. Would he try to make a good impression on me tonight? The way Gramps and I had tried for him.

I make my way onto the porch that wraps around to the back of the house. I admire the pretty white spindles and the detailed brackets that pull it all together in the corners. I study the swirling designs with one hand on a tall, Corinthian column to keep me steady. The first-floor bay windows sit protected under the porch roof. I hadn't noticed before, but the glass flashing of each window is intricately detailed. The glass is trimmed in royal-blue, and red roses sit at different intervals with frost-colored leaves and vines. I bet it's amazing with the early morning sunlight shining through.

The house is beyond beautiful. I've never seen so much detailed work on a single house. Even the fish scale shingles, with their robin's-egg color, popped. Each piece is astounding in its beauty. I could sit on the lawn out front, studying the facade for hours and continue to find new details. I can't wait to see inside.

I ring the doorbell, a tinny sounding ring that I hear from outside, then wait, fidgeting, until Gramps opens the door. I giggle, not expecting him.

"Long time no see, stranger. Thanks for the pancakes this morning. If you keep making those, I'm going to gain a hundred pounds. How's the library stuff going?" I ask, then give him a quick hug.

"Oh, Vale, you have to see it. It's exquisite. There are Byron originals. Come and see," he says, then he's off, taking me into Oliver's house as if he owns the place. Why did he answer the door anyway? Maybe Oliver's still cooking even though I'm late.

Gramps leads me straight to the library, though I really want a tour of the whole house. Most of all, I want to find Oliver. I follow Gramps and pretend to march behind him like a good soldier. I take in the foyer with its dark wood paneling that shines, dust free in the mellow Tiffany lighting. It's so nice, and for the life of me, I don't understand why someone like Oliver would want to have a house like this. It seems too traditional for a single guy.

I look up at the antique, floral runner on the stairs, knowing his bedroom is up there. I wonder if he's in it. I start to walk in that direction, but Gramps interrupts my thoughts by tapping my hand. I follow him through a formal living room, then past several rooms with carved doors tightly closed.

There it is, through decorative pocket doors made from dark wood and stained glass. The stained glass is decorated with a gold shield and bright, blood-red roses, the same color as the ones outside. I wonder if it's some sort of family crest. There's definitely a theme inside and out. The roses must be important. I smile with the memory of the rose he left at my bedside and how it'd been stripped of all its thorns.

I step through the doors, and Gramps closes them gently behind me. *Holy shit!* There's no way this has always been here. It couldn't have been. "Did he build the library on to the house or is this original?" I ask as I stare up at the domed ceiling that must be at least thirty-five feet high. There's a second floor at the base of the dome where beautifully hand-carved bookshelves line the wall.

I can't believe my eyes. It's magical. The space is huge, probably bigger than Silver Springs' public library. How is this here? It doesn't make sense. I swear the house is the same size as Gramps's house. I've never seen the dome. Surely no amount of trees and shrubbery could have covered all of this up.

"I think he added at least part of it on. I'm not sure. You'll need to ask him. Isn't it lovely. Come over here, come and see," Gramps says with excitement and joy in his voice. He loves it here.

"Now I know why Oliver needed help. Gramps, this is something else." I gasp in awe as I study the painted dome above me.

The dome is painted to imitate the sky above with pale blue and brushstrokes of creamy white meant to mimic the clouds. There are many small gold fleur-de-lis medallions, each like a star, and tiny lamps that glow and come down like rain at different intervals. I bet it would look like the night sky when the rest of the lights are off.

I turn in a circle underneath, watching as each angle changes it. Not only are the medallions a map of the night sky, but the lights are meant to look like meteors. They put the glowing plastic stars in my bedroom to shame. Is this what people say is a sign? If so, what's it a sign of?

For a moment, I can't look away. I'm in shock, awed by the

library's beauty. I've never seen anything like it. The dome itself may be the most beautiful piece of architecture I've ever seen.

"Gramps, who designed this library?"

Gramps looks up, joining me while I stare at the dome. "I knew you'd love that. Oliver designed it. He's an architect. Didn't he tell you?" he says, and all I can do is nod my head. He did tell me that, the night we met, but I hadn't thought anymore about it.

It is a sign. It must be.

Gramps grabs my hand and tugs me forward, jerking me out of my reverie. I follow him into a reading nook that happens to have several yellowed, handwritten pages protected in a glass case. I study it, but the handwriting is curled and slanted, slashed across the page—not exactly readable.

"What are those?" I ask, curious why these would be protected so.

"Those are Lord Byron's works, written by his own hand. And those are love letters to his muse. I can't imagine any reason these shouldn't be in a museum somewhere, but Oliver insists they must stay here. Some of these poems have never been published. I don't understand why they don't share them with the world," my grandfather explains, and I pat him on the back to comfort him.

"What Nick didn't tell you of course, is that these pages aren't mine to share with the world. I'm only their keeper. They belong to my mother," Oliver says, and I immediately turn toward the sound of his voice.

My cheeks heat when I take him in. He's leaning against a finely carved mahogany bookshelf, wearing a black apron that says KISS THE COOK in bright red letters. I try to calm my treacherous heart and the giggle that wants to bubble up because of that apron. How does he do that? You think you know a man and how serious he is, but suddenly he's got a man bun and a KISS THE COOK apron on.

Every time I see him it's something different, which doesn't fit in this puzzle. I wish I knew him better. I wish I understood him more. I have to look away, back to the precious pages that have my Gramps so enthralled. If I don't, I'll be stuck staring at him and Gramps will be pissed.

"Obviously Oliver can't part with something which doesn't belong to him, Gramps. His mom might kick his ass." I chuckle and Gramps sighs sadly.

"You're right. I know you're right. Oliver, I hope your mother comes to visit soon. I need to talk to her about these." Then, before my grandfather can continue, Oliver excuses himself.

Gramps is staring down at the pages lovingly or longingly, I'm not sure which, so I ask him where the kitchen is so I can offer Oliver my help. He tells me the direction, and I leave him there, a bit worried about the look in his eyes. I understand Gramps thinks this knowledge should be shared with the world, but this is their family business. They should decide the fate of those pages, not him.

Outside the library, there's a small dining room to the left that opens into the kitchen. When I get to the open door, I'm hauled through it. I'm pressed against a wall so suddenly the breath leaves my lungs entirely. Oliver leans over me, his eyes wide as he says, "I want to suck your blood," in a fairly comical, Lugosi-esque accent.

Who is this man?

I can't help it, I laugh so hard my eyes tear up. "God, Oliver you're such a weirdo."

The look in those unique green eyes is anything but amused. Then, as if he can't control himself, he's on me. His lips and teeth are at my neck. His gentle bites over my sensitive flesh set me aflame. He increases the pressure in warning, but he doesn't hurt me. I can hear him inhaling the scent of my skin, breathing me in. I reach out for him, but he's gone before I can wrap him up in my arms. I'm left leaning against the wall, aching for those lips once again while he's behind a stone kitchen island, chopping lettuce like nothing happened. How is he able to hide this so easily?

I take a deep breath as I watch him, my world turning on its axis. Whenever I'm around him it's like I'm high or dizzy. Will I ever stop feeling this way? Do I want to stop feeling like this? Finally, I'm able to calm my heart.

I clear my throat. "Do you need any help?"

When he looks up from his lettuce, his pale skin is flushed a bit at the top of his cheeks. Then he smiles at me and his whole face lights up, and I swear it's like he was made for love. Beauty seeps out of him.

I feel special when he looks at me. But when he smiles at me, I feel like a god.

As I watch him in the fading light that's cascading through the windows around the back door, it occurs to me that that's his super-power. He can make anyone fall in love with him. He's beyond beauti-ful, like an angel birthed from the exquisite intricacy of the cosmos.

My heart aches in my chest, seeing him like this in the watery light that spills across his head, his shoulders. He's something ethereal—not of this world.

I feel lucky to be able to witness him existing.

It was easier in the dark last night, when he kissed me, when he touched everything, maybe even my soul. It's harder in the light, harder to deny how much I want him. No, it isn't easy. It's more than the pressure and heat it takes to create a diamond. It's painful looking at him but not being able to touch him.

I want him so badly. I want his body against mine. I want his hands all over me. I want to feel his breath against my skin, his demanding kisses. He was right last night, but I was so willing to deny it. In this moment, I acknowledge his power over me, this intoxicating man. I want everything, all of him. He should be mine.

It feels like we were meant to be. It feels like fate. Oliver is my destiny. I know it in my soul. How do I show him the truth that I already know deep inside?

I breathe calmly, deeply, shoring up my courage. I step over to him and tug on his apron, turning him to face me as if I'm in control for once. I need that power too; I can't let it fall through my fingers. I can't stop. I wouldn't want to. I lift up on my tiptoes and wrap my arms around his neck, pulling him forward. I kiss him right there in his sparkling, chef's dream kitchen. He doesn't have a moment to stop what's happening.

I taste his lips as he wraps his arms around me, pulling me closer. I can't get close enough. I never can, and those touches, so fleeting, they're never enough. The kiss only lasts seconds before he pulls away.

I'm devoid once more of the warmth and safety of his arms as he steps back on his heel to look at me with a gentle smile.

"You're a bad girl," he whispers, shaking his head as his eyes linger on my lips. "We can't do this now."

"I know," I tell him. It breaks my heart all over again. He's right of course. We can't, yet it's all I want. "But I want—" I stop because I hear footsteps. "Pasta," I say as my grandfather steps into the kitchen.

"We'll dine alfresco," Oliver says as he gathers several covered dishes, placing them on a tray. He steps out the back door quickly, like he needs to escape. Sadly, I think it's me he needs to escape from.

I stand at the counter and continue chopping the lettuce as Gramps grabs another cloche covered tray. He follows Oliver through the back door. When the door shuts, I drop the knife and step over to the window to look out. Oliver sits the tray down, then turns to look out over the backyard. Lights come on and start to twinkle like tiny stars around him.

With the sun setting behind his head, for a moment, he looks like an angel, a halo of orange light clinging to him. His cheek twitches, and I realize he's trying not to smile. He's fighting it, but it's there all the same. This smile isn't for anyone else, just for him, a secret I'll keep forever.

Gramps walks up to him and pats him on the back. He turns toward Gramps, but his eyes slide to me at the window and I jump. I've been caught. Then his smile changes, his eyes light up. Gramps starts to turn back to the door, but I rush back to the counter to finish chopping the lettuce. It's what I should have done from the start instead of ogling him.

23

I CAN'T UNSEE THAT

VALE

Oliver was true to his word. He'd cooked way too much food. You'd think he was cooking enough for an army, not just the three of us. He's a fine cook though. He'd made fresh pasta by hand, and it makes me wonder if there's anything this man can't do. He seems too perfect to exist in this world.

Over the hours, I've learned Oliver's an architect who has a passion for historical homes. He specializes in historic preservation and restoration, but he's also been studying sustainable building models in Europe. He explained how these Victorian homes would one day fade from existence if people didn't make them more sustainable. He didn't want to see them disappear. I understood what he meant. These houses are unique with a chaotic character that doesn't exist anymore.

Oliver is very funny when I'm not stuck in my head thinking about his lips, his body, the way he kisses, or how his ass looks in those well-tailored pants. He's clever, with a quick-biting wit that intimidates me. I could listen to him duel with Gramps over literature and history for hours. They quote pieces and discuss them at length like philosophers. I don't step in often, but I admire them both for their easy banter.

I'm not like that. I wish I was, but I think too much before I speak.

I analyze the situation to death because I learned fear at a young age. I learned that my opinions were not and never would be appreciated by my parents. So now, I turn words over and over in my head, making sure they're safe before I speak. I'd assumed everyone was like that, but Gramps isn't, and neither is Oliver.

I feel safer here in Silver Springs, but old habits die hard. I can't break out of my shell enough to join in their conversations even though I know many of the subjects they've discussed. I ask a few questions about Oliver's job, but I can't make myself jump in more. The fact is it takes a kind of emotional toll on me after a while.

"What about you, Vale? What are your plans for college?" Oliver suddenly turns to me and asks. "Let me guess, astrology and astronomy. Am I right?"

Gramps laughs, but he doesn't say a word as he waits for my answer. I'm in the hot seat, and I don't like it. I wrap my finger around and around in the skirt of my dress while they both stare at me.

"No, not astronomy and astrology, although if I didn't hate math so much, I'd want to study astrophysics and aerospace engineering. Since algebra is my worst nightmare, I think I'll stick with a general education degree until I can figure out if there's a gateway for female pilots."

Oliver narrows his gaze on me while Gramps seems happy with my answer.

"You want to be a pilot in the military?"

"It's one of the only ways to become an astronaut, and that girl is going to space," Gramps explains with a genuine smile. He must have had too much wine because he never agrees with my plan.

"Can't you become a pilot without the military?" Oliver asks.

"In all honesty, I don't know what I want to do. Some days I want to be an astronaut, then some days I want to rehab old cars. When I figure it out, I'll let you know. How about you let me do some job shadowing so I can rule out being an architect?" We all laugh at that.

"I don't work for a traditional firm, so it wouldn't be a problem to show you the ropes," Oliver offers with a smile. "There can be a lot of math involved though."

"Thank you. I'm curious about what you did to this house and the whole process behind it. It's beautiful. I love the idea of bringing old, broken things back to life."

For some reason Oliver blushes. "I do too. When you find a project you love, like this one, it's not work. I wish I could've been here throughout the entire remodel, to see it all take shape. That's the problem. I design, but I'm rarely there on the build site these days."

"I got to see it," Gramps says, then he starts telling Oliver about the construction crews and how the front yard turned into a muddy bog in the spring. I bow out of the conversation.

The backyard is lit up by inviting fairy lights, and when the fireflies come out, the contrasting colors of their light makes the night wrapped around us seem magical. It's so beautiful here. Oliver has created a slice of paradise in southern Georgia.

It's not long before I start getting antsy. I'm fidgeting with the tie of my dress when I look down at the pool. I've hit my limit with the amount of mental energy I've used to sit at this table. I'm ready to move. I'm ready to dive in.

"Oliver, is it okay if I jump in the pool?" I interrupt when their conversation lulls for a moment while Gramps takes a drink of the no doubt expensive red wine Oliver's been serving all evening.

I was served wine, but I only took a sip. I don't like the way alcohol can take away inhibitions. I could get in a lot of trouble drinking, and it has nothing to do with Gramps saying no. He hadn't stopped Oliver from serving me, and he never said a word when I took a sip.

"It's getting late, Vale. Are you sure about swimming tonight?" Gramps asks.

"I'm sure. I haven't been all summer." I hope he doesn't make me point out that he's been at Oliver's house till late every single day since they met.

"It's fine with me if it's okay with Nick."

"I'm going to head home. I ate too much. Vale, it's okay with me. Just be safe. Get home before Oliver goes to bed, alright? I don't want you swimming alone."

Oliver points toward the path and offers me directions to the pool house where I can get changed and find a towel. I give my Gramps a hug good night, then thank Oliver when he stands like a gentleman. There's a moment when his hand lifts at his side like he's going to take my hand, but it falls quickly. I give him a weak smile and walk away.

I head down the path to the pool house. This isn't a changing room, it's an entire separate house. When you enter, there's an open concept kitchen, dining, and living room. And there's a wall of glass overlooking the pool. It's much more modern than the main house. There are multiple bedrooms, but I choose the first one to change in.

Why would he need so much space? He's a single man. I think. I never asked him if he was married or if he had kids, but here he is with this huge house and no one to share it with. It's either sad or he's hidden something from us. Gramps didn't tell me he was married. *Please don't let Oliver be married.* I don't think I could cope with the guilt if he was. It would make all the shit my father spewed true. I'd have done exactly what he said.

I slip out of my dress and into the black bikini, then take the clip out of my hair and leave it on the counter in the bathroom. I grab one of his fluffy white towels and head toward the pool, barefoot. I'm so excited to swim tonight.

As I get closer, I no longer hear Gramps and Oliver talking. Oliver probably escorted him home or maybe he's watching me from the veranda and I just can't see him. The thought of him seeing me in this bikini is scary. I don't think I've ever been so naked in front of someone. What if he saw my unfashionable curves and thought I was fat? What if he never kissed me again? What if he didn't want me? In the end, I don't want to think about it. I need to have fun for once.

I walk over to the diving board and step up. I haven't jumped off a diving board in years. Not since I was banned from the gym pool by my dad. I stand on it, admiring the huge pool, then I close my eyes for a moment as a warm wind blows. It sends ripples that expand across the crystal-clear water. I take a breath before jumping in. I drop down and down into the deep water. When I hit bottom, I kick up and swim upward as fast as I can.

The water is warm and as soon as I break the surface, I see the lights in the pool have come on. They must be motion activated, like the lights of the pool house. I float on my back and study the sky, smiling as I look up at the stars and admire the happy twinkling of Antares, one of my favorite stars. It's a tie between Antares and Sirius, both twinkle and flash in a multitude of colors. I'm happy. I love this place.

After doing a few laps from one end of the pool to another, I'm out of breath, so I swim to the shallow end, step out, and stretch my arms above my head and arch my back. Wondering if I can still do a flip into the water, I head back to the diving board.

As I ready myself to jump, I see Oliver watching me from the gate, and I lose my train of thought. Flailing, I'm surprised as I hit the water back first, screeching before I sink. I'm in shock for a moment and sink lower. Then strong arms wrap around my waist, and I'm being pulled to the surface.

I cough when I hit air. Oliver pulls me up and out of the water, lifting me up onto the edge of the pool. I'm sitting there trying to catch my breath when I hear a wet slap and look back at him. He's there, stepping out of his pants, and my eyes widen like saucers.

"What are you doing?" I choke out, panicked.

"Getting out of my wet clothes. Are you okay?" he asks as if he's worried about me, but the man is stripping.

"I'm fine," I bark, unable to make eye contact as the last piece of clothing lands on the concrete with a loud *smack*. My cheeks heat so much I think they might melt off.

Is he naked? Did he just strip in front of me? I can't look. Then again, he could still be in his underwear and technically it would be safe. I mean, all his bits would be covered, and that's safe, right? But do I want to play it safe right now? I've never been in this situation before. I don't know whether to look or be respectful and look away.

Oliver laughs and I can't help myself, I want to see his face, his smile. I look up and there he is, water dripping from his long hair, slicing down his body in rivulets that reflect the pool lights, a bright smile plastered to his lips. I take in a deep breath as my eyes wander over his body. My jaw drops.

His body looks like it's carved from pale stone, defined by strong muscles. His shoulders are broad, and his abs are cut deeply with shadowed grooves that lead down to the *V* of his hips as it disappears into his underwear. Oh, my God, that's his . . . my brain is officially broken. I stare at his crotch for much longer than is strictly necessary. Days could have gone by while I stare at it. It's huge. It's not normal to be built like that. Although, he *is* tall, and Kat told me about tall men and shoe size.

"Penny for your thoughts?" he says, and I struggle to understand his words. They don't exactly hit home.

"Uh-huh," I mumble because I can't look away, I can't form a coherent sentence. Oliver Byron has broken me.

"Dammit, Vale. I didn't want to do this."

He gets down on his knees beside me and no matter what he does, I can't unsee the outline of his cock in those black boxer briefs. I can't unsee his perfectly chiseled body. I can't unsee the red dragon tattooed on his sculpted chest. I can't unsee any of it. It's burned into my memory.

I'm burning, the sight of him has set me ablaze. Will I burn hotter if he touches me? I'll burn to ash and cease to exist at this rate. He's the most beautiful man I've ever seen, and my brain doesn't know how to process the knowledge.

Of course he pushes me into the pool like an asshole. As I bob out of the water, he jumps in beside me. The water splashes me in the face, but I wipe it away before he surfaces close to me.

"The way you look at me—" His voice is breathy and hoarse. "The need in those huge, innocent eyes, begging me to dirty you up. You're killing me," he growls the last words. His voice travels down my spine, making my thighs clench together.

Oliver closes his eyes for a moment as if he's trying to find strength. When his eyes open, it's all heat, boiling fire. "I want to drag you in the house and spread your legs. I want to lick and tongue fuck that tight little pussy of yours till you're screaming and clawing at my back. I want to fill you up and make you come. Then I want to do it all over again. I want to escape Hell just to show you a dark little piece of heaven, beautiful."

For some reason, my mind sticks on the word "beautiful." I look up and suck in a deep breath. "You think I'm beautiful?" I ask, and it's barely a whisper. How could he think that?

"That's some selective hearing you've got. That's all you got from that?" he asks, brows knotted together. "Come here."

It's not so deep now, so I walk over to him in the water. He wraps his arms around me, lifting me up, and I wrap my legs around his waist. He's so warm and suddenly I'm shivering. He didn't answer me. Why didn't he answer me?

I grab his face in my hands, and I know he can see the awful desperation on my face. He doesn't understand. "There's been no one —" I clear my throat, trying to get the words right. "No one has ever thought I was beautiful."

Oliver clenches his jaw at my words. I want to scream because he isn't saying anything. God, I wish he'd say it. I'd give anything for Oliver Byron to think I'm beautiful. I'm ashamed that I need to hear it, but he doesn't answer me, and I think my heart cracks a little bit. Why does that word mean so much? Why do I care what he thinks about me? He's perfect, and I'm just me.

He tightens his arms around me as he carries me out of the pool and into the pool house. Like a doll, he sits me down on a bed, then he leaves, shutting the door. It's the bedroom I left my dress in, so I stand up and start stripping out of my bathing suit. I'm stepping out of the bottoms, completely naked, when he returns.

"I didn't know if I could die until this moment," he says in a strangled whisper. There's longing in his eyes, but there's lust too, and it's stronger, turning his eyes black like in my dream.

I'm shy by nature, but right now, when I see how otherworldly his eyes have become, it takes away my nerves. His darkness is like the vacuum of space, it calls to me. I stand up straight, kicking the bikini bottoms away. I turn to face him so he can see all of me. This is my truth. I might not be perfect, but this is me, this is my body.

Look at me, Oliver Byron. See me.

There's a sudden buzz in the air like electricity sizzling. My skin heats, and that fire that's been trapped in me my whole life is burning me up, begging to escape, to be free. I want to be free!

He takes one step closer, and so do I. The devastation that's about to happen is exhilarating. It's exciting even though my world is about to crash down in front of me. Everything I've believed, everything I've known is about to be destroyed because of him. I can't stop it. I don't want to.

It's at this moment, although I hate to admit it, I know my father is right. I'm bad, ungodly, unholy. I'm a monster and, without a doubt, so is the man in front of me. I want to dance with that beast in my flames.

Oliver takes a deep breath, his body tense, as he starts clenching his fists at his side. I see the war waging in his eyes and his desire to stop the madness. I also see the part of him that's more beast than man. That part of him needs me; it's growling from within his chest, trying to claw its way out to get to me. I can hear its begging inside my mind, *Burn with me*, it growls. What could he be?

"I'm sorry," Oliver says, then he rushes me. I feel weightless when we collide. He lifts me into his arms, holding me up by my thighs as our lips crash into each other.

He's mine. Come hell or high water, I'll never give him up. He's my fate. We're meant to be. But then I feel his body tense up and he jerks his lips away from mine.

"I can't do this," he growls, but I don't believe him because he stares at my mouth before leaning back in. He bites into my lower lip, sucking it into his mouth.

"I need you. Make the pain go away," I beg him. Why won't he do this for me?

Oliver is the only person who can help me. I need him to stop this constant hurt that's bloomed between my legs. This new, exquisite torture he brought out in me. It's there, humming incessantly. Sleep can't take the thoughts of him away because he's there in my dreams. His very existence is an assault on all my senses. How can he fight the pull when I feel like crashing into him, destroying everything just to feel his lips on mine?

He sets me onto the edge of the bed and quickly backs away, his hands out before him like a shield. I lean back, my legs spread as I show him all of me. There's no modesty, not when my own monster claws to get free. The need claws at my chest, paining my heart, which beats too fast with the sight of him.

"This is yours," I remind him, sliding my hand down my body, smoothing my fingers between my slippery slit. "Only yours," I say and mean every word.

The muscle in his jaw ticks as he tries to gain control. I can hear the grinding of his teeth. "You have to go," he says, then takes another step back. "You need to run away home, right now. You need to get away from me because I'm not in control right now. I'm not entirely—"

"Not entirely human," I finish for him. "I've always known. Since the first time I saw you in the shadows. The way they embrace you. The way your eyes change. I've always seen you, Oliver. Maybe I'm not entirely human either. Did you ever think about that? My father said I was a demon. He might be right."

He shakes his head, refusing my words. "You don't feel like a demon, Vale. Not like me. I'm built this way to attract you, to seduce you. You see what you ache for, and I can give it to you, but in return I get to feed. There's a high price for giving into a monster like me. I don't know if what you feel is real." He looks sad for a moment, shaking his head.

"I want it to be real," he whispers, his eyes full of anguish. "With you." He looks like he's surprised by his own words, as if he hadn't meant to speak them.

The pain in his eyes hurts my heart, so I go to him. He thinks he's only a monster, but he's so much more than the horror show he thinks he is. "It's not all you are, Oliver. You're not a monster to me. You're real to me," I say and hope he believes me. Kissing his chest, I lick the salt from his skin.

"Please," I whisper, desperate. My lips hover over that red dragon, over his heart. I need more. I always need more.

His skin is warm now, as if he has a fever. He's burning just like I am. Does he hurt the way I hurt? I continue to kiss down his stomach and over each toned muscle, sliding my tongue through the deep grooves of muscle until I get to those black boxer briefs. I fall to my knees in front of him. Looking up at him, I lick my lips. "You taste like sin."

He inspires such lustful words in me.

I take each side of the elastic band in my fists and pull, over his hips, and down to the floor at his ankles. He doesn't move, and I'm able to stare at what I've uncovered.

"Fuck," I gasp when I see his cock for the first time. Now, I'm not a connoisseur of cocks, but what I'm seeing is extraordinary. It's long and thick, veins bulging out with a deep ruddy crown that makes my mouth water. I kiss the slippery tip. He's sweet and salty as I lick over the head. "You taste so good." I open my mouth wide to take him in, suckling the head, then moan around it.

But then he presses the palms of his hands into my shoulders, digging his fingers in. "Don't," he says, and it makes tears swim in my vision.

Why doesn't he want me? Why?

I love him.

24

CRAZY BEAST

OLIVER

I don't know what to say or do. I don't know how to fix this. I've tried to control my every action or walk away for so long that this frenzied lust . . . it scares me. I covet this girl and all she is. I want to tie her to myself so my darkness can consume her. I struggle to hold my hunger at bay, but it's harder with the beast. He wants her just as much as I do.

I want her more than I've ever wanted anyone. There's a part of me that doesn't want to touch her in case she ever touches another. I'm afraid the beast would destroy any man who dared touch her. But she doesn't belong to us, and I don't want to take advantage of her. If she was experienced, then maybe it'd be easier to have this with her, but she's not.

The way she looks at me with those sad aqua eyes, like I'm her entire fucking world, it blows my mind. I don't think anyone has ever looked at me like that. She looks at me like she loves me, and it makes me question everything I've ever known, everything I've ever wanted.

This seems like a karmic setup. Somehow the fates have decided I'm well worth fucking with. If I touch her now, I may not end up with her, but I need her. I need her like I need air to breathe. She was made for me. My soul screams, and the beast roars, *I need her*.

Why did I have to meet her now? I'm not ready for her. *We are!* the beast insists. Why do I have to be a monster? Why can't I be like the rest of the Lilu?

She's on her knees, kissing the tip of my cock, and I swear I'm about to get off before I've had a moment inside her. I want her mouth on me, and it's like she hears my desire because, just like that, she suckles the tip. My hands are shaking at the wet heat of her mouth, and I'm struggling to hold back from thrusting down her throat. Somehow I've got to get control of myself. I dig my fingers into her shoulders, and it takes all my will to pull her off me.

"Don't," I demand. I see in her eyes that my denial hurts her. It hurts her so much more than I could have imagined.

This thing between us has a life of its own. It feels so right but also wrong. Oh, but I want her. I need to be inside her. I need to be one with her, the only way I know how. I clench my jaw as tears fill her eyes.

I coax her up my body and wrap my arms around her, giving her support. "I don't want to hurt you, but we can't do this. You're too precious to me."

What I really want to say is, *If I fuck you right now, I'll never be able to touch you again, and I can't lose you.* I want to say how I'm the kind of monster who could kill her by loving her. I want to make her understand my predicament, but in the end I don't. I say nothing else, and her tears fall onto my chest. I hate myself for causing her pain.

"I know." Her words wobble with defeat. Vale just gave up on me, and it sends a pain directly into my heart like a bullet. I deserve that pain. She steps away, leaving me there to stew in my own self-hatred. She slams the bathroom door, and when the lock engages, it feels like a second stab to my chest. She's locking me out. Smart girl.

I grab her bathing suit from the floor. The stupid thing should be destroyed after what it did to me earlier. I found it hard to breathe when I saw her wearing it. But who am I kidding? It's hard to breathe with her just being in the room. I hang it to dry on a rack, then grab her dress, shoes, and bag and take them to the bathroom door.

I have every intention of leaving it there, hanging her bag on the handle, and walking away, but then I hear the shower running. She's trying so hard to hide her sobs.

I'm done for. I drop the bag on the floor and grip the handle, knowing I'm going to have to explain this later. I slam it downward with enough force to break it with a loud snap.

I walk into the room and find her sitting on the marble floor, knees pressed up into her chest as steam rises around her. Her hands lift from her face, and she looks up at me. When she sees me, she covers her breasts with her arms. She's hiding now, her fire having burned out without fuel. The beast inside, the one that pounds away at his cage, trying to escape, to get to her, rears its head, acknowledging her pain and, before I can stop myself, I move too quickly to be human.

Vale squeaks in fright when I enter the shower. I grab her, lifting her up and shoving her back against the marble. I press my hips into hers and growl next to her ear. She tries to push me away with her hands against my chest, but she's no match for me.

"Get away from me," she yells as I pin her against the wall. I trap her wrists in one hand over her head, then lift one of her legs to the outside of my hip, spreading her sex. I've got her trapped, completely at my mercy.

Her breathing ratchets up. I smell her arousal and fear mix in a heady perfume that makes my cock throb and leak against her hip. The vampire inside me wants to devour her blood. The Lilu wants to bend her to my will, forcing my cock in all her holes while she screams in pleasure, giving it all to me, letting me feed.

"Why are you doing this to me?" she cries, and I wonder that myself. I wonder why I've got her pinned to a wall. I had released her, sent her away. I should have walked away.

I lean in and press my forehead against hers. "I can't stop myself," I groan. "I warned you."

"You already stopped yourself when you turned me down. Just walk away," she screams in my face, tears leaking out of her eyes. She's right. I must look like a crazy bastard right now. It's that push and pull between us. I don't know how to control it. For so long, my life has been entirely about controlling myself, but I can't with her.

"Let's make one thing crystal clear, Vale. I want you. This—" I reach between her legs and press the tip of my index finger inside her gently. "This is mine." I lean forward as I pump my finger shallowly inside her. I take one taut, berry-pink nipple into my mouth, suckling it.

"These tits are mine." I drag my lips across her chest to suction the other nipple into my mouth. She cries out when I suckle too hard, her back arching against the marble where she's trapped.

I let her go and turn her around, pushing her body against the cool stone. As I lean over her, I bite the back of her neck, accidentally nicking her skin. There's barely a drop of blood in the shallow wound, but I tongue it, consuming her taste. Her blood tastes crisp and sweet like fall apples. She's delicious everywhere. I don't take blood from my lovers. This is new. I search for the Lilu or the iron-less sweetness of vampire blood, but neither are there. She tastes unique.

I move her wet hair around to lay over her shoulder, then lick down her spine and nip at the skin of her ass. I dream up things I'm going to do to that ass while I massage the thick globes in my hands. I growl when she tenses up and tries to pull away.

"Are you afraid of what I'll do here," I ask as I kiss and suck at her soft skin. "This is mine to play with. This is mine to fuck. Every inch of your body is mine, inside and out. You'll never belong to another. Do you hear me?" She tries to buck me off, but I hold her still while I lick down over the cheek of her perfect ass.

"You had your chance. I'll find someone else. Don't torture me. Please, Oliver, it hurts. Stop doing this to me."

End them all, no one but us. She belongs to us. His growls are getting angry, but I'm angry as well. I actually speak back to him, acknowledging the beast. *Same page*, I tell him.

"There will be no one else. It's too late. I'll be the only man inside your body. Do you hear me? No one else, Vale. You're mine," I growl. I can't believe she said that to me. Someone else. Never! If another man touches her, I'll rip them apart. She belongs only to me.

25

SKIN AGAINST SKIN

VALE

Oh, my God! Oliver is licking and biting at the cheeks of my ass. I think he's losing it. It's so wrong how he touches me, but if I'm truthful, his mouth on any part of me feels exactly right. I'm freaking out. I don't know which way is up. I don't know what to do or how to move. I don't know if I want to stay in his grasp or run away. No, that's a lie. I want him, but he pushed me away. Now he's acting like he owns me. The man makes my head spin.

I'm close to exploding. I can't do this. I can't breathe. He's so focused on how he's touching me I take the chance to move. I turn my body and look down at where he's on his knees on the stone floor. His dark hair is wet and long down his back. It curls around his face in dark tendrils, sticking to the drops of water that glow in the overhead light.

Oliver looks up at me through his thick lashes. His eyes are dark as night now, his pale cheeks flushed, his mouth partially open with those fangs showing. He's not human. "Are you going to hurt me? Will you let me go?" The words come out in breathy pants as I stare at this magnificent male on his knees.

Oliver smiles. "Never," he answers, and his voice is an octave lower than normal, so gravelly it makes me shiver. He grabs his cock in a tight fist, and I suck in a deep breath as he strokes himself. I'm enamored by what I'm seeing, studying the way his fist pumps up over his thick girth. I have to know how he likes to be touched.

"So this is what you want?" His strokes get faster. "You like watching."

I shake my head before I can say anything. "No, I don't want to watch." It's the truth. "It's too late for watching." There's safety in watching, but I don't want to be safe. I want the danger. I want to touch him. I want him in my hands, in my mouth, inside my body where he belongs. I want him to brand my body in the basest of ways. I want to be his.

His smile falters at my words, but before he can say anything, I sink to the floor in front of him. The water is still warm and flowing over both of us. I reach out my hand and hold his cheek in my palm. I halt his hand on his cock with my own, then look into his eyes, hoping against hope he understands that it's him I want.

"I want you. Do you understand that? I don't want someone else touching you. I don't want to watch you touch yourself. I want to touch you. I want to be the one who makes you come. I want to feel everything. You were right last night, I do want it all. I want every single piece of you."

I want to be his reason for smiling.

"Oliver, I don't have a lot to offer you in return. Just know that I offer every single piece of me. You don't need to threaten that you own me, I'll never deny it. I'm yours."

"Come with me now."

Oliver turns the shower off, then lifts me up, cradling me in his arms, against his warm chest. I think he likes holding me. I place the palm of my right hand on the base of his neck and his lips twitch. I wrap my arms around his neck and hold on as he speeds back into the bedroom we started in. He throws me down on the bed and I laugh. I make my way up the bed and lean back into the large, fluffy pillows.

He crawls on his hands and knees toward me. Each movement is controlled, each muscle contracting and relaxing as he makes his way slowly closer. The look in his eyes is all demand and possession. Oliver wants me and I want to be his, only his.

"I need to taste you." His need isn't like my own. It's not like the need I have to be normal or the need for acceptance. No, his need is for survival. He needs to taste me now to live through this moment. The desperation in his eyes overwhelms me.

I spread my legs for him, but he grabs my thighs with bruising fingers. He pushes my thighs farther apart, stretching my muscles tight. Up until this moment, his eyes were meeting mine, but now they're drawn to my center. He gasps before licking his wicked lips. The sight makes my inner muscles clench.

"Such a pretty little pussy. I dream about how tight you're going to be around me when I'm balls deep inside you." He takes a deep breath, then our eyes meet. "One day, I'm going to let you have all of it, every single inch." Those dirty words come out between smirking lips, and his look nearly undoes me.

He won't take my virginity tonight. Not yet. I don't want to wait, but for some reason he does. I've heard such awful things about guys rushing girls to fuck them that his denying me throws me off. It doesn't make any sense why he isn't giving in. I want him to give in.

Oliver kneels between my legs, bowing over me, his mouth an inch from my center. Each breath against me is teasing and makes me wetter and wetter. This anticipation is as sweet as it is frustrating, but he never seems rushed. When he takes one long swipe between the lips of my sex and my entire body reacts. My thighs twitch around his head as my breathing picks up.

He pulls back after that first swipe, and I sit up on my elbows, eyes wide. He watches me with those fathomless, alien-black eyes. If I was a smart girl, one with any sort of self-preservation, I'd have been afraid. Instead, I get lost in them. Those obsidian depths call to some darkness within me.

I grab his jaw and glide my thumb underneath his bottom lip. "How are you real?" I whisper. He doesn't say anything, so I lie back again.

Oliver takes a quick lick, then lifts up again so he can watch me lose it. "Good?" he asks, but I can't speak. I just nod my head, too overwhelmed by his presence, his touch. "I've been thinking about doing this to you all day," he admits.

He drops down, licking around my folds, sucking my clit between his lips. Then his tongue goes farther down, circling my entrance while my body quakes with an impending orgasm. He pulls back again and smirks devilishly, his lips and chin shining with my wetness.

"Please, I don't want you to stop," I beg, and he presses a gentle kiss against each thigh. He's teasing me, and it's lighting an angry fire in my chest.

When he leans forward again, I grab his head. I dig my fingers through his hair, grasping his scalp and holding him to me. He chuckles against my core. "No patience," he says, and it vibrates through my center, making my stomach muscles tighten.

Oliver tongues my hole. Round and round he circles it, teasing me. I'm so hot and frustrated I tighten my hand in his hair. It urges him on, and he thrusts his tongue inside me till it hits the barrier of my virginity, never breaking through even though I want him too. In and out he thrusts, humming as he fucks me. But it isn't enough, and I lean back against the pillows, hissing in frustration. I lift my hips toward his face and try to grind against his mouth.

"I need," I gasp, not knowing what I needed, only knowing I needed more of it.

"I know what you need," he growls against me, making me twitch with need.

He pulls his tongue out of me, flattening and dragging it up over my sensitive flesh. Then he changes direction and firms his tongue up while circling my clit. My hips shoot up from the bed. I start to move with his tongue as I reach for that pinnacle. He thrusts a finger inside me, then two, but he's careful not to go too deep. He's being so cautious. But he doesn't understand the utter emptiness inside me where I ache for him. He doesn't understand this pain. The pain I've had every day since I met him.

I'm burning inside. Flames are licking every inch of my skin, which feels too tight with this coming storm. My thighs are shaking, my heart pounding in my chest, my jaw is tight, and I feel the pressure inside me build more and more.

He growls, "Come for me, love," against my pussy and that's all I need. Only his demands for my pleasure.

Then I truly scream, my hips bucking against his face. I can't hold on to his head any longer. I'm lost as I arch my spine and clench my fists. My head flies back and I cry out to the heavens, shaking as he pulses his tongue against me.

"Oh, my God," I cry, tears filling my eyes. But he doesn't stop. He continues licking and sucking at my clit, ramping the pleasure up till I don't know if I can take anymore. I'm weightless, lost in the universe, floating on the pleasure he's forced me to feel.

Little aftershocks fill me as he climbs up my body. He kisses me hard, our teeth gnashing together as he tilts my chin so he can take charge. I taste myself on his lips. Why do I like that so much, knowing he's been there? My body is still climbing higher. I'm losing myself in this man.

Oliver lifts up on his elbows and stares down at me, smiling. Gently, he caresses under my eye and over my cheek with his thumb. I kiss his fingertips and smile back at him. He makes me so happy. I want to fade into that dizzy feeling he creates in me. I want to live there always, in the warmth of his eyes.

His long hair is still damp, curling around his cheeks, the elastic long gone, and he looks out of this time, out this world. He looks like some heathen warrior god above me. It falls in a curtain around his face, draping us in shadows as he studies my face. He sees more of me than anyone ever has.

"You're so beautiful," I say, unable to hold the words in. He's perfect, on a level that shouldn't exist.

I reach for his body, feeling his ribs and hips, then I wrap my fist around his thick cock and mimic what he was doing to himself in the shower. He's hot and heavy in my hand, and I can barely reach my fingers around him. I try to be gentle.

"Thank you." Oliver doesn't deny his beauty. He knows exactly what he is.

I'm surprised when his eyes close. He's lost in my touch the way I get lost in his. I lift up and kiss him as I stroke. His hips buck into my fist as he licks at my lips. His skin is soft and smooth, but underneath he's hard like stone. He feels so good against me, skin against skin. I wonder if I'll ever be able to go without this.

"You feel so good," I whisper against his ear, then drop down to lick at his neck, tasting the salty sweetness.

He shifts, taking my hand away from his cock and I frown. He gets off the bed. For a moment it's as if my greatest fear, that he'll walk away from me, is about to happen, but then he drags me by the ankles to the edge. I almost argue, but he spreads my legs wide and leans forward, pressing his dick into my wetness.

There's a soul-shattering moment when the crown dips and spreads me open. It feels like he'll never fit inside me, and I'm suddenly intimidated by his size. I think he's going to fuck me, steal my innocence and my soul. If only he knew, for him, I'd willingly part with them. I lied when I said I'd find another. There is no other, he's all there is.

I force him to look down into my eyes. "Oliver, you can take it. Please, take it. I want you inside me," I plead even though I'm afraid. "I need you."

He pushes his hips forward and I think this is it. He's going to make love to me—no, he's going to tear me open so no one will ever fit. He stretches me open, and I hold my breath. I'm about to levitate off the bed with anxiety, with the threat of it, but he stops, and I release my breath.

"Not yet, baby. But soon," he says, lustful promises in his eyes.

When he leans over me, I bend my legs and press my knees to the sides of his hips, trying to pull him closer. I hold him to me as he notches his cock in between the lips of my sex. Oliver grabs my hands and holds them above my head, pressing them into the mattress so I can't move.

"I want you to feel me," he growls over me, his eyes so dark and desperate. "Feel me, and let me feel you."

He starts pumping his hips, sliding his cock through my slippery lips. The underside of the crown hits my clit and my eyes widen. His smile is menacing as he watches me, knowing exactly what he's doing.

"I feel you," I gasp.

My wetness is all over him. He pumps his hips over and over as he grinds down into me. It feels so good. I can't take it anymore. I let go.

His hold on my wrists loosens as he continues to slide against me. My core is contracting muscles I'm not entirely sure I've used before, and warmth is spreading low in my belly. For a moment, I wonder if I'll pass out. The room spins while I succumb to the fire that's been building inside me.

"Look at me when you come." His voice breaks as my body trembles. "I want you all over my cock when I come."

Oliver's thrusts get faster and my insides clench, demanding his entry. I'm needy with lust. I'm losing my mind as he leans in and sucks one nipple into his mouth. He bites down, the pain a juxtaposition to my pleasure. Then it hits me. The way his thick cock is pushed against my clit, the way his hot skin burns mine where we touch. His hips mimic the sex we would one day have. I feel everything. I'm a live wire. Pleasure fills me. I suck in a single, deep breath, filling my lungs.

"Oliver!" I wail as tears fill my eyes. My hands are freed so I wrap my arms around him, pulling him closer and kissing his lips. I close my eyes and feel him move against me.

"Open your fucking eyes," Oliver growls against my lips. "I need to see you come undone. I crave it."

I open my eyes for him, and he studies my face, my eyes as I come. Pleasure envelopes me, and he groans as if he's the one feeling it. I feel love, suddenly a tangible, physical thing, bursting from my soul and I push all of it into him. I know he tastes my truth in the air. I'm his, from this moment until the end. He takes my offering, his skin glows with it, and his eyes light up with my release.

I see the moment things change as his eyes go from bright to dark again, the man dueling with the monster. Then they fill with so much lust I swear it spills out of him, into the air we breathe. I feel his power, feel it melt against my skin. It shimmers across every inch of my body.

"All that I am," I cry out. "Is yours."

He hears my words and rears back with a roar like a beast. His thrusts gain momentum, speeding up. My orgasm continues just when I thought it was over. I'm shaking when he suddenly stops, and I feel liquid heat spread over my stomach.

Oliver grabs my hand and wraps it around his cock, coaxing it up and down his shaft. "Feel me," he says, and his words are as soft as a summer breeze. His chest heaves and his eyes are so intensely focused on me that my cheeks heat even more.

He squeezes my fist around him, slipperiness coating my palm, then shoots more of that fluid out onto my stomach. I reach my other hand out to dip my finger in the small pool of it, then bring it to my mouth. I want to taste him the way he tasted me. Oliver wraps his hand around my wrist as if to stop me, but before he can explain, I lift up and suck my finger into my mouth.

My head falls back as I'm overpowered by his sweet taste, and I'm coming again, squeezing him between my legs and convulsing while he chuckles. He props himself up on his elbows as he watches me come and come, writhing against the bed unable to stop the pleasure flooding through me.

"Not human, remember?"

I laugh as he kisses me with every ounce of passion inside him.

I could fall in love with Oliver Byron. Who am I kidding? I've already fallen. I love him. I have since the moment I first saw him, but he just gets better and better.

26

WHAT ARE YOU?

VALE

It's late, but Oliver has been holding me for a long time, stroking my skin and placing little kisses against my spine. He's unable to stop touching me, and I'm unable to move away from his attention. We haven't spoken since he said he wasn't human. That should worry me, but it doesn't. I wish he would tell me what he's thinking, but he remains quiet.

"Are you a vampire?" I ask, breaking the silence while he rubs his hand down my spine. I arch into his palm like a cat. He lies back on the bed, and I turn to my side to watch him. "You don't have to tell me if you don't want to."

He turns his head slightly, those bright green eyes focusing on me. "You would accept it, if I had secrets? I don't think so. I think you want it all. You want every secret, every touch. It's all or nothing with us."

My cheeks heat because I know he's speaking the truth. He sees through me so easily. I want it all. I want all his secrets, the way I gave him so many of mine. I want every touch. They belong to me, just like mine belong to him. But I also know how hard it is to offer up your secrets to someone. This feels like a test. If I love him, then I should be patient with him. I can hold him close in my heart until he trusts me.

"If you don't want to tell me, that's okay. We haven't known each other long, and trust is hard won. I'll be there when you're ready."

Oliver offers me an understanding smile and caresses my cheek. "You're so sweet. I want to tell you, but this isn't something I normally talk to mortals about. I'm worried you'll never look at me the same way." Oliver looks up at the ceiling, deep in thought. I don't want him to be afraid of telling me.

"There's nothing you could say to make me look at you any differently, Oliver. I like you, and I accept that you're otherworldly. I knew that from the night we met."

"Vale, when I tell you I'm not human, I mean that. I wasn't turned into this by some magical force. I was born this way. This is who I am."

"Are you okay?"

His eyes connect with mine, his brows knitting together. "I should be asking you that," he says as if he's failed me somehow.

I give him an excited smile. "I'm great. I've had the most amazing experience of my life. I don't know how to express my awe of you. I've never done anything like this. You're the only one, and every touch is perfect." My words make his fists clench and his jaw tick. Why? I press my palm to his chest, over his heart where the red dragon rests. "I'm so grateful for having these experiences with you. Thank you." I want him to take all my firsts.

"Do you feel strange?" he suddenly asks.

"No, I don't, but I can see you're worried about something. Tell me what's going on. If I've done something wrong, tell me what I can do to fix it." I don't want to lose this afterglow. I don't want him to pull away again, but it feels like he's about to.

27

WHAT I AM

OLIVER

Vale is naked beside me, her leg draped across my hips, and her palm over my heart as if she owns it, and maybe she does. She owns something inside me, that's for sure. My beast is in love with her. There's a cynical part of me that can't believe in love, not for someone like me. Lust I can accept, but love has never existed outside of my family.

She doesn't act like an addict, but I'm still worried. She sees that and thinks she's done something wrong, but it isn't her. This beautiful girl before me deserves to know the danger she's in. She should run from me, even if it's the last thing I want.

"I assure you, you've done nothing wrong, sweetheart. It's what I am that worries me. It's what I could do to you. I'm not exactly a vampire, I'm different. I'm also part Lilu or, in other words, an Incubus. My father is a vampire and my mother is a Succubus or a lust demon. I'm of two species that humans can become addicted to. It's rare with vampires, the addiction, but a Lilu rarely, if ever, fucks the same person twice. I don't want to take your will and turn you into a puppet who only wants me for my body." I lie to her then, because I can't bear the thought of explaining the real reason I can't be with her.

My greatest failure, my greatest shame, the monster inside me, created by the abuse which fractured my mind.

"I wanted you for your body the night we met, what's the difference now?" she asks with a smirk. "We haven't had sex yet. Oh, my God, you feed through sex!" Vale sits up and looks at me with huge, innocent eyes.

"I can feed during sex yes, but it's not the sex itself that I feed on. It's the life force, essence, spirit, or sexual energy. It's pleasure that feeds me, but it's part of the spirit. It drains the person I'm feeding from, and it could kill them if I feed too much or too often. Just like a vampire taking too much blood. Vale, I feed on mortals. It's not often that Lilu murder donors, but it's dangerous."

I sit up and face her.

"That's why you had sex with that woman, wasn't it? It's why you didn't bother learning her name. You'd never see her again." She puts it all together flawlessly.

"Yes."

"Did you feed from me?" she whispers, looking at me shyly, cheeks getting red. "When you touched me."

"Yes, but I never intended to. I swear, Vale, I've never tried to take your energy. You fed me yourself, as if you could control your spirit."

I've never explained this to a mortal. It's taking conscious effort to find the right words. "Think of it like this, if your essence was a signal, then I would be the receiver, like a satellite dish. Vampires drink blood, and it's a physical thing, but the essence of your pleasure is spiritual. I absorb it into myself. I don't actually have a choice when you do it. Not that I dislike it. I assure you, I do like it, so much. Did you realize you were doing it?"

She smiles shyly, looking down at her hands. "I've felt it every time it's happened. I was giving it to you, but it wasn't like I knew what I was doing. It was supposed to be there. It felt like the right thing to do. Is that weird?" She looks at me like she's in trouble, and I lean in to kiss her lips gently. What's Vale's obsession with being normal? She's amazing and I wouldn't change her.

"Honestly, I don't know. I've never met anyone who could do that. Did you feel drained after?"

A smile grows on her face, lighting her up. "I felt energized. Did I take your essence too?"

I chuckle as I shake my head. She seems so excited, but then her face falls.

"You have sex to feed, don't you? You're going to be with someone else, it just won't be with me." Her words are sad and for the first time in my life I wish I wasn't like this. I've always enjoyed what I am, at least the Lilu side, but seeing it hurt her upsets me.

I'm about to speak, but Vale surprises me by jumping up onto my lap, straddling me between her thighs. "Don't feed from another. Take me. I want you. I like it when I share it with you. Taste my blood, my essence. I want to feed you."

"I don't need to feed every day. I can feed like a vampire, but it's not my first choice. While you're here, that's what I'll do." I shouldn't promise her anything like that. I can control myself. I have for millennia, but I don't want to feed like a vampire.

She bends forward and cups my head in her hands while she stares down at me with sad eyes. "I'll be gone in a few weeks and it's likely I won't be back for a while. I wish I could stay. I hate leaving."

I'm sure she hates leaving Nick, but I hear the words she doesn't say. She doesn't want to leave me. She doesn't want to lose me. I worry about losing myself if I can't have her. I worry about what I'll do if someone ever touches her. Can I wait now that I've touched her? Now that I've witnessed her glorious abandon as she cries out in what seems like agony but is pure bliss. How can I let her go when I know deep in my bones that she's my fate? She's my beautiful star in the sky. She's my future.

I don't know if I can accept that she isn't going to be mine right now.

28

DAWN

VALE

Oliver takes me to the shower. He washes me with loving, gentle hands, his every touch reverent. He's taking care of me. He dries my body and slides my dress back over my head. Then he leads me out of the pool house and up to the kitchen. I sit at the kitchen island nursing a bottle of cold water while he excuses himself to get some dry clothes.

It takes him five minutes before he's back, wearing ripped jeans, a tight black T-shirt and a pair of combat boots I'm surprised he owns. He's dressed down for once. Is this how he looks when he's alone? His long dark hair is down with a few thick strands caressing his cheek. He rarely leaves it down, but I wish he did.

Oliver smiles at me. "You're blushing," he says, and I look away quickly, bringing my hand up to my mouth. I don't want him to see my humiliation. I feel his arms around me in a soft embrace. "Don't hide from me. You never have to hide anything from me, Vale, not ever. Tell me what has you blushing."

He turns the barstool so I'm forced to face him. He leans in, his focus entirely on my eyes. He isn't going to give in. He wants to know everything, but it's hard to be so vulnerable with him. I barely know him, yet it's like I've known him my entire life.

"Your hair, I like it down. You look very handsome right now. That's all." My cheeks heat farther. Oliver wants no secrets between us, while I want to hide most of the time.

I reach up and grab one of the thick strands that curls at his cheek. I wrap its silky softness around my finger and twirl it. "I might be jealous of this strand and how it touches your face so freely." I say.

I can't believe I just said that. It may be my truth, but it's ripped from me without any conscious effort. I look down at my knees, my embarrassment grating against my nerves. My heart throbs in my chest.

Oliver lifts my chin, forcing me to look at him. His smile is the brightest I've ever seen it. He looks genuinely happy. That's the moment I realize that woman before hadn't given him happiness. She didn't, but my crazy-ass words did, and he's all the more attractive for it.

"Touch me, I'm yours," he whispers as he brings my hands up to his cheeks and holds them there with his own. I cradle his face in my trembling hands, then close my eyes as my heart sings at his words. I can barely breathe because of the fluttering in my chest. Oliver being mine sounds good, it sounds right. It sounds like fate.

My head is spinning. "Sometimes I think you must be a dream. Just being with you, feeling your skin against mine. It's too much, yet not nearly enough. I'm sorry. I'm not making any sense."

He stops me with a kiss, his lips gentle at first, then tugging at my bottom lip. He pulls me into his embrace. The heat from his body seeps into mine, waking my heart and filling me with bliss. Why does he feel like this? When he pulls back, he lifts my chin to look at him.

"Give yourself some credit, Vale. You make perfect sense. I get it. I don't think I could ever get enough of you. You're more than I could ever have asked for—" He stops and I have a feeling he wasn't finished. He doesn't say the words, but I hear them echo in my head, *More than I've ever deserved.*

"Come on, let's go for a drive," he says.

But I yawn before I can stop myself.

"You're tired," he acknowledges, his lips trying to tilt into a frown.

"No, I'm fine. Let's go." This is nuts, it's almost morning. The birds have started singing. I should have been in bed hours ago, but I can't tell him no. I don't want to tell him no.

"Are you sure? I can walk you home and hold you till you fall asleep. I can take a rain check. I won't mind." I love it when he holds me, but I don't want to miss a second with him.

"I'd rather be tired tomorrow than miss a moment with you."

"Alright, I'll not argue with my lady."

Oliver grabs my hand and pulls me off the stool. He leads me out through the back door as I try my best to keep up with his long legs. Instead of going directly out through the veranda, we turn left and walk around the border of a formal garden. It's too dark for me to see much detail. When we make it around the edge, I look over my shoulder at the house. I notice a tower that must face the front, one I've strangely never seen.

"Oh wow, that would make a good observatory. Do you have a telescope?" I ask, knowing he doesn't.

He looks back at the house, noticing where I'm looking, and smiles secretively. "Maybe one day I'll get one and you can show me how to use it." I crack a smile, hoping he does get one. Then he continues down a path to a large garage. Not once does he let my hand go. At the door, he presses in some numbers on the keypad, and it unlocks. When we go inside, lights come on automatically.

I'm shocked by the large space. He's got at least ten cars in here. But I know which one we're taking because it's the car that always sits in front of his house. I head straight for the pretty silver car.

Oliver laughs. "You know me already. It's a '59 Ferrari GT California Spyder," he explains as if I should know exactly what it is. Everyone should.

"I've never seen a car like this before. It's beautiful," I tell him as I lean over the passenger door and look at all the small dials that cross the dash.

Gramps and Oliver are alike in this, the love of classic cars. Gramps has a 1967 powder-blue Mustang he drives to all the local car shows and a boring hybrid he drives around town when he regrets the cost of gasoline. The Ferrari makes you question why modern cars have lost their souls.

Oliver pulls me back against him and opens the door. "My lady," he says, then holds his hand out for me as I sit down against the buttery soft leather. He shuts the door, steps around the car, then sits in the driver's seat. I search around for the seat belt, turning to my left and right, but I can't find it.

"No seat belts," he explains like it's normal.

"Oh, okay. Is that even legal?"

"Probably not, but I'll drive safe. No worries."

I sit back and he starts the car, the rumble of the engine loud in the enclosed space. He shifts the car into Drive, then pulls out of the garage. As Oliver turns toward a driveway I've never noticed at the back of the sprawling property, I tilt my head back and look at the stars.

I love this car.

As we get to Little River, he slows down. I don't understand why they call it that because it's huge. He turns onto a side road that leads under the bridge. I sit up at the crunch of gravel. I've been down here many times, fishing with Kat's family. He parks the car and sets the brake right under the bridge.

Where we're parked, the river expands in front of us. There's a gorgeous view of the sky above the water. In the distance, the dark sky is slashed with deep purple as the day fights away the night. Stars twinkle in the darkest parts of the sky, almost telling the world good-bye. It's a beautiful view I've never seen before.

"This is . . . amazing. I didn't realize . . . " I don't have the words. I've been to this exact spot many times but always during the day.

"I thought you'd like it."

I turn in my seat to face him. He wraps one arm around my waist and lifts me up onto the console between the seats, pulling me closer to him like he can't stand the distance between us. I lean my head against his shoulder, content to be in his arms.

I love him. I wonder if I've ever loved someone more. He leans in, kissing my hair.

"Why did you have to be so perfect?" he asks with pain in his eyes that claws at my chest even as it creates that fluttering feeling. He needs to be loved. I hope he accepts mine because it's there, growing, gathering momentum every second.

His words overwhelm me. I reach out and push a strand of hair away from his face, tucking it behind his left ear. I pull at his neck and kiss him. This time he lets me take charge. My lips are timid against his. They're soft while his can be hard and demanding. I suck at his bottom lip, pulling it into my mouth, sliding my tongue against it. He doesn't close his eyes the way people in the movies do when they kiss. He likes watching.

I draw away nervously, but his arms tighten around me. He pulls me closer and tilts his head a bit to the side. He claims my lips as his own. He bites at my bottom lip hungrily, and I can't stop the soft moan that escapes my throat. I'm helpless in his kiss. I lean back as he kisses along my jaw. His teeth glide over the sensitive skin of my neck, and I jerk my legs together. My breathing speeds up and he notices. He always notices, every single reaction. Maybe that's why he never closes his eyes. He needs to see it all.

"Do you like that?"

I reply with a breathy, "I really like it."

He smiles against my neck, then he nips me with his teeth. I don't know why the slight pain lights up all my pleasure sensors. "Do it." I want him to bite me, taste my blood.

Oliver pulls back and the monster inside him rears its head, darkness spreading out from his pupils. His breathing has picked up. He's affected by his hunger. In that moment, all I want is to give him all of me. I want to offer myself to him, my sex, my blood. It all belongs to him.

"What do you want me to do?"

"Bite me, taste me," I whisper, lost to the vision that swirls inside my mind of his teeth sinking into my flesh as I moan in pleasure. It's a wonderful vision.

"Spread your legs, Vale." His voice is gravelly, and it makes me shiver, but I do as he demands. I turn my hips away to comply, drop-ping my shoe as I lift my foot onto the passenger seat.

I'm sitting there awkwardly, my right foot propped up in the seat, my left draped around the shifter. He yanks me over his lap, and I turn my body into him a bit. This probably isn't the best car for a tryst.

He grabs my knee in his right hand and starts to glide his index finger over my thigh, pulling up the skirt of my dress as he goes. He nuzzles at my collarbone, his breath loud in my ears, then licks the top of my breast. My dress is bunched at my thighs where his hand slips under my panties. He swirls the tip of his index finger over my clit, making me hiss out a breath.

I lean my head back against the door, but he maneuvers my ass over his lap to sit against his hard cock. It's too much. His warmth seeps into me as he circles my clit, making me moan.

For a while, all I am is sensation. His lips and teeth nipping at my neck, his fingers toying with my pussy. He's playing me like an instru-ment, music he knows well. A tune he hums to life, a delightful, blissful song that throbs through my entire body.

"I need to make you come," he growls, losing a war with the monster inside him.

His hips jerk forward, making his cock bump against my ass. I look at him as best I can. His lips are red and swollen, his teeth clamping down on his lower lip. His skin is flushed with heat. I ache for this man. I need him filling me up.

"I need you inside me."

A look of understanding crosses his features. I try to spread my legs farther, and he prods at my hole with a finger, dipping in and out, deeper each time.

"This might hurt," he says before pressing against that barrier inside me. Slowly working it inside, I feel the give when he penetrates it. My mouth falls open, and I screech at the sudden pinch of pain. But it's not bad, I'll survive.

"It's taking all my willpower not to bend you over and stuff my cock inside your tight little cunt. I want to be inside you," he growls, and I love it when the monster talks to me. I love the filth that flies so easily from his mouth. I can imagine all of it.

"Show me with your fingers," I whisper, trying to be brave. "Show me what it will be like." He starts moving his finger. I'm sore inside already from the intrusion, but I don't care. I lift my hips for more.

"One day, I'll spread your legs and dip my cock inside. I'll go slow, getting your slick all over my dick before I penetrate you fully. At first, you'll squirm on me, you won't be able to take it. I might even make you cry, but I won't stop till I bottom out where that precious cunt ends. Baby, I'll ruin you with how deep I get. You'll never want anyone else." His words are so hot. And the way he lifts his hips, rubbing that very thick cock against my ass is hypnotizing me, pulling me deeper into those words.

"I don't want anyone else," I cry as he bends his finger, stroking the upper walls of my sex. My hips jerk in reaction and I moan.

His mouth slams into mine. He devours my cries as his tongue presses into my mouth. I fully open for him. I'm paralyzed with the feel of his tongue in my mouth, his devious finger penetrating my sex. "Beautiful," he growls between his kisses along my jaw, but I'm too lost to understand what it means.

His teeth are back, and another word slips free. "Divine."

Oliver's fingers work me closer to that pleasure. My hips jerk with every thrust. Now his thumb works my clit as that solitary finger works another spot inside me. I cry when the pleasure is too intense. The duality of the sharp pain from his teeth at my neck and the pleasure between my legs is beginning to scare me.

I feel like I'm going to pee, and I try to jerk my hips to the side, trying to get away.

"Don't move," he demands.

"I can't, Oliver," I tell him, panicking when I'm so close to the edge.

"You can," he yells into my neck.

He continues, that finger inside me about to do irrefutable damage to his upholstery. I'm so embarrassed my cheeks heat and tears form in my eyes. It starts the insanity. The fire inside me is about to explode.

I'm shaking, my thighs trying to clench together around Oliver's hand to stop him, but he doesn't stop. He gives me no quarter while I writhe in his arms, my body losing it, unable to get away, not wanting to go.

"That's it. Come for me. Now!" The words are a monstrous growl that tenses my spine.

I slam my head back against his shoulder. I look up at the fading stars, my body throbbing, quickening. I feel it everywhere, even in my temples. Fireworks explode inside me. I'm screaming at the top of my lungs, but he turns my head and muffles my mouth with his.

"That's my good girl. Come all over my hand," Oliver says, and I feel the gush of fluid from between my legs. I can't be embarrassed anymore, the pleasure is too great. It's too much. I'm going to die. I'm crying with it, my entire body shaking.

When every touch of his finger is painful in its intensity, I squirm to escape, and finally he lets me retreat. He looks down at his fingers, and they're wet and streaked with blood. He pulls his hand to his mouth, then gives me a dark look, that monstrous, knowing smirk as I stare at him and pant out of breath.

When he licks his finger that's slathered in my slick and streaked with my blood, I almost come again. I tense my thighs in anticipation as he gorges on my essence. He trembles for a moment, his green eyes flashing bright in the swirling, smoky darkness. That buzz in the air is back, surrounding him. He closes his eyes with such a gentle, serene smile, like the taste of me is everything pleasurable. I'm in awe of this man.

I'm breathing hard, taking in huge gulps of air as my skin cools, but I'm still too far gone to move my body away. Oliver smiles like the devil, dimples in his cheeks getting deeper.

"Did you like that?"

"I wanted you to bite me. I didn't expect whatever that was."

He'd wrung out more pleasure from my body than I thought he'd be capable of. I'm spent in a way I've never felt, barely able to hold my eyes open even though I don't want this night to ever end. I don't want to lose him, not even for a moment.

Oliver chuckles. "I need to take you home."

"Will you taste me one day? My blood? I want you to."

"Do you like the thought of me biting your neck and drinking your blood?" he asks, not looking happy about it.

"I enjoy the idea of sustaining you, of giving you some part of myself. I like your teeth against my skin. I'm sorry. I'm weird, huh?" I'm embarrassed because I don't want him to think I'm strange.

I want him to be the vampire he is. I want him to bite me. The urge is so strong. I want him to lick and suck the blood that streams from my neck. I want to see his lips slick with it. I want him to moan at my taste because it's so good. I want him to enjoy all of me. Okay, I am strange. I shouldn't want those things.

"You're not weird. Never be ashamed of your desires, especially not with me. I heard you've read *Dracula* three times this summer. Who wouldn't want to be bitten after that?"

I shake my head. "Have you been talking to Gramps about me?" I ask, my cheeks flaring hotter.

"Yeah, I have. He thinks you're in a romantic mood." He chuckles. "Whatever that means."

We both laugh. "If I'm in a romantic mood it may be because you showed up. What does poor Dracula have to do with it?"

That makes Oliver laugh, and I swear he's even more beautiful. "Poor Dracula, now that's funny. People who knew him wouldn't have called him that," Oliver says, still chuckling like it's the funniest thing he's ever heard.

"Did you know him?" My question makes him stop laughing. "Don't tell me he's actually a vampire. Is he?" I'm suddenly excited at the prospect of meeting the real Dracula. I bet he's hot.

Oliver looks at me seriously now. He's no longer amused at what I'm saying. "I didn't say I knew him, and I didn't say he was a vampire. I meant, historically speaking, he was kind of an asshole, you know because he impaled people. The obvious thing. They didn't call him Vlad the Impaler for nothing." He's staring me down, and the look is so serious I can't stop the laughter that bubbles up from my throat.

"Oh, Oliver, don't judge Dracula. You have to remember, I've seen you fuck a woman. I know you like impaling things too." I try to keep a straight face, but I can't. I laugh so hard tears brim in my eyes and spill over. He's smiling again, laughing with me. It's a great feeling to make him laugh.

"That's my naughty girl." He looks proud of me for some reason, and I can't fathom why. "I like it when you're fierce."

"Thanks. I just like you," I tell him as he leans forward. He kisses me sweetly once, then lifts me over into the passenger seat. I take one last look at the lightening sky as he starts the car. I'm so tired that once we start moving, I fall asleep.

29

A WHISPERED I LOVE YOU

OLIVER

I place a sleeping Vale in her bed after sneaking her back into Nick's house. She smells like the combined scent of our arousal and pure, unadulterated sex. I've made her come so much tonight I should be smiling. I should be happy. I know she is. I edge my knee forward onto the bed, hovering over her as I watch her breasts rise and fall with each calm breath.

Something happened out there tonight. I couldn't stop the beast from coming out. He took over in my human form. He took her to the very edge of pleasure and pain. He forced her to come on our hand. I swear he's still purring like a cat inside me, so pleased with himself. He's content now, not trying to escape. It's a new feeling, one I don't necessarily trust.

I lean in closer, pressing my lips over her heart just like she did to me the night before. I hope she never guards her heart from me. I want it to beat for me, only me. Her skin is cool from the night air, but it warms under my touch. Her heart speeds up though she sleeps soundly.

When I pull away, she grabs the back of my neck with a desperate hand. Her eyes open, bright with what I think is hope. She searches my face, my eyes, as one palm comes up to cradle my jaw. I'm taken aback by that look. It's something I've never seen in all my life, all these long years. She takes my breath away.

"I love you too," she whispers. Then she lies back, a content smile on her lips, her hand falling from my face, and her eyes closing.

By the time she hits the pillow, it's like it never happened. Her heart is calm again and so is her breathing. I can see by the movement in her eyes that she's dreaming. She must have moved in her sleep or maybe I'm seeing things. Maybe my age has finally caught up with me.

"Oh, God." The words flee from between my lips. My heart hurts, and I slam my fist against my chest, trying to breathe. Her words sear into my soul. Vale can't love me. She can't.

I run as if the Angel of Death is quick on my heals. I escape her bedroom, diving off her little observatory, moving so fast I don't notice the person in front of me till it's too late. She stops me in my tracks with a hard, bruising palm to my chest. When I crash into her all the air in my lungs is forced out. I almost crash into the ground, but she grabs my T-shirt, tearing it as I come to a stop.

"I heard those whispered words of love. Why did you run?" she asks, and I shake my head in denial. I take a step back. My mother opens her fingers, freeing me. I have to hold myself up. It's dizzying, the sudden stop after moving so fast. I shake my head again, trying to get control of it.

"Tell me why you ran," she demands. And there's her power, tickling at my senses, trying to loosen my lips and tell her truths I'm not ready to speak aloud.

"The third degree already. That didn't take long, Mother. Forgive me, but I can't answer that question."

"Then I will tell you. You fear that girl. You fear that demon within you, of what it could do. You fear hurting her. You just fear! Get over it! Stop running scared when everything you've ever wanted appears at your doorstep like a gift from the Light. She's the one. Don't deny her because it's you who will lose. I don't want to lose you again, son."

When I stare at her, I see that, to her, this is an easy choice. It's easy because she longs for her mate. She longs to be one with him. She longs for her children to be happy. I know what she wants, but it hurts just the same. I can't believe she used that word against me, as if I'm weak with fear. Father thought I was weak.

I shake my head again. "I never said I would deny a bond, but she's young, too young, for something like me."

"You're not a monster, Ash, and she isn't a child. Believe me! Don't let her go. Show her you're her future and don't deny her love. She knows what she wants."

"I'm a monster! I will always be a monster. I can't offer her anything that makes up for the beast inside. She deserves more." I force the words out, staring up at the sky because I can't look at her anymore.

"You're not."

I deny it of course. "She doesn't know what she wants yet. She was dreaming." My words are a lie. Vale's never denied what's between us. She feels it as strongly as I do. It's me who denies it because I can't bear the thought of hurting her.

I feel weary as I look back at my mother. Now she shakes her head, and a few strands of her golden-brown hair escape its bun and fly out on the breeze. "She feels your lips on her skin, even through her dreams. She felt them over her heart, a promise of your love. That girl loves you. I saw it before she forced me out." My mother smiles, impressed by Vale's strong mind. I'm proud of my girl for impressing her, so few can do that. "Promise me you'll give her a chance."

When I don't say anything back, I see the moment she concedes. She knows I won't promise her anything when it comes to Vale. I don't make promises I can't keep.

"We'll speak of this later. Now show me this house because I thought I was in the wrong place when I got here. You did such a beautiful job, son. It breathes new life."

I let my mother place her palm on my forearm as I lead her to the house. Most people have never been able to see all of it, otherwise they'd see the mismatched age of the facade. They don't see the old stonework, the tower on the east side of the house, or the southern wing. Vale hadn't seen it through the enchantment until she'd been invited inside.

We make our way into the house, and I show her around, but I can't get Vale out of my head, or her whispered *I love you*. To hear those words from her lips meant something to me. Whether she was dreaming of loving me or not, it changes nothing. It made her heart sing. She would be mine one day, I knew it.

I need to face facts. Vale isn't going anywhere. We're connected, whether it be by soul bond or first love, I didn't know yet. My heart is stubborn and yes, I'm afraid. I don't want to confuse lust with love. I want to know what lies between us is real. I want to know that what she feels for me is true and has nothing to do with me being a Lilu.

30

YOGA SHORTS AND JUMPING A FERRARI

VALE

I'm deep in thought, unable to get out of my own head. It's been two difficult days since I've seen Oliver. I'm lying on a mint-green yoga mat, eyes closed under dark sunglasses even though I'm hiding in the shade. I'm on the wooden deck behind Gramps's house. The sun is shining brightly overhead, heat and humidity a burdensome weight against my sensitive skin. The sunlight is so strong today, the shade isn't much cooler than being out directly under it. But I have to do it to protect my pale skin. If I don't, I'll be forever known as the lobster woman of South Georgia.

I contemplate, not for the first time, why I'm out in the heat. Why am I out here half dressed, wearing sticky sunscreen that smells like coconuts and absolutely fucking miserable? I could have been miserable in the house with air-conditioning. My misery deserves air conditioning at the very least.

When I came outside in my tiny pink shorts and my charcoal gray sports bra, I'd planned on doing yoga. I was moving slowly, but efficiently through the poses I'd only learned this morning. For two days, I'd searched the internet for methods to deal with my constant, painful state of arousal.

I was delirious at this point.

I had good intentions, tiny shorts not included. Honestly, that's for Oliver. I hope he sees me. I want to get his attention somehow. I miss him. Absence, or is that abstinence, really does make the heart grow fonder.

I've texted him, telling him about what I was reading, what I was doing. I'd flirt and send cute emojis. Sometimes I'd send pictures. Oliver always replied, but his answers weren't the heated replies from before. He was suddenly so distant, a million miles away, even though I felt his presence right next door. I hope he's okay. Would he tell me if he wasn't?

The first day we went without seeing each other, I questioned if I had done something wrong. I thought maybe what happened in the pool house had upset him. He had told me the truth about what he was and maybe he was regretting it. I don't want him to regret anything with me.

I wish I could control myself the way he can. It seems he's able to ignore the draw altogether. Whereas I'm over here with wet shorts, wishing he'll find me, throw me up against a wall, and destroy me for all other men. Oh, how I want to be destroyed by Oliver Byron. I bet it'd be worth every bit of heartbreak when it was over.

Yeah, Oliver did that to me. The attraction was intense before he kissed me, but after . . . I find myself in a perpetual state of arousal, daydreaming about how he'd fuck me. No joke. Just now, downward dog, has me thinking about Oliver propping himself up against a wall to gain leverage while he pounds into me. That visual just pops in to say hello.

What the hell is wrong with me?

I've never been so desperate as I've been with him. It takes a lot of mental and physical energy to stay aroused all the time. I feel drained. I find myself dehydrated, constantly craving water so my body doesn't turn to dust. Here it goes again. I imagine riding him in a huge bathtub, then how I'd lick the water droplets from his cheeks while he smiles with those sexy, bedroom eyes.

"Goddammit!" I yell as I lift my hips, trying to release the tension in my lower spine.

"Was it a bee?" Oliver asks.

I open my eyes, looking for him as he laughs.

"What bee?" I have no idea what he's talking about.

He squats down at my left side. "Were. You. Stung. By. A. Bee?" he asks slowly, spacing each word out as if I'm some sort of nitwit who only exists to agitate him.

Ugh! He makes me as angry as I am turned on.

I give him a scathing look I hope he can see through my sunglasses. He seems to be getting what I'm putting down. "No! Why would you think that?"

"Oh, you know, the fact that you're screaming goddammit at the top of your lungs while you're doing your pelvic thrust exercises. I figured one might have crawled under those teeny-tiny shorts. You know maybe it stung you somewhere very private," he explains, his green eyes focused on me, a dark eyebrow cocked up and that kissable dimple in his cheek showing his amusement.

What the fuck is he talking about? Pelvic thrust exercise? Is everything about sex with him? I like Oliver, but he's a perv. In truth, it's one of my favorite things about him. That and the stop-you-in-your-tracks, make-a-woman-drool sexiness.

He's so sexy. The thought makes my cheeks flush as if it's not hot enough out here, over a hundred degrees. I'm so frustrated I take it out on him, but he deserves it. That's what I tell myself at least. I have to justify my crazy somehow.

He's still squatting beside me, and I want to knock his arrogant ass over. He doesn't even see it coming. I jerk up off the yoga mat, grabbing his ankle and pulling his leg out from under him before he can stop me. *Yes!*

His eyes get big and his sunglasses fly off the top of his head as he topples over onto his back with a loud, hollow *thunk*. He lies there, blinking up at the sky like he doesn't know what happened.

I laugh so hard, tears well in my eyes. I hold my ribs when they start to ache because I can't stop the laughter bubbling up. I don't think I'll survive it. Best day of my life!

"I got you, you little bitch!" I yell like a championship wrestler while I bend my arm, showing off my fabulous muscles, of which there are none. I'm a strange person, but I won't let it get me down.

He lies there while I cackle like a cartoon witch. "What's wrong, don't like being beaten by a girl?" I say with my best pouty voice. I'm still snickering. This is the most fun I've had in two days. I'm desperate for a good time.

"That's not it," he groans like I actually hurt him.

"Oh, my God," I shriek and jump off the mat, crawling over to him to check if he's okay. "Are you alright? I'm sorry. I was joking around, I didn't mean to hurt you." I reach my hand out, not knowing where to check him for damage. I cup his man bun in my hand, patting his head lightly with an awkward smile.

Why the fuck am I patting his man bun? I'm such a weirdo. I also hurt him. Shit!

"Should I go get Gramps? I'm so sorry."

I bend forward, leaning over his chest, checking the other side of his head. That pained mouth perks up in a devious smile, and his eyes show his delight of this outcome. He grabs me around the waist, pulling me hard against his chest.

"Apologize," he demands with a huge, shit-eating grin. I want to punch him in that gorgeous mouth.

"No! I will not. You're an asshole," I yell at him as I struggle to push away from his chest. His grip is so tight I can't get my legs underneath me.

"Apologize or I'll do something very bad, Vale." The way he threatens me makes me wet all over again. That's not the reaction a normal person would have. I like it when he threatens me, at least he's showing desire again, and not that horrible aloofness from his text messages.

I stop fighting, my muscles lax but for the strength it takes to stay up on my knees. He looks confused. I get in his face, so I'm all he can see. No more than an inch separates our lips. I smile at him with all the menace I can muster. *Can you feel my flames, Oliver?* I want to say, but I don't.

"Fuck you," I growl between clenched teeth, drawing each word out in agitation. I smile down at him with bright, hungry eyes, then I flip him the bird with both hands—double the fun.

The laughter that suddenly escapes him is some of the most beautiful music I've ever heard. This man, every part of him, is gorgeous. His voice is sexy. His hair is sexy, even in that silly man bun. Those kissably soft lips are sexy. Even the deep, shadowed grooves of his abs, hidden under that plain white T-shirt are sexy.

I look around, searching for something to slap him with, maybe a stick. But there it is, woe is me, my one weakness! He's wearing those heather-gray exercise pants again. How many fucking pairs of these things does he have? Someone should burn them because he's a danger to all when he wears them.

I should have said *fuck me* instead of *fuck you*. I tense in his arms as I look down at that bulge between his legs. He's turned on. He so hard the outline of his cock is detailed in those cursed pants. I don't know what to do, but I can't start making sexy eyes at him out here on the deck. It's daytime! Anyone could see us!

"So, you're not gonna apologize, pretty girl?" he asks, his voice cutting like a razor's edge, deep and dark. Lustful. I'm screwed.

He called me pretty and, under any other circumstances, I would have been shocked by it, but I was in some type of strange mood. I'm fierce and insolent. I'm full of flames. That fire burning inside me is making me unafraid. It's likely heatstroke-induced insanity.

I shake my head, then start tickling him, hoping it loosens his grasp. Yes! He jerks at my touches. I have to get away from those gorgeous dick pants. I mean cock pants. I mean . . . I mean . . . um . . . oh, yeah, exercise pants. Fuck my brain that only wants to focus on his dick! It really is a great dick though.

The minute I try to tickle him under his arms, he releases my waist. I take no time to think about it. I bolt off the deck like a jaguar into the rainforest. I don't know if I've run so fast or jumped so far in my life.

I take off across his front garden. When I see those red roses, I remember my thoughts from weeks ago and know without a doubt that I'm going to fall into them, so I run away from the house. I run away from rosebushes and the karmic thorns that will definitely pierce my flesh if I get anywhere near them.

"Stay away, sucker," I yell back, not looking because I know I'm screwed if I look back. I'll stumble into the nearest rosebush. I know it!

I'm running in an arc in his large front yard, laughing like a loon. This house is so much bigger than it used to look. I'm going to lose steam soon if I don't find a place to hide quickly. I finally make it to the opposite end of the house and stare in fright at the formal garden full of roses. Fuck! Fuck! Fuck! I turn a sharp curve back to the front yard, and that's when I see him.

"No!" I yell with my hand out to stop him. "We can't. These rosebushes have a bone to pick with me. Trust me when I say I need to run away from them." I'm yelling this stupidity out and it doesn't occur to me that he doesn't know what I'm talking about.

He stands there watching me bolt from left to right, trying to figure out which way to get around him. His eyes are a beautiful bright green, so unique I believe it's truly a color that doesn't exist in the real world. He's all lit up with mirth, and he's so gorgeous. His man bun has fallen to the side, so I point at the crown of my head, bend forward, and start laughing hard again.

"Oliver, please, your hair." I laugh as tears start streaming down my cheeks. Tears of absolute, utterly amused, delight. If I don't stop this crying-laughter, snots going to start flying, and it's not going to be sexy.

He falls for it and grabs his hair, taking the elastic out. As he's trying to fix it, I dart left and right, waiting for him to give chase. He's distracted, thinking something's in his hair, so I fake left and run around him back to the front yard, back to the evil roses. I'm out of breath when I get close to the front door.

He yells, "You cheat, get back here."

It renews my vigor, and I keep pumping my legs, feeling like I could fly. The sun is shining so his fancy, vintage Ferrari is out front in the circle with the top down, waiting to go. It's blocking my way.

I hear him behind me, and it inspires me to fake left toward his front door, but at the last minute I go right toward the car. I jump over the front end so he can't grab me. My ass comes down on the hood. I lift my legs, sliding across and praying I don't damage it. I hadn't meant to touch it at all. I was trying to jump it like a hurdle because, duh, I'm suddenly athletic. For some reason I thought I could do it.

"Oops!" I screech as my sunglasses fly from my face and fall to the faux cobblestones. I don't stop to grab them.

"Different game now, I'm going to kill you," he growls, and he actually sounds angry. I refuse to fall for it.

I know how much that car means to him, but I can't find it in my heart to care at the moment. I don't give two shits that I may have scratched the paint on his fancy car. I'll care later.

I'm laughing again, tears streaming down my face (or is that sweat). "Come at me!" I yell and make it around the other side of the house where there are no roses. I hope there's not, at least.

"Baby, you promised you'd never hurt me. Remember?" I say, then start chuckling again.

"Leave the car out of this."

He sounds so close. I pump my legs harder. "Yep," I agree. It's all he's getting from me as I round the house. I run toward the pool house instead of the veranda that will take me back to those evil rose bushes and the formal garden I almost ran into.

"Fuck you, rosebushes!" I yell with laughter, flipping them off while I run toward the woods.

I can get lost in the woods, meaning I'll find a place to hide. I feel powerful. Who knew being chased was so much fun? I would have knocked him on his ass earlier had I known. This is the best. I'm happy, like a child suddenly. The world is at my fingertips even as my sides start to protest. I can't even let the memories of what happened in the pool house distract me. I'm giving it my all as I try to escape.

"What is it with you and those roses?" His voice sounds farther away now. I'm getting away. He must be getting tired too.

I pass the pool house, running left. There's a small, covered patio in the back, but I don't linger. I have to make it to the tree line so I can lose him. I'm a jungle cat, all lean muscles and coiled power. I can outrun this Lilu behind me. I already have. I don't hear him anymore as

I make it to the line of beech trees covered in Spanish moss. I slow down enough to jump over a fallen log. Then I take off again, toward a large oak. It's so different from the forest on the other side of the street that's mostly pine.

My feet slap against sticks and forest debris, making all kinds of noise, but if I can get behind that wide oak trunk, surely I can hide. I can be still and quiet, then get away when he passes me.

I make it around to the back of the tree and stop. I'm about to peer around the wide trunk, but instead I take a moment to catch my breath. I'm leaning right to see where he is, when my chest is suddenly thrust up against the rigid bark, my hands stretched high over my head. Oliver steps into me, pushing me harder into the tree so every breath is a struggle to expand my lungs. His chest is heaving against my back, his breath hard against my ear, my neck.

"Thought you could escape?" he asks, his voice so gravelly and low that I shudder. "You'll never escape. Now bend over, Vale. I win."

A shiver runs up over my spine. I've imagined this very scenario. I've imagined him fucking me against a tree, bound and helpless. Fantasy number three hundred twenty-two, I think.

He releases my hands, and I grab the tree trunk the best I can with my fingertips. I walk my legs backward so I'm bowing. He drags me by my hips back against his, and the palms of my hands slide down the tough bark. I want him to see me bent over. I want him touching me. I want him just as crazed as I am.

I'm breathing so hard, trying to catch my breath, but his fingers at my hips, those that are caressing gently under the elastic waistband of my shorts, are ramping it right back up. We stand like that for minutes. Time begins to move slower and slower in my brain. Why is he just standing there?

Move! Do something! Say anything!

I press my hips against his, rocking. I'm so turned on I can't stop moving. My frustration is only amping up.

"Vale." He says my name like a prayer, his voice deep and sexy. "You've been a bad girl." His words are like a fiery caress over my too sensitive skin, creating fire in its wake. We're still playing a game. *Okay, I'll play.*

"Have I?" I ask with a smile on my face. I'm going to win this time.

Oliver growls like a beast. His fingers wrap around my ponytail, then he rolls it around his fist so slowly I want to scream. I love it when he does this. He presses his hips into my backside. I feel that rigid, thick hardness. I weep for it. I'll get on my knees and beg for it. I'll do anything.

He yanks my hair back so fast the breath comes rushing out of my mouth with a whimper. My body is arched back at an unbearable angle. My hips being held back against his cock. Who knew he could bend me to his will so thoroughly?

"Yeah, Vale, you have." His words are so low, rumbling deep from within his chest.

I try to tilt my head to the left with the little slack he's given me, but he doesn't let me move very far. I'm on fire, burning so hot one stroke and I'd be coming against his hand. That's all I need. I'd say please, but there's a part of me that's still fighting.

"What are my crimes?"

I can barely see his lips, but what I do see is an incensing smirk. He sure is cocky right now. Does he think he has me? I'm ready to play some more.

"You existing so close to me is a fucking crime, especially dressed like this. I imagine you knew that though when you decided to work on your core strength out on the deck."

I smirk right back. "I'm a free woman. I can do whatever I want, baby." My voice is breathy with desire and a wee bit of confidence. Why is it so hot for him to have such complete control over me?

"Is that so? So you think you're free of me? You think I don't own this?" He lets go of my hip before stroking up over my belly, the rung of each rib, until his hand slides right under my sports bra. "You're saying I don't own these tits?"

I can't speak as he pinches my nipple. It hurts so much I cry out. Soon his fingers journey back over my rib cage and farther down till he cups my sex in his hand, squeezing it tightly. I try to push myself into his hand harder, rocking my hips, needy for the smallest amount of friction. That's all I need. Why won't he give me what I need?

"Is this hungry pussy not mine, baby?"

My breathing is so fast I'm dizzy. I think I'll hyperventilate if he doesn't stop soon.

"You better fucking answer me," he demands next to my ear while I squirm against him. He's never been so rude to me, so demanding. He talks dirty, but this is different. His words wrap around me, choking me where I can barely get enough oxygen, much less speak.

"You've got five seconds to tell me I own your pussy or I'll punish you. Do you understand me? On the count of five, got it?" he asks, but there's no use. I can't answer.

I try to nod my head but the fingers in my hair have gone tighter, tugging at my scalp. I'm trying to think. I'm trying to get my brain to work, but the world's spinning around me. I have no control.

"Five," he says against my temple. "Four," he whispers at my ear.

He removes his hand from cupping me over my shorts, and I groan in pain, my pussy throbbing at the loss. I ache.

"Better hurry. Three," he says, his hot breath pressing against my neck.

"You," I gasp. "You . . . " I can't get the words out. God help me, I can't do it.

"Yeah, baby, that's it. Tell me what I want to hear. Be a good girl, tell me I own it," he says so sweetly against the back of my neck, his lips against that sensitive skin.

"Two!" His teeth scrape over my neck to where my shoulder meets my spine. My heart is pounding. I'm trying to put the words together. It's what he asked me to do. I'm trying to answer. I want to answer.

"Bad girls get punished, and you've been"—his breath comes hard against my skin—"a very bad girl. One."

I'm in trouble.

Oliver lets go of me so fast, I almost fall. He rips my shorts down and they drop around my ankles. I'm toppling sideways, but it feels like everything is happening in slow motion. I can't stop myself, but he reaches out and steadies me.

"Do what I say. Now. Hold on to that tree as best you can. I want you to keep your ass out for me. I want it on display, or it gets worse. Remember baby, it can always get worse." Impossible!

Oliver's hands feel like the stinging zap of electricity when they move over my ass cheeks. He's rubbing them, squeezing them while I pour sweat in the heat of their all-consuming possession. I feel so weak while he does it.

I hear it before I feel it. He slaps my left cheek. The sting makes me gasp long after I hear the vicious pop. My eyes are open now, the swirling world suddenly, deeply focused. All I feel is the sting he left against my skin, the deep fire blooming, growing ever higher.

The muscles in my core clench, like their revving up to run away. "Oliver," I gasp. I'm shaking like a leaf when he slaps the right. I cry out and arch back farther into him. I can't stop it. I swear if I didn't know any better, I was about to come. I'm supercharged, hypervigilant in the absolute worst, torturous way.

"Does it hurt?" he asks sweetly, like he actually cares about the pain blooming between my legs.

I nod my head, but it's not the slaps on my ass that hurt. It's the constant clenching of muscles, unused inside me. It's my clit that's so swollen and engorged I don't know if I'll survive not being able to come. I need it to breathe. I need it to survive.

"Want me to make it stop, sweet Vale?" His tone is all seduction.

"God, yes. Please, Oliver. Please," I beg him with tears in my eyes.

"Then tell me what I want to hear." He's growling again, a grumbling sound that makes me shiver.

I lick my lips, trying to focus. "You own my body. You own every inch. You own my pussy. No one else ever will." My words rush out, and I recognize them as the absolute truth they are. I never denied it, not really.

Oliver kneels behind me, then tells me to lower myself so my knees are bent, my legs spreading farther apart. He holds my hips steady with the palm of his hand as I sink.

"Can you take one more?" The question makes those tears fall, streaming over my hot cheeks.

I'm throbbing. He's killing me. I hate this as much as I love it. "Yes." I weep with the lie when he has me exactly where he wants me.

Then he does something I don't expect, he presses his lips against my left ass cheek. My skin throbs where he touches me. One of his hands comes up between my thighs. He holds it flat against my belly. My abdominal muscles clench in time with my core.

"This is really messing with you, isn't it? Do you like losing control?" he asks against my ass. I wish I could see his face.

I tilt my head back, licking my lips. "I do, Oliver. You're touching me. It's all I want," I say with a sniffle. "It's all I need."

When his hand moves, sliding across my abdomen, I squeak. My entire body is overstimulated. I'm drowning with how each touch feels. My legs are starting to shake with the strain, and I worry I won't be able to hold myself up much longer. I feel Oliver smile against my bum. He bites down on the skin, shocking me, and suddenly his hand at my belly isn't sliding over skin, it's slapping my pussy so hard my head flies back and I scream.

The pleasure erupts unexpectedly, like a volcano—absolute violence in its destruction. Hot tendrils shoot out from my core into every inch of my body. I'm screaming so loudly Oliver has to cover my mouth to muffle the sound. I scream and moan into his palm like some kind of lust-crazed maniac.

My knees straighten, shooting me to standing, bringing him with me. I fall against the tree, breaking bark as my nails dig in harder like claws. My hips are bucking though there's no more touch. Pleasure continues to build within me, then release, over and over again like a never-ending orgasm. I slam a fist down onto the bark as it gets so intense I almost lose my mind. I can't control it as it floods my system like a tidal wave.

What the fuck did he do?

Then that energy buzzes, my own electrical current, building inside me. I turn against the tree quivering, swallowing through the pleasure, trying to control it. I'm balling it up. I want to show him the same.

When he lets go of my mouth, looking at me with insanely pained, lustful eyes like he can't take anymore either, I lose it.

"Get on your fucking knees," I groan as the orgasm ramps up at the sight of his heaving chest. It's as if I'm being throttled by all the pleasure that exists in the world, and it's suddenly exploding inside me. My stomach muscles clench as I try to hold it inside.

He sees something in my eyes, and he doesn't argue. He does what I told him to.

"Show me your cock, baby. Touch it for me. Do as I say!" Demands fly from my throat like I've become someone else entirely. Do I have a monster?

It's taking something of a miracle to hold that pulsating energy inside and not force it into him before it grows any stronger. But it does grow stronger. My legs are shaking as sticky wetness spills down the inside of my thighs. I may faint if he doesn't hurry up.

Oliver lifts his cock over those evil fucking pants, then watches me as he starts to stroke. I smile as the orgasm spasms through my pussy, making me clench down on nothing because he isn't inside me. He isn't inside me where he should be. That's where he belongs.

The ball of energy is so large, so strong as it pulls the pleasure from within me. I think it might kill me when I release it, but I don't care. Nothing will stop this.

I smile at him as he pants. "Yeah baby, you ready?" I ask sweetly, but I don't let him answer. I force it all inside him, focusing on his cock and hoping it goes deep inside his hips, making him feel everything I've felt in the last few moments, everything I've felt since meeting him. All my love, the lust and pain from being denied, I put into that energy. Oliver needs to know what he does to me. He needs to experience that exquisite cruelty for himself. I have something to prove.

"Vale," he groans as the clenching inside me stops suddenly, shutting off like a tap. The sky tilts, and a dark halo surrounds my vision as I take my first deep breath.

Oliver's head slings back with such force it looks painful. It's such a beautiful sight. I almost come again. "Fuck," he groans, his jaw tightening, lips pulling back, showing his teeth.

"You feel that, baby? That's me coming inside you," I say with a devious smirk. "Feel good?" I sound like a monster. I sound like Oliver, and it makes me smile wider.

He's shaking, still stroking his cock. I pull up my shorts and step closer on wobbly legs. I get on my knees next to him in the brush. With the sticks and dirt strewn across the forest floor, I'm suddenly reminded that the price for living is death.

I force his hand away and grab his cock. I stroke him. "Now look at me, Oliver."

He's shaking when he lifts his head. His swollen lips trembling, his Adam's apple bobbing when he swallows. Now he knows how I feel. Now he gets to learn how hard it is. Poor Oliver and the vengeance I offer, a pleasure so intense it's painful. He did this to me.

When our eyes meet, I feel his cock jerk in my hand, so hot and heavy. He's full of my fire. "Now come for me!"

I hear his teeth clink together and his nostrils flair as he tries to breathe through it. "Vale," he whimpers, and it's so sweet. Just like I used to be before he turned me into this creature full of need and lust.

"That's how I feel." He spills his hot, sticky cum against my wrist. He groans. His mouth is slightly parted, showing those canines that make my heart speed up. *There's my monster.*

When I let go and stand up, Oliver is clearly shaken. He watches me, still on his knees, unable to speak as he swallows hard. His eyes are glowing inhumanly green, appropriate in this chaotic woodland setting. The color surprises me, the darkness hasn't filled them.

I move to step away, but he grabs the wrist that isn't soiled with his pleasure.

"Where the fuck do you think you're going?" he asks, and his voice is deep again. He's coming back to himself.

I smile down at him, then shake his hand off my wrist, like it's nothing. Like I'm completely unaffected, strong for the first time in my life. It doesn't take much. He drops my hand as if he doesn't have the energy to fight me for once.

"I'm going to wipe your cum all over your precious upholstery. I win." I say with a cavalier smile, uncaring of his anger.

I take off. I run like the wind. I'm strong. I'm a wild cat, all lithe muscles and grace as I escape Oliver's sexual thrall. I feel so mighty, impervious. I'm finally in control, and it feels so good. I run around the pool house. I don't look back. I want him to chase so the next time he catches me he's so excited he forces his cock inside me. He can deny it all he wants, but we both know where this is leading.

"Don't you dare, Vale!" he yells.

I start laughing. "Why not? Mine is there."

I'm running, but I know I can't keep it up forever. I'm only human. All the muscles in my body are on fire, wanting to seize up. I've burned through more energy than I've taken in today. I'm so sweaty I feel the forest debris sticking to my knees. But I keep running. Nothing will stop me.

"Yours belongs there." He's so close, those words so surprising my legs slow. Then I make a mistake, I look back.

He grabs me with the force of a linebacker, slamming into me, stealing my breath. I scream like I'm being attacked, and we go flying through the air. I close my eyes as he cradles my head, protecting me. I'm scared for all of a tenth of a second before we crash into the pool.

Oliver tightens his grip around my waist and forces me up out of the water. I gasp for air as I push against him trying to get away. I give him a dirty look even as I laugh. He presses me up against the wall of the pool, then holds my jaw between his thumb and index finger as we tread water. He forces me to look into his beautiful eyes. There's a moment of capitulation between us that drags on and on, seemingly forever, as he studies me. The only sound is our harsh, mingled breaths.

I open my mouth to speak but my words get lodged in my throat. He presses forward, and I spread my legs for him. When he slides between them, where he belongs, I wrap my legs around him. I press my palm against his chest where his rapid heartbeat gives me a sense of pride. I did that. I made his heart race. He's always done that to me, but now I've done it to him. It gives me hope.

"Vale," he whispers against my lips. "You're something else, something amazing and wonderful. You're so beautiful." His words are genuine, and it makes my heart sing with a different melody. There's admiration in his eyes I don't understand and affection for me that I'm so grateful for.

Tears leak from my eyes. "Oliver," I cry, ruining the mood. I don't know what to say. I've dreamed about him telling me I was beautiful. He looks at me with his loving, beautiful green eyes that speak volumes without saying a word. He knows how the word "beautiful" makes me feel. He knows how I need to hear it.

Oliver cups my cheeks reverently, making me feel precious. We stare at each other for so long, our breath melding, our bodies wrapped around each other. Then he says the words I've been dying to hear, "I want you, Vale, all of you." It's a painful confession against my lips. The need in his voice is so overwhelming it shocks me.

Oliver Byron wants me. He wants me!

He kisses me and at first it's so gentle, like that first touch. I wrap my arms around his neck. I need to be closer, always closer. I try to hold every part of him with every part of me.

There's no denial in this moment. It's too precious. There are no maybes, probablys, or perhaps. I love him. I love Oliver Byron with all my heart, my soul. I love him with every piece of me.

"Oliver," I moan against his lips, the kiss getting more heated. I need to tell him. "I—"

"Vale! Oliver! Are you two alright? Is everything okay?" Gramps yells from the veranda, and I lose my chance.

We smile at the same time against each other's lips, then break apart after the quickest of kisses. I swim toward the shallow end, putting space between us. Space I don't want. I need him closer always.

"Fine, Gramps!"

"There was a bee," Oliver and I yell out at the same time.

Our eyes meet, then laughter bursts free from both of us. I cradle my forehead in my hand, shaking my head and laughing so hard. I'm so impossibly happy. Joy, like I've never felt, is filling me up. I feel weightless and light. He does this to me. I've never felt this way, not once in my life.

I splash water at Oliver as he swims closer. I'm wrung out, but I still want to play. I still want the chase, the colliding, the aftermath of us. I don't want to lose the joy we've found today.

Oliver splashes me back. When I wipe my eyes and look at him, his smile is only for me. It's so beautiful. There's joy in those green eyes I haven't seen before. It's new, and I worry Gramps will see it too. He'll see what it is, and he'll know what we've done because, for the first time, Oliver isn't hiding his feelings so well.

"That must have been one huge bee," Gramps says, then laughs as he gets to the pool, taking a seat on a lounge. "I heard you scream and got worried. You sure it wasn't a wasp? Nothing inspires more fear in a grown man's heart than a red wasp. Even I run from those buggers and I'm sixty-eight."

31

SUPERNOVA

OLIVER

eed her. Our mate, the beast cries inside me, but he's not clawing at my resolve. He knows I felt it. He's left us alone to experience it, to figure out what's between us. He tells me about her, how he wants her, how he needs her, how he loves her, as if there's some camaraderie between us. So much has happened in the past hour I don't feel so threatened by speaking to the beast. I can't fight with him. I can't or Nick might see how my eyes change. It's full daylight; he could see the truth.

"Well, I better go get a shower and change. Vale, feel free to grab a towel from the pool house," I tell her as I step out of the water.

I'm facing her and for a moment she looks like she's upset. She doesn't want me to go and under different circumstances, I wouldn't. I would take her with me. She quickly hides her disappointment, and I hate myself for causing it.

Nick can't see my face, so I try to give her an apologetic look. I mouth the words, *Call me*, and hope she actually does. I need to explain why I'm walking away. I want that carefree smile back on her lips.

"Thank you for saving me," she says, and the words hit funny. I don't understand what she's trying to say. Did I save Vale? I think she's trying to save me.

"The bee," she says as if reading my look of confusion, but that's not what she's actually talking about. I know there's something else. I hope she'll tell me one day.

I turn away because if I don't, I'm going to drag her with me. Then Nick would lose his mind, and I'd lose a friend.

"What time are you two going shopping tomorrow?" Nick asks.

Shit! I forgot to ask if she wanted to come with me. I was supposed to pretend I needed something unique from the gourmet shop downtown, then we'd actually go to the DDS, where I'd made an appointment for her. It's her birthday surprise, since Nick thought if it was a gift she wouldn't refuse it. But I'd talk her into getting her license in the parking lot if I had to.

"Vale, I forgot to ask, do you want to come with me tomorrow? I want to go to that European market on Tremont. Nick told me you could show me the way. I'll treat you to lunch and we can hang out downtown if you want." The words fly out of my mouth, and I hope she's convinced.

When I look back at her, she's sitting on the edge of the pool, pulling her waterlogged shoes off. She looks up with a bright smile that steals my breath. She's so impossibly beautiful. The upset from a few minutes ago is gone. There's joy once more, like my simple question meant so much more.

"Of course I'll come! I've been dying to get out of the house. I've been so bored lately," she says. "Can we check out that thrift shop Once Used Twice Loved? Kat says it's awesome."

She's so excited. Her happiness makes me smile. I feel it blossom deep in my chest, making my heart thump. I'd do anything to make this woman happy. Her smile alone is worth the effort. *She's so beautiful*, the beast whispers. *Look at her. She's ours.*

"Of course we can. Let's make a day of it. I'll text you later to let you know when to be ready," I say, then turn on my heels and walk away.

"It's a date then," she says, and I feel the muscles between my shoulders tighten. I don't acknowledge her words. I continue up the path in my own squeaky, waterlogged trainers.

I hear Nick apologize to Vale, about how he feels bad for not doing more with her over the summer, but I don't hear her reply. I see my mother standing at the kitchen door, and I speed up. Vale doesn't know she's here yet. With all the chasing I didn't get the chance to tell her that she was in town and that's why I haven't been around the past two nights.

When I get to the door, she points at my shoes with an irritated look while she shakes her head back and forth. I don't say anything as I step out of the shoes and walk into the house. I expect her to follow me up the stairs before we speak a word about what just happened. I know she heard us. She's ancient, her hearing better with age instead of worse. My siblings will tell you she knew when we were up to no good.

I make it to the top floor, my floor. These are my private quarters. I don't usually have guests here. I can feel Mother's energy at my back, but I can't hear her steps or her breathing. She doesn't make a sound as she follows me into my bedroom.

It's a bit disturbing after only being around humans lately. Humans are so loud, when they breathe, when they walk, when they move. The way I can tune into their crazy rhythmic heartbeats. I get used to it after a while and don't pay as much attention, but then when I get around a vampire or a demon again, their silence is irksome.

I walk straight into the bathroom before she can speak.

"What the fuck was that?" she asks.

I pull the T-shirt over my head and hang it from a towel rack. I pull my pants down and do the same. I grab a towel and slide it onto the floor underneath so the water won't make a mess. "I don't understand the question. What the fuck was what exactly?" I ask, annoyance clear in my tone.

"I heard you two. I was in the kitchen making tea for Nick when you two decided to have very loud sex in the backyard. One minute she was screaming, and the next you sounded like you were in pain. It was strange. That girl messes with my senses. Her mental blocks are strong, but I didn't think they'd block our bond.

"I thought she'd hurt you. It felt like an explosion of power, then I couldn't feel you anymore. Next thing you know, you two were screaming and chasing each other again. Was that the energy she feeds you?"

Her words are excited, intrigued, and my cheeks flush. I've never been embarrassed of my sex life around my mother. If anything, she's one of the only people who understands what I've gone through. That hunger. She has it too. But as I think about what Vale and I did in the forest, I find I want it to be private. I wish for it to remain only between us. I wish my mother hadn't heard any of it. No, it's not embarrassment. It was a cherished moment between two lovers lost in need for each other.

"Are you alright?"

I wrap a towel around my waist and step out. My mother is worried. I can feel it through the bond and see it on her face. For the first time in a long time, she looks afraid. Did Vale scare her?

I think about how I can explain the energy she forces into me. It doesn't make sense to me either, but this time it was wholly different. This time I felt her yearning, how much it pained her to be denied by me, I felt her orgasm. She showed me exactly how it felt, and it did hurt me. It was never-ending pleasure mixed with never-ending pain. Oh boy, it was like something out of this world different. The pain she feels for me, the pleasure, it's so extreme. It was the purest form of need I'd ever experienced.

"We didn't have sex," I tell her as I make my way to the closet. I step in, closing the door behind me, and move to the dresser to grab a pair of soft lounge pants.

"I don't believe you. That kind of energy exchange doesn't come from foreplay." Her words raise my hackles.

When I step out of the closet, she's sitting in my favorite chair, her legs crossed, and she looks irritated. I sit across from her on the sofa, crossing my arms in defiance. "Do you know why I don't want to tell you? I'm serious, I don't want to share with you for once." She looks hurt but hides it quickly.

"So, she fucked you," she says, and that irritation returns to her voice. "I heard what she said. She said she came inside you. It's alright. No reason to be embarrassed."

I'd thought Vale had said that, but I was so overwhelmed by her release of energy inside me that it was like a dream. I wasn't sure if it actually happened or not. It didn't seem like something she'd say. Then again, she was so different today, so assertive. She was unapologetically doing what she wanted, and it was spectacular. She was so gorgeous when she was running from me. I let her get away, of course, but I wasn't going to tell her that. I had more fun in those moments than I've had in the entirety of all my years.

"Ash," Mother says. "Truly there is no need for embarrassment. I promise."

"I'm not embarrassed. She didn't fuck me either, not exactly. There's no exactly about it. She didn't physically fuck me. Ah! She wasn't even touching me when she said that. It was her energy. It was intense. She controls it somehow, and this time it was different than before. I felt her pleasure, her arousal, I felt her pain at being denied. It was so extreme I thought I was going to pass out."

"This girl hurt you."

I shake my head. "Not at all," I say, but it's not quite true. Her emotions flayed me. "I felt her emotions, her pain, her desire for me, the ceaseless longing, the agony when I've told her we can't have sex. I felt the rejection of it. It felt like she had taken all the pleasure and pain in the world, melded it into a powerful, pulsating ball of light, then pressed it deep within me and let it explode outward so I felt it all simultaneously. It was a supernova inside my soul. It was everything, yet there's no evidence of it. I've fed so thoroughly I'm full. Mother, I hunger no more."

I look up at her as tears make my vision swirl. Her stiff demeanor changes, and she looks at me with such a warm smile.

"I love her," I say, and the words escape outward into the world. I do nothing to stop them even though it scares me beyond belief. I love

Vale more than anything in the world. It's a love that's incomparable, remarkable, and new. I love her, and that knowledge makes my heart ache. I hold my fist to my chest.

"I know, son. I'm glad you figured it out."

Mother stands and steps forward. She pats my hand, and I stand up. I wrap my arms around her much smaller frame as my chest shakes. When was the last time I cried in her arms? When was the last time I was free to be vulnerable, even with her? I've felt like the world weighed on me, crushed me for so long. I hadn't realized how painful the loneliness was till I felt the same in Vale. I hadn't noticed at all until today, after being so wrapped up in the fear of what I felt for her. Is that what I'd saved her from? Is that what she'd meant?

Mother holds me in her arms, and I feel like a child again as I cry. She doesn't leave me. She doesn't run away from the scary, overpowered emotions that erupt from me like a volcano spewing hot lava.

I rant about my fear of hurting Vale. I tell her how the monster inside me claws to get out, how it wants her. I tell her how frightened it makes me. I tell her about how badly it hurts to know how much I love Vale. To love a mortal is beyond stupid.

I cry about how Vale will die one day, leaving me alone. How would I live without her? I can't leave her alone for more than a few hours now. I hate being separated from her. Even when Vale doesn't know, I still check on her. I watch her from the windows just to get a glimpse of her beautiful face. How could I survive losing her? I wouldn't.

"You can't think about the future, Ash. You can't. You'll only lose the time you do have, worrying about a future that you can't do anything about."

I know she's right, but now I'm flooded by my staggering emotions. These things I've never felt before. We both sit on the floor, my head in her lap, while she brushes her fingers through my hair, trying to comfort me.

"Just be with her. Don't take anything for granted. Embrace every precious second you have with her. Show her all the love in your heart. Do your very best to make her feel loved and special. None of us are guaranteed tomorrow, not even immortals. So why worry about the future. Just live, son."

I want Vale to know how special she is to me. One day, if someone asks her if she's known love, I want her to think of me fondly. I want her to picture me loving her. She should never doubt my love for her. I sit up and look at my mother. I realize she's never stopped parenting me, no matter how old I've gotten. She's tried so hard to be there for me, through everything, even when I push her away.

"Will you help me? I'm taking her out tomorrow. I want to make her feel special. I need advice."

Mother smiles brightly. She's so happy for me. "Of course I'll help you. I've been waiting for this day for centuries!"

32

BEAUTY IS THE WRONG WORD

VALE

I've tried on every outfit, every combination of every piece of clothing I own. Nothing's right. I've put a lot of thought into what I'd wear. I thought about what we were going to do and the weather. I thought about how I would style my hair. I searched for makeup I knew I didn't own. I have a couple things, including a lip stain, some mascara, and a tinted lip gloss, but that's the extent of it. Point being, I'm beyond anxious.

I don't know where Oliver and I stand after yesterday. I don't know if this is a date or if we're just friends. I don't know what we are. I've gone so long not being interested in the opposite sex, I'm not prepared to go on a date.

Where Kat had been using makeup for years, I hadn't done more than experiment with it. She'd bought sexy clothes, but I hadn't bothered because it didn't seem like it was ever going to happen for me. Who would ask me on a date? I barely know anyone around Silver Springs and it's not like I'd be going on a date when I was living with my parents.

I stand in front of the mostly empty closet, staring at the charcoal-gray garment bag that's hanging there. I can't look away from it. I'm tapping my foot nervously, shaking my head. "Nope, I'm not doing it."

I pace across the room, then I pace back, giving the garment bag a dirty look. "Ugh!" I cross the room again with folded arms.

"They're just clothes. They have no power over you. You're choosing this, not them," I tell myself. "Fuck it!"

I run back to the closet and grab the garment bag, tossing it down on my bed and unzipping it. Most of the skirts are black or brown and boring. I flip the hangers to the side, one after another, until I find the one I'm looking for. It's a navy-blue and white polka dot, A-line skirt with tan buttons that fasten it together down the center. There's a tie at the waist instead of a belt, and it falls just below my knees.

I admit it's cute, a rarity amongst the clothes my mom normally buys me, but I'm still ambivalent because this is from the real world. Normal life and summer vacation, may the two never meet. I narrow my eyes at the skirt, then decide right then and there that I won't be cowed by some cotton and buttons. In fact, I open every single tan button with a devilish smile on my face.

I put the skirt on and twirl in front of the mirror. I like the way it shows my legs, but when I catch a glimpse of bright red bush, I decide to close a few buttons. No reason to go to jail for indecent exposure. The skirt looks so nice, I decide to find the matching white dress shirt. When I realize it has long sleeves, I stick my tongue out at it. Can't win them all.

I grab the camisole from underneath the blouse instead. The camisole is cute with a pretty lace trim at the top of the jersey knit. I grab a white satin strapless bra and the sexiest panties I own, just in case he sees them. They're sheer white panties I'd bought when Kat was on a lingerie kick. She hadn't liked them and said they were too modest for lingerie. I didn't think so. For goodness sake, they were transparent and pointless, just like most of the lingerie I'd seen her buy.

I shaved my legs and contemplated shaving my pubic hair till I realized it could go so badly wrong. Thank you, Kat, for your horror stories in grooming that prevent me from doing stupid things.

I leave my hair down long, curling it with a very old curling iron that belonged to my grandma. It's not uncommon to find things that belonged to Grandma. I don't think Gramps had the heart to throw her stuff away and neither do I. He kept her perfume on his bedside table and more than once I'd taken a sniff just to remember how she smelled. We both miss her.

When I've tortured myself long enough with an eyelash curler and mascara, I give up. I use the lip stain and check my face for tiny black spots of mascara. Makeup is torture for me. I don't know how to use it, and it probably shows. I want to be pretty, but is it worth the annoyance? My lips look like I've been kissing though, and that I like.

Finally, I'm ready. I grab a pair of sunglasses, a hair tie, and my purse, which has all the essentials. I'm waiting in the kitchen for Oliver, when I'm surprised to see Gramps stroll through the back door.

"Gramps, do I look okay? I didn't know what to wear." I frown down at myself, questioning my choices for the millionth time.

Gramps's face lights up when I step around the kitchen island. "Pretty as always," he replies. Gramps is so sweet, but it's rare when he says anything about my appearance.

I used to get very upset when Grandma complimented my appearance. She said such nice things about me, but it hurt to hear it, and I'd run away, panicking. So both of them had stopped complimenting my appearance. I'd done that. My anxiety had done that. My fear of being prideful had done that. I wish Grandma was here now. I wish I could apologize. I wish I could hear her say those sweet words again.

"Why so dressed up?" he asks as he makes his way to the fridge to have a rummage. Lunch it is.

"That market we're going to is full of rich people. I don't want to embarrass Oliver. He's always dressed so nice."

"Honey, I don't think you would embarrass Oliver with cut-off shorts and a baggy T-shirt. I think he's got more substance than that. Anyway, he's young too, I'm sure he gets it." Oliver wouldn't care about what I'm wearing, but I do. I care because I want him to think I'm beautiful. I want him to want me.

"Oh yeah, before I forget—" Gramps reaches into his back pocket and pulls out his wallet. He grabs a wad of cash and holds it out. "This is for clothes and whatever you want to get while you're out. I hope you two have fun."

"I don't need that, Gramps. I brought some money with me." By that I mean I put two hundred dollars in my wallet. My parents send me with a thousand dollars every summer so I'm not a burden on Gramps, but he refuses to take it. Anything left at the end of summer goes into my hot rod fund.

"Vale, I have money for you to take, no chores needed. Your birthday is coming up and this way I won't get you something you don't need. You can get whatever you want." His smile is so sincere it makes me feel bad.

I stand there, not knowing what to do, then my phone rings. "Hold that thought," I tell him. I grab the phone from my bag, tossing it onto the counter. The screen flashes, *Hot Neighbor* as the contact name. When had he done that? I try hard not to laugh because I don't want Gramps to ask questions.

"Hello," I answer cheerfully.

"So, in case you want to drive today at some point, which car would you feel the most comfortable driving?" Oliver asks.

"The Ferrari," I blurt out immediately even though I know he'll refuse.

"Ha, ha, ha, very funny. That's a big fat no. She's still mad at your ass. Anything else?"

"It doesn't matter, truly. Gramps doesn't let me drive in town, much less downtown. So whatever you want to drive is fine. Surprise me."

"You two could always drive the Prius. She's driven that," Gramps offers.

"No!" Oliver and I say in unison.

Gramps chuckles. "I heard that."

"You were supposed to, Gramps, trust me."

They're both laughing. Gramps loves the hate toward the Prius. He thinks it's hilarious. I think it's the only reason he drives it. You see, Gramps might be in his sixties and a stodgy, gray-haired professor, but he's actually a cool dude. He's cool in an understated kind of way that sneaks up on a person. People love him.

"Seriously, it doesn't matter. Gramps taught me the art of manual transmissions, so if it rolls forward and has brakes, I can drive it. I think." Gramps made sure I knew how to drive a manual because so many young people couldn't. Always preparing me for life, my Gramps.

"Surprise it is. Be there in five," he says, then hangs up.

Gramps is leaning on the countertop on the opposite side of the island smiling like the cat who ate the canary. He's studying me like he knows something is going on. My cheeks flame, and I don't know what to do.

"That Oliver Byron is very considerate, don't you think? His mother is too. I like her. She's just brilliant."

What?

"You've met his mother?"

"She's been in town a few days, I think. He didn't tell you before you were being chased by killer bees?" He looks amused.

"We didn't have time, you know, running for our lives, away from monster bees and all that." It's the truth, kind of . . . well, the running part, not the monster bees part.

"Soon you two will be telling tall tales about how the murder hornets were trying to, well, murder you." Gramps laughs loudly, finding the whole "bee situation" hilarious.

"Yeah, yeah. Anyway, he's coming. Maybe I should go wait outside." I point my thumb at the door as if I'm trying to hitchhike, which makes Gramps narrow his eyes on me.

"Vale, a gentleman will come to call at the door, not honk the horn from the driveway like trash. Stay calm and make him wait. It's your first date after all." I try not to blush more as my eyes get big. Shit!

"It's not a date. I said that because I was messing with him. No reason to worry."

"I'm not worried about Oliver, he's a good man."

"So you're saying I can date him?" I ask, though this feels like a trap. "Not that he would ever date me. We're just friends."

"I knew you were reading *Dracula* again because you have a crush on him. Romance is in the air." He chuckles.

"You didn't answer me. I thought you said I can never date. Why are you acting so silly today?" I ask. "I need to know the answer, by the way. Because if you say yes, I'm going to ask him out on a date. It'll be all your fault when I fall madly in love with him. I'm going to blame you."

"Ask him out, I dare you. I'll give you my answer after he says yes. It won't matter though. I think you're already in love with him." My cheeks couldn't be more red at this point.

"Gramps, he'll never agree to it, he's scared of you," I explain. Oliver knows Gramps doesn't want me to date.

He opens his mouth in a wide grin and stares at me. He's happy Oliver's afraid of him. Men are weird. I think he's been drinking because his cheeks are flushed and he seems almost giddy talking about Oliver and me dating. The fact that he's smiling about me asking Oliver out isn't normal.

I change the subject by refusing his money. "Oh yeah, I don't need the money, Gramps. Maybe you can take me shopping. We can go together. I'd love that."

"Already in your wallet. Shouldn't have answered your phone," Gramps says, then he stands up straight, grabbing an envelope from the counter. "There's your date."

Oliver is standing at the back door, his hand up about to knock, when I turn around. I wave at him as Gramps steps around me, opening the door. I grab my bag and follow him outside into the heat. The sun is so bright I pull my sunglasses from my bag and tug them down over my eyes.

When I look up, Gramps is handing Oliver the envelope. He holds it in his hands like it's important, then Gramps pats him on the back. Oliver looks him in the eyes and something unsaid passes between them. What are they doing?

Gramps turns toward me. "Good luck, Vale. Pick me up some madeleines if that shop carries them. Have a good time." I narrow my eyes on Gramps. He's up to something. I know he is.

"Thanks," I say, though I don't like how they seem to be scheming together.

Oliver takes my hand, wrapping my arm through his and placing my palm over his forearm. I'm taken aback by his sudden gentlemanly nature. I crack a smile, but I don't look up at him as he leads me to a charcoal-gray SUV. Oh damn, it's a Jaguar. He's going to let me drive a Jag. Sweet!

"Nice wheels."

"Thank you," he answers softly.

Oliver removes his hand from my arm and opens the door for me. When I finally look up at him, he's smiling shyly, unable to make eye contact with me. He's blushing, and there's something so innocent about that. I can imagine him looking like this at my age when a pretty girl came along and caught his eye. It's adorable.

He wears one of those perfectly pressed shirts in a plum color that makes the unique green of his eyes pop. The sleeves are rolled up to his elbows, showing off his powerful forearms. He always looks so perfectly dressed, but today he's wearing jeans and that's a rarity. Did he have trouble choosing what to wear as well?

"You look beautiful, Vale."

My heart speeds up so fast I feel dizzy. I lay a palm on his chest to steady myself. Heat singes my hand, and I jerk away. I get into the car quickly before Gramps has a chance to see me touching him. I have to get away because I know I'm about to kiss him. I want to kiss him. I don't want to hide how I feel about him anymore.

Oliver closes my door, and I grab the seat belt, pulling it over my chest. I take a deep breath before he sits down in the driver's seat and starts the engine. Are we on a date? Is that why he's nervous?

"Thank you, Oliver." I say, my voice so quiet it's almost a whisper.

"Are you ready to go?" he asks while he stores the envelope in the console between us.

I nod my head, then I blurt out, "You look handsome, but then again, you always do." I take in a deep inhale, feeling embarrassed. What happened that we feel nervous around each other?

We weren't like this yesterday. I was so confident and demanding. I felt strong. Now, I'm having a hard time telling him he looks handsome. Oliver knows he's handsome, I don't have to tell him, but I want to. He doesn't say anything, just shifts the car into gear.

Oliver's movements on the steering wheel are graceful. He moves so confidently all the time. Those beautiful hands have touched me. He's held my hand in his. They've made me feel such glorious pleasure and also love. Every single part of him is beautiful.

He brakes at the last stop sign on Hudson Street and slams the shifter into Park. His seat belt is released before I know what's happening, then he grabs my jaw, pulling me closer. I pull my sunglasses up to the top of my head, so I can look into his bright green eyes. There's so much happening in those eyes right now I wish I could read his mind.

"Beautiful doesn't begin to describe what it is I see, what I feel, when I look at you. There are no words, Vale. Not one single word comes close to your beauty. So every time I say that word, understand that it's a lie because it doesn't come close to how exquisite you are to me. Nothing has ever come close."

Shallow breaths escape my trembling lips. *I love you!* Those are the words I'm dying to say, but I stop myself because I'm afraid he doesn't love me. He thinks I'm beyond beautiful, but does he love me? Could Oliver Byron ever love me? He said it himself, that's not who he is.

I wrap my arms around him and slam my lips against his. Everything is right in the world. His lips are against mine, and it feels so good. My hands travel up so I can twine my fingers into his bound hair. We're clinging to each other, lost in the kiss. Those words try to escape again. I want to tell him. I want to scream them out at the world so they can be free. I want him to know that I love him. But once again, it's not meant to be. Someone honks their horn behind us.

"Later, I promise. I'll kiss you all night if you let me," he says against my lips, and the words tear at my soul.

I feel the kind of emotion in my chest that is so strong it brings tears to my eyes. I hold it together for once, like the strong woman I want to be. I hold it together because he offered me all night. I want that. I want to be locked in his arms, trapped against his body, our hearts syncing up, his mouth against mine.

I want every night. I want to wake up in his arms and know I'm loved. I want to be there when he needs me, and I want him to be there when I need someone.

"I don't know when it happened, but you've become everything to me, Oliver," I say because it's as close as I can get to telling him that I love him. "Everything," I repeat.

He buckles his seat belt quickly and the car lurches forward, both of us quiet. When we get to the highway, Oliver grabs my left hand with his right. He holds my hand with care, and I can feel I'm important to him. He needs to touch me.

"I want to be your everything," he says, and his words make my heart swell.

This time, the tears form in my eyes. I open my eyes wide so they don't fall. *Don't cry, Vale! Don't! You're wearing mascara!*

"What is it, baby?"

"I'm trying not to cry because I'm wearing mascara. I never wear makeup, and now I'm worried I'll look like a raccoon." I lean my head back against the headrest, then turn to look at him.

He looks at me for a second before focusing back on the road. "I never want to make you cry. Not ever again."

"I don't mind crying happy tears."

Oliver brings my hand up to his lips and kisses it. "If they're happy tears then cry away." He smiles against my fingers. "I hope you cry happy tears when I surprise you. We're taking a bit of a detour."

He exits the highway quicker than we should and makes several turns. Let him surprise me; nothing could ever surprise me more than meeting him this summer, touching him, falling in love with him. Nothing could be as great as all that.

33

SURPRISE!

VALE

Oliver tells me to close my eyes when we get near the surprise. I do, with a silly grin. Then I feel the car come to a stop, and he's pulling the emergency brake. That strange, hydraulic hissing sound letting me know it's electric and not mechanical. "Here's the deal, I thought a lot about your birthday. I thought about what I could get my girl, that's super special. Something she'll remember, something she needs. Something she wants so badly—"

I interrupt him. "Are you going to give me your dick finally because it's just about all I want these days." The moment the smart-ass comment flies from my lips, he growls, and I get goosebumps.

I hear paper tearing. "Open your eyes," he says.

I open my eyes and blink a few times. We're parked in front of a familiar brick building. I know this place. I look at the glass doors and read, GEORGIA DEPARTMENT OF DRIVERS SERVICES.

"We've got an appointment in fifteen minutes for you to take your driver's test. Nick filled out all the forms," he says, then hands me the application. "Here's your proof of residence and your birth certificate. Trust me when I say this is the easiest DDS visit you'll ever go through. Mayor Ingram pulled some strings, so no one's here. Only you. No waiting for hours."

I look at him for a moment, then I look at the door again. I look back at him and back at the door. What was he thinking?

"You're very sweet for doing this. I appreciate it, but I wasn't going to get my license this summer. I was going to wait till I got back."

"Listen, when I asked Nick about it, he said I might get push back. I see it as a win, win situation. You're a grown woman. You need a license. You don't have to tell your parents if you don't want to. You wouldn't be doing this for them, or me, or your grandfather. You would be getting your license for you."

Part of me wants to walk in that door and do exactly that. If I do this, then it's over. I don't think I'll be able to go back. One last time, I'd told myself. I'd go back one last time to prove to them I'm good, that I'm not evil. I'm still their daughter. I want them to accept me, who I've become, though I know they never will. I want them to love me. I swallow hard.

"Do I need to sweeten the deal?" he asks, and I look back at him, confused.

"Maybe," I say, wondering what he'll offer. Could it be worth disobeying them? I'm the one who'll have to pay the price for it when they find out.

"I'll make you dinner for a week."

I wave my hand and shake my head. "I know how to cook."

"Alright. How about I let you drive any of my cars, except the Ferrari."

I smile as my confidence soars. I want to be devious. I want to push him. I want to drag his mind down into the gutter where mine tends to stay these days. "How about you let me drive us somewhere in that Ferrari, then you can take my virginity on top of the hood?"

"That's a lovely picture. However, the paint job has seen enough of your ass. It might have scratches. I was too afraid to look."

I pout at him.

"I'll buy you a car, anything you want," he spouts next. "I'll fuck you on it, but I won't take your virginity like that."

I shake my head. "That's ridiculous. You didn't put a price tag on that offer. I could want a Ferrari for all you'd know. You're a terrible negotiator, Oliver. Do you know that?"

"I'm not a terrible negotiator if you're thinking about walking into that office and taking your driving test. I'd do almost anything for you. I want to see you succeed. You deserve that. If it takes a six or seven figure car, it'd be worth it because you're worth it."

Six or seven figures? What the fuck has gotten into him? My cheeks heat. He's being so sweet today, even if he's lost his damn mind. "Oliver, we're not even together. You can't offer to buy me a car. I'm not a good investment."

He grabs my chin and forces me to look up into his serious eyes. "Don't you ever say that to me again. I think you're a good investment. I think you're worth it. I want you to believe you're worth it. I want you to believe you're worth walking through that door and getting your license. I want you to know that I believe in you, your worth, your value which is exponentially more than all the money I could ever have."

His eyes are so intense. He seems upset at my lack of self-worth. It's a surprise to be honest. He genuinely believes in me and that's so hard to overcome when I don't always believe in myself.

"Don't make me cry," I say with a sniffle.

"I'm not trying to. I need you to know I'm on your side. You have to know that. I want you in my life. We haven't defined our relationship together, that's true, but it isn't because I don't want to be with you." His eyebrows pinch together; he's worried about something.

"Tell me," I say, mimicking his past words. "Tell me your secrets."

Oliver takes a deep breath, staring at the roof for moment. It's like he needs to fortify himself before he explains. He looks back into my eyes for only a second, and I know what's happening. I've been there. He can't look at me when he tells me the truth.

"When you leave, you're going to break my heart." He's sitting back, head tilted back, his eyes closed. Did he just admit he loves me? Did Oliver say I could break his heart, meaning his heart is already mine?

"I'll be back," I say, defending myself. "It was always my plan to come back, Oliver. After meeting you, I'm not exactly sure I want to go anymore. It'll break my own heart to be so far away from you." I take a deep breath and watch him, but his eyes are still closed, his jaw tight. "I'll do it. I'll go in there and get my license. You don't have to sweeten the deal."

I reach to open the car door, but he yanks me back. He wraps his arms around my shoulders and pulls me against him. I feel his lips at my right ear. He's breathing hard, taking in my scent. "I want to sweeten it. Ask me for something, anything. I want to make you happy."

I don't know what to say at first. I don't know what I want other than him. Then I remember our chat in the street when I was so mad at him. "I want to dance under the stars like no one's watching. I want to be free." I turn back toward him. He looks so nervous. I've never seen him like this.

"Look at me."

When he looks into my eyes, I cup his cheek. "Don't buy me a car or let me use yours. Don't offer me presents. I don't want any of that. You already know what I want and that's you. Make love to me, not to sweeten the deal, but because you want me."

"I want to," he says simply. "I will." He grabs my face in his palms. "I promise you, I will." The look in his eyes is all desperation. He kisses me softly, gently. It's the sweetest kiss we've ever shared. We cling to each other, breath mingling, tongues tasting, hearts pounding.

"Right now, we have to get out of this car," Oliver says against my lips, but he doesn't pull away.

"I know," I whisper back. I don't want to let go. Will there ever be some moment in time when I'm not forced to let him go?

I don't know if he hears something, but he points at the door. I turn and see Kat's father, Albert (Alan for short) Ingram Esq., in a soft-blue seersucker suit, checking his watch nervously. Is everyone in town in on this scheme? I let Oliver go, though I don't want to, and I get out of the car. I walk up to the entrance.

"Hey, Mr. Ingram. How've you been?" It's unusual that I haven't seen him this summer. He's a busy guy, but I used to eat dinner with his family at least once a week. Kat and I had slumber parties in his living room. He's the man who taught me how to fish. He's family.

"For goodness sake, Vale, call me Alan already. It's been good, a little quiet around the house since Katherine and Raif have been away. I hear she's coming back early. Before you go in, I hope you file for your voter registration while you're here. I know I can count on you in the next election. You too, Oliver."

"I can't vote yet, Alan. I need the naturalization paperwork back before I can register. You'll have my vote though, no worries on that," Oliver says with a sincere smile.

I'd always assumed he wasn't from the US. He has an accent I can't place, almost like his tongue tenses to pronounce certain sounds. It's a light accent though, barely there. Sometimes it gets thicker when he gets angry, or when he's turned on. I don't know where Oliver is from. I don't know where he grew up. I don't know what his favorite color is or what his favorite food is. I don't know enough about him, but I want to.

We've never been on a date. I think that's how you get to know someone. That's how you form an opinion on the person you like, you have to spend time with them. That's how they do it in the movies at least. That's what happened with Kat and Brandon before she lost her virginity to the asshole. They hung out every day. They went to dinner and to parties together. They went to concerts and hung out long past curfew.

Oliver and I hang out, he asks a lot of questions about me, but I get so lost in him I don't ask him very much in return. I have to start asking questions. I need to know things about him, even if I've already fallen hard.

"Alright, Alan, let's do this," I say, and he beams when I use his name. Alan is a good guy, if not a little intense with his career. That's where Kat gets her attitude from. If she sets her mind to something, nothing ever gets in her way. I hope I can be that way one day.

34

FATE HAS PLANS FOR US ALL, EVEN IN GEORGIA

OLIVER

Vale takes the written exam with a clerk named Joe. He's also the same person who'll take her on the road test. When I ask her how the written test went, she refuses to tell me. I can't read her mind or the look on her face. I don't want to make her more anxious than she already is, so I just grab her hand and hold it until Joe returns.

Joe strolls out from behind the counter with a clipboard in his hands. I toss Vale the keys to the Jag, and she leaves me there. I hope she isn't mad at me for all this. She's been very quiet since we came into the office, only speaking to Alan about Kat, asking him when she'd be back.

I'm leaning against the counter, waiting for her return, when one of the clerks comes back in through a rear door. She's in her mid-fifties, though her tawny skin looks barely aged, with only little crow's feet around her unique silver eyes. Her tightly coiled black hair is streaked with pretty silver that shines under the fluorescent bulbs. I wave and say hello, trying my best to be friendly.

"You've got that look about you. It's that anxious, fell-in-love-for-the-first-time look. Don't worry, sugar, it's all gonna be alright."

"Is it that obvious?" I make my way closer to the counter.

"I see it all the time. You can't be prepared for love, but it happens every day. God willing, it happens to all of us eventually," she says with a thick, singsong accent that I've heard a hundred times. She's from Louisiana, Cajun country probably.

"Why are you so worried anyway? It's love, it's a good thing. Everybody needs love."

I shrug my shoulders as a strange need to spew my guts hits me. The feeling takes me over. "It's better than good, it's fantastic, but she's young. I feel like we've met too soon. She hasn't experienced life yet. I'm afraid she'd be living for me alone and not herself."

"Of course she'd be living for you, as long as you're living for her too, then you're gonna figure it out."

"You sure about that?" I look at her badge. "Davina."

"Is that your girlfriend? The young redhead in the Jag?"

I nod and look out the door, desperate for Vale's return. "Davina, is she too young for me?" I feel so comfortable speaking to her that I ask the question that's been on my mind a lot lately.

"It's not like you gonna find a soul your own age, sugar. You got an old soul. I feel it just as plain as day, like them vampires. The ones who walk round New Orleans as if they own da place. You one of those?"

I shake my head. "Not exactly." I don't know why I answer her question. I should be running. She could be one of those crazy hunters who've attacked vampires throughout the ages. Some mortals can sense that there's something different about supernatural beings. They usually just go crazy or are ostracized for being crazy. But there are a few who create sects of hunters, usually religious groups with fringe views. However, they tend to kill more mortals than immortals. It's hard to kill immortals who don't necessarily follow the folkloric rules, but who have extremely sharp senses.

"Don't be frightened, I won't hurt ya. My people know all about your world. We exist on the outside as well. You asked me if she's too young for ya. She ain't no sort of a thing. She got an old soul too. She's hidden mostly, but I see those flames clearly, like a phoenix about to rise and burn the world. If I were you, I'd be careful, she got more power than most. Angel Killer, they call them things, hadn't seen one in a long time."

"Vale is mortal," I whisper, knowing the lie as it escapes my lips. What's an Angel Killer? I've never heard of anything like that.

"I tell you now, she ain't. She burns from the inside. You don't sense it because her cleansing fire ain't for you. It's for the angels. Her kinds born to protect the balance in this world."

"What are you, Davina?" I ask bluntly. In polite supernatural society, one that doesn't exist, I wouldn't normally ask what she is, it seems rude. Most of us can sense others, the way I'm able to sense that Alan is a witch.

Davina laughs with a big smile. "Right now, I'm only mortal. Sometimes though, I see things. I see the threads of fate, all the tiny knots they weave. I was born of chaos and everlasting light, just like you."

Her eyes begin to glow white, and I close my eyes, unable to keep them open. I get it now. I've heard stories, but I've never been visited. I should be grateful for her presence. It's supposed to be a blessing.

"You're an Oracle," I whisper against her power that's pressing in on me like a heavy weight from all sides. Oracles or Fata are witches who get visions of the future or the past. They give up their lives amongst other witches to serve their visions. Her laughter echoes, and now I'm unable to open my eyes at all.

"Oh Ash, what they say is true. You are smart. Since you're smart, hear me now and remember it well. There's a fight coming to this world. One the chaos born can't fight alone. Only together will you win. You all gonna have to make peace." Her voice echoes all around me. Each word sounds like the voice of many, blending together.

"The fiery girl, she's important. She'll either save or condemn us all. Do you hear me? She could burn the world," she continues. "Let her burn. Mark my words, remember them true, she must burn within her own flame. She has to."

The thought of Vale being burned like the idiots who burned witches long ago hurts me. It hurts my soul, and my beast says the same. *Don't hurt her*, he screams at Davina, trying to escape, trying to claw his way out and fight.

"Is Vale my mate?"

The laughter mingles, their voices harmonizing together like a song. "You know I can't answer that, against the rules. Can't tell you who your mate is, only you can answer that. I got da feeling you already know though.

"Heed my words, Ash," she says, using the name my family uses. "You gonna need to fight. You gonna need to become one with that demon inside. You gonna need that power. Don't fight it down. No reason to be afraid when it loves her too."

Her oppressive power eases up, and I can breathe again. I open my eyes and look at the desk in front of me. There's a different woman, with red cheeks, who giggles at me. And just like that, Davina is gone, like she'd never been there at all.

"Thank you, Mr. Byron. You made my day," the young woman says. She hands my credit card back to me and a paper receipt.

"You're welcome," I say, even though I don't know what I said or did.

"You wouldn't want to go out sometime, would you?" Had I been flirting with her?

"I'm sorry, but I'm taken," I tell her apologetically. "Thank you for the offer though." I try to be nice. The woman can't help it.

The front door opens and I turn. Vale runs through looking upset. She gets closer and Joe enters behind her staring down at the clipboard. *Oh shit, did she fail?* I hadn't thought about that being a possibility.

"Everything alright?"

Her head comes up and there's a big smile on her face. She jumps into my arms, wrapping her legs around my waist and gives me a hard smooch. "I passed!" she yells, her arms flung wide in the air as I hold her up. "I have a driver's license!"

"Good job!" I say as Davina's words echo in my mind. My beautiful Vale, she's going to burn. I want to protect her. I want to love her and be with her always.

"We gotta move this along, Miss Granger. Head over there to Miss

Cathy, and she'll take your picture and give you a temporary license," Joe explains, seemingly annoyed at our public display of affection. He can fuck right off.

Vale looks at me with wide, happy aquamarine eyes. I let her go and her sandals hit the ground with a *thump*.

"Right over here, stand against that blue backdrop and smile for me," Cathy says as she points in that direction.

"Thank you, Cathy."

"No problem, Mr. Byron. Anytime," she says, unable to look me in the eyes now that she saw Vale kiss me. Vale watches the exchange and looks suspicious, but she doesn't say anything.

"Vale, you need to smile. Everyone hates their driver's license photo, but you don't have to," I tell her.

She nods her head. "Is this okay? Cathy, do I look alright?"

I turn to Cathy, waiting. "She looks beautiful, doesn't she?" I say in a strained voice. My heart and mind are in turmoil. How could Vale burn?

"Absolutely. It's going to be a good one. I can feel it. On the count of three. One, two, three." The flash happens, and I notice Vale staring at me, smiling secretively.

A moment later, Vale is standing at the counter as people start to filter into the DDS office. The clerks have come back from lunch. The sound is now overwhelming, all the voices and heartbeats in such a small area. I'm grateful when we finally walk out. Vale is silent as she stares at the temporary license. She leads me to where she parked the Jag but doesn't get in. She stands next to the passenger side, still staring at the card in her hands like it's something special. It is special. She's one step closer to the freedom she seeks.

"Hold it up," I tell her, and I hold up my phone. "I'm gonna send it to Nick."

Vale smiles brightly, teeth showing, cheeks flushed with heat. The sun shines in her copper locks and she beams with such joy. Then she holds up the card in her hand beside her face with a goofy smile.

There's something so genuine about the way she smiles. My heart hurts when I see her like this because I want to be the one who makes her look like that all the time. I want to make her happy. I want to make her smile. I'd do anything for this woman.

I send the picture to Nick, and she demands I send it to her so she can forward it to Kat. Her phone is ringing before we ever get into the car. Surprisingly, Vale hands me the keys and gets into the passenger side. I thought she'd want to drive right now. She's a woman with a license.

35

HUNGRY TRICKS

VALE

Gramps is calling before I'm fully seated in the car. "Hello," I answer, smiling. I put the call on speaker. "Congratulations!" his and another voice yell. I don't recognize it though.

"Thank you! Who's that with you?"

"Oh, I'm sorry. I should've introduced myself before now. I'm Lais Byron. I'm Oliver's mother." Her accent is much different from Oliver's, it's much thicker and very British. I look over at Oliver and see his shoulders stiffen.

"Well, I've heard so many nice things about you," I lie, and Oliver smirks. "It's nice to hear your voice. I'm sure we'll meet soon."

"I doubt you've heard much about me at all, but I've heard a lot about you." Her words make Oliver blush. He told his mom about me. I wonder what he said.

"Hello," Oliver butts in. "You two can get acquainted some other time. Vale and I are going out to celebrate."

Gramps is chuckling in the background. "Congratulations!"

"Thank you, Gramps. I love you." I give Oliver a dirty look, eyeing my phone. "Oliver tell your mother you love her," I growl.

Lais and Gramps start laughing again. Are they drunk? It's only three o'clock.

"I love you, Mother," he groans with an irritated look on his face.

"Love you too, son." There's a hitch in her voice, making me think she's trying not to laugh. Why would she laugh at Oliver saying he loves her? Not sure I like this Lais so much.

"What's the plan? Where are you two headed?" Gramps asks.

Oliver pipes in. "Same plan as before, I imagine, unless Vale wants to do something else." He looks at me. "Downtown, food, shopping."

"Vale, your Gramps is currently getting drunk with me. So take your time. Stay out late, have fun, be young and stupid. We're being young and stupid, right, Nicholas."

"That we are, Lais. That we are," Gramps says, and I'm surprised. "Have fun." They hang up abruptly. *What on earth?*

"Should I be worried about Gramps hanging out with your mom?" I wish I was joking, but I'm not. Lais is a Lilu.

He says one word, "Definitely," then laughs. "She won't hurt him, but I'd be lying if I didn't point out that she has an effect on people. They can't help themselves with her around. Her draw is a lot stronger than my own."

"What do you mean by her draw?"

"You know what I'm talking about. It's why you're attracted to me. It's the Lilu magic. We are undeniably attractive. We ooze sex. We seduce. It's like some sort of innate magic."

I don't believe it was magic that attracted me to him. "If you had no magic at all. I'd still be attracted to you, Oliver. You're physically very beautiful. But if I was blind, I'd still like you because you make me smile. I enjoy being around you. It may have been your magic first, but I don't think that's what it is now. It's more than that."

Oliver stares at the windshield, jaw tight. I know he wants this between us to be real. He doesn't want it to be his magic, his draw. I hope he believes me.

"Okay, tell me what you want to do? Let's be impulsive," I tell him.

He shrugs his shoulders. "I think you should tell me. We can go downtown like we'd planned, but you realize it was all a ruse for your surprise."

"Wanna runaway together?"

Oliver turns to me, confused. "What do you mean?"

"Let's run away, find a hotel, and spend every second wrapped up in each other."

"Are you trying to seduce me?" he asks with a smirk.

"Always," I say with a smile and heated cheeks. "Make love to me," I beg. "I need you. I don't want anything else."

He breathes deep, closing his eyes as if he's considering it. "When I make love to you for the first time, it needs to be somewhere we can get lost in each other, no distractions. I want you in my bed. I want to be able to do anything to you. I want to share ourselves completely. I'm willing to, tonight even, but we need to be prepared for it."

"Let's go get condoms then," I blurt out, then start laughing nervously, holding my hand up to cover my mouth.

Oliver starts the car and drives out of the parking lot before I can get my seat belt on. He turns into an alley behind a nearby shopping center and slams the car into Park. My eyes get huge as he slides his seat back, then starts to unbutton his pants. He reaches inside his pants and pulls his cock out. What's gotten into him?

"I want you to look at my cock."

I look around at the empty alley, then look back at it. He's not even fully erect. My mouth waters as I take in the ruddy head and the flared crown. I don't know if it's because we're in daylight or because my brain hasn't turned into mush yet from his touch, but this is the first time I notice that Oliver is circumcised. I lean closer, across the console, studying it in the light.

"What am I supposed to be seeing?"

He grabs his shaft and pumps it once. It starts to grow. "Do you see how big I am? I want you to know what you're asking when you beg me to make love to you."

I've seen porn before, Kat showed me, so I've seen dicks, but none of them looked like this. None of them were as thick or rigid as his. They weren't as long. There's something very different about his, almost as if it seems more alive, more everything. I want to taste him.

I lick my lips and lean down to lick the tip. He tastes like salt, lust, and a unique sweetness I can't place. I open my mouth wide to take it inside, but his hand grabs the back of my head and lifts me up to look at him. I'm breathing hard, my mouth hanging open as he looks at me like I'm in trouble. I want to be in trouble.

"I didn't ask you to suck my cock. My point is I'm not small. You need to understand what you're asking for. I could hurt you the first time." His left hand comes up, and he points his index finger at me. "You barely took this, baby. Now look at my cock."

I look at that long finger and smile brazenly. That night was amazing. He made me bleed with that finger. He made me come so hard with it. Then I look at his cock and the only thought that flies through my mind is if his finger felt that good, his cock is going to be that much better.

I lick my lips, hypnotized by what I'm seeing. "I'm hungry," I gasp when his hand tightens in my hair. I lick my lips again, staring up into his eyes. "Give it to me."

His chest rises with a deep inhale as he studies my eyes, my mouth. "Fucking hell, woman, not here. I want you to understand. I need time to get your body ready for me. I want you to be able to take me without pain. I can't just stick it inside you. I want it to feel good."

"Yes, you can. You can do it right now. I could lift my hips, straddle you, and impale myself on it. I'd be riding you in less than a minute. That's what I think." Part of me actually believes what I'm saying. Another part thinks I'm a crazy woman who needs to shut her mouth before I do something stupid.

He lets my hair go. Shadows swirl around the green in his eyes. They're both there, the man, the beast. I want them both. "If you're so confident, get up there and take it."

He's trying to trick me, but that foolish confidence from yesterday fills me. I smile like I've won some type of award. "Alright."

In the passenger seat, I lift my skirt, then grab my panties and pull them down, sliding my sandals off. He watches my every move while he lifts his hips and pulls his pants down a little more. When I look back at him, he's breathing hard, his lips parted. His pupils are blown out wide, and they're almost hiding the bright green of his eyes.

I climb onto his lap, tossing the panties into the passenger seat and rucking my skirt up. "We don't have a condom," I point out.

"We don't need one."

"Why not?" I ask. I don't want to have a baby right now, I don't know if I ever will.

"Lilu carry no human diseases and the odds of me impregnating you is very low. Immortals don't breed as easily as mortals, we're not meant to."

"Okay," I say, accepting the explanation quicker than I probably should. But I want this, him. It's all I can think about.

He raises his palms to my backside, pulling me forward against his chest. One of his hands comes between us, under my skirt. He slides the tip of his finger through my wet slit and growls again. "Fuck, baby, you get so wet for me. You're dripping," he says with heated eyes.

He pulls his fingers up in front of him. We both zone in on the glossy wetness he moves between his fingertips. It's glistening like honey. He brings them up to my lips.

"Open your mouth."

He rubs my own fluid against my lips, then slides his index and middle finger against my tongue. I grab his wrist and close my lips over his fingers as I watch his reaction. I suction them into my mouth, then stroke my tongue over them, tasting my slick and his skin.

Oliver's cock is fully hard now and it hits my pussy with a thump. I smile around his fingers. He yanks them out of my mouth. He crushes his lips against mine, licking around my lips, tasting me, stealing my honey back. It's sexy the way he loves tasting me. It makes me growl like an animal, like he does.

He uses his free hand to hold his cock steady under me. "Are you ready to take it?" He smirks. He's so hot when he's smirking like a prick.

I don't say a word, but I feel for his hand below me, then I lower my hips against him. His cock is there, the tip sliding against me. I rock my hips a little because I'm not exactly sure how to line us up.

Oliver is still smirking. I bite my bottom lip as I press my hips down. He adjusts his cock, so we're lined up better, and I feel the squishy tip pushing through. It makes my limbs shake. I sink down a little more and the flared head makes me swallow hard as I clamp my teeth together. Oh, my God, he feels so big, and I question my actions for the first time since he told me I could do this.

"You alright?"

I take a deep breath. "Perfect, what about you?"

I lift my hips and press down harder. The crown slips in, that flare stretching me so taut it stings. I close my eyes and breathe. I need a moment because it doesn't feel good. He feels too big, too thick to take any more, but I'm not done. I refuse to give into the pain. I refuse to give up.

The steering wheel is hitting my lower back, and I can't take it anymore. I lean farther into him, and it makes him slide a little deeper. "Oh, God!" I cry out.

His breath rushes out against my face. When I open my eyes, he looks like it's taking everything inside him to hold back. I don't know why I ever thought he didn't want me. Our eyes lock, and I lift my hips, then press them down harder. He's maybe an inch inside me, not much at all, when he hits the barrier of my virginity. I feel it, a tightening, tugging at the intrusion.

I lift up again because I know he's going to break through. Oliver grabs my hips. "Stop, Vale! Please, stop. You win," he says, wide-eyed with panic, his entire body shaking. "You win."

"What? Why? You said." He shakes his head in a panic, stopping me.

"I thought you'd stop because it hurts. I thought you'd stop yourself." The words fly from his mouth, and he cradles my cheek. "I didn't realize you'd keep going. I feel your innocence and if you take any more of me, it'll be gone. I'll have stolen it in the seat of a car. I will not have laid you down and taken my time, touching and tasting every inch of you. I will not have had the chance to worship you properly. You don't want this, Vale. Tell me this isn't how you want your first time to be."

It's hard to think when I feel him there, throbbing inside me. It's hard to think when the sting of tearing is already happening. He feels impossibly big. I've been told it always hurts. I knew it was going to hurt. I'm not scared of the pain. I try to lift off, but he wraps his arms around my waist, holding me against him. He's still inside me, but he's not as deep. It takes the pressure off a little and I relax.

"I didn't know how I wanted to lose it. I didn't have a plan. I'm not against doing it this way. It does hurt, but I don't care. As long as it's you, I don't think it matters where we are."

"Then let's go. Let's go have dinner. I'll make sure the house is empty before we get back. I'll lay you down in my bed. I'll be gentle. I'll make love to you, baby. I'll make it beautiful. If we stay here, I can't guarantee I won't fuck you in front of that guy over there. He's been watching us, trying to get a peak."

I look over at the big green trash bin and see a young man who's smiling between each puff. The windows are tinted but he might have seen something. I jerk backward and Oliver slides farther in. I hear him hiss and feel the biting pain. He does his best to lift me off him quickly. Did he break my hymen? I thought he did with his fingers because I bled, but it was still there when I tried to impale myself. I don't think it's there anymore. I felt the tear, the give.

I drop into the passenger seat, then stare down at his cock. There's bright red blood on the tip. He wasn't deep at all. I can't believe how little he was inside me. It had felt like so much more. "Is that?" I question as I touch the blood with the tip of my index finger.

"Do me a favor, lick it off and feed it to me." His breath is coming fast, his knuckles gone white on the console. His body is locked down, his veins standing out on his arms and in his neck. I don't ask questions. I lean down and take him into my mouth. His skin is on fire, and he groans when I suction the tip in. I moan at the coppery taste of my blood, the swirling mix of salt, metal, and his sweet precum. I take him to the back of my throat, and he lifts me off him.

"You've got blood on your lips," he whispers and those sexy fangs are showing. I hope he bites me.

I lick my lips and he loses it. He pulls me forward so hard our teeth clank when our mouths meet. He's licking at them, moaning. He's feeding on my mouth because this isn't just a kiss. It's dark. He claims me with each lick, each pull at my lips. He licks at my tongue while he holds my mouth open. His tongue has to be longer than mine. It swirls against the inside of my cheeks, against my teeth. He's taking every drop for himself.

"You taste so fucking good," he growls into my mouth. "I want you riding my face baby, that pussy dripping into my mouth. I want to drink you down before I slide deep inside you. I'm going to, Vale. You're going to let me. You're going to want it. I'm going to fuck you with my tongue, then I'm going to slide in until your little cunt can't take any more. I'm gonna fill you up, over and over again. You're going to feel me inside you for days."

I love it when he threatens me.

I'm shaking in his grasp now. Eyes wild. "Why did I agree to go somewhere else when I need you right now?"

"You agreed to come home with me so I could give you every dirty, fucked up fantasy you crave."

I look at the man who's still standing there, trash bags at his feet long forgotten while he lights up a cigarette. I wave, wondering if he can actually see us. When he waves back, I drop to the passenger seat, sinking lower as my cheeks flame. I try to pull my panties on, but Oliver yanks them out of my hand.

"Can we go?" I plead. "He saw us."

"We can go, but I'm keeping these." He pulls them to his face and inhales, making my cheeks burn brighter. His lips tremble when he stuffs them in his pocket.

"You're so weird. That would've been super gross about a month ago," I say, then laugh.

"And now what's it like to see me inhale your scent? To huff in that rapturous, mouthwatering scent your pussy fills my car with."

"Now I wish you were between my thighs with that beautiful mouth cleaning me up, because watching you do that has made a mess." The words come out breathy and heated. I'm barely able to stop myself from jumping in his lap again.

"You dripping for me, pretty girl?" he asks, that smirk back. That dimple so kissable, lickable.

"You have no idea. My body is determined to ruin all your upholstery." I laugh. "Hope you don't mind."

"I love that idea. I'd like it more if you marked me."

"Yeah, I can do that," I tell him with a smirk of my own.

I slide my fingers through my slit, getting them nice and wet. There's very little blood on my fingers when I hold them up. I lean back in my seat and urge him forward with them. He leans closer, and I paint it on his lips. "You make me so dirty. You inspire me to do things I never thought I'd do."

He smiles as I paint. When I look up at him, that dimple is too close, so I drop down and kiss it, licking his face like an idiot. "Always wanted to do that. I love that cute dimple," I say, oversharing as always.

"You love my dimples. Anything else about me you love?"

I love you! The words scream in my mind to get out, to be free. "There's a lot I love about you, Oliver. I'll tell you all about it when you're inside me," I say, then smirk back at him.

36

KNOW ME

OLIVER

W e leave that alley behind, her slick still on my lips. The taste lingers pleasantly on my tongue. I drive downtown, licking them every so often, needing every single taste that clings to my lips. Nothing tastes like Vale. Nothing tastes like her arousal or her blood. At one point in my life, I would have been disgusted by my hunger, but with her, it feels inevitable. I'd gone so long without it, pushing that hunger down for fear it would consume me, but it's different with her. I'm jubilant with each taste.

I take her to an early dinner, near the market. It's a Greek place, little more than a dive. We sit next to each other on a green vinyl booth that's seen better days. It's possible to judge the restaurant poorly for its dated décor, but they serve fantastic food. Of course it made me miss the Mediterranean. I miss it eventually, no matter where I go. It's my constant. The place I feel the most at home.

Vale slides closer nervously. I'm stunned when she leans her head on my shoulder, and it occurs to me, as I lay my head against hers, that we are, in fact, on a date. I don't think I've ever gone on a date with the intention of seeing someone again. I'm nervous just thinking about it.

"Where are you from?" she asks out of the blue, her head still on my shoulder. "I don't recognize your accent. Your mom sounds like she's from England, but you don't."

I place a kiss on her gardenia-scented hair. "You want to know where I was born or where I was raised?" Those two places are very different.

"Either. Both. I can't figure your accent out. It's been going around and around in my head. It's familiar, like I've heard it before. I'm curious about you," she says when I sit up. She's looking up at me with those big aqua eyes now.

"My accent isn't from anywhere. I've lived all over the world. I've picked up different accents on the way. I lived in Greece till I was twelve, Corinth actually. I left Corinth for Bab—" I can't tell her Babylon. "I spent my teenage years in Iraq, near Baghdad."

"Oh, wow. Is Greek your first language?"

"I grew up with people who spoke many languages. I think my first language was Greek, but I also spoke a unique dialect based on Semitic languages, similar to Aramaic and Hebrew. My uncle and my grandfather are very good teachers." That's an understatement, having angels for family means they can teach you anything quickly. Almost like they can beam the information directly into your brain.

"You spoke multiple languages as a child? You must be very smart. I've never been outside the United States. My parents mission all over the world, but I don't go with them. I'd like to travel one day. I want to see the world."

I want to show it to her. "I don't live anywhere very long. I like to wander, always have."

Vale looks up at me sadly. "You won't be staying long in Silver Springs?" She thinks she'll lose me.

I get close to her ear and whisper. "I don't age. I can't stay anywhere very long before people notice."

"Oh, I didn't know that. How old are you?"

Vale's curious, but we don't tell mortals about ourselves, not often anyway, and only with a trusted few. I've never wanted to tell anyone everything about myself. It's a new thing for me, but most things are with Vale. I want her to know me.

"I told you the truth, I'm twenty-five. That's when I stopped aging and became immortal."

"When was that?" she pushes, but that part isn't something mortals understand easily. You can't tell someone you've been alive for more than two thousand years and expect them to understand. They don't get it because they can't fathom that length of time.

"Does it matter how long I've walked the earth?"

She thinks about the question, then shrugs. "It doesn't matter, not really. I want to know you. I want all your secrets," she whispers with a half-hearted smile.

There's some part of me that loves it when she uses my words against me. I love it when she stands up to me and when she gets snarky. She'd come so far in the last couple weeks, continuing to surprise me at every turn. She's so brave. She wasn't afraid when I told her what I was. She didn't judge me or run away. And, somehow, she still looks at me like I'm the normal one.

The owner steps over, food piled high on a serving tray, and I tell him thank you in Greek. When I met Alexander Dimitriou, he couldn't have been more excited that I spoke his language. That, in fact, I was one of his countrymen. That's how I saw myself at least.

Greece felt like home because it was the last place that I felt happy. I had an amazing childhood, one that was blessed by joy. Time didn't matter, and I yearned for that peaceful existence again. I returned again and again, searching, waiting, and hoping to feel it. I knew it wasn't possible. I'd never feel that innocent joy again because nothing would ever be the same.

"So this is your young lady friend. I'm happy you brought her with you this time," he says, hiding his words from Vale. At least now he won't ask me to marry his daughter again.

"This is Vale Granger, my girlfriend. Vale, this is Alexander Dimitriou, he owns this place."

Vale offers her hand. "It's a pleasure to meet you, Mr. Dimitriou," she says sweetly. He takes her hand in his, leaning over and kissing her knuckles while he looks at me. His thick eyebrows go up and down. It's hard not to laugh because he's trying to make me jealous.

"Call me Alex, no mister this and that. You make me too old," he says, giving Vale a playful wink. He tells us to enjoy the meze, then steps away. He meets up with his youngest daughter. She looks over at me with a sad smile and a wave.

"Who is that woman?" Vale asks when I wave back.

"That's Alex's daughter Daphne."

"It looks like her heart is broken. What did you do?"

"I did nothing. He told her that you're my girlfriend, and she missed her chance. He asked me to marry Daphne when we met. I declined obviously."

"I noticed you said girlfriend. Am I your girlfriend now?"

I turn away from the father and daughter, who're now arguing over grandchildren, and wrap my left arm around Vale's shoulder. When I squeeze her close, our eyes meet. I can't get over how beautiful she is.

"You're more than that. This, between us, is special. I want you to be my girlfriend and one day, if I'm lucky, you'll be my wife," I explain nonchalantly. My words shock her. I knew they would. She has no idea how much I want her to be mine.

"Do you love me?" she whispers, her cheeks heating, her heart beating faster. She turns away, unable to look at me. She stares down at her hands in her lap.

I swallow hard, then squeeze my right hand into a tight fist.

"You don't have to answer that," she says. And suddenly I hear, *Please, let Oliver love me.* It's the first time I've ever heard her thoughts. I can read many human thoughts, and immortals, but Vale's mind is strong and usually closed off. The way she begs, like it's a prayer to the Light, is painful to hear.

"I'll tell you everything later. I'll offer you all my secrets. If you loved me, would you tell me right now? Or would you wait till tonight when no one but us can hear our confessions?"

Vale tries to calm her breathing as she realizes what I said. I admitted I loved her without saying those exact words. Am I selfish not to tell her in a restaurant? She asked me, and I want to tell her, but I want it to be special, just us.

"Let's eat. Then tell me what's your favorite."

"I already know. Dolmades. Those are always my favorite."

I grab one between my fingers and hold it up to her mouth. She stares at me for a moment before she takes a bite. Her eyes close as she chews, and a soft moan escapes. I'm hard right away. I'm part lust demon, but I've never been so horny as I am around this woman. She fucks my brain all up. My body's constantly on fire when she's near me. It's been difficult to deny her. She thinks I'm not affected, but I am.

Vale wraps her lips around my fingers as our eyes meet. Her gaze is hot, hungry. She has no idea how desirable she is. She steals the last bite from my fingers. "Mmm. So good," she moans. It's such a simple sound, but my brain blanks for a moment as all the blood in my body rushes to my cock.

"You're so sexy right now," I growl, the sound vibrating in my throat like the purr of a wild cat.

Her body reacts. I can smell her desire in the air. She's getting wet, again. She bites her lip when she's turned on. In that moment, she sucks her own lip in and bites it hard. She's trying to get control of herself, but I don't want her to. I want her to lose herself with me.

"Tell me your favorite."

"That's easy, you," I explain as I lean in close to whisper in her ear. "Nothing tastes as good as you do. It's all ashes on my tongue in comparison."

"Oliver, stop. I'm struggling. Please," she begs, and it's so sweet.

"I'm sorry," I tell her until I realize I'm not sorry, not in the least. "I lied. I'm not sorry. I want you. I know how it feels, Vale. You showed me exactly how it made you feel. The only part I'm sorry about is that I haven't taken your ache away yet, but I will. I swear to you, I will."

Vale takes a drink of sparkling water, trying to cool herself down. She grabs another dolma, but I grab her hand and take it with my teeth, wrapping my lips around her fingers. Then I lick her fingers clean as she stares at me with wide eyes.

"Mmm, those are good."

"That was mine," she pouts, and I want to bite that lip. I want to make it bleed. Then I want to lick and suck it, soothing the pain away.

I grab another and feed it to her. Then it's her turn to feed me. It's foreplay, a dance. When we finish, she excuses herself because she can't take it a moment longer. Alex comes to the table and waves his hand in front of my face. "I should charge you extra for scaring off the customers," he says angrily, but laughs anyway.

"Sorry," I say, even though I'm not.

"Love is special," is all he says before he departs with the plates.

I call my mother while Vale is in the bathroom. "You gotta get Nick out of my house," I say the moment she answers the phone.

She starts laughing. "Why is that?" she asks, being irritating as always. It's not a great thing because I'm on edge.

"You know why. I can't wait any longer. I need you both gone. Please, Mother. Take him out. Night on the town. Get super drunk and stay in a hotel. I don't care, just make sure we're alone."

"He's already drunk. Half an hour before passing out, I'd imagine." I can hear him singing a Sinatra song in the background.

"Please! I need you to do this for me."

"Yeah, yeah, yeah," she says. "Nick, let's go dancing! Out to the clubs," she yells like a young party girl.

"That sounds fun. Can't drive though. Call a cab!"

"You owe me, you little shit," she groans. She's joking. This is the kind of thing she lives for.

"Right. Please feed him, give him some coffee. Don't bring him back till tomorrow evening at least. I need time with her."

"I know. I think we'll play, 'Woke up hungover in Savannah. Unsure how we got there.'"

Vale steps forward. "Gotta go," I tell my mother, then hang up.

"Who was that?"

"My mother. She's just letting me know that Nick and her are going clubbing tonight," I say with a chuckle.

"What? It's five o'clock on a Wednesday." She can't believe what I'm telling her.

"Yeah, they wanted to go dancing."

Vale shakes her head. "Is Lais trying to corrupt Gramps?" She looks amused and worried at the same time.

"Maybe, but she won't let anything happen to him. I'm sure they'll have a blast. No worries."

Vale stands there staring at me. "I need to get him some of those cookies, so we have to make a stop at that posh market. Is that okay?"

"Of course it is. I thought you wanted to go shopping. There's one place I want to take you before we go back."

I can't wait to get her into lingerie. I can't wait to rip it off her. I can't wait to experience everything with her. I can't wait till she's mine.

37

LINGERIE AND JEALOUSY

VALE

I'm standing in a dressing room staring in horror at my own reflection. Oliver is on the other side of the door chatting with a salesperson. Her giggling is getting on my nerves, but I can't do anything about it currently. I'm staring wide-eyed at the lingerie he chose, wondering how I got myself into this mess. It's just a bunch of straps. I don't know how to put it on.

"Can I come in?"

"Hell no!" I yell, irritated by my own predicament but mostly embarrassed.

"Open the door, or I will."

I open the door with a groan and scoot behind it so other people can't see me. I'm practically naked. Seriously, I can't figure out how to put the thing on, and the straps seem to have locked around my thighs. I shut the door when he's inside and make sure it's locked. He looks at me, then he starts laughing, eyes alight with glee. I want to slap him if I'm honest. This is all his fault.

"What happened in here?" he asks as he tugs one of the little black straps that's knotted between my thighs, holding my legs together like one of those finger traps you can win at the arcade.

"*What happened*? I'll tell you what happened. You handed this to me over the door without an explanation or an instruction manual. I'm currently stuck in it because I had no idea how to put it on, and now I can't take it off."

Oliver falls to his knees in front of me, his lips smirking. Arrogant prick. "Let me see if I can help you out with that," he says, his chest shaking. He's trying not to laugh. I should appreciate that, but I still want to slap him all the same.

He unclips one of the straps—I didn't even know it had clips—and pulls one strap over the front of my left thigh. It starts to loosen, thankfully. His fingers brush against the lips of my sex. I try to stop the breathy sigh that comes from my throat, but I can't. I have to look away as he adjusts the other straps. He stands up, looking like a smug asshole. Have I slapped him today?

"Hold these."

I grab the clip and strap in one hand. He lifts my hair, dropping it to the side before pulling a strap over the side of my neck. He grabs the clip from my hand and snaps it into place. He takes the fastener side and clips it on another, then gets behind me and clips another at my waist.

"There you go. It looks good on you, baby," he says as he appreciates his handiwork. His eyes move to mine in the three-way mirror, and he stares me down, making me horny and nervous.

He's behind me, his palm possessively flat over my belly. I stand there with leather straps crisscrossing over my hips. Three large, silver grommets are placed in strategic positions. There's one grommet for each nipple to poke through, then a third over my mound where multiple straps attach.

"Imagine for a moment that you're on your hands and knees," he says as he pushes me down, taking my weight right before my knees hit the floor. I land gently with a gasp. He looks like a god behind me, so strong, fit, and fucking gorgeous.

"Do you see how the straps connect above your pussy?" He bends down to whisper in my ear. I look in the mirror at the thickest metal grommet over my mound.

I can't speak, so I nod my head as I lean my head back on his thigh.

"Wanna know what that's for?" he asks, and I nod again.

Oliver grabs the straps at my waist and tugs. The straps on each side of the lips of my sex tighten, spreading me open, and it takes all the strength I have not to moan.

"Now, stand up," he demands, and I get up quickly. "You see these straps over your breasts?" He grabs them and tugs. The straps press against my breasts and tighten against my sex.

I hiss. "I can't take anymore. I'm dying. Please, Oliver, you have to stop."

He smiles sadistically in the mirror. The look is so feral, like at any moment he'll attack me. Instead of attacking, he growls, "You can't take it? I haven't even started." Those words make my skin prickle with gooseflesh and I shiver.

He gathers my hair into his fist, then looks up into the mirror as he angles my head to the side with a devilish smile. I watch helplessly as he licks up the side of my neck, never losing eye contact. I quake in the wake of that single taste. The way he looks at me so possessively, like he owns me. I want him to own me.

"I'm going to teach you such filthy things. Make peace with the fact that you won't be innocent in the morning. Also—" He gets real close, nipping at my earlobe, tugging on it with his teeth, never taking his eyes off me. He loves teasing me in the mirror, forcing me to witness my own downfall. "I don't get tired. I don't have to sleep. I can come over and over again and still be hard," he whispers, threatening me with that pantie-melting smirk.

Oh, my fuck! That smirk is deadly. His words scare me. Does he want me afraid of him? I'm turned on and frightened in equal measure, a unique, exciting combination to be sure.

"Don't threaten me with a good time." I smile back, proud of myself for being able to get the words out.

"Then pack it up because I'm buying it all. I don't want you to be sad when I rip it off you and we start over." He walks around the dressing room, looking at the other things I've been trying on, then he rips the tags and walks away like nothing happened.

How is he so calm about this? He says he aches for me, but he can't. It's not possible because he's still able to function, while I'm a soaking wet, mess of a girl unable to move.

Oh, my God, he's going to fuck me till I can't walk. I'm only human. Can I handle him? Once or twice, yeah, okay. But if he fucks me all night, I don't know if I'll survive it. I'm going to need a lot of electrolytes tomorrow, maybe even some painkillers.

Is he going to hurt me? He's been so possessive since we left that alley. I've never seen this side of him. If another man looks at me, he steps around, blocking me from their view. It happened in the market. Then again at the thrift store. Outside on the sidewalk, we were just walking, looking at the shop windows, and he told some guy, "She's taken, pal. Move along."

I'd like to think I'm a modern woman, that I should be mad that he's being like this, but I'm not. It makes me hot. Oh, that possessive streak makes me so wet. I'm so hot and bothered right now I'm sizzling with heat. I don't think I can take much more of his teasing.

Every little thing he does makes me throb, makes me ache and clench inside. All I have to do is look at him and I'm horny all over again. He doesn't have to touch me to send me into overdrive, but he can't seem to hold himself back from touching me either.

My hands are shaking when I figure out where the clips are, and I remove the crazy straps from my body. I get dressed, then grab all the lingerie as I step out of the dressing room. Oliver is at the counter waiting for the clerk to scan all the tags. He won't let me pay for anything even though I told him I have money. He insisted on buying me everything I picked out to purchase for myself. Then he started buying me things I only glanced at. He's being ridiculous.

Oliver is chatting with another lady I can't see on the opposite side of him. He's so friendly to most people he meets, unless they're of the male persuasion and looking at me. He looks so at ease, even in a women's lingerie store. Of course he is.

I take a moment to admire him. My man is a hottie. I don't blame people for wanting him. I want him too. I want him to be mine forever, not for the rest of summer, not for a little while. Forever.

Then I hear a familiar, nasally voice. Oh no! I have a slap my forehead kind of moment. Shae is standing beside him, hand on his arm like she owns him. Flames lick over my mind as I grind my teeth. He's mine! I have to calm the anger inside me, but she's standing too close. She's touching him, and he doesn't belong to her. I hate it so much.

I drop the lingerie on the counter in front of him. The cashier packs it up in such a wasteful manner, wrapping each piece in tissue paper and tucking it into different sized, pale blue boxes with gold lettering. I'm not actually annoyed with the clerk, but the fact that Shae's still touching my man is making it difficult not to go nuclear.

Oliver wraps his other arm around my tense shoulders, pulling away from Shae to my absolute delight. He turns us to face her, but Shae doesn't seem to care that he's touching me. She tries once more to grab his bicep. I try to stay calm, I really do.

"When are we going out?" Shae asks as her eyes zoom to me, squinting in barely concealed anger.

I press my palm on his chest. "Where are you two going?" I ask innocently, trying not to smirk as I look up into his mossy-green eyes.

"We're going on a date," Shae says it so matter-of-factly, I'm surprised she can keep a straight face.

I shake my head. "Shae, you know he doesn't date right?"

"No returns," the cashier interrupts our glaring contest, looking uncomfortable.

I keep my eyes on Shae. "Trust me, you wouldn't want me to return it." Shae's eyes flair. She knows what I'm insinuating.

Oliver snickers as he pulls his arm away from Shae. Again. "Yeah, you don't want those back." He smirks and hands the blushing clerk his card.

"So where are we going on our date?" Shae says again, butting into our sexy-time joke.

"Yeah, baby, where *are* you taking her? It better be nice. Not some shithole."

He grabs my chin between his finger and thumb, lifting my mouth up. My lips separate on a sigh, and he leans down, licking up over my bottom lip, then the top with dark promise in his eyes. Then he kisses me hard, fucking his tongue into my mouth like he owns it. He's never kissed me like this in public.

I moan into his mouth. I don't want to hide what he does to me. Let her see. He's mine. I grab his neck and pull him closer. When I finally pull away, he's staring at me with heat in his eyes the likes of which I've never seen. Is this an act? Is he acting for my benefit. Then again, he might be turned on by my jealousy. Is that it? Does he want me to be possessive?

The clerk waves his card around in front of him, but he doesn't look at her as he grabs it and places it in his wallet. He continues looking at me as if he's trying to tell me something, but I can't for the life of me focus on anything other than that smirk and his flushed cheeks.

"Take me home," I say, loud enough for Shae to hear.

"I'll take you home if by home you mean my fucking bed," he growls, grabbing my ass in one hand and lifting me against him like I weigh nothing. I let out a giggle as he holds me awkwardly against him, only one of my feet touch the floor. He's hard, and when I realize he's using me as a modesty shield, I burst out laughing.

"You're crazy," I say. "Good seeing you again, Shae," I lie as he grabs the bags, supporting me in one arm while also trying to drag me out of the shop caveman style.

"Oliver, wait!" Shae yells, and now I've had enough. Doesn't she understand what we're doing? I didn't want to be rude, but he's mine.

He knows it, and he drops me so I land on both feet. "Tell her I'm yours," he whispers into my ear. "Tell her you own me."

"Just stop," I tell Shae with my hand up. "Oliver is nicer than I am. He's trying to let you down easy, but he's not yours," I try to explain, but Shae doesn't let me finish.

"He isn't yours either, you trashy, little bitch. He doesn't do relationships," Shae says in a desperate, high-pitched voice. She's so smug that a part of me doesn't mind setting her straight.

Oliver steps forward, but I hold my hand out against his chest, stopping him. I can handle her. Confidence fills me, and I don't cower like I did before. I make a promise right then and there that I'll never cower to her again.

"I don't appreciate you calling me a bitch, but I'll let it slide because I know how easy it is to fall into this one's web—" I use my thumb to point at his chest. "But you're wrong about something. He's already mine. I hate to break the news to you like this, but he belongs to me. I own that sexy ass, don't I, baby?"

"You do, my love." Our eyes meet and there's a look of pride on his face. Then he looks back at Shae. "I belong to her. Vale and I are together. I'm sorry if I misled you, Shae. That was never my intention," Oliver says because he's nicer than I am.

Shae stomps her stiletto-heeled foot and again she reminds me of a rabid Chihuahua. She's super pissed. If it were me, I'd be crying of embarrassment and running away, but not Shae. She's used to getting what she wants and she wants Oliver. She can't have him.

"You're really with her now?" She gives me a disgusted once-over, like she doesn't understand. I see it in her eyes. He's too perfect, too sexy and I'm not enough to lock someone like him down.

"Vale told you, we're together. You'll accept she's right. She's the most beautiful woman I've ever seen." He's speaking to her, but he's facing me now. "We were just two stars that collided in an explosion of blinding light. She's my everything. I hope you find that one day."

I want to cry at his words. They're so sweet. I love him, and I see so much love in his eyes. I've seen it before, but I didn't recognize it. I think Oliver Byron loves me.

"Well, it's your loss buddy," Shae says before stomping away.

"Not really. I've gained the entire universe."

I take in a huge gulp of air and swallow. Tears shimmer in my eyes.

"Don't cry," he says gently. "Mascara." He points at his eye.

"You're too much, Oliver."

"As long as I'm enough for you, then nothing else matters."

Does he realize what he did for me? He pushed me to speak our truth. He pushed me to have a voice and claim what was mine. But then he did something that no one ever has—he told her I was right. He told someone he was with me and that I was more than good enough. It didn't matter what Shae thought of me.

He chose me.

Oliver thinks I'm good enough to tell the world about us. He did it in the restaurant, and he's done it by being possessive. I feel like the luckiest woman in the world. I feel powerless when it comes to loving him. I couldn't stop it even if I tried.

"Take me home. I don't want to shop anymore." I don't want to wait anymore.

38

EXQUISITE AGONY

VALE

We walk a few blocks to get back to the garage where he parked the car. He places the bags in the trunk and offers me the keys again. He's been so good to me today, so loving and generous. He waited for me in the thrift store, in the market. He took me to a hippy bead shop where I got Kat a bracelet and smelled all the home-made soaps. He didn't seem to mind when I tasted all the ice cream flavors at one shop. When I didn't order anything, he dropped a huge tip in the jar for their trouble because he's nice like that.

Every day we spend together, I love him more. I love him so much, it's a struggle to hold it inside. I want him to know that he's precious to me. How can I show him how wonderful I think he is?

"I don't think I can drive right now, I'm a little on edge."

He's got a boyish grin on his face. "Are you that hot and bothered?"

I huff and walk around to the passenger door, shaking my head. I can't talk to him about this because it'll make the throb between my legs worse. He'll do something that makes me suffer more, and I'll get even more frustrated.

"Wait!"

I turn around in time for him to grab my thighs and lift me up. He presses me into the car door, his hips notched between mine. "Tell me why you can't drive." He knows exactly why I can't.

"I'll crash and kill us both imagining what it'll be like when you're inside me. I don't want to kill us both. Okay?" I snap at him.

He thrusts his hips between mine. "This the cock you're thinking about?" He smirks, always smirking this one. If I wasn't so frustrated I'd appreciate it.

"Oliver," I moan and lean my head against the car door, closing my eyes. "Save it. I can't take much more. I'm this close to being committed to a psych ward—" I hold my hand up, my index finger and my thumb smashed together, illustrating just how close I am to losing it.

"What happens if I keep going? What would you do if I keep teasing this tight pussy for the rest of the night?" He rolls his hips, his hard cock teasing me through our clothes, and I want to scream.

"Immortality won't mean anything because I'll kill you. If I were you, that's what I'd be worried about right now." I give him a dirty look when I lift my head.

Oliver sticks his bottom lip out and pouts. I grab his shoulders and lean in closer. I grab that lip with my teeth and bite down, making a threat. His breath rushes out against my face, and I feel his cock twitch against me. "Be good," I growl without releasing his lip. I wait for a moment, then I suck his lip into my mouth, licking at it, tasting him.

When I release him, the fire burns in his eyes. The color swirling between green and black, a pulsating inferno that makes my core clench with need. I want him so fucking much! I can't handle this. I can't handle any more.

"Are you sure you want me to be good right now?"

"No," I blurt out, but then I shake my head. "Yes, I do. Don't you want me?" I say as my hips jerk, sliding against his hardness, making myself wet all over again.

He gets in my face. "I've never wanted anyone more. Not once in my very long life, Vale." He slams his lips against mine before I can process what he's said. He's showing me his desire, his pain. He wants me too. When he drops my legs, I stand on unsteady feet, worried at any moment I'll tip right over. I get this dizzy feeling around him way too often. I worry that it'll never go away.

"Allow me," he says, and he opens my door. He stands back, shifting his erection under his jeans. The bulge looks uncomfortable. I hope it is.

When I get into the car, I lean my head back on the headrest, smiling up at him with a horny, lust-filled gaze. "Does it hurt, baby? I want it to hurt for me."

Oliver leans in and over me. "Trust me when I say that you have your wish. I ache for you. It hurts because I'm not already buried in that tight, little cunt. I'm going to be. Don't you worry, beautiful." He grabs my pussy over my skirt, his fingers possessive as he squeezes and smirks in my face.

"I'll fill you up." He kisses my left cheek. I turn into him, but he pulls back before I can kiss him. "I'll stuff you so full of my cock you won't be able to walk." He kisses my right cheek innocently, smirking like the devil as my heart races. "Oh baby, you'll be so sore, so full of my cum. Mm-hmm, I can see it now." He closes his eyes and hums.

Oliver takes his hand away, but I grab his wrist. I place his hand under my skirt. "I'm going to die if you don't make me come. Please. Right here, right now. Make me come because I can't take it anymore. I've hit my limit."

He continues to smirk before pulling away. I swallow hard as I try to get my body under control. I rearrange my skirt to cover my legs, but when he opens the door and jumps in, I change my mind. I undo the top buttons so that all that's left is the tied waistband keeping it on me.

He already has my underwear stuffed in his pocket somewhere, so I prop my foot up on the door. Watching his every tense movement, I spread my legs and toss the fabric to the sides of my hips. He closes his eyes, drawing in deep, steadying breaths.

"Don't do that," I say, my words the gentlest whisper in the air. "Look at me." I don't think my voice has ever been so low, so sexual. It sounds strange to my ears.

Oliver turns to me, right as I place one hand on the inside of my thigh. He looks down between my legs. I'm sure the view isn't the greatest for someone like him, someone who wants to see everything, but I have to do this. I'm going to die before we get back. I can't wait.

I slide the fingers of my right hand up the inside of my thigh, watching his eyes follow my movements. Normally, I'd be full-on begging him to touch me, but since I failed at it, I'm going to show him what he's missing out on. I get to the edge of my mound, then slide them back to the knee. Oliver's eyes get wide, and he looks at my face, nostrils flaring. I can finally make him crazy with it. I can make a lust demon, well, lust. And that makes me so fucking happy. I smile at him when he bites his lip.

"Have you resorted to teasing me, Vale?"

I lean in and he does the same, propping one elbow on the console between us. I lift my fingertips up to his lips with an innocent look on my face. "Well, you see, I'm so wet right now, but my fingers"—I hold my middle and index finger up—"they're not. I thought maybe you could help me with that first."

Oliver grabs my wrist and brings my fingers up to his mouth. "All you had to do is ask, baby. You know how much I like getting you wet." He smirks at me before he slides my fingers inside his warm, wet mouth. His tongue swirls over my fingertips, pulling them deeper. I pull them back and he slides his mouth back up and over them, taking them deep.

Memories of the night we met, how he healed me when I got burned, make me grin. "You don't have to heal me this time." I pull my fingers out of his mouth and slide them to my pussy. His lips twitch for a moment when he realizes what I'm talking about.

"You knew?"

"I thought you had magic saliva," I say, and it makes him laugh.

"I do," he says, then continues to laugh. "Just a little bit."

I slide my wet fingers up my slit and press down on my clit, the same way he taught me. I'm still close to his face, looking up into those gorgeous eyes. I can tell he's having a hard time deciding whether to look at me or at what my hand is doing. My breathing hitches when I circle my clit.

My hips slide forward with a jerk. I lean back into the seat, pressing my back against it hard. I close my eyes because it feels good. I want to make myself come. As much as it's for me, to get me through this moment, it's also for Oliver. I want him to see me touch myself.

I hit the wall though. I can't get over it. It's like my body revs up to the point that I'm going to come, but I can never achieve it. He claims I'm not broken, he felt it. He's seen my clit, he should know, but I can't manage to do it on my own.

I open my eyes and look at him. Oliver looks up from my hand and frowns. "Oh, baby," he says softly, reaching for my cheek. "You can do it, keep going. Let me watch you. Keep your eyes open and focus on me. See how much you're turning me on. See how much I want you."

Even though I haven't stopped circling my clit, I want to. I don't want to continue. "Why is this so hard? When you touch me, it happens so fast. You're so much better at it than me."

Oliver chuckles and my cheeks heat in embarrassment. "I'm not laughing at you, Vale. It's just that you said I'm better at it than you, and I suddenly felt giddy with power."

"You have power, Oliver. Why don't you use it for good right now and make me come."

"You don't know how badly I want to watch you make yourself come," he says, and he's so close his breath is against my lips. "Get out and get in the back seat because I want to see it better."

I don't think twice. I jump out of the car and hop in without buttoning the skirt. The fact is there's more room back there and we can get closer. It does occur to me that we're in a parking garage, but I'm done caring. I need this.

Oliver slides the seat forward before he follows me into the back seat. The moment he gets in and closes the door, I jump onto his lap. I grab his face in my hands and kiss him. It's so fast. I'm already losing it. "I want you," I cry out against his mouth.

Oliver pulls back. "And I want you, but I need to see you make yourself come. I want it so bad," he says while he holds my hips still. "Now it's all I can think about."

I let out a huff of frustration. "Fine!"

He hauls me off his lap and tells me to lean against the opposite door. I struggle to get comfortable against it, but when I do, he bends my knee and props my foot up on the seat next to him. I spread my legs as wide as I can, then I flip the two sides of the skirt over. He hisses as he stares at what I've revealed.

"What a pretty pussy you have, all slick and wet for me," he growls while he palms his cock.

"Show me how hard you are." I'm not surprised when he opens the button of his pants and slides the zipper down.

He grabs my hand before sucking my fingers in between his lips with a wink. Then he goes back to what he was doing. He's staring at my pussy when he grabs his cock and pulls it out. I moan when I see it. He's so fucking big and hard that my core tightens up at the sight of it.

"Oh, my God, you're dripping, baby. You make my cock so fucking hard. Do me a favor and slide your finger inside you, let me see how deep you can get them," he growls between clenched teeth.

I lift my hips and swirl my fingers through my wetness, then I press at my entrance, sliding one finger inside me. I take it out and slide another in to join. I can't work them in very deep, I don't even get them in past my first knuckle, but it feels good. I keep going, in and out, focusing on him.

"It feels good when you're watching me. Can I see you touch yourself? Will you show me?" I ask him and my breath is so uneven it sounds like I'm actually in pain.

He nods his head in agreement, then he does something that makes me laugh. He licks the palm of his hand and slides it over his cock from the tip to the base, then back again.

"That's really hot." I'm biting my lip as I slide my fingers out and circle them around my clit, making my hips jerk forward.

"I knew you'd like this. The naughty girl that watched me do this in her dreams." When he smiles, I start panting. He starts stroking the wide crown of his cock, focusing the motions there. He's right. I do like it. I don't think I'll ever get tired of seeing him like this.

"In my dreams, you were on your knees between my legs." I sigh, seeing it in my memories, picturing it so clearly.

One moment he's sitting in the seat, the next he's on his knees, leaning forward, still stroking his cock. I tremble as I look up at him, gasping for breath at the heat in his eyes.

"Like this," he asks, low and guttural.

"Oh, God, yes. Just like that," I cry out. "You're so beautiful. You were meant for love."

Oliver closes his eyes for a split second, and I swear it looks like he's about to cry. There's some great pain in his past that's written on his face. Why would my words make him hurt? My words are the truth, he was meant for love, and I'm going to prove it to him one day.

"Vale, where did I come?" he asks and my own touch gets firmer as his breathing picks up.

I swallow hard because I feel like I'm going to scale that metaphorical wall. "You came inside me. Oh, fuck," I cry out the last words as my body spasms with it. I feel my inner muscles clench as I come. I moan through it and for a moment light blasts through my vision like stars. The pleasure is so focused and deep my entire body shudders with it. "Oliver," I gasp as the bliss fills me, heating me from the inside and wringing out every bit of agony from moments before.

My vision clears. He's still there above me, watching me. He's sliding his palm up over his cock and back down. His movements speed up. He falls on top of me, his lips so near my own, one hand on the back of the passenger seat so he can keep his full weight from crushing me. He sucks in a deep breath the moment he nudges my entrance with his cock. I grab his cock with my hand, knocking his away, stroking as I pull him forward, lining us up. He's breathing so quickly, trying to control himself, but I don't want his control. I want him to explode.

"Push into me and come. I want you to come inside me," I whisper desperately and grab onto his shirt, over his heart. "Please come inside me."

He slides his hips forward, barely an inch. I'm so wet that the tip slides inside easier than before. He's shaking with the oncoming orgasm. I keep stroking him and our eyes meet. "Now, give it to me. Come for me," I demand. "Oliver, baby, come for me."

His spine goes tense and his head falls between his shoulders. He's trying so hard not to go deeper, but I feel him throb against my innocence as he slides farther in. Oliver's mouth opens, and he moans softly before he gasps. He's shaking, and finally I feel him spill into me. I feel his heat pool in my core.

I open my mouth, a discordant moan escaping because suddenly I'm right back there, pleasure filling me up. My energy floods outward, sinking into him. My core spasms around him and I come again. I wrap my arms around his waist and stare up into his eyes, overcome by it. He's the most beautiful man I've ever seen, and it brings tears to my eyes. My heart hurts when I look into those gorgeous green eyes.

"Oh, God, Oliver. You were meant to love me," I cry out, tears of pleasure, of happiness covering my cheeks. I don't tell him I love him. I tell him he's meant for me because that's the truth. I feel it in my soul. I grab his hand and press it to my chest, desperately looking into his eyes. *Please see it.* I reach up to place my palm against his heart. I'm shaking, searching for love in his eyes. "You were made to love me. Me," I sob, completely overwhelmed by the love swirling in my chest. I swear the weight of it is heavier with every second that I don't tell him.

"I know, baby. I know," he agrees against my lips.

I focus on those beautiful eyes that glow for me, and it's on the edge of my lips. *I love you!* My soul screams it to him. *I love you!*

He sees it. He sees everything.

"Not yet," he says, shaking his head. "Please, Vale, not yet." The words stutter out from his lips. I think we're both shaken and for several minutes all either of us can do is stare at each other. We exist in each other's orbits.

Everything comes to an end so quickly. We hear people in the garage, and Oliver sits up to look around, but I cower down lower in the seat, afraid of being caught. He says they didn't see anything, but now I'm not comfortable.

Oliver pulls away and glances between my legs. He pulls my panties from his pocket and brushes them over my sensitive skin, cleaning up the mess we made with gentle strokes. "Are you okay?" he asks. "That was a lot more than I thought it would be." His cheeks flush as he hides his cock once more and zips up.

"I'm alright," I say, though I don't know if I am actually.

"You did it, baby. I knew you could," he says, his smile so sweet. Then he reaches out to caress my cheek. "Do you feel better now?"

I have to think about the question for a moment. I have to consciously connect my brain and my body. There it is, the throb, the ache deep inside. I shake my head. "Not at all."

"Did you think it would put the flames out?"

I shrug sadly, staring down at my knees, then out the window to hide my face. "I don't know what I was thinking, honestly. It made sense at the time. You know, that if I had an orgasm, I wouldn't be hurting, but it's still there. The pain. The ache inside me. Oliver, I'm not lying when I tell you it hurts to wait for you. It feels like I've been waiting for you my entire life." I wipe my eyes and see the mascara on my fingers. I let out a deep sigh. "I didn't make it. Please don't look at me. I'm a mess."

"You're not a mess, Vale. You're the most beautiful creature I've ever seen," he says, grabbing me and wrapping his arms around my shoulders.

I lean into that comfort. He feels like home. There's something about Oliver that calls to me, urging me on. It entices me closer, taking all my will, to the point that I'll never be able to let him go. I can't imagine a world without him in it. I turn to him, then look up into his swirling eyes. I lift my chin and kiss his lips.

"How do I look?" I ask him with a half-hearted smile.

"No less beautiful for the tears you've shed," he says, his voice suddenly deeply accented and gruff. "You're still the woman I want, tears and all."

"Well, you're the man who's supposed to fuck me later, so take me home."

"Anything for you, my lady." He kisses me one last time before we part.

Oliver is going to take me home, to his bed. He's going to make love to me.

Finally.

\#

Oliver

When she cried, "You were meant for love," it was like a wound opened up in my chest. It hurt so fucking bad I'd do anything to be what she wants, what she needs. When your world claims that your kind is incapable of love, you start to believe it after a while. They say Lilu can't love but it's a lie. I do love! I can love. Because I love Vale.

Had anyone else said those words to me, I would have laughed like an asshole and walked away. I would have run from the words because only a short time ago, I wasn't capable of loving anyone. I believed my heart would never be moved by another, but here she is, this beautiful girl who looks at me as if I'm her entire fucking world.

How did she tear down my walls?

"You were made to love me. Me," she said, and I realized she was right. I've never loved anyone the way I love her.

She may be human, or at least part human, but she feels it too. I think she's known all along. It's only been me who was in denial.

You're the asshole in denial, not me. I've always known she was ours, the beast explains. He thinks this whole situation is funny, when he isn't growling inside my head begging me to fuck her. *I've always loved her*, the beast claims. *I've always known she was our mate.*

He did know. He tried to tell me so many times, but I thought it was hunger drawing him to Vale, not a mate bond. He's right. I'm an asshole, but I'm not in denial anymore. I know Vale is my mate. She is. That's all there is to it. I was made to love her and there's no room in my heart for denial. It's filled with her.

Finally! he growls. *It's about time you pulled your head out of your ass.*

39

CONFESSIONS

VALE

I've been sitting in the car silently, fidgeting with my skirt for the last half hour. I'm full of anxiety. It doesn't help that we've barely spoken to each other since we left the pleasure in the back seat. Oliver must have noticed something's wrong. He's tried to hold my hand, but I can't stop fidgeting. I pull away because it's all too much.

The garage door opens and he drives in. When the car is shifted into Park, I jerk to attention. I'm freaking out. It's time. We're here alone, but I can't get out of my head. I'm so worried about what's going to happen between us. What if he hates it? What if I do it wrong? What if he's bored and he never wants to touch me again?

"Vale, are you alright?" he asks, reaching for my hand again, but I jerk away.

I nod my head and remove the seat belt quickly. "Of course I'm fine," I tell him, then I jump out of the car, purse in tow, trying to escape. I shut the door and he's around the car in an instant. He's not hiding how fast he can move now, not when we're alone. I stare up at his beautiful face as he steps forward. He grabs my hand before I can run away.

"I won't hurt you. I swear it." He looks so sad right now. He thinks I'm afraid of him. I can't stand it. He's wonderful.

"I'm not afraid of you, Oliver. I . . . " I don't have the words because I don't know what's happening. I was fearless earlier. I asked him for what I needed. I want him, but the desire has cooled to a rumble while my anxiety takes over. Now I can't stop thinking about everything that could go wrong and how huge this moment is.

"Tell me what it is," he pleads, stepping closer. He deserves to know.

"I think we're about to do something that'll either change the entire world or completely change us. It's something so special, and it feels so final. I think it's supposed to feel like that, but it makes me anxious. Then there's the fact that you have all this experience and I don't know what I'm doing. I don't want to disappoint you, Oliver. I want to make you happy, the way you've made me happy. I want to touch you and make you feel good. I feel inadequate because I don't know how to do that."

The pad of his thumb slides across the top of my cheek softly. I lean into his warm touch. He looks at me like I'm the most precious thing that's ever existed. I want to scream that I love him because the way he looks at me, it fills my heart to the brim.

"You will never disappoint me, Vale. Not ever. I understand the fear of not being good enough. I do. I'm afraid of disappointing you too. When we take that step, I imagine we'll both be lost to it. There won't be any control. We'll both let go and feel it. We'll take care of each other. I'll take care of you."

I nod up at him, taking his words as the truth. I don't think he would ever steer me wrong, not about sex. What surprises me is the fact that he's worried about disappointing me. How could he ever think that? "I don't think it's possible for you to disappoint me, Oliver." He smiles at my words.

"You and I, we are always. We go on and on. Our flames don't burn out. They are forever, Vale." His words are powerful, and I believe them. Oliver feels like forever. Being with him is as natural as breathing.

He wraps his arms around me, and he feels like heaven. Those strong arms were built to hold me close. We were always supposed to be in this moment. It feels right. So why am I still so worried?

"Vale, come with me. Take a chance on being mine. Please, take a chance on me," he whispers against my ear.

Oliver squeezes my hand, and I nod in agreement. We link our fingers together and I follow him. He puts in a code on a keypad next to a metal door. It unlocks with a *click*. I follow him down the steps and into a dimly lit tunnel. There are lights on the walls, leading the way, but they aren't very bright.

"Taking me to your bat cave."

Oliver stops. There's a serious look on his face when he says, "You know I can't turn into a bat, right? I don't have rabies if that's what you're worried about." He loses it by the end, and we both start laughing.

"I was just implying you might be Batman, not an actual bat," I say with a snicker.

"Not Batman either, just making sure no one sees us. Tonight, you're mine and I don't want to share you with anyone. I'm making sure of that," he says, but he doesn't look back at me when he speaks. He starts walking again, focused on where we're going.

We walk farther and farther through the tunnel. It opens into a cellar filled with wooden crates and shelves filled with what looks like wine or liquor. Some of the bottles are coated in a fine layer of dust, while some have cobwebs like they've been here for ages.

"How long has this tunnel been here?"

"This is part of the original house. It was built a hundred and seventy years ago. It's been here a while. You'll have to ask my mother about it. That was back when this was her house."

"It was her house?"

"She was the original owner. When she left, she willed it to one of her lovers with the intention of coming back one day. There's magic here, Vale. More than half of the house is hidden until you're invited inside. It's a spell from a famous Louisiana coven of witches. People only see an illusion, not the actual house. It's rare magic. Powerful stuff to last generations."

"I knew it'd gotten bigger. I thought I was crazy at first. I didn't see it until you invited me for dinner. Suddenly, I could see the turret, the south side, the library. So why did you decide to buy the place?"

"I had too. If they sold the house, then all the knowledge in that library would be in human hands. That can't be, Vale. Humans can never know about us . . . well, they can't know the truth." The word "human" stops me in my tracks.

"I'm human. Why would you show me any of this? Why would you tell me what you are?"

Oliver finally turns to face me. His face is half cast in shadows, the tendrils trying to hide him in their darkness. "You're different. You're my mate," he says, but he doesn't look into my eyes. He waits for those words to sink in.

"What's a mate?" I ask even though I have a feeling I've known it all along. I knew something was different between us.

He turns his back to me once more, like he can't bear to look at me when he explains. I hear his deep inhale, the way the air sputters out from his chest when he exhales. He's nervous. For once it's not me. Still, I'm on edge waiting.

"When our souls are created, immortals of any kind, we lack half. We're not complete. If we live long enough, if we fight long enough, we find them, the one who completes us, our other half. The only way to complete each other is to be together. It's almost a compulsion. That's who we are, we are beyond lovers. We are one, separated in the beginning, who now are blessed to come together." He says the words like they hurt him.

My heart is pounding. "I knew it!" I yell, my voice echoing in the tunnel. Why did he hide it from me? I'm shivering as if the temperature has plummeted. The heart in my chest feels like it cracks, pain spreading through my sternum, stealing my breath. My lips tremble when I look up at him, but he stands with his back to me. I drop his hand and step away. I have to.

"I've been waiting on you my entire life. None of it made sense until you showed up. I never desired anyone. I didn't want anyone! That's the truth. I told you at the bluffs that it was only ever for you.

Do you know what that feels like? Just knowing I wasn't like other people. I wasn't attracted to others. I knew though, when we met. We found each other and it felt right, but you refused me over and over again. I knew from the moment I met you. I fucking knew!" My voice cracks with each word.

"I'm sorry, Vale. I knew there was something, but I never knew I'd have a mate. I've never done anything worthy of you. Lilu aren't as common as other immortals. There is only one other Lilu with a mate in the entire world. My mother. But my father has never accepted their bond. Many immortals believe Lilu can't have mates. They believe we can't have them because we feed on lust. They think we're not capable of love and that's been true my entire life. So, yeah, it was hard to believe you could be mine. It felt impossible that I could be so lucky."

His shoulders are slumped like gravity is dragging him down. He stands four feet away in those shadows that slither between the lights. The distance between us suddenly feels like it's much larger, an impossible feat to cross.

"I've been living in absolute hell," I cry, tears streaming from my eyes.

His shoulders stiffen. "I didn't know for certain. Yesterday, when you showed me how you felt, I thought you might be, but I didn't know for sure. I swear it. Had we not been interrupted, I believe we would've figured it out."

"I knew the night we met. I knew the first time I saw you, that I was yours. I've held my emotions back my entire life. I learned to block it all to survive. I've breathed through that suffering. I've stuffed it down until it silenced not only my voice, but also my entire being. I found the silence within me to survive.

"Then you showed up and you drew out every emotion in me, everything I tried so hard to bury and hide. Nothing was the same, the world became a loud and confusing place. I couldn't silence those feelings anymore. Even with all the noise, I knew, Oliver. I knew you were mine," I yell, my voice echoing in the tunnel.

He turns to look at me, finally. I see the hurt on his face. My words are hurting him, but I'm so angry, so hurt, so blown away by his confession that I don't know what to do with it. The fiery rage is burning through me. I feel it filling every limb, every inch of skin. I have to let it out. Not for him to steal my truths, but for me to free them on my own terms.

"Night after night, I hurt. I ached for you. I watched you with them. I saw you touch someone else. I saw you fuck someone else! You fucking broke me!"

"You're not broken. You're perfect, Vale. You're everything." He shakes his head, denying my words.

"You asked why I was crying after seeing you with that woman in the window. The truth is I loved you from the moment I saw you. It hurt so bad to see you with her, but I was willing to take the scraps of your affection because it was better than having none. It was better to dance in a tiny bit of your darkness than exist in the full light of the sun. You're not the only one who feels worthless." My words are spiteful, just like the hot tears that streak down my cheeks when I look at him.

"Oh, God, Vale, I'm sorry," he says, his words high-pitched with agony. It hurts to hear it. I never want him to be in pain. "I didn't know. I swear it. I never meant to hurt you. I'm so sorry."

"I'm angry. I'm hurt and yet none of it matters because I still love you! You know that, right? It's so easy to love you, Oliver Byron. You're amazing and you make it impossible not to love you. I've never known what it felt like to be special, to be beautiful, to be wanted, not until I met you. It doesn't matter how we got here. None of it does because the truth is I'm hopelessly in love with you. I love you with every single breath, with every heartbeat, with all of me. The thought of not seeing you, not touching you, not being by your side, that's what scares me most in all the world."

One minute he's several feet away, the next he has my cheeks cradled in his hands, forcing me to look up at him. "I denied your love and I'm sorry for that. I don't know if I'll ever be able to make it up to you, but I want you to know, I believe you, that you always loved me.

"One night, I kissed you over your heart. You were sleeping, I didn't think you'd know. You opened your eyes long enough to tell me you loved me too. It was like you heard the words I was unable to say. You knew all along. I wanted to be worthy of that love, worthy of you. I wanted to give in, but I was afraid. I thought you were dreaming. Well, listen to me now, wide awake. I love you, Vale."

I gasp at his confession, tears streaming harder over my cheeks. I'm gulping down air trying to breathe. The truth is spilled out into the world. We're laid bare, torn open. They say the truth shall set you free, and right now, my heart soars to the sky with the glorious feeling of freedom. I hadn't been freed by turning eighteen or becoming an adult. I'd been freed the moment he said he loved me.

"You love me?" I question through the tears, still struggling to believe it. *Please let this be real.*

"I swear to you. I love you," he says, then kisses me, his lips fiery, branding my own. I'm free upon wings of glorious love.

I cry harder even as our lips press against each other's. "Then I'm the luckiest woman in the world because I get to have you."

"I'm yours. Only yours." I can't help it. I cry harder.

Oliver scoops me up in his arms and carries me like I'm precious cargo. He's so strong and his arms make me feel safe. Not once in my life have I ever felt safe the way I feel with him. I feel like the entire world could crash down around us and, as long as he held me, we'd be protected. I try to stop my tears, wiping my eyes as we enter the house. He holds me closer as he carries me up a set of stairs I've never seen.

"The third floor, Vale. This is my private space. I don't let anyone in here but family. You should remember the code. It's 0623. Remember it in case you want to get in here without me. You're welcome here, anytime. You never have to ask," he says sweetly, his smile so sincere even though there's still sadness in his eyes. I want to wipe that sadness away for all time. I hope he never feels it again. I want to make him happy always.

He opens the door into his room and welcomes me inside with a dramatic bow and flourish. I'm astonished at the large space. There's a small sitting area with a few chairs around a coffee table. The furniture is antique, with a Victorian style that suits the facade of this house.

The room is long, the bed facing the east. Maybe he likes to watch the sun rise from the bed. The bedspread is burgundy with gold embroidery and looks familiar.

"Your picture, you were here when you sent those photos. I thought you weren't in your room. That room I could see through the window, it had a navy-blue bedspread. I thought you were with someone else."

Oliver shakes his head. "I was here. This is where I sleep when I succumb to boredom," he says, then chuckles like not sleeping is normal.

I take in the creamy wallpaper and the ornate mahogany wainscoting that leads farther into the darkness. The room is an old-fashioned type of masculine, cavernous and lonely.

"You were alone?" I ask, though it's a feeling in the air. It permeates the space. I recognize that loneliness as if it were my own because it is.

"Always."

I stare longingly at the beautiful bed. I can't move any farther into his room because I'm stuck. There are four delicately woven iron columns, and each one is draped with creamy sheer fabric. It's so romantic I'm surprised he chose to decorate his room like this.

"Your bed is pretty."

I look over my shoulder at Oliver and his cheeks flush. Is he embarrassed? "It would be infinitely more beautiful if you were in it."

I walk over to the bed, leaving him near the door. I step out of my shoes, then remove my shirt. I drop the skirt onto the floor, kicking it out of the way. He's at my back in an instant. Oliver brushes my hair aside with his fingertips, then kisses my neck where it meets my shoulder, sending chills up my spine as I arch back into him. His tongue licks and laps at the tender skin, making my heart race.

He's a sneaky Lilu while I'm distracted. My bra falls to the floor. The way the fabric rasps over my sensitive skin makes me let out an unsteady breath. His hands slide along my waist, up over my ribcage, then back down. I'm lost in that gentle, reverent, and loving touch.

"I would worship every inch of you," he whispers against my neck. "I've waited so long for you. Two thousand years of waiting, wanting, and hoping even when it hurt. You're the only woman I've ever loved. You're finally here with me. I'm in awe of you."

Pain prickles at my heart, making me gasp. I feel it, the time he waited. Oh, my God! He waited two thousand years. I feel selfish for being upset about my own experience. I suppose longing is subjective. Forever is the time we recognize, the time we know. Eighteen years seems like an eternity for me, but his time has been unending.

I turn in his arms. "I'm sorry you waited so long, but I'm here now, if you'll have me."

"I couldn't have dreamed up a more perfect creature. I know it hurt you to wait, but I'm glad we waited till I knew, without a doubt, that I love you. Isn't it better this way? We both know it's love that brings us together." Oliver might be a closet romantic.

I'd always be able to look back on this night, knowing that I was loved. I'd know the man who took my innocence was worthy of it, that he thought it was a precious gift I gave him. He'd cherish it. He'd cherish me. He was the only person who could ever be worthy of that part of me, my innocence.

I love him, this absolutely wonderful, amazing person. My everything, my beautiful Oliver.

"You're right, but then everything is better because you love me. Thank you for loving me, Oliver."

"You're very easy to love."

His love is precious, given to me so freely now. He'd been showing me since the night we met, even if he didn't know it himself. I make a silent promise in that moment, that I'll never take his love for granted. I will keep it and grow it. I will do everything I can to be worthy of him. I want to be a woman deserving of him.

40

MY BEAUTIFUL LOVE

OLIVER

Vale stands before me, bare as the day she was born. She's not modest because, unlike my own stubbornness, she's always accepted us. She knew. Of course she did. When she lets go, she's all passion. She's lit up with it in a way no one else in the world is. She embraces that part of herself with me, even when it makes her nervous.

The heart wants what the heart wants, but what if it's the soul, and all you lack is right there in front of you, if only you're brave enough to take it. I don't want to exist in an imagined future. I want to revel in this moment we're sharing, every second precious.

Vale had been silenced, hidden in the beginning, but now her lust for life burns and she's too bright to go back into the shadows. I don't think she'll ever be able to hide again. She shouldn't have to. I'll be strong for her. I'll lift her up when she's down. I'd give her the world if I could.

I've no hope of trying to hide how I feel for Vale, not anymore. She's my mate. She's meant to be mine. She owns my heart. I'm hers, till the end.

"I want you in my bed." My words are clipped; I can't take much more. The need inside is so great, ramped up because she's finally here.

I'm so impatient, before she can move, I grip her behind the thighs and lift her body onto the bed. As I set her down on the edge, she grabs the elastic in my hair, tugging it out and tossing it onto the floor. Then she slides her fingers through the dark strands. I lean into her touch, closing my eyes in pleasure. Her nails are a gentle scrape over my neck as she pulls me closer, always closer.

Vale brings her hands to the buttons of my shirt. She wants me as naked as her. No secrets between us, no fabric, no lies. We're done with all of that.

"I want every inch of you against every inch of me." Her voice is a breathy, lusty whisper. "I need to feel all of you."

I lean into her, kissing her temple first, then her cheek. I nibble at her right ear. "You shall have all of me. I'm all yours, only yours."

Vale trembles like she can't hold it together. She's so torn up with desire she's struggling to control her fingers as they fumble over the buttons. I love how desperate she is for me. I love how her body trembles at my touch. Every single detail is special. Every shiver, every moan is exquisite.

I put my hand over hers. "I can do this if you want. You can lie back and enjoy the show."

"I think that's a good idea."

I step away from her trembling hands, then study her movements as I undress. While I take off my shirt, she leans back on one elbow and spreads her legs. My God, I've never seen such a beautiful woman. I mean it. She's flawless in her beauty. She's gorgeous as her fire shines from within, lighting her up in desire that's only ever been for me. I'm the lucky one.

I'm ready to feel those flames against my skin. I'm ready for her desperate pleas. I want her so badly. I need her like I've never needed anyone or anything. Before I met her, I was alone, only surviving, never truly living. Moving through the motions of an empty existence. Then she appeared like the answer to a prayer, and suddenly I felt purpose again.

She licks her lips, and I groan. "You're so fucking beautiful, sitting there showing me everything. Spread your legs wider, let me see how wet you are for me."

She does what I ask without protest, her eyes on my chest, on the dragon that guards my heart. I take my eyes off her for only a second to tug my pants down and drop my shoes beside the bed. That's all the time she needs to surprise me. When I look up, she stares down at my cock, mouth agape, eyes lidded low. She has two fingers pressed against her clit, moving in slow circles. The top of her cheeks are flushed, her lips red and swollen already.

How I want to fill her up with ecstasy and show her everything she's missed. "Do you like what you see?"

Her eyes close briefly and she bites her bottom lip. She's lost in it. Her desire is thick in the air, the sweet smell of her pussy making my mouth water. I throw her hand off. She'll come on my tongue, my cock, but not by her own hand. I'm done with the games we've been playing. She's mine to pleasure, mine to love.

"Tonight you're only mine."

Vale watches as I kneel between her thighs. Her legs are spread wide, bent at the knees, feet flat for leverage. I swipe my tongue through her slippery folds, all the way to the top where I circle her clit, and her hips lift off the bed. I smile as thoughts of fucking her with my tongue slither around my mind.

She runs her fingers through my hair, then grasps my head in one hand. She wants control. I'll give it to her. I don't mind. If I've learned anything about pleasuring a person in two thousand years, it's to be flexible in my roles. One person wants to submit and another wants control. Then there are those rare few who want it all. Vale wants no less than everything and fuck if that doesn't turn me on more.

I kiss her beautiful glistening cunt. I make love to it with my lips, teeth, and tongue. I give attention to all its pretty folded petals, worshipping it, worshipping her. When she's moaning, rocking her hips against my mouth, trying to use me as her own personal sex toy, I pull away. I like making her desperate.

Her eyes flash with fire. I want her to burn me. I want her name branded into my skin so everyone I ever meet knows that I proudly belong to this woman.

"Don't stop," she begs.

"I won't, but I need your eyes on me. I want you to see what I do to you. Tell me you like it, tell me you want more. I want to hear you scream for me." I open those petals up gently. I swirl my tongue up over her engorged clit. "Don't close your eyes," I say, then swirl my tongue over her tight little hole. Her hips jerk while her breathing speeds up. "You like that?" I ask. "Tell me you like my tongue inside you and I'll fuck you with it."

I watch her while I slither my tongue over her clit, then move back to circle her hole. She's so tight, I need to loosen her up. I need to take my time and make her body relax. If I don't, it's going to hurt when I enter her.

"I love your tongue. Now fuck me with it," she demands, and her hand tugs at my head, pulling me closer.

"That's my good girl. Demand what you want. I'll do anything to you. I was made to pleasure you, only you."

I suction on to her clit, drawing the little nub out, making blood rush to the surface. I flick my tongue, left, then right. Her body shakes with every swipe, the muscles in her thighs twitching. I stop the suction, and she moans in frustration. But then I thrust my tongue inside her. I look back up to see her mouth open on a silent moan, eyebrows high in awe. I roll my tongue left and right, going a little deeper with every move, tasting the clenching walls of her sex. I can taste the blood still inside her from earlier, her arousal, and my cum. I lick at the tiny tear she made when she slid down onto me in the car, making her let go the cutest little whimper. I bet it stings, so I tongue at it some more, soothing the ache.

Her eyes glaze over, lost to the feeling. I'm losing myself to her taste. I'm drinking her down, when she lifts my head suddenly, stopping me. She's shaking her head. "Please come up here, with me." She's desperate to come, so I'm surprised she stopped me. Vale releases me and scoots back on the bed. I lick my lips before climbing up beside her.

"I need to touch you."

I reach for her, yanking her forward, against my body. She's so warm, her skin as hot as a roaring fire. Vale burns hotter than most mortals. As I lean over her, we simultaneously grab and tug at each other, pressing our lips together. I lick at her lips, and she opens for me. She tastes so good. She feels so good. I don't know how I'll ever survive being inside her.

"I need your cock inside me, take my mouth, take everything, just let me taste you too."

I grab her hips, turn her around, then lie back, lifting her onto my face. She screeches before she realizes what I'm doing. I smile against her slick pussy.

"Suck me while I fuck you with my tongue."

Vale doesn't reply, only leans forward and takes my cock into her hot mouth. She's been wanting to do this since the pool house. I don't know why I ever tried to stop her. Now none of it makes sense. Why did I deny this? I was an idiot, but I'll make it up to her.

I thumb circles around her clit while her hips twitch and jerk. Then I lengthen my tongue, which is something special Lilu can do. It's not a joke when I say I was built to give pleasure. I was built to seduce, to fuck. I was built for lust. Most of all, I was built for Vale.

I reverently brush her hymen with my tongue. I feel scarring from where I fingered her roughly in the car. I taste the tiny tear from earlier, which has healed with my saliva. Our story is written on that tiny membrane. I find the hole right in the center, where she's naturally open. I thrust through it while she moans over my cock and her hips tilt.

I was never the kind of man who put such importance on a hymen. Some men put a price tag on opening a woman for the first time. Personally, I never went for virgins. I believed women showed their value with their character, not an intact hymen. However, I devolve into a lower creature when I think about hers. I value this tiny piece of flesh. I value it because it's hers. I value that I'm her only man. I value that she'll never have another. And some awful, animalistic thing inside me values her virgin's blood as my prize. My one sip of her innocence.

I spear the membrane over and over with my tongue, stretching the tiny hole, hoping it helps her when she takes me. I make my tongue longer, thicker and slide it in and out. I can't stop smiling as her hips rock over my mouth. I want her to lose control.

Vale suctions the tip of my cock into her mouth and swirls her tongue over it. Her hot mouth burns with such intense heat it makes me pull my tongue out of her. I can't think when her mouth is on me. She takes my breath with each stroke of her lips. I lift my hips, not meaning to. She lifts off, then she's back down, going deeper, taking more and more of me with every downward stroke. I groan against her pussy as the head of my cock hits her throat and she swallows around it.

"That's so good," I growl into her cunt. The moment she realizes she can't take me any deeper into her throat, she adds a heated fist to pump my shaft in time with her mouth. "Fuck, Vale," is all I can say.

I lengthen my tongue farther into her tight hole. I fuck her with it when I can, when I can think. I don't feel like a very spectacular Lilu in this moment. I'm losing my mind, distracted by those plush lips. She moans around my cock head and the vibration makes it even better. I speed up my movements on her clit with my thumb.

We're ouroboros, feeding off each other's lustful energies. She moans against me as she takes me faster. I swallow hard removing my tongue. "Vale, fuck. Wait!" I growl, but she doesn't stop. "Vale, I'm going to come in that pretty fucking mouth if you don't stop." She goes harder, squeezing my shaft tighter.

So I give it my all. I start sucking her clit, then add a finger inside her, then two, stretching her open, but not going too deep. Her hips start bucking and so do mine. We're devolving into baser creatures, together. She smiles around my cock, her lips tightening, and I come hard. The moment it hits her tongue, the moment she swallows my release, she jerks upright, hands slamming down on my hips. I replace my fingers with my tongue. She's screaming through her release while she rides my tongue.

I open my mouth, letting her sweet cum drip. I feed on it. I take every little twitch, like it's the word of the divine, and I devour her. I devour that pussy. I lick and suck and fuck her until she's screaming louder and louder. Until she stops screaming altogether and falls onto me, her breaths heaving from her lungs. The muscles in her stomach twitching.

Vale rolls off me and looks up with hot, hooded eyes. She licks her lips, and it makes her body jerk and her head fall back. "You're a goddess," I tell her.

"You taste so good. You always taste so good."

My cock twitches at those words, still ready to go. "I'm glad you like it. I love the way you taste."

Vale gets comfortable beside me. Her eyes are closed, her whole body flushed now. Her nipples are hard, pointing at the ceiling as her head hits the bed. I wish I could take a picture of her just like this. She's perfectly, happily, debauched.

"What is it?" she asks me with those sexy, fuck-me eyes.

"I want a picture of you, like this. You look so pleased. It's a very attractive image."

"Then take a picture. I don't mind. I like the idea of you looking at me when I'm not around."

She bites her lip. She's so gorgeous. Her eyes open, glowing aqua-marine as she lifts her head. She's waiting, but I can't move, not yet. I want to watch her, be with her, experience all there is with her. When I don't move, she crawls up the bed to my side. "Too slow," she says, then chuckles.

Vale leans over my chest and kisses above my heart. "Marking your territory, my little vixen."

"Yes," she says unapologetically. She laps at my chest with her tongue, then she bites my nipple, tugging it and making me hiss. "Because you're mine." I love how she says it.

I run my fingertips over each of her breasts, then I place my palm over her heart where it thumps harder against my hand. "You are mine, and I yours, always, my love."

"Always and forever," she whispers as she presses another kiss above my heart. She's right, always and forever.

41

LOST TO NEED

VALE

There's a moment of absolute calm. We're bare, touching each other with gentle strokes, exploring each other in no hurry. I lick, suck, and taste his skin. I learn his body. My hands learn each dip, the softness of his skin, the hardness of his muscles, and each spot that makes him laugh. I'll never get enough. Will I feel this after he makes love to me? Or will this fire become more of a smolder?

We've not had sex yet, but I realize the difference between making love and fucking now. This isn't just new to me, it's new to Oliver. With each touch he watches, memorizing every single detail. I don't want to forget a single second of this. I lick the shadowed grooves of his abs. I press kisses into his skin. I lick each fingertip. I caress each muscle. I make love to him with every touch.

"This is the difference between fucking and making love. I'm making love to you, Oliver. I'm giving you love with every kiss, every touch. I give you my body. I give you all my love. It's intention, which has meaning, and I intend to give you every piece of me."

I kiss his chest again, over the dragon that guards his heart. I turn my head to listen to each beat while he slides his fingers through my hair, a content smile on his face. Each resonating thump is so strong.

"I think you're right. Do you hear that?" he whispers, then grabs my chin to tilt my head back so I'm forced to look at him. I look into his beautiful, bright green eyes so full of love. I've never been able to truly compare that unique color of green to anything else. "My heart, it beats for you."

Tears fill my eyes. "I love you," I gasp. I jump on top of him and press my lips to his. "I love you, so much." Note that once I've said the words out loud, I can't stop saying them. I'll never hide those words again. I won't be afraid to say them.

I kiss his mouth, his cheeks, his chin, and his forehead. I even leave a kiss for the tip of his nose. I stare into those eyes and they're glowing, lit up just for me. "Tell me you love me," I say as I straddle his hips. I roll my hips forward over his length. "Tell me you want me, only me." I'm desperate for his words.

"I love you, Vale. I want you, only you. You're mine." His words are possessive, and I love that. I don't mind belonging to him. I want to be entirely, irrevocably his. He lifts up enough to lick my bottom lip, then he sucks it into his mouth, nipping at it. I rock against him, his cock notched between the lips of my sex, lighting me on fire once more. He runs his palms up the curve of my waist, cradling one breast.

My mouth drops open when I move at just the right angle, so that the flared head hits my clit. "Oh, God, I need you. I need you so deep, where it aches. I never knew desire could hurt so much."

I'm like a demon possessed. I lift off his chest, grabbing my own head, squeezing my eyes shut as I rock my hips against him, getting his cock wet with my slick. I shiver over him, my hips vibrating with the energy building up inside me like a static charge about to explode into the world. I cry out a desperate moan to the heavens.

"Please, I need you inside me. I'm dying. You have to make it stop! Please, baby," I beg. I'm so overwhelmed, so lost. My core clenches and my hips roll over him.

Oliver grabs my hips, stalling my movements with strong fingers that might leave bruises. I drop my arms, ready for a fight. But when I open my eyes, he's watching me, and his look says it all—he knows that pain. He feels it too. He's taking it all in. Eyes hooded in lust, Oliver Byron wants me.

"How do you want me, Vale?"

I smile, and without hesitation I say, "I want you on top, over me, filling me up. Don't you want to know what I feel like wrapped around you?"

He moves like a monster with infinite speed and strength. He grabs me and hauls me off him, then lays me down before him. He smirks at me, showing a hint of fang. It's so hot when he gets cocky. I love his cocky mouth, his kissable dimples. The way he threatens me with those sharp canines. I want those fangs buried in my flesh.

Oliver leans over the edge of the bed and opens a drawer. I'm curious about what he keeps in there, but that's for another time. When he's back, he has a small tube of something in his hand. I think it's lube, which doesn't make sense because I'm soaking wet. If I were any more wet, I'd drown the both of us.

I feel the knot form between my brows as he notices my confusion. "It's lube. It'll make it easier for you to take me. Trust me," he says, needing me to trust that he knows what he's doing. At least one of us does because I didn't expect that.

"Have you been making plans?" I grin at him.

"Absolutely. I've been planning every way I'm going to take all your holes," he says. When my eyes go wide, he smirks again. "I want all of them."

I swallow nervously. I don't think I can take him in every hole. He seems too big. I worry my lip for a moment, then blurt out, "You'll only fuck me in the ass if I can fuck you. Fair is fair." My face feels like it's on fire. I can't believe I just said that.

He smiles as he pours the lube on his fingers, then he leans down, demanding my attention. "You surprise me. I didn't think you'd be into that. I thought you'd shy away from it. I should've known better." His smile is demonic, his lust so great it washes over me in an instant, creating visions. I blink hard, trying to break away from the image.

I hadn't meant to say what I said. I was intimidated and scared of what he threatened. I should have known he'd call my bluff. I'm about to lose my virginity to a Lilu, a lust demon. I shouldn't be surprised that he'd be into something like that. He's probably into all sorts of things.

Oliver leans closer to my ear, making it where I can't see his face anymore. I feel his breath against my ear as his cold, lubricated fingers push into my body, so silky and smooth. The temperature difference makes me buck my hips.

"I'd let you fuck me. It'd be my pleasure," he says, and his words make my pussy clench around his fingers that are massaging gently inside me. Oliver chuckles softly. "You like that thought, don't you. Do you like it when I offer you control?"

I can't speak, so I nod my head. He smiles against my ear, then nips my bottom lip with his teeth. "My innocent girl and her dirty thoughts. I love that about you, Vale. I love your dark, little fantasies. I love how much you want me. My only question is are you ready for me? Because I'm ready to be inside you."

He crawls over my body, and I spread my legs wider, tilting my hips. Once again, he drops lube on his fingers and spreads it around inside me, pressing it up against that barrier. I'm going to come if he doesn't stop. I don't want to come till he's filled me with every glorious inch of that cock.

"Oliver, stop," I gasp. "I'm going to come, and I don't want to without you inside me. Not yet."

He removes his fingers and pours more lube for the third time. He massages it gently into my labia and finally over my clit. There's a lot of slipperiness happening between my legs. It's making a terrible mess on his bed.

Finally, he fills his palm with more lube and closes the cap, tossing it to the side. He cups his hand around his shaft, working it up and down, coating himself in that slipperiness. He works his fist over the crown, slathering the tip while I watch, my mouth watering at the sight.

"I want you inside me, please." The words come out without any control as I stare unabashed at his thick length. His cock is beautiful. The head is ruddy with color, almost red. His shaft is thicker than my fist can wrap around, lined with bulging veins that throb as his blood rushes through it. He's even more beautiful when he strokes himself, a forbidden sight. Some beautiful art hidden away from the world that only I get to see.

Oliver is on his knees between my thighs, waiting. When I finally look up, he leans forward, placing gentle kisses over my hip bones, my stomach. As he gets to my ribs, it makes me giggle, and I jerk away.

"Ticklish," he says with a content smile, and I nod my head.

When he gets to my breasts he presses slightly at my entrance, letting me feel him. His mouth opens so wide that his jaw pops. He suckles a nipple and at least a quarter of my breast into his mouth. My hips react to this new feeling, lifting to take more of him. He lifts his head and my nipple pops free from his mouth. "Be careful, baby."

"I can't wait anymore." I'm doing my best not to cry because I'm on fire. I grab his ass cheeks, arching my body into him, yanking him closer. He sinks in maybe an inch, but it's not nearly enough. I scream with frustration, losing my ever-loving mind. He rocks his hips back and takes all the air in my lungs with him. "Please, Oliver!"

"Vale, we do this together."

When I look into his electric-green eyes my heart calms. "Together," I whisper, and he slides inside a little farther. I tense because it's uncomfortable. He feels too big. I'm worried he'll never fit.

"I'll do my best not to hurt you," he says the words against the center of my chest. "Tell me if it's too much, too soon. I'll stop."

I gulp air into my lungs as he slowly sinks deeper. He hits the barrier inside, and I reach for his shoulders, sinking my nails in, holding him there, tears filling my eyes. "Oliver," I cry. "It hurts." To his credit, Oliver backs off a bit, relieving the pressure, easing the pain. I sigh in relief while he studies my face.

"Women are cursed to hurt," I tell him as tears slide down over my temples into my hair. "I'm sorry." He adjusts his body so he can reach for my face with one hand. He's all I can see and it makes the tears come harder. Why does it have to hurt?

"You're not cursed. You and me, we're blessed more than most. We've found each other. We are love. We are one. I was built for you and you for me. I'll ease your pain," he tells me with such a sincere look.

"You have," I cry. "You don't know how bleak the world was before I met you. I died a little, every day." I brush his hair back from his face and smile up at him, tucking the strand behind one ear. I grasp his head in my hands. "You saved me."

His eyes go soft, and he nods his head. "That's what you meant yesterday. You must know that you saved me as well, Vale." I do know. I felt his loneliness, the pain inside him.

"Do you want me to continue?" he asks, searching my eyes for the answer.

"I do," I say. "Kiss me."

I gasp when he presses his lips against mine because the movement makes him slide in deeper. One of his hands slides between my legs. He pets my mound softly, calming me. His finger glides through my slit and he touches my clit. I arch back into the pillows. I stare up at him while he slides out and back in, hitting the barrier.

Let him in, I tell my body. *Please let him in.* I tense, but I don't ask him to stop. He swirls his fingers against me, and I moan, tilting my hips higher. He pulls back and we both realize the next time he enters me he'll break through.

"Thank you for this precious gift," he whispers against my lips. "I love you, Vale. Hold on to me. Squeeze me to your body and don't let me go. Don't ever let me go."

I wrap my arms around him, squeezing him against me. "I love you."

He doesn't stop circling my clit as he sinks in faster than before. I swear the pain is delayed. It doesn't hit for a moment. Both our eyes widen when he sinks deep, breaking through. I suction in air. My jaw drops, and I scream when I feel it. He's too big, too much to take inside and it's tearing me apart. He slams his mouth against mine and I cry into it. He takes my pain. He lets it bleed into him as I sob into his mouth, clutching him against me.

I get lost in the feel of that pain. How he fills me to bursting. I'm so overwhelmed by it I can't feel anything else. I can't take anymore. I'm lost in the sensation, eyes squeezed tight. When I open my eyes, he stares down at my chest, breathing hard, eyes wide. His mouth is open, chest shaking with every breath. There's a lonely tear sliding from the corner of one eye. That tear makes a path down his perfectly straight nose and drops to my chest.

He looks so lost. He looks hurt. Did I hurt him?

I take a deep breath, trying to calm my heart. I press my palm against his cheek. "Oliver, baby, what is it? What's going on?"

"I didn't want to hurt you," he says, unable to look at me. "I thought I could do this without hurting you, but I failed."

"I'm okay," I try to tell him, but he shakes his head even as he leans into my palm, receiving just a little comfort in my touch.

"You feel like heaven, but I deserve to be in hell," he whispers into my palm. "Oh, God, Vale, I didn't want to hurt you, not you."

It takes a moment for him to gather the courage to look into my eyes. "Feel that? You're inside me." I smile up at him. "You have been so gentle with me, so kind and sweet. This moment is perfect. Thank you for being my one."

Oliver leans in, kissing me. "I love you. You should never know a moment's pain, only pleasure." If only that was the way the world worked. But the pain makes me appreciate his love more.

I smile against his lips because he's the sweetest man in the world. "I love you. I don't mind the pain. It's mostly gone now. I'll survive. It's not pain exactly, just that you feel bigger than I thought you were, like there's not enough room inside for the both of us." Then I moan into his mouth, letting him know exactly how amazing this moment is.

"You feel so fucking perfect." His voice is unsteady. He kisses my lips and down over my jaw to my neck. "You burn for me, but do you know I burn for you?"

He runs his teeth over my skin and my hips move. "Oh, God, Oliver. I need more!"

"Baby," he growls. "For once, I know exactly what you need."

I want to wrap my legs around him, but he places the palms of both his hands flat, one on each thigh. He presses his weight onto them as my legs spread farther apart, each of my knees hitting the mattress as my hips tilt up, taking him just a bit deeper.

He's staring between my legs, where he entered me, a beautifully content smile on his face. I want to melt into his happiness. I want to be inside him, warm and loved.

"Don't close your eyes. Feel me, all of me," he says, his words choked with emotion, with lust and love. "If it's too much or hurts, tell me. I only want to make you feel good."

His hips roll back, pulling almost entirely out. It makes my mouth hang open in shock. Then he snaps forward, sinking himself so deep. There's very little pain left, just a sting to know he's been there, but it's an intense feeling when he bottoms out. I cry out, not in pain, but surprise.

The feel of him is a profound experience. He's so slick, sliding against my internal walls, massaging each pleasurable nerve ending. It's so much; I'm overwhelmed by all of it, every single sensation. I'm trapped below him, in awe of him, the way his body stretches me open, the way he shows such love in his eyes. There's a gentle storm in his hips as he plunges in and out. My body reacts to each thrust, clenching down on him, wanting him to sink deeper. It feels so strange, yet breathtakingly wonderful.

"You feel . . . oh, God . . . you feel so good," he groans. "So fucking tight, squeezing me over and over. You feel so perfect, made for me."

At first his thrusts are long, piercing me each time with poignant, sharp pleasure, but then he releases my thighs, lifting one leg to wrap around his hip. He slides closer while he licks and sucks at my lips. He thrusts back in and grinds his hips into mine. I remember this from my dream, and I'm lost to it.

Flames of delectable sensation start to center inside me. I can't breathe when our eyes meet. There's a rhythmic heat spreading outward, through my entire body, pulsing, flowing toward him. It's that energy, but it's not rolled into some contained ball this time. It flows out, golden, light-like tendrils escape my body, reaching out to him. My light glows against his skin, lighting us both up. What's happening?

"Oliver, baby, please," I say, though I don't know what I'm begging for. I jerk my head to one side, then the other.

He grabs my chin in one hand. "Look at me, Vale!"

When my eyes focus, shadows swirl in those green depths, that monster trying to escape the man. I want them both. I need all of him. He grabs the back of my head, forcing me to look into his desperate eyes. "Beautiful," I moan up at him. He's beyond beautiful. There are no words, just like he said.

"Now come for me. Show me how good it feels. Show me how much you enjoy me inside your body. Give it to me."

His body is taut, using every muscle to power into me. Then that slow, deep grind undoes me. I scream to the heavens. I growl out such filth as I come, the pleasure filling me, then releasing, filling, then releasing. I wrap both of my legs around him. Oliver smiles proudly, those sharp fangs showing. He's so fucking hot and he's all mine. This amazing man is all mine.

"I own your pleasure. It's all mine."

The tendrils of my light wrap around him like arms, holding him tight, piercing through his chest, into the dragon, past the blood and bone. The moment it touches his heart, things change. His eyes get wider as the ecstasy releases from me into him, but because we're still connected we both feel it. I think he'll have to shut his eyes, but he stops himself at the last second. He licks his lips like he's hungry, and I need more.

I tilt my head to the side offering my blood. "Give me everything, Oliver. I need you to bite me."

For once he isn't thinking, he's lost in his lust as he strikes. His fangs sink deep into my flesh. There's a pinch of pain and an audible pop before he lifts those razor-sharp fangs and suctions onto my neck. I feel the blood flow into his mouth. There's a beautiful sound that escapes him, part moan and part whimper. He's devastated by it, and that fact brings a smile to my lips.

The moment my blood is suckled into his mouth, fire sizzles over my skin, growing. The tendrils grip his heart like a fist, and I come. I come again and again, showing him what it feels like for me. I thrust all my pleasure into him. We're connected at the core, at the heart, by blood.

Oliver's hips falter, and he cries into my neck. He rears up suddenly, roaring like a beast, head slung back on his neck. The feral animal that I've only now witnessed is dark, tempting, utterly captivating, and oh so fantastically beautiful. It's so perfect the way he comes inside me. He's completely overwhelmed by it.

"You're mine entirely," I demand possessively. "Body and soul."

42

NOT THE ONLY ONE

VALE

Oliver tilts his head forward. He smiles darkly with hooded eyes, his chest rising and falling so fast. His lips are covered in my blood. It drips down his chin and onto his heaving chest, evidence of our exuberant lovemaking. His eyes are the purest black, a limitless night sky without stars. His face is without flaw, his skin so pale and pristine it's unnatural. If he didn't have that blush at the high points of his cheeks, he'd look like one of those classic marble statues. His long hair is down, cascading over his shoulders in soft waves. He's beautiful in a way that shouldn't exist, it's too perfect.

He looks like a demon straight from hell's nightmares, but he's smiling with an exalted sort of bliss, showing those perfectly white teeth. I'm not afraid, I'm in awe of him. I've never seen such a lovely sight. This is his truth. Oliver is as beautiful as he is monstrous. I love him more for allowing me to witness it.

"You're so fucking sexy right now." I love the way he looks. I love his nubile body, his substantial cock. The beast that rears its head to see me. When I look into those eyes, I know he sees who I am. Oliver's beast loves me. Those looks in his eyes are addicting. I hope he always looks at me like that.

I've hit my limit. I can't just admire him. I lift up, capturing his neck in my arms, and pull him forward. Our lips crash together, and I taste the copper tang of my blood on his tongue, and it urges me on. I'm squeezing him against me, trying to disappear into his mouth. I need to be closer.

"My blood tastes good on your tongue." I nip at his bottom lip and gaze into those black eyes.

He smiles against my lips, his lower lip popping free of my teeth. "Every part of you tastes good on my tongue. I want to devour all of you."

Oliver's hips jerk back, then he slams into me. I fall back into the pillows, tilting my head back, my spine arching as my fingernails anchor into the skin of his chest. I close my eyes as he rocks in and out, feeling every thick inch of him. I open my eyes as our bodies slam back together. He's deeper than ever.

My feet fall to the bed, and I lift my hips to rock against his. Oliver tries to keep my body pinned, but I can't stop moving. I can't get enough. I want more and more until I'm completely lost in him. Till the world around us floats away and he's all I see, all I feel. He's all there is.

"Such a greedy little pussy," he growls in a voice I've never heard before. The monster is speaking, and it makes me shiver.

"It's definitely greedy." I lift my hips and swivel on him. Fluid gushes from between my legs. "I'm so fucking wet for you. Can you feel it?"

"Oh, I can feel it. I can feel you grip me. The way you tighten up feels so good around our cock," the monster says. And I'm not afraid.

He wraps his arms around me, one under my head and one under my ass as he lifts me up over him. He suspends me there with the tip of his cock barely inside me. I know this monster from my dreams. He wants to torture me till I give him the sweetest of surrenders.

It's a miracle I don't fall and impale myself on his cock. He's so strong. I wrap one arm around his neck and place my right palm against his heart.

"I need you," the monster says against my mouth.

"I need all of you."

Then he starts to lower me down. It's a slow descent into madness. I clench my teeth, head falling back as he spears me. His cock burrows inside me, and I don't understand how he feels so much larger this way, so much deeper. "So good," I whimper as he lowers me, my entire body trembling with the feel of him. "You're so deep."

"Wanna stay buried deep inside you forever," he snarls as he lifts me off his cock completely and drops me onto his bed.

Oliver shakes his head, his eyes closed. He's fighting the beast inside. I see it so clearly now. I do the only thing I can think of to get their attention. I spread my legs wide and slide two fingers through my slick folds. I cry out as I make contact with my clit.

Oliver opens his eyes, green and black swirling. They both see me. They're both there. "Don't make me wait. I want you both." I put that truth out there with a grin.

"You know?" he says, his voice weary.

"I've always known. Your darkness visits me in my dreams. Who do you think fucked me like a selfish beast on the platform? I can hear him screaming inside you to get to me. I want his darkness. I need it."

"You're not afraid." It's not a question.

"I want it all."

I get up on my knees in front of him and I push him back onto the mattress. I crawl over his hips. I grab his rigid cock in one hand and force myself down, taking him to the hilt. "I'm not afraid, baby. I can take it. That beast inside you wants me. He wouldn't hurt me, would you?" I ask and pat his cheek with my palm. Oliver lets out a feral growl that makes me smile. "You wouldn't hurt your mate. Tell me you won't hurt me."

Oliver grinds his teeth together. "I can't always control it, Vale."

"I don't want you to control it."

I grab both his hands in mine and pull them above his head. I use my own weight to hold them down. He's done this to me before and I show him the same courtesy. I get a thrill from the payback. He lets me control him. When he seems so helpless below me, I rock my hips back and forth.

"Teach me how to fuck you. Let him see it, let him feel it. Then let him go because I want him too. I promise you, I want it all. I want every torturous thrust, every single groan. I want you to howl my name. I want to be your little doll. I want you to control me. I want your fucking lust, your love. I want your darkness and your light, so just fucking give it to me." The desperate words Oliver inspires in me are surreal. Maybe I'm the one with a monster inside.

His eyes swirl as he stares up at me in awe. I lift off his chest and rock my hips on his cock. I grab his hands in mine and flatten his palms against my breasts. "Tell me you both want me," I demand. "Tell me you own this body and I own yours."

Oliver's eyes are wide as he watches me, his mouth open, revealing those sexy fangs. I love those fangs. I love how they break my skin and make me bleed. They felt so good when he sunk them into my neck, when he drank from me. The thought of them makes my pussy spasm, clenching down on him.

"I want all of you, baby. Remember it's all or nothing with us," I tell him.

Oliver lifts off the mattress and grabs my hair, wrapping it around his fist. "How I fucking love you. You're exactly what I need. All I want. You're everything beautiful and good in this world. How lucky I am to have found you." He licks and sucks at the marks he made on my neck. My hips jerk. I feel him smile against my skin. "So fucking tight," he growls. "Squeeze me again."

I do it again and his fist in my hair tugs harder. "I'll squeeze you all night."

"Your pussy is perfect. I want you again and again. I want to be trapped inside you, baby." His words are like gasoline on my flames, and they grow hotter, bigger, ready to engulf us both.

I turn my head toward his. He lifts up long enough for our eyes to meet. "Fuck me," I demand. "I need more."

I'm lifted up and he drags me off the bed, leading me farther into his room. The breath is forced from my lungs as he leans me over one of the arms of the sofa. My palms come out in front of me instinctively to hold myself up.

"What a beautiful ass you have," he says with a laugh.

When I turn back to look at him, he's standing behind me, the sweat of his skin glowing in the soft lamp light. He stares down at my ass, and the look of abandon is beautiful on his face. He runs his palm between my shoulders, down my spine. I arch into his touch like a cat, leaning my head back. Each touch is gentle, exploring, and I burn hotter. He moves his hands on my hips and I swallow hard. The muscles in my core are so tense it feels like they'll break if I don't get relief. I'm ready for more.

Feet flat on the floor, body bent over the arm of the sofa, my ass up suggestively, and I finally understand why sex can be such an all-consuming thing. I feel the force of nature between my thighs, the gentle start of subtle longing that grows into an exciting crescendo of anticipation. It consumes me. He consumes me.

"Spread your legs for me."

I do as I'm told. I spread my legs as far apart as I can without losing my balance. Then I feel his deep inhale of breath against my slit. I drop my forehead to the sofa seat, overwhelmed by the feel of his breath alone. He kisses the lips of my sex reverently. My inner muscles clench and spasm, fluttering like delicate butterfly wings. I whimper at the gentle sweep of his lips. Liquid spills from inside me, dripping down the inside of my leg as my cheeks heat.

"Baby, you're bleeding."

I squirm in his hold. "I think that's normal."

The next thing he does makes me squeal—his tongue licks up the blood that trickles down the inside of my thigh. "Oliver," I cry out in shock. Then his tongue is there against my slit, soothing my swollen sex.

"Innocent girl no more," he whispers. "I broke you."

I lift off the sofa arm. "You told me I wasn't broken," I say, then moan as his tongue slithers inside me. For a moment, I try to fuck myself down on it. It feels so good.

I look behind me where he's on his knees. He pulls away, standing up. His lips shine with my blood and cum. He looks wild and hedonistic when he smiles at me. "I can heal you."

"Why would you heal me if I'm not broken?" I ask, turning toward him.

Oliver shakes his head and several strands of his long hair fall down over his shoulder onto his chest. I reach for it, twirling it around my finger. I smile up at him, overcome by memories. "Kiss me," I say before he can answer me.

"Vale, you're hurt. I need to heal you."

"I'm not in pain."

"You're bleeding inside, let me heal you, please." Oliver looks like he needs this for some reason.

"You can heal me, but I'm telling you, I don't feel hurt. Everything is right in the world for the first time in my life."

Oliver smiles sweetly, his head cocked to the side. "I can do both at the same time. Kiss you and heal you." He brings his finger up to his mouth as he steps forward. He bites down, and I wince. Blood wells at the tip. I grab his hand, jerking it forward.

"Oliver, no!" I cry out. I bring his finger up to my lips, then take the injured tip into my mouth. He jerks his hand away, but it's too late. His blood is in my mouth. I swallow it down. He's supposed to be inside me, all of him. His blood doesn't taste like my own. It doesn't taste like copper and salt. It's sweet, with a subtle spice that makes warmth spread through my belly.

"You weren't supposed to drink it," he says with worry in his eyes. "I've never shared it with anyone, Vale, I don't know what it could do."

"You taste so good." Why would his blood taste good to me? I'm not a vampire. "Why do you taste so good?"

He nicks his finger again, then forces it up inside me. I gasp when the heat starts to grow there, but this time it's painful. I try to pull away, but he grabs me and holds me still.

"It feels like fire," I gasp as I squeeze my thighs together. I tilt my head back. "I'm burning."

"My blood will heal you."

"I need you to make it stop!" I scream. I sit on the arm of the sofa and lift my legs around his waist. I wrench his body forward. Oliver lifts me into his arms, holding me up while I rock against him. "Please make it stop."

I look into his eyes for only a second before his lips crash against mine. I thrust my tongue against his as he tilts his hips and enters me. My head falls back and I moan as I lose my grip on reality, my vision clouded by a rosy, euphoric haze. He pulls my hips forward to meet his and all I can do is feel. There's no pain, no sting, just heat and that pleasurable stretch as he spears me open. It's as if his touch alone can heal me. Oliver walks with me, but I can't focus on where we are, only the familiar feeling of floating. I close my eyes.

"Are you okay?" he asks as he presses my back into the cool wall, a shock to my system.

I lift my head up, opening my eyes. He looks ethereal. Golden light halos his head from the lamps. His lips are swollen and a dark pink, his cheeks flushed. Oliver looks innocent and heartbreakingly beautiful. Two thousand years this beautiful man has existed, and I never knew it. I should have known he was out there in the world. He's too beautiful to hide.

"Oliver—" I swallow before I can get the words out. "Never been better. I feel whole. I feel loved. I feel beautiful. You make me feel that way."

"You are beautiful, Vale. You are loved beyond reason. You are loved beyond what I thought myself capable of providing," he says before pressing a gentle kiss over my heart.

Oliver pumps his hips as he kisses up my neck. His breath is loud against my ear. "You feel so wonderful. No one has felt so wonderful." He places a kiss under my ear.

I lean my head back as he enters me, over and over again. I tighten around him with every forward thrust. I hear his jagged breathing, his honest reaction to the feel of me. "Do I feel good?" I hate that I need to push him into telling me, but I want to hear it again.

He pulls back and looks into my eyes with an understanding smile. "No one has ever felt better. I will want no other, Vale. You're my mate in every way. You feel perfect." His words make me blissfully happy.

"Do you like how I feel?" Oliver asks with a smirk as he thrusts deep inside me, bottoming out.

"Well, I don't have any way to compare it—" I start, but he growls and his thrusts get harder.

"You never will," he says, his voice deep and low. His jaw is clenched, and I see jealousy in his eyes. I float ever higher on his possessive words.

"How could I want another when you fill me so completely? You feel amazing. There's no room left in my body for anyone else. I knew you were the only one for me. You're all I want, all I need. I belong to you. I exist to be yours, only yours."

Oliver places his hands under my thighs and lifts me higher, my knees up under his arms, my back forced against the wall. Then he slams into my body. My mouth falls open, and I release a harsh breath.

"That's right, Vale. You belong to me. Only me. I'll never share you. Do you understand? This body is mine to fuck, mine to hold, mine to fondle, and make love to. It's mine. You're mine."

He pulls almost entirely out of me, then thrusts in deeply. His thrusts speed up. He's fucking up into me, then stealing away. My inner muscles can't keep up, they just quiver and vibrate around him rhythmically. It's not long till my fire spreads, making me sweat and swear. I scream his name as I claw at his neck.

"Come on, baby," the monster growls, those eyes completely black again.

I'm losing my mind as he moves so gracefully, so fast. He's more in control than any human could be. He's fucking me so good that my inner muscles squeeze tightly, clamping down hard. I squeeze him like my pussy is a vice. Oliver grabs my left wrist and bites it without looking away. My body arches against the wall, and I scream with the pain as it ratchets up my pleasure.

The pleasure isn't only in my core, it's all over, every single inch. Pleasure licks me with burning flames. It's ecstasy and energy building as I twitch and jerk in his hold. Blood stains his lips and the sight is beautiful. My golden energy suddenly floods from me. I fill him up with it. He starts to shake, and I notice his eyes start to glow. He's feeding on my pleasure.

His lips tremble. "That's what I feel like to you?" he asks, and he's barely able to whisper the words. Tears shimmer in his eyes.

"Yes."

Oliver's head falls forward, his breaths panting against my open mouth, his forehead against my own. Neither one of us can look away while we come undone together.

We stay that way for what feels like forever. When he does finally release inside me, he squeezes me so tightly I can't breathe for a moment. His arms around me feel like love.

"I love you, Vale. Thank you for showing me."

I smile against his lips. "It doesn't feel like I have a choice. I need to share it with you. I can't contain it all. You make me feel so much. I love you so much."

43

GIVE HER THE WORLD

OLIVER

I'm sheathed fully inside her. Our mingled release, her blood, it seeps out around my cock, dripping onto the rug as we calm our breathing, our hearts. Her legs are wrapped around my waist, her back against the wall. We're breathing each other in until we're dizzy and our skin cools. Vale's pussy continues to suction down tightly onto my cock, pulling me deeper. It feels so right. She feels like heaven. I'm still hard, filling her up. I'm home.

Vale looks dazed or dazzled, lost and drifting on the moment we've shared. Her long copper hair is a tangled pillow against the wall. Her head is tilted to the side, her neck exposed as she watches me with hungry, aqua eyes. She's a sight to behold in this quiet moment, even more beautiful for her vulnerability.

My blood hasn't hurt her. It pumps through her veins for now, giving her enough energy to keep going. I know without a doubt that we'll fuck until she's exhausted all the energy inside her body. Even then, I might bury my cock inside her as she sleeps. I don't want to be outside her anymore. I need to be filling her up, every waking fucking moment. I need it to live, to survive.

Vale told me in the car that a physical release hadn't helped her. That she still ached for me. I feel the same right now. I'm buried inside her, having come inside her not once but twice and still the compulsion to mate with her is there. I don't want to stop.

Vampires have a word for it, a frenzy. I've heard stories over the years. When mates come together for the first time, they get more possessive, unable to fight the urge, unable to stop the delirious need for each other. It's instinctual, not something that can be controlled. They have to get it out of their systems. Sometimes it can take days.

Will Vale be able to handle this if I can't stop?

I wrap my arms around her tightly, my precious gift. I lift her off the wall, one hand lifting her ass and the other hand on the back of her neck. She tightens her arms and legs around me, and I walk with my cock buried inside her, where it's supposed to be.

Where we should have always been, the beast purrs inside my head.

Vale presses gentle kisses against my neck, then drags her blunt teeth over my skin. I let out a harsh breath. It feels so good. I wish she had teeth capable of breaking through my skin more easily because the thought of her drinking from me, taking it, is something I didn't realize I'd yearn for, but I do now.

We enter the large en suite, and I sit her down on the long marble vanity. I thrust in and out of her shallowly for a few minutes while she nips at my neck. I pull away, our bodies separating as she tries to suction me back inside her tight cunt. She whimpers at the loss and the sound makes my cock twitch.

Vale leans back against the mirror above the vanity as we study each other. Her eyes wander down my chest to my cock, and her eyes fill with a powerful kind of lust. She spreads her thighs provocatively, trying to seduce me back inside.

I look down at her swollen cunt, pride filling my chest. Her pretty folds are red and puffy. Her clit engorged with so much blood it looks painful—definitely not broken. Her little hole clenches as I watch. My cum leaks out streaked with more blood.

"Clench for me," I whisper, but she hears it well enough because she squirts more cum out onto the marble vanity. This Vale, who's squirting out our shared release all over my vanity, is decadent, she's perfectly debauched. She blows my fucking mind. Her fingers dip down over her clit and she shudders at the feeling. She's such a beautiful mess right now.

"You really filled me up," she gasps as she slides one long finger inside. The fluid spills out around the digit.

"I did."

She adds another finger and pumps them inside. I step back, but I don't turn from the sight of her. I reach to turn hot water on in the bath. I need to get her clean so I can get her filthy all over again.

"I plan on doing it again." I growl at her like an animal.

Vale's body tenses against the mirror as her body trembles harder. She pumps her hand, forcing her fingers as deep as they'll go while I watch. She wiggles her fingers inside and gasps. I watch in awe, when she pulls those wet fingers out of her tight cunt, she looks at them with a devious smile. I step forward, but I don't make it to her before she's got them in her mouth, sucking them into her heat. Her eyes go big as she comes again. She's already learned my Lilu tricks.

Vale's head is tilted back against the mirror, mouth agape, eyes heavy, and her breaths like tiny pants. I grab her fingers, licking them clean, then I kiss her, sucking at her lips, taking every drop of us off her tongue. I suck her tongue into my mouth as she moans.

When I release her, she says, "I love your cum."

She hops off the counter and sinks to her knees in front of me, licking my hard cock. She bobs her head up and down, taking me deeper and deeper till I bottom out in her throat. I growl as she swallows around me. I grab her long copper strands, wrapping them around a fist. I hate to do it, but I lift her off my cock.

Vale whines like I've stollen her favorite toy. Her cheeks flush deeper. "Tell me what you want."

The sound of water rushing into the tub floods the room around us. She smiles up at me like she's so happy. "I want you to fuck my mouth. I want to make you come again," she says, then bites her bottom lip like she's recalling the memory vividly.

I hold my cock in one fist, her hair in another. I smirk. "Open your mouth for me." She licks her lips, then opens her mouth wide for me. I slip the tip of my cock between her lips.

"Suck it, lick it, get it nice and wet. Then I'll fuck you with it." My words make her smile around the tip. She's gorgeous like this, on her knees, begging me to fuck her. I love this woman. She licks the head of my cock and sucks it between her lips, but when she tries to lower her head I don't let her. "No, no, no, baby. You said you wanted me to fuck your mouth. You don't control this now. I do. Is that still what you want?"

Her lips are red and swollen as I pull out. Vale breathes deeply, her hooded eyes never leaving mine. "I want it. I want you."

I thrust into her open mouth, and she gags at first. "Too deep," I say, but I do it again before she can answer me. There's some sadistic part of me that's enjoying the way her throat spasms. She doesn't give up, not even when I gag her with it.

Vale is panting when I pull out, but she smiles wickedly. I shake my head, surprised once again by this amazing woman. It's my turn to bite my lip. I guess it's true that mates are perfect for one another because she's perfect for me in every way. I realize right then, while I look at her on her knees, this girl can handle me. I questioned it before, but I don't anymore. She can handle every inch because she was built for me, body and soul.

"Such a dirty girl. You like me taking over. You like being my little plaything. So much time we've wasted when I could've been inside you. I want every inch, every hole. I want to own your entire body." I feel those possessive words deep in my soul.

Her eyes become dark and heated. "Then own me," she replies, a supplicant at my feet.

I lift her up and press her body down onto the vanity, tits first, head down with my hand on her neck. "Stay there," I demand.

I open a drawer and grab more lube. Should I tell her I have it stashed all over my house? She's going to find out that I'm a very prepared Lilu. She was right, I'd been making a lot of plans.

I halt in front of the mirror, taking in the way she's bent over. Her thighs are trembling with urgency. She looks so turned on. I want to dive into her flames and live there always.

She lifts up on her hands, impatient for me. I'm at her side less than a second later. "I told you to stay there." I slap her, right on that round, fuckable ass. She cries out, and the way her eyes close, head flung back, is spectacular. All her reactions are so honest.

"I'm sorry," she whimpers before opening her eyes once more to watch me in the mirror.

"I should stuff my cock in your tight little asshole for disobeying me," I tell her, my voice gone raspy thinking about it. I wouldn't punish her with it though . . . well, the truth is I would punish her with it, but not tonight. I like her reactions to my threats, the way her eyes get wide.

But that upsets her. She shakes her head and lifts up again. "Absolutely not," she says as I grab her hands and tug them behind her. She arches up as her breasts hit the vanity. She's ready to fight back. I love it.

"You'll take me, maybe not tonight, but you will. I'll make it feel so good." I lean against her hot skin, pressing my face into her hair. "Don't you want me to fuck your tight little asshole. Don't you want me deep inside it. You want me filling it up." I breathe deeply, nudging her hair away from her neck. "I want to show you how good it can be. Let me play with it. I'll wait to fuck you there till you beg me, but rest assured, you will beg me, Vale. I know you, you want everything I can give you."

Vale tilts her head down as she draws deep breaths into her lungs. Her hair spills down and hides her face. I let her hands go so I can sit the lube down in front of her. She stiffens when she looks up at it. Her cheeks flame. She's embarrassed, turned on, and mad all at the same time. "You can touch it, but I don't think I can handle all of you there tonight. I don't know if I'm ready to do that. Can that be okay?"

"Of course it's okay, baby. You have all the power. Your word is my command when we come together," I tell her and she nods, so innocent, so trusting.

I grab the lube from the counter and pour some on to one hand. I pull back looking at those lush hips. She doesn't want it tonight, but I'm going to show her what she's missing. "Spread your legs wider," I demand, and she does without question. "You're so beautiful here," I assure her.

I wreck her when I drip the lube over her tiny, puckered hole. She jerks her hips forward and I smile. "I promise I won't hurt you. I promise I won't fuck you till you want me to, but you'll feel my fingers."

"Okay," she moans as my slick fingers rub a gentle circle over it.

Vale's eyes are closed as she shudders. That's it, she's relaxing into it already. I'm so proud of her I press my cock against her swollen pussy. She wiggles her hips so she can line me up. She's a natural at accepting all the pleasure I offer her.

I press my thumb against her asshole and apply a little pressure while I dip my cock inside her slick cunt. Vale hisses when I don't fill her up. She needs more. I grab more lube, squeezing it out over her cleft. I dip my thumb into her hole as I press my cock in and out in tiny increments.

"Fuck!" she cries. "I can't take it, Oliver."

I smile at her like a sadistic bastard and she sees it. I slide my thumb through that tight ring of muscle, turning my wrist as I back it out. I dip the tip in more of the lube, then thrust it all the way inside as I thrust my hips forward. I fill her to the hilt and wiggle my thumb inside her ass.

Vale lifts her chest, arching her spine. There's a sound I've never heard from her before. She's keening, a high-pitched, wobbly cry that shakes her with its ferocity.

I lean over her and lick up her neck to her jaw. "Feel good?"

Vale's eyes flutter open. She shakes her head, and I worry I've screwed up. "What are you doing to me?" she asks almost sadly. I stop moving and study her. "Do you want to make me just as filthy as you are? What if I'm worse? I might be worse, Oliver." She giggles after that last question, and I smile in relief. Like I said, absolutely perfect for me in every fucking way.

"You can be filthy with me, Vale. You can be anything you want with me. Trust me to give it to you. I want all of you, and I hope you wouldn't ask anything less than everything from me. I want to show you everything. I'd give you the world."

"Are you going to show me all of it tonight?" she asks, and her eyes seem worried, like the thought is overwhelming her. I feel a bit guilty. Perhaps, I'm moving too fast, but I'm so excited by the prospect of teaching her.

"I'd need a lot longer than one night," I say, then smirk at her. "This is just a little fun." I pull my thumb out and slide my index finger deeper inside her.

This time she can't stop her reaction. She lifts off, slamming her body back into mine. Her head falls back onto my chest, and her hair is a messy halo of coppery-red waves. Her mouth is wide open, surrounded by those puffy, berry-stained lips. Her cheeks are stained with the flush of her desire. She's overcome once more.

"Open your eyes and see what I see," I whisper against the crown of her head. When those bright, aqua eyes open to meet mine, I'm overcome by all that passion. "Do you realize how fucking beautiful you are right now?" I ask, then thrust inside her till I bottom out. "Nothing compares, Vale."

Vale tilts her head, and I see the tears swell in her eyes. She reaches up to cradle my jaw. "You're the most beautiful man I've ever seen. I thought this would be impossible, us, but it feels so right. Everything with you feels so right, so good. Why do you feel so good? Is it because you're Lilu? Or is it because you're mine?"

"Are you Lilu?" I ask as I smile against her hair.

"No, I'm not," she whispers sadly. "Sometimes I wish I were."

"You're perfect. No need to be Lilu. I believe that rightness you feel must be because we are fated to be together. We're meant to be one. I feel it too."

Vale turns around, and my cock slips out of her tight pussy. We both gasp. She wraps her arms around me, laying her head against my chest. "I love you," she says, and her cheeks blush even more when she looks up. "I can't stop saying it. I'm sorry, but it's hard to keep it inside."

I kiss her lips gently. I want to support her so she knows it's more than okay. "I like hearing it. I'll never get tired of hearing it, sweetheart. I love you, my beautiful mate."

I tug her toward the bath. We step into the warm water, and when we sit across from each other, the water sloshes over the rim. I turn the taps off before we flood the house. I don't care about the mess we've made everywhere; I don't care about anything other than the woman in front of me.

"I'll do all I can to make you happy, my love. I'll make it my sole purpose in life to give you everything you want, everything you need," I promise her because she is my purpose now. I've lived for thousands of years, aimlessly wandering the world. I had no purpose. I had no reason for being, but with her I feel it. I feel a reason for living, a reason to go on.

Vale looks at me from the opposite end of the tub. She takes in a deep breath, tears falling down her face. "All I need is you," she says, then sniffles. "You're all I need."

44

EVERY MOMENT, I LOVE YOU MORE

VALE

Oliver dips his head into the water, wetting his long hair. When he sits back up, it's slick against his skull. He reaches for the mass of curls, pulling it over one shoulder and wringing it out. He looks beautiful with those wet tendrils dripping over his chest, curling up at the ends against his pale skin. He cups water in his hands and lifts it to his face, closing his eyes. I do the same, hoping the mascara is long gone. I lie my head back and smile. I take a moment to be happy, enjoying this massive bathtub.

When I sit up, he's watching me intently. He washes his body with soap that perfumes the air, woodsy and dark. I'm fascinated by every single stroke of his hand. I've lost my virginity to the most beautiful man to ever exist. I'm so grateful for the experience. I'm grateful for how sweet and gentle he tried to be with me.

"What are you thinking?" he asks with a tilt of his lips.

"I love you more with every second we spend together," I whisper, knowing he'll hear it. He grabs my hand and tugs me toward him, sloshing more water and bubbles onto the bathroom floor.

I collide with him, my palms sliding up his wet chest. I wrap my arms around his neck, then spread my legs on both sides of his hips, keeping him imprisoned between my thighs.

"Love doesn't feel like an adequate word when it comes to what I feel for you." He presses the gentlest kiss against my lips.

I told him earlier that this felt so final, what we were about to do. It was the truth then, and it's true now. I know he's my forever. I never want to be with anyone else, and I never would. It's not something I have to make peace with; I accept it fully.

I grab his face in my hands and lift it so I can stare into his eyes. Then I swivel my hips over his cock that's always hard and ready no matter how many times he comes. When he's notched into me just right, I sink slowly onto him. Breath is freed from both of our lungs like neither of us can hold it back. My lips tremble as I rock against him slowly.

He bathes my body with soap that smells like him. He takes great care to clean my shoulders, my neck, my breasts, and my back. His thumbs glide effortlessly across my nipples, back and forth, while I glide my hips forward, rocking over every thick inch of him.

"Nothing feels like this," I cry out. "Nothing."

I lean forward and take a single lick up his neck, then his chin. I kiss his lips as one of his hands slides down my back to rest at the base of my spine. At his urging, I tilt my hips forward and pull up, then crash back down against him. Oliver's cock bottoms out and for a moment I close my eyes. My head tilts back as I shiver at the weight and fullness I feel.

"I feel your heartbeat inside me." I gasp because the feeling is so unbelievably amazing. I lift off, sink again, and there it is. Every time I seat myself onto him, the beat of his heart throbs inside me.

He smiles. "That's it, use me, make yourself come on top of me. Fuck, you're so beautiful like this." He moans as I lift off and fall again.

I grind my body over him, placing my hand on each of his shoulders to gain leverage. I lift my hips almost entirely off him, then crash back down. His head falls back as he releases a sigh. He's content to be used by me.

"Fuck!" he growls as I swivel my hips over the tip of his cock, experimenting. "How are you so good at this? You're going to make me come again, baby."

The smile on my face is full of pride. I'm going to make him come. I'm going to rock his fucking world, and that alone makes me smug. That's exactly what I wanted. I was afraid I wouldn't pleasure him, but his words of approval are everything to me.

I clench my inner muscles around the flared head of his cock as I swirl my hips. Narrowing my suddenly cocky gaze, I lean against his chest and pull my feet below me. I take him deeper, grabbing the edge of the tub so I don't hurt his shoulders. I clench and release as I hop on his cock. Every inch of my body outside of the water is covered in sweat. I'm breathing hard as my thighs twitch and burn with the effort.

Oliver lifts his head and his teeth are bared, as if he can't take a moment more of my sweet torture. "Feels so good, baby. Fuck me harder, I can take it."

I'm so out of breath I sink all the way down on his cock. I tilt my head back and gulp in air. He feels so overwhelmingly huge inside me. I shake over him as I feel the flames of my own pleasure dance against my skin. When I lift back up, he sits up straighter. He grabs my hips and helps to lift me. I roll them as I get to his tip, clenching those muscles. He groans again.

"Faster," he growls. "Take me deeper. Oh fuck, that's it. Just like that." His words send pleasure spiking in my pussy. I take him deeper, and I swear he swells inside me, thicker and thicker. I scream with my next breath.

As I watch him, my mouth hangs open, my lips tremble, and my thighs burn. My muscles are clenched so tight around him that I'm going to break if I don't come soon.

"Come with me," he whispers on a shaking breath.

Oliver's hands roam, and he grabs each of my breasts in his palms, squeezing and pinching my nipples between his finger and thumb. I cry out from the pain and pleasure. He leans forward sucking one berry-colored nipple into his mouth. He smiles around it when I clench, my muscles sucking him deeper into my body. Oliver lets go of one breast and slides his hand down over my ass.

I clench and release when he penetrates me with his finger. I bite my own lip until blood wells. I feel so full; the stretch of it is intense. When he wiggles his finger in my ass, I grab his shoulders, lift up, slam back down, then swivel my hips as I pop back up. It's so good I get lost in the pleasure. He fucks me with that finger while I hop up and down on him, losing my mind. It's all too much.

"Oliver, I'm going to come!" I scream as I start to shake with the impending orgasm.

I feel the rasp of his fangs against one breast. Blood wells up to the surface, and I watch with a sick sort of obsession when he sees the blood on my skin. He licks it up, and that's all it takes. I slam my hips down, taking him as deep as he'll go, over and over, until Oliver's yells meld with my own. He spills inside me as I force my pleasure inside him. I feel his cock swell impossibly bigger, then he spills again.

I scream, breath rushing from my lungs, riding his thick cock into a heavenly orgasm that continues on and on, seemingly endless. It's my energy, it's keeping us tethered in this moment, forcing a pleasurable feedback loop from me to him, then back again.

"So fucking good. I want you to fuck me for days, till I can't come anymore. I need more. Fuck me!" I'm still coming, still riding his dick like a desperate bitch. I don't know what on earth is happening to me. I'm lost to the beat of our fucking, utterly addicted to him.

I'm floating on a wave of ecstasy that won't let me go. There's no hope of surfacing again; I wouldn't want to. I can get lost in him forever, and that's my idea of heaven.

He pulls out, and I scream, "Need you, please!" He lifts me up to the edge of the tub, bending me over it. Then he fucks into me so deep I scream at the depth. His hands are on my hips, pulling me back with every forward thrust. I'm like a helpless, fucking doll. I couldn't hold myself up if I tried.

He growls against my spine, "You're so fucking slick and tight. I can't get enough. Tell me to stop! I don't want to hurt you." His pleas are desperate. He's losing himself, just like me.

I shake my head as I lift my hips higher. "It feels so good, please, baby. Please don't stop."

I'm coming when he lifts me up against his chest and bites my neck again. I shout and shout, barely able to fill my lungs with oxygen because we're tethered once again by my energy, locking us into place.

Oliver is suckling at my neck, his hands bruising my hips. It's so good, the pain, the pleasure. He's everything, it feels like he's everywhere. I tilt my head back over his shoulder, closing my eyes. "Don't ever stop."

The growl that comes from him is entirely his monstrous side. "I won't stop until you pass out, baby. Then I'll fuck you while you sleep. I won't be able to pull out. You'll only wake up to come on my cock. Would you like that?"

I moan at his filthy words. "I like it. Need more. Need it all," I cry out as he seals the wounds at my neck and pulls out, leaving me painfully empty. Oliver lifts me out of the bath and stands in front of the mirror, and I'm shocked by the sight.

It's not Oliver at all but his demon, fully formed.

Oh shit, the monster is here. He's finally here. The weird thing is I already know exactly who he is. I've known him most of my life. I take in the beast and tears swirl in my vision.

45

MY BEAUTIFUL MONSTER

VALE

"Hey there, lovely one. Miss me?"

There's a familiar demon holding me in his arms. Water droplets drip down, rivulets sliding down over his broad, muscled chest. His eyes are completely black, sclera and all, just like his skin, and the long hair that slides down his back. This monster disappears into the shadows, becomes one with them. He's a predator, a corrupter.

"Oliver?" I say, eyes wide as my heart beats frantically.

The demon shakes his head with a sadistic smile. "You know exactly who I am. Remember me," he growls and there's a golden light behind the darkness in his eyes, but it can't quite break free.

Tears fill my eyes as dreams play out in my head. I'd dreamed of this demon since I was a little girl. He was never like this though. Now he stands here, hands on hips, completely naked, his wings sitting close to his back. The beast is so tall, so broad and beautiful. He always had been.

"The biggest, baddest monster of them all. My beautiful monster, my Ashmodai," I say when the tears spill. "I thought I made you up."

One of the reasons I'd believed my father was right, that I had a demon living inside me, was because of this creature, this demon who lived in my dreams. It'd been easy to believe because I *did* have a demon inside me, Ashmodai. He was always there, my hero who fought the nightmares when I was a child. The beast who held me in his arms when I was a confused thirteen-year-old, wondering why I was so different from everyone else. Then it was the beast who took me so selfishly in the rain on the platform wearing Oliver's face. It took a couple days to understand Oliver had another side, a monster, but I didn't know he was my monster too.

I try to wrap my arms around his neck, but he has to lean down. He's probably seven feet tall. "I remember you. Were you really there?"

"I was. I am him, and he is me. Though we are separate," he explains, and it's hard to make sense of what he's saying.

"I remember, Ash. Why didn't you tell me who you were? Why? You know I love you. I always have." The love I had for him was not a romantic love, but he is Oliver, and Oliver is Ash. I knew exactly who he was. I knew the monster because he had been my friend, and now he's my mate.

"Your Oliver doesn't know how to enter dreams. He wouldn't understand why I was there. Vale, you called me to you, in your dreams. When I felt you in the world, I had to get to you the only way I knew how. I had to. There was no choice."

"How can you enter my dreams if Oliver can't?"

"We may be the same, but we're split. Two different consciousnesses. We shouldn't be this way, Vale. We should've never been this way."

He's so much bigger like this, but I manage to lift my lips to his. This precious being who saved me from the nightmares. They've been there, waiting, all along. He found me. "I've missed you, Ash," I say, and it's the truth. As I aged, he'd come to me less and less often.

He lifts me easily, like I weigh nothing, and I wrap my legs around his waist. I slide my fingers into his hair as he steps out of the en suite. I press my lips against his, feeling his energy pulsing against mine. I feel power radiating from within him.

He sinks to his knees in front of an unlit fireplace, but when he snaps his fingers, flames grow from within. His skin glows in the firelight, and the world around us fades. He sits back on his knees, studying me as I study him. I swallow nervously before I spread my legs wide. I give him a good view. I'm throbbing again, though I'm just as scared as I am aroused. This massive demon is about to make me his.

Ash continues to watch me, his great wings rising, then flinging out behind him. Droplets from the bath sling out into the air and glitter like stardust. He's magic. His shoulders are broad, his body so much larger than Oliver's human form. His cock stands straight up between his legs, dripping fluid from the slit. I bite my lip as I take him all in.

"I've watched him with you all night, but it's my fucking turn with our mate. It's my turn to love you," he growls and it makes me smile. "Spread your pussy open," he demands, his voice much lower, more gravelly, and more accented than Oliver's.

I spread my legs wider, then place my hands on each side, using my fingers to open myself up. "Is this good?"

"You're so swollen. Are you sore, sweetheart?"

"No, I'm not sore. I'm ready for you." I run one finger up over my clit and shiver. "Will my beautiful monster touch me?" If I was a sane woman, maybe I'd be afraid of him, but I wasn't. I wanted him.

He grabs my ass in both hands and lifts my center up to his mouth. "Hold your cunt open. I'm going to feed," he growls against my center. I scramble awkwardly to do as he asks.

His tongue is thick and almost rough as he brushes it over my clit. My hips shake in his huge hands as he supports my weight. He sucks my clit into his mouth, pulsing his tongue over it. Then his sharp teeth take over. I scream when they sink shallowly into my oversensitive flesh.

I come undone. I'm coming already when he chuckles against my hot core. Then he thrusts his tongue deep inside me. His tongue curls upward, pressing against my G-spot. I scream, the pleasure ratcheting up so great I see stars. I'm going to faint. I'm dripping into his mouth. He groans as his fangs tear the sensitive skin of my pussy again. My hips jerk against his mouth.

"Damn, damn, damn!" How does he make that feel so good?

"You taste like heaven, everything I've always been denied."

When I come down from my orgasm, he drops my hips to the floor. I didn't expect this. How could I? He was supposed to be a dream. He's spectacular, otherworldly, and very fucking real. He's going to fuck me to death tonight. I'll die a happy woman.

"If I fuck you to death, I won't get to come play again. No baby, I won't hurt you anymore than your body can take. I'll take you to the edge though. I'll make you beg for it." He smiles and those eyes fill with such promising heat.

"I don't long for death. I long for you. Tell me you want me."

Once again, my monster lifts my hips, but this time he comes forward. He's kneeling between my open thighs. Close enough to slide inside me, but he doesn't.

He grabs his cock in one massive fist and strokes it, smirking. "I want you. I want to fill you up. Do you think you can take me?" He angles the tip at my entrance so I feel the size of him.

I study Ash, he's much larger everywhere and that includes his cock. It's much thicker than Oliver in his human form, but I'm so, so wet and dripping, surely I can take it all. I want to take it all. I don't care if it hurts. I'm being drawn into a lush haze where all I see is visions of sexual decadence and surrender.

"Ease it inside, be gentle, and I'll take it all," I say, though I have doubts.

He drags my body against the rug, jerking me closer. It burns the skin on my back, but I don't care. None of it matters. I tilt my hips back as he lines us up, then smile up at him as he focuses his attention where his cock head is currently dipping into me. Ash's eyes are at half-mast when he thrusts in. I moan even though the stretch of him burns. Thankfully it doesn't hurt, not yet anyway.

"I want to force it inside you. I want to make you bleed around me. I want to make you scream for your pretty boy to save you. I want the inside of your thighs to be black and fucking blue," he growls as he sinks deeper. I shouldn't trust this demon because he does want to hurt me. His words sound like threats, and it makes me worry if some part of Oliver wants to destroy me. I wonder if it's because he really is a monster after all.

"Are you going to hurt me?" I ask, worrying my bottom lip between my teeth. "Is that what you want? I want you to love me."

He looks up and for a moment he disappears into the darkness around us. It envelops him, hiding him. The same way it clings to Oliver; in the end, they're the same person. I wish I knew how they split into two parts. I wish I could piece them back together.

His eyes glow with golden fire, pulsating through the darkness, and it's the first part of him that reappears. "I'm supposed to be the monster, Vale. I'm supposed to be evil. You know this already. That's who he thinks I am, and therefore I am. I've taken on his views. I'm the aggressor, the bad one."

I shake my head. "I don't believe that. You're not. You're the same. You look at me just like he does. You love me."

"You're the only being I've ever loved," he growls as his hips press farther, and I wince. He feels impossible to take. "I waited so long for you to come back to me. My love has never faltered, I swear it."

His words are strange. They make me feel dizzy, and I have to close my eyes as I try to flee from the images his words create in my head. I don't want to see it. I don't want to remember. When he sinks farther inside, stretching me wide, taking my breath away, the images start to fade. I breathe around the stretch as he works inside, making me forget what he said altogether. I refuse to think about anything other than how good this is.

"If you love me, then you'd never hurt me. I know you won't hurt me. I'm your mate. You know that, right? You feel it the same as I do."

He lifts over me, pressing down against me, and my breasts smash against his muscular chest. My hips arch upward as my legs are propped over his thick muscular thighs. He's all hardness to my softness. He feels so heavy, so dark, and so right. My beautiful monster.

"I have always known you were my mate, but he doesn't listen to what I have to say. He fears the truth, and he fears me. I knew you were mine. I've always known, since the moment you were back in this world," he whispers against my cheek. "I've waited for you, Vale.

Do you understand that? I let him take over, I let him live just so I could await you."

"Thank you for waiting for me, for seeing the truth." I wrap one arm around his neck. I press my fingers into the leathery wings that sprout at his back. I run my fingertips over those wings as I thrust my left hand into his thick hair. "Tell me you love me," I beg him.

The monster pulls out and thrusts deeper than ever. I scream as he fills me. It's that evil dance where he doesn't want to hurt me, but he has to get inside. Ash shudders as I run my nails over his wings.

"I love you, my fiery Queen," he groans, and his shoulders shake as if it's all too much.

I press my lips against his cheek. "Tell me again," I moan. He pulls out, then thrusts back in.

"I love you!" he yells against my lips. "I fucking love you."

He pulls his knees under him as he licks up the underside of my neck, to my lips. "I can't stop. I need to be sheathed in your fire. I need to come inside you. Will you stay still. I promise I'll fuck you so good, but I'm going to come deep in this tight cunt first."

I moan and slam my lips against his. I'm shaking when he pulls back. He sits up on his knees again and lifts my hips. He's moving inside me with that impossible, supernatural strength. He's fucking me but not going very deep, just the first six inches at most. I'm covered in a sheen of sweat. He watches where he disappears inside me, just like Oliver did. They like seeing it. His chest heaves with effort. I think the look of him alone is enough to make me come.

"Tell me you're ready to take it all!" he bellows. "I'm going to come buried all the way inside you. Breathe through it."

"I'm ready," I moan, and he thrusts forward so fast it scares me.

Stars dance around in my vision as tears fill my eyes. There's a deafening roar in my head and my eardrums crackle at the sound. Then I feel liquid fire fill me, deep against my womb. I clench down. He's roaring, his mouth wide open, his head thrown back. He pumps deeper still, pouring his heat into my body. It goes on and on.

My pussy flutters with pleasure, and I suck in a breath. "My monster," I cry out, and he opens his eyes. I come, sucking him deeper into me. My hips start jerking, and I scream, "More!" I reach for his body, lifting myself up onto his lap. "I want more."

"You like how I fill your tiny cunt up?" he asks with a sadistic smile that should scare me. I nod my head, and he wraps one arm around me, pressing my small body against his much larger one. His hips rock up into me as he lifts me on and off his cock.

"I want you both, let him see," I demand. "You're the same. He needs to see how we are with each other because I'll die without you both. I need you. I need more. Fuck me!"

"I thought it was us who fed on pleasure, but now I think it's you, and you've been starved for too long." He throws me down on the floor, flipping me over roughly. He lifts my ass into the air. My flames grow higher as I clench and let him see me drip with him. He uses two fingers to press his cum back inside me, and I moan.

"I like you dripping for me, but I like it better when I'm filling you up." He thrusts into me so hard I scream for him. "Sing for me, my fiery little bird." He yanks my hips back against his.

I come so hard my vision nearly blackens. I get lost as he pummels me with exquisite, tortuous pleasure. Orgasm after orgasm, he draws them from my body like magic. I come so many times I pass out in his hold.

Awaken

When I come to, the first thing I see is my own reflection. I'm confused at first. My cheeks are flush, my hair a tangled mess. My breasts are red with large handprints. I smile because they're everywhere. My thighs are red with welts that should bruise by morning. Yet I feel more beautiful with his marks on me than I ever have.

My legs are spread wide, my feet flat on the floor, his muscular thighs keeping me spread apart. My pussy drips over that thick, dark cock covered in pale white cum. Suddenly, his hips lift and half of it disappears inside me, stretching me wide. I whimper as he fills me.

Ash's long fingers are around my waist. He lifts me up and down over him. "I thought I lost you for a moment. Are you okay?"

I look up into the mirror. "Is he here with us, I'd like him to see this. Call him forward."

"Baby, he's here. He watches," Ash says and those huge fangs slice the skin at my throat. "Turns out he likes watching too."

"Feels so good," I moan as he licks the blood welling at my throat.

I watch in the mirror as he disappears inside me, shocking me with the depth. It's hard to believe my body can take all of him. It's a miracle. I gasp, mesmerized by the sight as he disappears between the swollen lips of my sex. I love the sight of my slick dripping down his shaft when he lifts me up, how it's covered with both of our releases.

Then he lifts me off completely. Holding me above him, I squeeze those muscles. I'm sore inside, but they do what I want. I squeeze the cum out and the monster growls when he sees it drip onto him. He drops one hand to my pussy and coats his fingers.

"He watches me play games with you." He smiles darkly, then he brings those wet fingers to my mouth. "Suck it off me," he growls.

Our eyes meet in the mirror. They're so bright green right now. "Feed it to me, Oliver," I beg, and he does. I suck his fingers into my mouth. His sweet cum hits my tongue and my head snaps back. When he drops me onto his cock, I scream out my pleasure and come again.

"Oh, God, yes. Fuck me. Both of you, fuck me," I cry as I spasm around his thick shaft, trying to suck him impossibly deeper into my body. My body doesn't want him to ever be free of it.

They bring their hands around my waist and fuck me on and off that thick cock, over and over again. "So good," I moan.

This isn't what I thought my first time would be like. I thought if I ever lost my virginity, it'd be with some fumbling college guy who'd hurt me, thrust twice, and come. But this, this is something else. I couldn't have dreamt this madness up.

"I'm so glad I got to pop your cherry, Vale. This pussy is perfect, and it's all mine. This body is all fucking mine."

"I belong to you." The words burst from my lips. "Both of you, all mine. Do you hear me? You both belong to me. Do you accept, Oliver? Do you accept I'm bonded to the monster? You better because when I want him inside me, I'll have him. He'll come, won't you?"

The monster grunts against my neck. "I'll come, come deep inside this tight pussy. I'll come down your fucking throat and deep inside that ass. I want to make you drip with me."

I shiver with his dark words as his fingers go tighter at my waist.

"I accept." Oliver's voice comes through the growl, and I smile. I pull his hands off my waist and fall forward on my palms, that huge cock still buried deep. I start riding him, rocking over his dick.

"Good, baby, now I'm gonna fuck you."

I slide over him as he sits there and takes it. I pop my hips up and off his dick, taking him to the hilt with every downward thrust. All the while he watches in the mirror. When I'm almost there, that energy pulsating inside me, balling up and glowing so bright, they squint their black eyes, and I scream. I watch as it barrels out of me, sinking into his hips. I smile when it detonates inside him and he roars.

I feel him come inside me. His hands hold my hips down onto him. It doesn't matter. I don't want to move. I can't anymore. That was the last bit of energy I had, and it's growing inside him as my hands falter, then I crash onto the cold floor. "I love you."

46

MAKING LOVE

OLIVER

Vale crashes to the floor as her energy continues to pulse inside us. I hold her hips down, keeping her there as I come so deep inside her. It feels like my balls tighten up until I squeeze out the last drop. I don't think I have anything left to give my mate, which has never happened before.

The energy doesn't seem to dissipate. I stand up as it makes its way into my chest, wrapping around my heart. I hold one hand to my chest as it squeezes, taking my breath away. I've never taken so much of her energy, but tonight she can't stop feeding it to us. My other hand flies out, hitting the floor-to-ceiling mirror to steady myself, and I see her. She's sprawled out on the floor. Her heartbeat may be steady, but I believe she's unconscious. She's not moving.

Feed her, the beast snaps at me.

Oh, God, I've hurt her.

Blood! You idiot! Feed her your blood.

I pull her into my arms as I tear open my wrist with my teeth—Or is it the beast? I struggle to find where I end and he begins—then press it to her mouth. Her eyes flutter as her lips open around the wound.

We did it! We're the same!

I shake my head, trying to push the monster down deep so I can concentrate on Vale.

I will not be pushed aside. She's our mate!

"Shut up then so I can concentrate. She needs us."

Complete the bond, she'll be fine. Little one is strong this time, he says, but his words don't make sense.

"What do you mean 'this time'?" I ask, but all he does is growl. He's getting angry and pushing at my mind, fighting me.

Complete the bond! he roars. *Do it now!*

I lift Vale up higher into my arms as I sit against the mirror. Her head is in the crook of my arm, and that's when I notice how pale she is against my midnight skin. My jaw clenches at the sight. I take in a deep breath as I press my wrist closer against her mouth.

"I need my skin back," I say, the words tumbling out.

This is your skin!

I clench my jaw. "It isn't! I'm not a monster!"

Vale's mouth suckles harder at my wrist, her blunt teeth abrading the wound, making it sting. Her mouth is hot, searing the skin. Her eyes open wide as she stares up at me, then she narrows her gaze. For a moment, I swear flames dance in her eyes.

My skin heals, and she kisses my wrist. "You're not a monster, Oliver. You're the most wonderful man I've ever known. You're so kind and loving. You're the best, no matter what skin you're in. I love you. You're beautiful as a man and you're beautiful as the demon. That's the truth. I want you to see what I see when I look at you."

Vale smiles with a calm I wish I knew. I'm worried for her, though she just snuggles deeper into my arms. "I love you, Ashmodai."

"You know my name?" It's all I can think to say. I should be expressing words of utter love and devotion, but that name on her lips distracts me.

"Is that the name your mother gave you?" she asks as she burrows into my chest, trying to get closer, always closer. She doesn't explain how she knows it.

I nod my head. "When she was pregnant with me, she was very sick. We very nearly died. My grandfather saved us, and she honored him by giving me his name," I explain, hoping she won't have questions about him.

Vale reaches up and cradles my jaw in her palm. "I'm glad he saved you so we could find each other one day. I don't want to be in a world without you." She yawns and stretches her arms above her head. My blood has healed her body. Her thighs are creamy without my handprints now. There's a part of me that's almost sad that the evidence from our lovemaking is gone. I want my mark on her skin.

"Feel better?" I ask as I stand, then set her on her feet.

Vale lifts her face to look into my eyes and smiles brightly. "I'm great, just tired. I think you exhausted me," she says, then giggles. Her cheeks flush a delicious shade of pink that makes me hard again.

"Come, let me clean you up, then I'll take you to bed. You'll sleep beside me tonight."

"We won't get caught? Not that it matters now."

I shake my head as I turn the water on in the shower. "Not tonight. Tonight, you're entirely mine."

I gently wash Vale's body, being careful in this form. I'm stronger as the demon. I've never lived in this body, not truly. The beast coos at Vale, growling low in his throat when she moans. He loves her.

She tries to wrap her arms around my neck, but I'm so tall she can't. She gives up and wraps them around my waist as I wash her long hair.

"This is nice," she sighs against my chest. "Every touch feels so good. I don't want you to ever stop touching me."

Her words fill me with pride. I don't want to stop touching her either. I'm finding it hard not to continue fucking her. In fact, even now I wish I was buried inside her.

"Was this night good for you?" I ask, hoping I haven't ruined it. I hope it's been special. I hope I've given her what she wanted, what she'd dreamed of.

I feel her smile over my sternum and feel an ache in my chest. I have to breathe deeply to calm my heart from racing. "I can count the best days in my life on one hand. Tonight is number one. Everything else pales in comparison to being loved by you," she explains as she wipes her eyes. "You're in all my best days now."

I lift her chin and bend forward. I kiss her reverently. She's right. I've lived for two thousand years, and these past few weeks have been the best of my life. I love knowing that we share a future together.

The night I met her she couldn't have told me what she needed. She was quiet and nervous, full of anxiety. Her hand shook in mine. But Vale's grown so strong. She called me out on my bullshit. She drove me wild. I love her for it. If I'm honest though, I loved her then as well. I think I've loved her since the moment I first saw her. I didn't know it could happen to me. I had to learn how to accept her love.

"Vale," I whisper against her lips, then kiss each cheek. "You're the best thing to ever happen to me. You're part of my best days as well."

She tries to wipe her eyes again, but I grab her hand to stop her. "Don't hide those tears. Don't hide what you feel. Don't ever hide again."

She blinks up at me and there's a soft smile on her lips. "I'm not sad. These are happy tears. These are tears of gratitude. No one has ever loved me the way you do. My whole life something was missing, it was you. I'm happy you found me, Ashmodai."

"Me too."

I rinse her hair and wrap her in a thick towel, then I lift her into my arms carefully. She feels so small, so fragile in these demon-strong arms. I want to protect her from anyone who would hurt her.

She's stronger than both of us, the beast growls into my mind. *She is fire.*

Vale's asleep before we make it to the bed. It's awkward to hold her in one arm as I pull the ruined duvet off the bed and toss it to the floor. I lay her gently onto the cream-colored sheets, then study her face, not for the first time. I swallow hard. She's the most beautiful creature I've ever seen. She glows with beauty. My chest aches as love fills my heart to bursting. I run the tip of my index finger over her delicate jaw. I trace her swollen red lips.

When I press one hand over her heart, the towel falls and her eyes open. I swear they've changed. Maybe my vision is different because

I'm seeing through the eyes of my beast, but I see the flames within her eyes grow. She watches me for a moment while her eyes glow brighter. What's happening to her?

Vale isn't human. She can't be. Davina said she was an Angel Killer, but I've never heard of that. *She is fire,* the beast repeats in my mind.

"You're so beautiful," I say as she watches me. "I love you."

The fire calms in her eyes, the glow dissipating a bit. "I know you do," she whispers. "I love you too." Her eyes close, and it's like she was talking in her sleep again. I don't want to let go, but I have to. I turn all the lights off but for a solitary lamp so she can see if she wakes.

"What do you mean by 'she is fire'?" I ask the beast, but he says nothing. "What's an Angel Killer?" He gives me nothing; the beast has gone silent as if he's gone to sleep.

I toss towels over the soaked bathroom floor, then leave her to get her bags from the car. I throw the new clothes and lingerie into the washing machine, rushing through the house, so I can get back to her.

When I get back, she hasn't moved. I toss the towel from around my waist onto a chair and get into the bed beside her. There's a strange moment when I don't know what to do. I've never slept beside a lover. But the beast takes over and grabs Vale around the waist, pulling her closer, not caring if he wakes her up or not.

Vale jerks awake, and I wonder if she can see me in the gloom. I look into her eyes, but there's no acknowledgment, so I tell her, "I'm here, my love."

She smiles, then presses me back into the mattress. My wings spread out below me so they don't take the entire burden of my body weight. I wish for my body, but the beast is determined not to let me change. I watch as she straddles my hips, then grabs my cock. She hisses out through clenched teeth as her hips fall and she sinks down onto me. She's so tight, like a glove, surrounding me in her precious heat.

"I thought you wanted to sleep," I whisper.

Her chest heaves with quick breaths filling her lungs, and her head tilts back like the feel of me is so much more than she could've imagined. Vale slides her hips forward, then back, stealing my breath. I reach for her, one hand on her hip, the other over her heart. She tips her head forward and our eyes meet.

She licks her lips before she speaks. "I don't want to feel empty ever again."

Tears prick my eyes as I watch my mate rock her body over mine. Her movements are gentle and unhurried. She places her hand over my heart and shudders. I lift my hand from her hip and place it between her shoulders, pulling her down onto my chest. She slides a hand under my neck and cradles my head, her fingers sliding through my hair.

"You'll never feel that way again, I promise."

She hovers above me, and our breath mingles as she rocks against me. Her whole body trembles. I feel her shaking from the inside. She feels so good. I'm in awe of her. She's all mine. I feel blessed.

I run my hand down her spine, spreading my hand wide over the base of it. With every rock of her hips, I press her forward, giving her my strength as she makes love to me so achingly slow and soft. I wonder if she can come like this, but her desire fills the air. Her wetness slicks my cock more and more, gushing out of her.

I lean in closer as she supports my head with her hand. When our lips meet, she moans into my mouth. I tighten my hold against her lower back as she rocks forward, and when I tilt my hips up into her, her breath comes hard against my lips. I lick at her mouth, tasting her lips, nipping at the bottom one with my teeth. Her heart speeds up and I feel her inner muscles clamp down on me.

The way she makes love to me is like floating on a gentle sea. Our bodies get lost in the rhythm as we become one. My tongue is inside her mouth, tangled with hers. Our breaths mingle, but still we don't pick up the pace. I lift my hips when she rocks forward, but it's all I offer her. We move like a wave for what feels like hours. I lose time while we're wrapped together so tightly.

Our skin is heated, slicked with sweat, sticking together. And still she rocks. Both of her arms are around my head now, her breasts smashed flat against my chest. As we kiss, I have one arm wrapped around her waist, while the fingers of my other hand thread through her hair, curling against her scalp.

I'm not trying to force her into another orgasm, and she isn't trying to force me to have one either. It's just easy. She's loving me, showing me how beautiful this can be. My heart fills, and I gasp against her lips when it hits me. I've never done this. I've never been so close to another. I've never felt so fulfilled by the act.

Sex has always been a rush to make my partner feel more pleasure than they've ever experienced, to feed, but this, this is a thoughtful kindness. This is the ultimate beauty when it comes to lovemaking. This is something I could never have with anyone else. My Vale offers all her love so freely.

Tears fill my eyes, and she backs away from my lips. She looks at me in the gloom, the look so desperate, like she can't possibly take it a moment more. "Do you feel it?" she asks, her voice a barely audible whisper.

I do feel it. Maybe there aren't words to explain this all-consuming love, this feeling of oneness, this ache inside that's being filled for the first time, but I know exactly what she means. I feel it so completely that I never want it to end.

"I feel it." The words stutter from my lips like I don't have the strength to speak them.

I pull her back, pressing my lips to hers. "I feel everything," I say against her mouth. "I've never felt the like or equal."

Breath is sucked into her lungs and her hips falter. She moans against my lips, tightening her hold on me. Her muscles quiver inside, and I feel the gush of her slick. Her entire body starts to tremble harder over mine. "Oliver," she cries, and I feel her clench so tight around me, it sets me off.

"Yes," I groan into her mouth, pleasure spiking inside me, but it isn't a violent storm of an orgasm. It's sweeter and it continues on and on as I spill into her.

As Vale comes, that beautiful energy inside her glows through her skin, lighting her up from the inside. She rides me through it, her body so loving and tender.

"I love you," she gasps.

We cling to each other as the orgasm goes on, unhindered. I wish I could show her the way she shows me, but I truly believe she already knows. We are one.

"I love you," I moan into her mouth, my own body trembling at the pure power and intensity of this shared moment.

I couldn't say how long it lasted, the pleasure that filled us both, but it felt like an eternity, like time had no meaning while we were locked in each other's arms. When it was over and our breaths calmed, we both smiled. We held each other close and she kept me buried inside her body. I would stay for her because, for once, I didn't want to go.

I feel the dawn creep forward as she falls asleep on top of me. Her face is buried in my neck, her lips against my skin, her palm over my heart. Even in sleep she claims me. I hold her with my wings folded around her, keeping her wrapped up in a tight cocoon.

I tighten my hold on her as tears fill my eyes, and I let them come. I don't fight it. I cry for my past and mourn the man I was before her, the one I'd never be again. I leave that man there, the one who was empty inside. The one who'd never loved. I cry for the painful memories, the things that happened and made me that apathetic creature. I finally feel able to leave it behind, to let it go.

This woman, she's my future. I no longer have time to duel with the pain in that past. I don't need it anymore. I won't cling to that trauma because all I need is her. I need her love. She's more important, and I'll never let her go.

I'd thought I could let her go at the end of summer, but now I know I can't. She's mine, and I'm hers. We belong only to each other. I don't know how to explain it to Nick, and I don't know what tomorrow will bring, but I know it's a future with her. We're intrinsically linked for all time, our souls will bond eventually.

I've known love this night. And I'll embrace her love because she's mine, always and forever.

47

CRADLED IN THE WINGS OF LOVE

VALE

I wake up in a warm cocoon, my body relaxed. For the first time since I met Oliver, I didn't dream about him. I'd been exhausted from last night's exertions, my mind finally able to rest. We got lost in each other last night, and it was perfect. I tilt my hips, stretching my spine. Oliver's still inside me, still hard. I can feel his heartbeat there, throbbing in a calm beat. His heartbeat is comforting.

I've never seen him sleep, so I lift up to study his face. Oliver's long hair is wild around his head, spilling across his forehead and onto the pillow. His eyes are closed, his thick, dark lashes fanning out and creating shadows. His cheeks are flushed at the tops, his lips sleep-swollen and pink. The angular shape of his jaw is softened by the peaceful look on his face. He looks younger in sleep, innocent, though I know he isn't.

He's back in his human skin, yet his wings are still stretched out, cradling me to him. The man, the monster, they both protected me, loved me. He held me captive in an embrace that I'd never want to escape.

Gently, I push his hair off his forehead. I slide my fingertips over one dark brow, then down the bridge of his nose and across to his high cheekbone. His cheeks and jaw, which are usually smooth, shaved close to the skin, are now dusted with stiff, dark hairs that tickle my fingertips. When I get to his lips, they tilt up in a sly smile. He's awake.

With his eyes still closed, Oliver opens his mouth and bites my finger. Of course he wakes up as beautiful as when we went to sleep. No marks on his face or drool on his chin, always perfect. I hadn't expected any different.

He lazily opens his eyes, they're half lidded and sweet.

"Sorry for waking you. You looked so pretty. I couldn't help myself."

Oliver moves so fast, flipping me onto my back under him, causing me to shriek. The movement takes him out of me. I jerk my head back and hiss.

"I want you back, please," I beg him because there's something about him being there, even when he isn't fucking me. He tethers me in this world.

I watch as his beautiful, leathery wings sink back into himself. He sighs, arching his spine when they disappear. I reach one hand around his back, searching for them with my fingers. He laughs like I'm tickling him.

"How can you do that? Where do they go?"

"Here I thought you were going to beg for my cock again, but no, you want to know about wings," he pouts.

"What did you think would happen? Those wings are impossible. I don't understand how they sink into you and disappear. You're bigger in your other form. Can you fly? What else can you do?" My eyebrows knit together and I frown as my sleep-addled brain tries so hard to make sense of what I've just seen.

"Don't you know? It's magic," he says with an obnoxious smirk that makes my heart pound.

"I don't believe you."

"That's too bad. There are things stranger than me in this world. I don't have all the answers. It's easier to say it's magic. You ask me how I change my body, but I don't know. It just is. I thought those wings were too heavy, and they sunk back inside me. Do you know how your body changes? How it ages?"

I shake my head. "No. I don't know exactly how it happens. Maybe it's hormones," I say as I shrug my shoulders, giving him my best guess. "I was only curious. I love your body. I find you fascinating. I'm sorry if I ask too many questions." I hope I haven't offended him.

"When you're not bound by mortality, it makes you seem different, otherworldly maybe. There's no need to apologize. I know this is all new to you. Ask your questions and if I have answers, I'll give them to you. "

"Will you live forever?"

"Possibly, as long as I'm not damaged beyond my capability to heal. I can heal from most damage, given enough time and enough resources. I would need to feed more if I was damaged very badly."

"Do you have any superpowers?" I ask, more excited by this question.

He tilts his head to the side. "I'm physically much stronger than a mortal man. I'm faster. I can read the thoughts of most mortals and some immortals. The older we are, the more gifts we gain. I have a favorite gift though. People really want to fuck me. I'm supernaturally hot, which makes feeding easier." Oliver smiles down at me, trying to hold in the chuckle, but he can't.

"So you'll be young and beautiful forever. Can you turn people into Lilu or a vampire?"

He doesn't seem so amused now. He shakes his head. "I'm a hybrid and unable to turn someone into something similar to myself. Only vampires can do that, Lilu cannot. The vampire must be very old and near the original line, close to Lilith. Though it's not done often, only in rare circumstances because the made vampires lose much during the transition. They lose the sun. They lose the ability to bear children. Some of them lose humanity all together. It's not a good thing necessarily to be turned."

"Are there more than vampires and Lilu?"

He nods his head. "There are witches, which are higher in number than most other beings. There are fae as well, although they are exceedingly rare. There are many different beings. Probably some I don't even know about. Nothing in this world is impossible, Vale."

"I see that now."

I grin up at the most beautiful man I've ever seen. I'm grateful he's willing to talk to me about it. "Does everyone fall madly in love with you?"

He gets in my face, our eyes meeting. "Only you." I don't believe that answer. Not even for a second. I bet everyone falls in love with him. He's so easy to love.

"I love you." He kisses my chest between my breasts. "I love you," I say again as he kisses my neck. "I love you," I moan as he runs the tip of his nose along my jaw, breathing me in.

When he's back in my face, I grab his waist with my legs and pull him closer.

"Say it again," he growls as he pushes his cock inside my body, taking his precious time to fill me.

"I love you, Ashmodai. I love you, Oliver. I love all of you. I love every single inch."

"I love you, Vale. I love all of you. You're mine." His words make me so unbelievably happy. Every time he says it, the words ring true. Oliver Byron loves me!

"Tell me you need me to fuck you."

"Oliver, sweetie, would you please fuck me. Then you need to feed me because I'm starving." I laugh as the words leave my mouth, but he pulls his hips back and thrusts so deep my laughter stops and he makes me sing.

#

Oliver dries my hair with a fluffy towel as my stomach rumbles. I smile up at him awkwardly as I sit on the counter where he put me. I laugh as he twirls the towel over my head, then leaves it there covering my eyes so I can't see. When I get it off, I throw it at his chest as he laughs.

"Do you understand how beautiful you are?" he asks as he steps forward and runs his fingers over my messy hair. I lean my head into his hands and close my eyes in pleasure.

"I didn't think anyone could see me as beautiful. It didn't matter though, not until I met you. Then I thought I was completely inadequate compared to you. It hurt, how much I needed you to say it."

"Do you believe me when I tell you that you're beautiful? I think you're the most beautiful woman I've ever seen," he says, then steps forward between my legs. He tilts my head up with his hands, desperate for me to believe him.

I blink my eyes to stop the tears from spilling over when I look up into his earnest eyes. "I believe you think so."

"It's the truth, Vale. I'll tell you so every day for the rest of our lives. I'll do anything to make you believe it because it's the truth. You're so lovely, sweetheart." He presses a gentle kiss to my lips.

"Do you believe me when I say you're the hottest piece of ass I've ever seen? It's true, you know? You're super fucking hot. So hot you make me wet when I look at you." I struggle to say the last bit as my cheeks burn.

"If you want to eat, you have to stop saying things like that. You realize when I get hungry, your pussy will do just fine, but you actually need to eat food. I can't believe you're still upright to be honest. You need to let me take better care of you," he says as he lifts me from the counter and carries me out of the bedroom and down the stairs.

"The thing is I believe the best way to take care of me is to give me, many, many orgasms." I pretend to be serious as a silly grin creeps onto my face.

"I succeeded last night. Don't you think?" he questions, one eyebrow cocked up as he waits for my reply.

"Oh, Oliver, you know how I am. I'm ravenous for you, absolutely starving. You could give me a thousand orgasms"—I lean in closer to his ear, nipping at his earlobe with my teeth—"and I'd still need more. I'll never get enough of that beautiful cock. I'll never get enough of you. See now, I'm all wet again."

"I try to be good, but you don't want me to be good, do you?" He's right. I don't want him to be good.

He sets me down in the middle of the landing, and I watch as he shakes his head. He's breathing deep, forcing my monster down, or at least I think that's what he's doing. They seem closer somehow, as if they've accepted each other a bit more. It seems like Oliver's natural response to Ash is to hold him back, pushing him down, but that part needs to stop.

I drop my towel to the floor, then jerk the towel from his hips. Oliver narrows his gaze, but I just smile sweetly, innocently up at him. I step back, making my way to the far wall where I notice a painting of a man who looks a lot like Oliver. The man looks out of a different time, refined, wearing over-the-top blue satin brocade. His hair is down, long and ebony-black, just like Oliver's, but his eyes are molten gold. There's something mischievous in those eyes. I get trapped in them.

As I watch, the painting changes, flowers blooming around the man, happily bobbing in a breeze that can't exist. The man turns toward me and smiles with a devious grin. I back away, afraid of what I'm seeing. "Oliver," I gasp, my heart speeding up as the painting beckons me with fingers that move in a come-hither motion.

"Oliver," I gasp again. I'm afraid if I look away it'll disappear.

"Vale, what is it?"

"Do ghosts live in your paintings?"

I feel Oliver move around me as I stare at it. The man inside the painting changes. His eyes get heavy as he studies my naked body. I cover my breasts with one arm and cover my pussy with the other.

Look how pretty you are, a deeply accented voice rumbles inside my head. *Move your hands, let me see you,* it hums, and when I search the painting, the man has his hand over his cock, rubbing over the stiff length while he smiles wickedly. He's a rakish beauty. The kind of man you know will ruin you in the most amazing of ways, just like Oliver.

"Ghosts?" Oliver questions. "Oddly, I don't believe any ghosts are in this house, but perhaps I'm wrong."

"Who is that man in the painting?" I ask as it changes once more and the silk-clad gentleman grows larger. *What the fuck?* Huge, feathered wings flare out and up behind his back. He morphs into a huge demon. Thick horns grow, curling back from his temples like a crown. Suddenly the sharp tips shine with the bright light that expands above his head. I squint my eyes as it almost blinds me.

Those eyes shine like melted gold, swirling with a familiar darkness I've seen inside Oliver. His body still grows across the canvas, his skin turning a deep shade of darkness. The absolute lack of light is in deep contrast to the halo that glows brightly above his head. The clothing melts like wax from a candle, and he's exposed, completely nude. A violent desire blooms and throbs between my legs as I watch. He's beautiful just like Oliver. It hurts my eyes to look at him.

You sure are pretty when you're turned on. I can see your pussy dripping from here. I like that, he moans into my brain, then suddenly I feel fingertips all over me. It's as if a thousand hands caress every inch of my skin. I feel them everywhere.

"Fuck!" I gasp. "Oliver, who is that?" I ask again, but it's like I'm in a bubble and he can't hear me. My eyes can't escape the demon in the painting.

Every inch of my skin is set alight and I moan. It feels so good. I know it'll only be seconds before he makes me come. This is bad. I feel so guilty, though I don't know how to stop it. "Oliver!" I cry out and try to look away. I can't though, I'm enthralled by him.

My body is lifted into the air, and I'm slammed up against the opposite wall. My legs are spread wide around familiar hips. Oliver enters my body all at once, slamming into me. My head slams back against the wall. With Oliver touching me, I'm able to close my eyes and finally break contact with the painting.

"Dammit, Vale! I want to be good for you, but you're so fucking wet," he growls against my ear. "I can't help myself. I can't get enough. I'll never stop wanting you."

His hips thrust faster, his cock spearing me as the demon's laughter fills my head. I try hard to ignore it. My muscles flutter over Oliver, ready to come as he bottoms out inside me over and over again.

"You feel so good, baby. Never had better," Oliver groans as he bites my neck, and I fly apart, screaming with the sudden overload of pleasure. I come so hard.

When I open my eyes the energy inside me grows, swelling with the orgasm that lingers. I force it into Oliver and feel him spilling inside me even as the demon winks at me with a knowing grin. The demon laughs and the painting morphs back to the rakishly handsome man in the colorful satin brocade. Once again, he looks like Oliver, but it can't be, it's something else. I wasn't hallucinating, was I?

"I love you," Oliver whispers into the sensitive skin of the crook of my neck. He drops me and my feet hit the floor. My legs wobble as his cum spills down my inner thighs.

"I think there's a demon in your painting. Who is it?" I ask. But this time the painting doesn't move, it's back to normal.

"Oh, it's my grandfather. That's Asmodeus, he's an archdemon in Hell," he explains.

My head slings to the side, and I look up at Oliver. "That's your . . . Asmodeus is your grandfather! He just, he just, I felt him all over me. Oliver, I . . . " I don't have the words. I'm disgusted with myself.

"He likes to play pranks, sweetheart. I'm surprised it took him this long to fuck with you." Oliver reaches out for me. "Don't be scared. He won't hurt you."

"I thought he was going to fuck me," I blurt out, and that laughter fills my head again. He's still there, somewhere.

"What?" I can tell he's angry because of the frown on his face as he searches the landing. He grabs the towel and thrusts it at my chest.

"Is your grandfather a Lilu?" I ask as the demon chuckles again.

I'm not a Lilu. Oh, Vale, I'm so much more, he says, laughter in his voice. I feel a finger press to my lower lip. I pull away from the feeling, wrapping the towel around me tightly. This being shouldn't see me like this.

"No, he isn't. I'm not sure how to explain what he is. He's the manifestation of lust. Fuck, I don't know exactly. You'd call him a demon but he's actually—" Oliver's cut off by the glass in the ornate frame cracking. "He doesn't want me to say. Come out if you want to talk to Vale. Don't scare my mate!" Oliver yells, his voice loud in the enclosed space.

"Your mate?" The voice booms in my ears. "I didn't know if I'd ever see the day, Ash. I apologize for my behavior, sweet Vale. Worry not, princess, I'll leave you in peace."

Oliver laughs. "Yeah right. Why are you here, old man?"

I search the landing, then look back at the painting. Where is he? Does Oliver normally have discussions with the disembodied voice of a demon? No wonder kids thought this house was haunted. "Where are you?" I ask the demon, my hackles raised as if he's going to burst out of the wall that holds his likeness.

"Firstly, I came to see your mother, but she isn't home. Second, I'm everywhere, all the time, all at once." Asmodeus continues to laugh like this is a funny situation. "I'll be in the kitchen with breakfast," he says, his voice not nearly as loud as before. Thank goodness because I was worried it would burst my eardrums.

I start to walk back up the stairs, but Oliver grabs my wrist before I can get more than two steps. I turn back to look at him, and he shakes his head. "I need clothes before I meet—" I say, but then suddenly there's an audible snap. Silk slides over my breasts, falling to my knees. I suck in a deep breath as it slides over my nipples like a warm caress. My eyes get wide as I look at Oliver, who's now wearing a pair of black silk pants that match my gown.

"What the fuck?" I gasp as the gown tightens at my back.

"He's a fan of the theatrics. I'm sorry," Oliver says as he reaches up to my cheek. "Don't be afraid. This is a world you'll need to get used to. Suspend your disbelief for a little while. I promise he won't harm you."

I step closer to him. "I felt him touch me. It was . . . " I try to explain as he caresses my cheek.

"Don't be ashamed of how he makes you feel. Most can't help it. He's not human, not at all," he says. "Stay with me. Don't be alone with him."

"Alright," I whisper, then he grabs my hand and I follow him down the stairs.

Oliver straightens his back before he opens the door into the kitchen. Bright light cascades into the dark stairwell, and I have to squint my eyes. He pulls me behind him as we enter the room. I didn't know what to expect but the light is giving me a headache.

"Tone it down a bit," Oliver groans, and I realize it isn't the sun. The light is coming from Asmodeus.

"Oops," he says with a jovial chuckle. "Forgive me."

The light dims, and I blink, trying to focus my eyes. Across the room, the demon stands on the opposite side of the long, stone island. He doesn't look like a demon. He looks like a young man, like he could be Oliver's brother. Now he's the beautiful young man in the painting.

There's something too perfect about the way he looks though. His features are perfectly symmetrical—fake. It has to be an illusion. I'd seen the night-skinned demon in the painting. I'd seen the horns that'd sprouted from his head like a crown. I felt his power slide across my flesh. I knew this vision was false. It irritated me, tickling at my brain, setting my body on high alert. My muscles tense as if at any moment I'd have to fight my way out of the room.

"See something you like?" he asks and my cheeks flush and my heartbeat speeds up.

"Don't tease her," Oliver says as I cling to his arm.

The demon smiles brightly at me, fangs on display. "I won't hurt her, Ash. She's just curious. Isn't that right, Vale?"

I think long and hard before I speak. As beautiful as he is, as familiar as he seems, he's hiding something from me. My body responds, overwhelmed. I don't know whether I want to run away, stay and fight, or fuck him. I hate it. My body aches in a way it's only ached for Oliver. The sensations conjured, make me feel guilty, like I'm cheating. It doesn't matter that it's due to his power. I feel guilty all the same, for the throb between my legs.

"Show me who you truly are," I demand with a scowl.

His smile vanishes. "Is that an order? I do love it so when women boss me around."

I roll my eyes. "It's only a request, but one that would make me feel better. I think this"—I wave a hand around—"is all a lie. So I request you show me the truth because you're fucking with my head."

"Please don't. She's mortal, only human," Oliver says, and I let his hand go, looking up at him with anger in my eyes. *That hurt.*

"It's fine, I'll give her a show. Will you escort her into the library, son?"

Asmodeus walks away, stomping off through the pocket doors like he's angry with me, but even that feels like a lie, like he's putting on an act. Oliver takes my hand, but I pull away, shaking my head.

"I may be human, but I'm not weak. I might not be as strong as you, but I'm not weak. I'm here, aren't I? I didn't like it when you said it that way. Mortal or not, I need to see the truth because something he's doing doesn't feel right. It's hurting my head."

"I'm sorry. I had no intention of making you feel less than. I don't think you are. I told you, he's lust. He isn't the same as mother or me. He affects people differently. He's trying to look human for you, to ease you," he says. He steps forward and wraps his arms around me. "Trust me."

"I do trust you, but something isn't right. I need to see this through," I try to explain, but he doesn't get it. This isn't my world, it's his, and he's used to it.

"I don't have all day," Asmodeus's voice booms through the house, making me wince.

I rush toward the pocket doors, letting go of Oliver's hand as I walk down the hall into the library. The demon stands under the massive dome, but he looks the same as before.

"Are you ready for this?" he asks with a familiar smirk. I don't know why that expression eases me, but it does. Maybe it's the dimples on his cheeks, just like his grandson's.

I nod my head. "Probably not, but show me anyway," I respond with plenty of snark, matching his tone.

48

ANGELS AND DEMONS

VALE

The library is lit up in golden light when I step in, but darkness pulses around the edges of my vision like smoke like a dark vignette. I watch the demon in front of me carefully. He seems to be going over something in his head, as if he's thinking of the best way to show me who he is.

"Who are you?" I ask. That makes him focus on me, and the darkness becomes absolutely complete around us. The library disappears.

He smiles at me with excitement, one eyebrow cocked up. "I am Asmodeus, a king of demons, the manifestation of lust. Have you heard of me?" The question barrels through my brain, lighting up memories I'd long tried to forget.

My father had told me about him, how he corrupted everything he touched with sin. And there were stories about how he could take your will, break you, and you wouldn't even realize he'd damned you. Then I remember my father's words, "Women are his children, his corrupters in this world."

"You can call me Oz, the great and powerful," Asmodeus says, then chuckles. It grates over my nerves as his body starts to change, melting into another form.

Light floods my vision, blinding me once more. When my vision clears, he's flashing in and out of existence, warping the world around him, like he doesn't belong on this plane, in this dimension. This world struggles to contain him as if he shouldn't exist.

I stare up at him in awe. He takes my breath away with his beauty. He's so tall he towers above me like a giant. He has dark horns that wrap around his skull, then curl up, holding a golden, pulsating halo in place. It reminds me of the solar crown of Horus.

Great black wings sling out with a snap behind his back. Unlike Oliver's, his are feathered like a bird. They're large, lush, muscular wings, powerful enough to create the winds that shape the world. He seems too large for this room, and his essence presses against me, dwarfing me, making me feel small and fragile. I feel my own mortality when I look at him.

His skin is so dark the light disappears against it. It doesn't shine with life or reflect his halo; it's devoid of all light. His hair is long and curls down his back in beautiful ebony ringlets. Some cascade over his shoulders onto his large, defined chest.

That chest is as wide as two men, and his nipples are pierced by silver barbells that shine, catching the golden light from above his head. Oliver looks so much like him in his demon form I'm surprised he doesn't have a crown of horns just like his grandfather.

My eyes travel down the length of his chest, down over his muscular abdomen. His hips have that defined V that leads my eyes down even farther, and I take in the largest cock I've ever seen. It hangs long and heavy between his legs. It's at least a foot long though he isn't aroused.

That intimidating cock is studded by the same silver barbells that are in his nipples. So many run down his length that I'm fascinated and horrified all at the same time. He could kill someone with that cock, but I knew they'd die willingly in his embrace.

"That must've hurt," I say as I feel Oliver's touch against my shoulder, pulling at me, trying to get me to turn away from the beautiful demon in front of me. However, I can't look away. This is some great truth I must figure out on my own.

Oz chuckles. "Don't be jealous, Ash. She's only curious, aren't you, pretty girl."

"Yes," I say, stepping closer to the mighty being, drawn in by his familiar power.

Oliver tries to stop me again, but I jerk away. Oz holds his massive hand out as I inch my way forward in awe. He's painfully beautiful, much like Oliver. I imagine at any moment my eyes will bleed because I shouldn't be seeing this.

"Do you want to touch it?" Oz asks, and I smile up at him, taking in those molten gold, pulsating eyes. They glow powerfully, just like the halo on his head.

"Yes," I answer as my body shivers. His power radiates across my skin. It feels electrical and alive, taking my will but also giving me something in return, something that wasn't there before. I want to succumb. I moan in pleasure as it spills through me, into me, bliss coursing through my entire being. Oz isn't evil, this power of his, it's good.

"Vale!" Oliver growls at my back. "Stop!"

I feel Amodeus's massive hands around my waist, and I'm like a doll in his hands as he lifts me higher. I hold my arms up, reaching for the halo that glows and pulsates almost like the energy that burns inside me. It feels so familiar. I recognize that power. I hunger for it. I need it.

The moment I make contact I'm filled to the brim with so much purely happy, beautiful energy that it bursts from my fingertips even as it sinks deeper, making a home inside my chest. It burrows inside me, finding a place to exist where it hadn't before.

I can't stop the pleasurable moan that escapes my lips as the tingling heat fills each molecule. I'm enchanted by all that power, in awe of it. I want to devour that halo. I want to bathe in its light for all time. It courses through me, changing me.

Asmodeus lowers me a bit, then kisses my forehead like I'm a child, his wild essence curling around me. That's when I realize he doesn't just look like Oliver, he feels like him. "You really are his grandfather. You feel like him." I had always felt that energy close to the surface, that awareness of him that I didn't have the words for, it was the halo, and somehow it was inside Oliver. I press my palm to his heart as I struggle to look into his eyes without crying.

"Your energy, it feels similar to Oliver, stronger, but it's also similar to my own when I . . . " I'm embarrassed to say what happens when I have an orgasm. I shouldn't be telling him this. It's private. But I feel the need to tell him everything, this being would understand.

The king of demons nods his head. He leans closer, next to my ear as if to tell me a secret. "I gave him part of myself before he was born. He was dying, and I couldn't bear it. You feel the part of me that's still inside him."

I turn so our eyes meet. I'm overcome by how grateful I am for him saving Oliver. I lean in and press my lips against his. I moan as pleasure fills me. Oz pulls back, and the look in his eyes is anything but innocent. He smiles, exposing his sharp fangs, making me shiver in his hold.

I feel like I'm floating on a cloud as we study each other. He seems equally as fascinated as I am. Every single touch makes my body sing. That's why my mind couldn't cope with seeing him as a human, he isn't one, and he shouldn't hide himself. The world should know this secret, they should know him. He's magnificent.

"Don't fall in love with me, Vale. I'll never be yours," he says, his warning gruff and affected. Is he as affected as I am? "I belong to another, and so do you." His words make me laugh.

I lean forward and whisper into his ear. "I feel you inside me, growing. Don't play games with me. I can't help my attraction to you because you're part of him and now you're a part of me too. Is it the halo? What will it do to me?"

Asmodeus smiles brightly. "Just a little piece of my power. I gave you what you needed to live, sweetheart. You'll see when the flames engulf you. You'll need my power, the echo of it will draw you back to this world. Don't you want to live forever? To never be separated from him. He can't lose you, Vale."

I grab his face in my hands. "You made me an immortal?"

He shakes his head. "I wish I had that kind of power. No, this changes you enough, just enough so your own power can be set free. You'll see."

"I don't have any power."

"That's not true, Vale. You must allow it to manifest inside you. That energy he brings out in you is something unique. When the time comes, don't be afraid of it."

"What am I?"

He shakes his head again. "It's not my place to tell you, but soon you'll understand."

"Should I say thank you? I don't know if it's a gift or a curse you've bestowed upon me. Everything comes out eventually. Do you know he wouldn't let himself love me at first? He tried to put space between us, but eventually he fell. Tell me, will you fall?"

"I already fell, but she's napping. Immortals can't fight their fate. We all have a purpose. He was made to love you, just as you were made to love him. Just as I have love for you and you have for me." He's strangely right. I feel a strong bond with Oz, and yeah, it feels a lot like love. Maybe things are meant to be, and loving Oz is just part of it.

"What's your purpose in this world, Oz?"

Asmodeus taps my nose as if I'm a child. His eyes glow with amusement. "My maker would not like it if I told you. There are rules. But I can tell you this, I was made to love humanity."

"You're an angel then."

He's surprised I figured him out. But it's pretty obvious he's an angel. He's got a huge halo above his fucking head, for one. But it's not the halo or the great wings at his back. Oz is not any of those things, not exactly. It's his energy, it's not evil at all, even if Oliver called him a demon. It's purely good. There's nothing bad about the light that comes from him, no darkness to mar that perfection. Is this what it's like to witness God?

"I am celestial, but mortals call me a demon. I've had a long time to make peace with that fact. You're a smart girl. I think you'll be good for Ash."

"I'll protect him with my life," I promise, and it's almost like my words come out as a threat. I'm drawing a line in the sand. If he ever tries to hurt Oliver, I'll destroy him. It's not that I believe he would, but I feel suddenly protective of what belongs to me.

His face changes into a deep frown. Sadness fills his eyes for a moment before he has a chance to school his features. "I know that, sweetheart. I've always known you would. It pleases me greatly that you found each other. He needs you, more than you know."

Oz shrinks down to near human size, but he still doesn't look like a human. He's an angel who has a duty that's much greater than all of us, and though I don't know this world, I get the feeling Oz is a good guy.

As he sets me on my feet, I realize he doesn't overwhelm me anymore, and for that I'm grateful. I feel at ease. Maybe it's because I touched his halo.

"Before I free him, I need you to promise me something, Vale."

I turn in his arms and see that Oliver is in his demon form. He pounds against the air, like it's holding him prisoner. "What is it?"

"Promise me you won't tell him what I gave you. He couldn't see what truly happened. What he saw was an illusion."

"Don't hurt him."

"I would never hurt him. You must understand, so much of what I do, what I am is to protect my family in this world. If you believe nothing else of me, believe that." Oz's eyes are earnest when I look back at him over my shoulder.

Oz seems sincere. His words feel truthful, but I was taught to fear demons and their lies. Are demons not evil? He's an angel, yet he's a king of Hell. But he is my love's family. I want to trust him, his word.

"I trust you, for now. Don't make me regret it." I don't know if I'm an idiot for offering him my trust, but I do it willingly nonetheless.

"Then promise me," he demands again.

"I promise I won't tell him you gave me part of your energy," I say. I make the promise and it's like something clicks into place inside me. Maybe I shouldn't have done it. I hope I never find out what happens if I break it.

Oz snaps his fingers and Oliver falls forward, barely catching himself. I run to him.

"Old man, don't you ever do that again," Ash growls. "She's mine."

Oz chuckles. "Don't worry, I know she belongs to you. I wouldn't take her from you."

"As if you could," I call out over my shoulder.

Oliver wraps me in his arms and pulls me against his heated skin. I wrap my arms around him and close my eyes as I press my lips into his chest. "I'm fine, he didn't hurt me."

I look over at Oz who's exiting the library. He winks at me, and it feels almost like a blessing. He wants me to be here with Oliver. He wants me to protect his grandson, and I will. Always.

"Let's eat," Oz belts out and disappears into the kitchen again.

Oliver pulls my head up to look at him. "Tell me you're okay." My beautiful monster came out to protect me.

"I'm fine. I promise. We just had a chat, that's all. Everything's okay," I explain, and he takes in a deep breath as his body returns to looking almost human.

"For a moment, I thought he'd take you away from me," Oliver says, his eyes lost.

"He could never," I tell him. "He could never hurt you that way, Oliver. He wanted to speak with me, and I needed to understand why he affected me so much."

"Do you understand it now? That he is lust."

"Yeah, he's the demon, er, angel of lust, and you share the same energy. No wonder I felt strange. It's like having two of you in the same house. I'm sorry it affected me so."

I'm attracted to Oz, which is beyond strange. It might be a hard thing to come to terms with even when I understand why.

"I told you, don't be ashamed of how he makes you feel. He can't stop it. That's who he is, his essence. He calls out to your soul. You feel the light, and you feel the darkness. I don't think you should feel guilty for it. I think most people feel some sort of attraction to him."

I grab Oliver's cheeks in my hand and force him to look into my eyes. "I was only attracted to him because he felt like you. It's you who I want. It's you who I desire. It's you who I love."

He lifts me up onto one of the tables, and when he spreads my legs, I giggle. He leans down between my thighs and swipes his long tongue over my sex like he needs to mark me. I love how possessive he is right now.

"Tell me you belong to me," he demands, and his voice is a deep, vibrating growl in his chest. He needs this.

"I belong to you, Oliver," I moan as he suckles my clit between his lips and my eyes roll up into my head.

His tongue swirls hot and slick over my sex so fast my thighs tremble around his head. I lift up and slide my fingers through his long locks, pulling him. His mouth suctions over my clit again, and that's all it takes to make me come. I cry out, trying to lower my voice, but I can't.

I rock my hips over his mouth as the orgasm slowly fades. I jerk away when he tries to suckle me again, and finally he lets me go. Oliver stands up and smiles with a deviousness I've never seen. I love it.

"Now come on, let me feed you," he says, then licks my slick from his lips, groaning as he tastes my desire on his tongue.

I don't care about food now. He's fucked me all up. Now I want him inside me. I want him thrusting deep. I want to be one with him.

49

WHO'S DESERVING OF HELL?

OLIVER

I worried for her safety when he held her. But I was more worried that he'd take her from me. When I got her back, I had to make her mine in the only way I could. I had to prove to her that I could pleasure her better than the demon who'd held her in his arms. She was mine, and I needed to mark her so Asmodeus knew who she belonged to.

I didn't like the beast I became, and it was the first taste of jealousy that did it to me. I hadn't been prepared for it, not in the least. I needed to mark my territory like an animal. And that's exactly what I did. I'd devolved into a beast for my love because no one's allowed to touch her. No one would pleasure her. No one would get a taste of her sweet cunt, only me. I owned her. I would make her scream so he heard what I offered her, what only I could give her.

When we enter the kitchen and sit at the island, my grandfather smirks at me, knowing exactly what I did, and I'm glad of it. My beast forces a low growl from my chest in warning, but Grandad just laughs.

"She's mine," I hiss at him, and he shrugs his shoulders.

"Of course she is, son. Don't ever doubt that," he says with a happy grin I haven't seen in ages.

"I can feel the testosterone in here. Chill out," Vale pipes up.

There's a plate sitting in front of each of us. Vale's is piled high with steak and eggs, chunks of fresh fruit, and toast. She looks at it with longing, her stomach rumbling, then a cup of coffee appears before her.

"That's what she really wanted."

"You know me so well for a man I only met half an hour ago," she says with a giggle as she brings the coffee up to her lips. She takes the drink and moans against the rim of the cup. "So good."

Then we hear my grandad's whispered words. They're not of this world, nothing I could translate. His hands are clasped in front of him in prayer. The only time you'll see him with his eyes closed is when he prays, although that's a rare sight for me these days. I wait till he's done, and Vale sits her cup down out of respect. She's blushing. I can tell she feels bad for drinking her coffee before he prayed.

When he finishes, he says. "Dig in everyone."

"I didn't know demons prayed, Oz. I'm sorry," she says. "I shouldn't have started without you."

Vale thinks she offended him, but I know that's not likely. Who can offend him when he's the one who enjoys offending others so much.

He shakes his head. "I'm grateful for this bounty, so I thank my maker for it," he explains with a wink. "No worries. I thanked them for you as well."

She smiles brightly. "So, when I pray, is someone listening?" she asks, and his face changes.

"Someone is always listening," he says, suddenly serious. "Now that you've met an angel who's also a demon who rules Hell, you must believe there's someone above. You believe, don't you?" I'm surprised by the hopeful look in his eyes.

My grandfather is an angel. I grew up knowing that truth, so I never doubted the heavens. How could I? Not that I grew up with any religion specifically, only that you can't deny the Light when you've seen it in an angel. But Vale, she's unsure about her beliefs. It must be hard to be faced with the divine all of a sudden.

"Do I belong in Hell?" Vale suddenly asks quietly and with a sad look in her eyes. Her words shock me. "My father—" She starts to explain, but Asmodeus holds his hand up silencing her.

"He's wrong. You're innocent. You've done nothing that would send you to Hell, not that I can see," he says, and I'm grateful for his words. "Hell is for true evil. Your soul shines too bright to have done anything like that. True sin is like a stain on your soul that can't be washed away. It spreads like a virus until it takes your Light over entirely. True sin grows for those who don't feel remorse or regret, those who feel justified in those actions that harm others."

The words make tears gather in her eyes. It breaks my heart to see her pain. All her life, she's thought she was evil. My mate was taught that she was bad, but she's not. She's so sweet. She is good. I know that without a doubt.

I look at Asmodeus. *Thank you for telling her that. Her father . . . he hurt her*, I whisper the words into his mind.

I grab Vale's hand and kiss it. When she starts eating, I look back at my grandfather.

I know some of what he did. He's the one who'll end up in Hell, Ash. Mark my words, I would take him there right now if it were his time, but you know I can't. He's damaged her greatly, son. More than she's admitted, even to you, he says into my mind, and I nod in understanding.

They're both quiet while we eat, and it's a strange thing, especially for my grandfather. Maybe he's trying to be respectful in my home, but I doubt that very much because he isn't a respectful person in general. He rarely minces words and if he does, he's hiding something. Angels can't lie, so they've gotten very good at circumventing the truth.

"Oz, my father tried to exorcise you from me, are you a part of all women?" Vale asks, and I'm truly shocked by what she says. What the fuck is wrong with her father?

Grandad shakes his head. "I'm no god, and I can't possess people. I do inspire lust, it's part of my job. Your father is very misinformed."

"His beliefs are entirely based on his hatred of women," she explains.

"That's one of the reasons he's so wrong, I love women. One day I'll tell you a story of how I became female for a little while." He turns to me, smiling. "It caused your mom to go into labor with you. We were being chased through Corinth, too hot to trot, caused a riot. Good times! I got a grandson and a vagina on the same day!"

Vale starts laughing hysterically, tears streaming from her eyes. "I wish I could've seen that."

After we finish our meal, I ask him, "Why are you here?"

"I was checking in on your mother. She was going to tell me about Gabby and the baby. Where is she? What's she been up to? I haven't heard from her in days. That's not like her," he says, but I'm sure he could find her easily enough.

"She's with my Gramps. They went out dancing last night. From what I understand, they're best friends now, day drinking and everything," Vale explains, trying to not laugh.

"My Lais has a new best friend? That doesn't sound like her at all, does it, Ash. Should I be jealous? I thought I was her best friend," he says, his eyes meeting mine.

"I asked her to take Nick out," I tell him, and Vale looks at me, studying my face.

"You did?"

I turn to her and cup her cheek. "I wanted to be alone with you."

She smiles up at me. "Okay, that makes more sense now. Still, why aren't they back, it's nearly noon?"

"They stayed the night in a hotel," I say. I feel guilty; I should have told her why they went out. "I told her not to come back till tonight."

"Well, well, well, Ash. I'm surprised. My apologies for interrupting your union. I didn't know the lengths you'd go to be alone with your lady love. Tell your mother I stopped by." He stands up and walks around me.

When he steps up to Vale, my hackles rise. I don't like how close he is to her. "It was lovely meeting you, Vale. I hope we meet again soon." He takes her hand in his and kisses her knuckles as a growl rises in my throat.

They both look at me like I'm the crazy one. Vale pulls her hand away. "It was nice meeting you, Oz. Please come visit again soon. I want you to meet my Gramps. He's gonna freak out if he meets an angel," she says, excitedly.

Asmodeus's smile turns down a bit. "I'm not supposed to interfere with mortals, Vale. I don't often meet them in this plane unless it's in the line of duty."

"He told me"—she points at me—"that immortals don't tell humans about themselves, but I'm mortal. How is it okay you can meet me, but not him?"

"I must go now. Perhaps I'll explain another time," he says, hiding something. He won't explain till he's ready. He waves at me, then shimmers a bit before he disappears. I feel his lips on my forehead.

Love you, I whisper in my head before his energy dissipates.

Love you, son. And just like that, his energy winks out.

"Did he really tell you to call him Oz?" I ask Vale.

"The great and powerful, but I think I'll stick with Oz. Anyway, Asmodeus sounds too close to Ashmodai."

"It's the same name actually, his is Greek, while mine is Hebrew. He's been called a lot of things through the ages. Lust is a constant in this world. Truthfully, I don't know if he even has a true name. But if he did, it'd be in the language of angels, and I can't speak it. Although we do call on him with a name, but I have no memory of it after I say it."

Vale's eyebrows come up curiously. She doesn't ask any more questions about him, even though I can see her wheels turning. She's seen something today few people ever do. I wonder if she's okay with all this. I can't imagine how it feels to suddenly be thrust into a world like mine.

"Did you really ask your mother to take Gramps out so we could be alone?" Vale asks with a smirk.

"Was I wrong to do that? All I wanted was a night alone with you. I didn't want anyone to hear you scream, baby," I explain as her breathing kicks up and her desire scents the air. "We have a few hours left. What do you want to do?"

"Hmm," she says as she hops down from the barstool. She steps toward me, and I spread my legs so she can slide between my thighs. With a look of lust so great it makes my breath hitch, she places her hands on my bare chest and says, "I think I want to do you."

My cock lengthens as she looks down at my tented pants. "You're not tired or sore?"

"I wouldn't care if I was, but no, I feel great. I'm ready for you," she says, and I don't know how I'll ever get the strength to stop fucking her.

"You know they'll be back soon. How are we supposed to hide this, Vale? I can't stop touching you. I'll never get enough, and they'll know. I don't know if I'm capable of hiding this anymore," I tell her. "I don't want to hide it."

"Let me take care of Gramps. Actually, would you go on a date with me?" she asks out of the blue.

My eyebrows knit together in confusion. "Yes, of course, anytime. Why?"

"Yesterday, before you came to pick me up, Gramps said to have fun on our date. I denied it, but Gramps didn't believe me. Then I asked him if he'd let me date you. He said I had to ask you first, and if you said yes, then come ask him." She's smiling so brightly.

"He's setting us up," I blurt out. "He told me you had a crush on me and I needed to let you down easy because he didn't know how to mend a teenager's broken heart."

"What are we going to do?"

"Tell him I said yes. I'll ask him myself next time I see him."

She smiles up at me. "What a brave man. Now stop thinking about him and start doing wicked things to me."

"You don't have to tell me twice," I answer and grab her up into my arms to take her back to my bedroom.

50

WHAT MAKES A WOMAN?

VALE

The sun went down while I was in the shower, sadly alone. When I return to the bedroom it's dark, barely lit by a single Tiffany-style lamp. I flick a switch near the bathroom door so I can see better, but the room is cavernous, so the lamps do little to light it. Maybe Oliver can see just as well in the darkness.

I look at the bed, but he isn't in it. In fact, it's stripped of everything but sheets. The pillows are missing and so are the blankets. Where did he go? He should have been back by now. I thought he just needed to make a phone call.

Searching for him, I open a door and find a small office. It has a rare overhead light that's bright, and there's a solitary drafting table and a few cabinets. The walls are covered with blueprints, some yellow with age, under glass. I'm drawn to the pages on his desk. His house is drawn neatly in pencil, detailed notes for trim colors off to the side. I lift the page to see the next one. It's Gramps's house with me sitting on my stool on the platform, looking into the telescope, face mostly hidden by my long hair.

I lift the next page, and the breath leaves my lungs. It's me. I'm standing on the platform at the top of the steps, my hand held up, hair wet, the rain coming down. It's from his perspective, his hand on the window, his thumb covering a part of my hand as if we were touching. My cheeks get hot when I see how my clothes are clinging to me, showing my nipples and the outline of the lips of my sex. It's so detailed it shocks me.

He's captured a look in this sketch, a sadness in my eyes that I feel deep in my chest. I was heartbroken, and he saw it, he knew it. Oliver sees everything I try to hide. I drop the pages, not wanting to get caught up in those feelings. I turn the light out and speed back into the sitting room.

Folded neatly, and spread across the sofa, I notice three sets of lingerie. I hadn't put any of it on last night. A note sits on top of a creamy lace piece: *Choose and meet me at the top of the tower.*

That's all it says, so I grab the satin nightgown the color of blood and its matching thong. It's not the sexiest thing he bought me; in fact, it's probably the most modest. I chose it because I'd liked the color and the shiny gold embroidery over each breast. It'll probably not last long enough for it to matter—he'd promised to tear them all off anyway.

I run my hand over the satin, liking the way the fabric slips over my skin. When I finish dressing, I step into Oliver's closet to see my reflection, questioning my choice.

I look so different right now. My normally pale skin is flushed—Oliver has that effect on me—and my hair shines against the scarlet lingerie. I swear it shines more than it did yesterday. Even the color has changed. I used to say it was just red, but now there are highlights of gold and lowlights of auburn. There's copper in the strands that seem so unfamiliar. And not even a bit of frizz sits at my temples the way it normally did.

I stand there trying to figure out why I look so different. Does losing your virginity actually change how you look? Even the way I stand seems odd, as if I'm taller, or my spine is straighter. I don't know exactly what it is. I lean closer to the mirror, looking at my eyes. The whites are unmarked by blood vessels, and they're so bright my normally watery-blue eyes look more like aquamarine gemstones. Everything about me seems in higher contrast, more colorful. Is this what I normally look like?

My lips are darker red, closer to the scarlet of my lingerie, but I'm not wearing lipstick, and my eyelashes look longer and thicker, even after I washed the mascara away. I shake my head and step back from the mirror.

I focus instead on what I'm wearing, making sure it looks alright. It lifts my breasts up high, so they look like round globes right below my collar bone. The skirt flairs out around my hips, giving me an hourglass shape that I like. I look pretty and feminine.

I look like a woman. Is that the difference I see in the mirror? Had I become a woman overnight?

I hope he'll like what I'm wearing. I hope he isn't disappointed in my choice. I want him to think I'm beautiful. He says it, but I don't normally feel it. I don't think I've ever felt pretty until this moment. I smile up at myself, then wink.

I'm having to hold back tears as I see myself in his full-length mirror. Did Oliver do this? Did he somehow make me believe? We don't have a lifetime of him assuring me that I'm beautiful, so maybe I'm finally ready to see it.

I leave the closet and search for the door to the tower. I find it on the eastern wall, in the center of some dark wood paneling. I hadn't noticed it last night. How different it looked from the rest of this room? It seems somehow out of time, out of place. I admire the beautiful masonry, where a tall, arched door sits in the center between carved columns. It looks like something out of an old, gothic cathedral.

This house is so strange. The door looks older than it should. It's made of dark wood that gleams in the lamp light as if it's been treated with penetrating oils to bring out the shine. A carving takes up most of the door. It's of the world tree, Yggdrasil from Norse mythology. The design tops out right below the gothic arch, its roots ending about six inches from the base.

I don't think I've ever seen a door like it. It looks like it's made from a single piece of wood instead of multiple pieces joined together. You can see the growth rings that would have been inside the tree spreading out from the center in ever expanding circles. The effect of the rings on the carving makes it look like the tree is glowing with life.

I get lost for a moment studying the light in the rings and the shadows of each dark, carved groove. The door is tall and intimidating, like an entrance into another world. I wonder if Odin himself awaits beyond it. It's stunning in its complexity, a work of art. I can't imagine how long it'd take to make something like that.

Where does he find this stuff?

When I grab the black iron knob that's shaped like knotted roots from the tree, it's warm, like Oliver had just been there and stepped through the portal before me. The warmth surprises me, and I jerk back quickly. I look at Yggdrasil's canopy and swear it sways as if the limbs dance in a breeze.

I'm creeped out by the door. It's just like seeing Oz move in the painting. Something strange is happening in this house. Oliver had said it was spelled by a coven, so maybe the magic affects the inside as well. I hope Oz isn't back to fuck with my head.

I take a deep breath, trying to settle my nerves, then reach for the knob again. I turn it, trying not to focus on the carved image. I linger at the threshold, heart pounding away. There's a round staircase leading up, disappearing behind a huge stone column in the center of the round room.

The wide, cylindrical tower is lit by old-fashioned hurricane lanterns sat in built-in nooks along the stone walls. Flames dance behind delicate, tulip-shaped glass shades, causing shadows to sway and linger in the stairwell. It's possible Oliver hadn't connected the electricity to the tower.

I search for Oliver in those writhing shadows. Is he hiding in here, ready to jump out and scare me? I hope not because I'm on edge already. The anxiety ramps up inside me. Should I call into the shadows to make sure he isn't there? Something is. I can feel it, a dark energy that sways unnaturally.

"I mean you no harm," I whisper before stepping over the stone threshold.

I force myself to go up the stairs as my scalp tingles with apprehension. The tower is so creepy. I get the feeling I'm being watched from the very walls that surround me. The stone itself feels alive with energy. I'm curious if those kids were right, that a ghost lives in this house.

Every step I take echoes. It's surprisingly loud for bare feet as the sound seems to travel up and back down as I climb. At some point it sounds like someone's stalking me in the dark.

I speed up the stairs unable to stay in the shadows. I have to get out. I have to escape. My heart races with fear even though my brain tries to rationalize that it's the sound bouncing around the circular staircase. I never liked being in enclosed spaces, much less creepy stone towers without windows.

When I get to the top of the stairs, I open the door to the outside, fleeing into the night air. The humidity hits me right in the face like a slap. I shut the door quickly, then breathe deeply, the fear dissipating just as quickly as it came.

There's a wall that wraps around the top of the tower blocking my view of the pine forest across the street. I could see over it if I was on my tiptoes, but I decide not to chance it. The adrenaline is slowly dissipating, but my legs are still trembling.

"Oliver, where are you?"

He slides behind me, one hand coming up to cover my eyes. "There you are," he says against my neck, his lips hot as I lean back against him. His presence makes any lingering fear disappear.

"Not fast enough for you?" I ask, and he slides his teeth over the sensitive skin of my neck, teasing me. It feels so good. I ache for his bite. I tremble at the thought of it. He slides one hand to my waist. His fingers glide across the slippery satin that clings to my curves.

"Any time away from you is too long. This is beautiful, by the way. You look absolutely edible."

"I thought it'd be too modest, that it might cover too much for your taste."

"I don't mind as long as you let me take it off you." He nips at my earlobe with his teeth, making tingles dance up my spine.

I lean my head back against his chest. "You can undress me anytime you want. You know that, I'll always be ready for you." The evidence is currently soaking through my panties.

His lips tremble against my skin as he breathes in my scent. "You smell so good. It's hard to keep my hands off you. You don't understand how hard it's been." He squeezes me closer, pulling my ass back against his hard cock.

"Is that why you breathe me in so often? What do you smell?" I've seen the way it affects him when he takes my scent in. I've always wondered why he does it.

While I wait for an answer, I focus on the night song blanketing us. It's louder up here. I hear the crickets sing. Their quick and bright tempo the current upon which the cicadas drop their drawn-out, echoing beat. Then the pine woods tree frogs start up with their short and clipped cadence, singing a familiar song. Their music flows, always in tune.

If I was able to see over the stone wall, there would be a light show in the pine forest to go along with the orchestra. The lightening bugs come out to find their own mates just like the insects who sing night songs. They call to one another in the darkness. Does my scent call to him?

The sound, the smell of pine in air, the summer heat wrapping around me is my idea of peace. I love it here, always have. It's a magical place. The thought of it comforts me when I'm away. But now it's Oliver who feels like peace and love. It's his arm around my waist, his expanding chest as he breathes in behind me. I'll never be able to leave him.

"You always smell like flowers, like late-spring gardenias and sea salt spray from churned up waves after a storm," he whispers into my ear, snapping me out of my reverie. "But when you feel desire, your body temperature changes, your skin heats up, flushing with blood. Your scent changes from a spring storm to warm, honeyed fall. The heat makes you smell sweet like warm caramel, ripe apples, and cinnamon, with just a touch of smokey midnight bonfires. I can taste your desire on my tongue, in the air. I can feel your temperature spike. I can hear your heart race, and each quick pump makes your scent stronger, deeper.

"I don't have to touch you to feel your essence, it's like an electrical current teasing me closer, flowing over my skin. I felt your current, could smell your scent, before I saw you the night we met. From the moment I stepped out of the car, my senses gathered you to me, taunting me, before I ever saw your face."

I pull his hand from my eyes, then turn in his embrace. "How do you sense all those things and have it not be completely over-whelming?"

Oliver eyes swirl, the green and the darkness. "It is overwhelming, Vale. My senses are heightened because of what I am. You feel like a freight train to the gut at times." The words are passionate and sharp, his jaw tensing.

"Does it hurt being around me?" I whisper as I stare into his eyes, searching for the truth.

He grabs the side of my neck, his thumb under my jaw, over my pulse, and his breathing ratchets up as he leans closer. "I hurt from the moment I felt you in the world till the moment I was inside you. He knew you were our mate and he wanted you. He'd never wanted anyone like that. I was fighting a battle, attacked from inside and out. A beast fighting to escape. One who I thought would kill you immedi-ately if he came out. I could feel your desire for me. I wanted you, but I didn't think it was safe. I was afraid. But I always felt that connection to you, even if I didn't understand it at first. You have no idea how I've hungered for you." His voice is low, his head tilted, as he whispers against my lips.

"I've never wanted someone like this. I crave you with an unquenchable thirst. Every time I denied you, I denied myself, denied my very nature. I ached to savor your blood and that in and of itself was a rare thing. My body was on fire, burning for you. Had you not miraculously fed me every time we touched, I think I may have gone insane, waiting, starving for a single taste. I felt crazed because I wanted you so much." His words make my chest ache.

"I didn't mean to hurt you, Oliver. I wanted to be with you. I felt crazy too. Every day I needed you more. Every touch just made it worse. I'm so afraid that being with you hasn't sated this desire at all. I need more. I ache for more. It's a hunger like no other. It hurts so much."

He grabs my face in his hands and bends forward, kissing me sweetly. His eyes are so full of understanding. Oliver gets me.

"I watched you like a stalker. I studied you from the shadows while you studied the stars. I heard you curse me every time I had a new visitor. I watched you dance through the house, singing at the top of your lungs the morning after I kissed you for the first time. I heard your misery and your happiness," he explains, and my cheeks heat with embarrassment.

"I hated seeing you with anyone else. I wanted you so much I cursed you and your visitors for it. I wished one, or both of you, would fall and get impaled on the thorns of your rose bushes. I knew karma would get me for wishing you harm. I may always be afraid of them," I say. He laughs, and it lights up his face. He is ethereal, beautiful. Such beauty shouldn't exist.

"I'll protect you."

"What's more embarrassing is that you saw me dance after we kissed. Had I known you were watching, I never would have." I don't think I've ever felt so embarrassed in my life.

"You were wearing a pair of tiny shorts and that big T-shirt with a fluffy gray kitten on it. Every time you'd spin, it would flow out around you, and I'd get a glimpse of those tiny shorts. I wanted to rip them off with my teeth," he growls, pulling me closer and nuzzling into my neck.

"You like my shorts, don't you?" I smile up at the sky as I lean to the left so he can get closer to my throat. It's instinctual, offering myself to him with that single move.

"In every instance I've seen you wear them, I've only wanted to tear them off you. I watched you frustrated and trying to work out in those damn shorts. I thought about all the ways I'd punish you for teasing me. I knew that's what you were doing, baby," he says, groaning the words against my neck, then nipping the sensitive skin with his teeth. "I think you like teasing me, Vale, but I wouldn't tease a monster if I were you. Sometimes we bite." I suck in a shaky breath.

"That's not a good enough threat, Oliver. I love it when you bite me. You're basically giving me permission to tease you till you can't handle it anymore." He sees my wicked smile and grunts as his cock grows against my hip.

When I reach down, I'm surprised he's covered. I see those exercise pants he wears to fuck with my head. "Who's the tease now?" I ask. "You wear these to tease me, don't you. Admit it!" I laugh.

"I like the way you stare at my dick when I wear them. So yeah, I guess you're right," he admits with a devious smirk. "I liked it when you watched me. I liked it more when you noticed I caught you. You'd looked so guilty when I caught you, but sweetheart, guilty you are not. I loved your eyes on me. I wanted you to see how hard I got for you. Did you know it was for you?"

I bite my bottom lip as I look at him. "I never knew that. I hoped it was, but I didn't know." I'd lucked out that he's my mate. I can't believe how wonderfully wicked he is.

I run my fingertips over his bare chest, then press one hand over his dragon tattoo. I feel his slow, methodical heartbeat against my palm. My hand sinks lower, and I brush my fingertips against his tight abs. I trace the sexy *V* of his hips, then step back to see exactly how hard he is in those pants. I see his bulge, but this is something else. It looks so big. I stare unabashedly at him and feel strong. He's mine.

"If you don't stop staring at my cock, I won't be able to show you your birthday present," he says as he pulls me close and covers my eyes again.

"I don't want anything else, only you," I whisper.

"We'll see about that. Keep your eyes closed and let me lead you. Remember, I'm already yours, Vale." He's the best gift of all, nothing compares.

51

DANCE UNDER THE STARS LIKE NO ONE'S WATCHING

VALE

The tower isn't a large space. It looks like it was built as a soldier's lookout, which is weird because it doesn't have windows. I'm surprised when he tells me to step down. I squeeze his hands tightly as I walk down a set of steps. Five in all. Then Oliver tells me to open my eyes.

The first thing I see are thick cream candles scattered around, their flames protected by deep glass shades. There's another burgundy bedspread laid out, creating a pallet on the floor. All the pillows that were missing from his bed are spread around it. It's romantic and sweet. It looks like he planned this. When did he have the time to think about it? I smile brightly as I look up at the stars.

Twinkling stars seem to pierce the heavens, lit up like diamond dust. The full moon is a cool white light in the distance. It's so big and bright with a rare lunar halo.

There's a gentle breeze that makes the candle flames flicker and dance, casting shadows across the rooftop. Music plays softly. Oliver tightens his hold on my right hand, pulling me around to face him. I almost fall into him when I recognize the song, "Wonderful Tonight."

"Dance with me under the stars, like no one's watching," he says, and the way he looks at me, as if with all the love that exists in the world, makes my heart speed up.

Oliver steps closer and places his left hand at the base of my spine. My hips tilt back to meet his touch. With his right hand, he takes my left and lifts it up to his lips. He presses a kiss to my knuckles, then he takes one step to the left.

I've never slow danced. I don't know what I'm doing, yet my body moves instinctively with his. It feels like a dream. I feel buoyant, floating along the current of his very existence. If this has all been a dream, I don't want to wake up. I want to feel this way forever.

I swallow hard while I look up into his beautiful green eyes. As he leads us in a circle, I try so hard not to cry. "I've never danced with a man. I don't know what I'm doing."

Oliver smiles, and it's that soft, content smile I rarely see. He looks so happy right now. "You told me you wanted to dance under the stars like no one was watching, but I've been watching, Vale. I've always seen you. I thought, perhaps, you'd dance with me."

The tears do come then. I can't help it. I remembered yelling those words at him. I'd been too afraid to tell him what I wanted, that I wanted him. I'd been so mad that night. I didn't want a chaperone. I'd wanted to be alone so I could figure out how I felt about him. I had wanted him so much. He'd been right next door, yet he'd felt a million miles away, completely unattainable.

"I said that because I couldn't admit"—I take a deep breath—"that I wanted you. You were all I wanted, all I needed, but I didn't know how to say it. I was afraid you'd run away," I confess.

"I knew that, sweetheart. You didn't have to say it. I felt it too. I can't guarantee I wouldn't have run away. I was afraid of what I felt for you. I would have come back to you though. I'll always come back to you, Vale. I promise," he says, and I'm grateful for that promise. I don't want him to run away ever, but as long as I know he'll be back, I'll be able to deal with it.

I wrap one arm around his neck. "Why are you so perfect?" I ask, fighting back more tears.

His smile gets wider. "I'm not perfect, Vale. Far from it."

I shake my head in adamant denial. "You are," I whisper, and the tears fall hot against my cheeks. "I love you so much sometimes it feels like my heart genuinely hurts. It's swollen with all the love I have for you. I didn't know it could feel this way."

He wipes the tears from my cheeks as the song ends. "I love you, Vale. I will love you when the world ends and the dust of our soul floats free out into the universe amongst the stars you love so much."

I drag him down to my level and steal his breath deep into my lungs, then brush my thumb across the top of his high cheekbone. The song repeats, and my smile gets bigger. This is heaven. I wasn't in Hell after all.

We're silent as we watch each other, still dancing. I can feel the magic all around us. I feel his love and isn't that magical enough? I have a soulmate and, by some miracle, we found each other in this life. I love him so much. I hope I get to spend the rest of my life with him.

I stand on my tiptoes and kiss him with every bit of love in my heart. That energy swirling inside me grows so bright I can see it even through my closed eyes.

"Vale, look."

I step back. "What?" I ask. His eyes are half closed.

"It's you," he says in awe, smiling sweetly. "You're glowing."

I lift my hand up and stare at my palm. The energy is flowing over my skin, like gentle flames. I smile as it twirls into the air above my palm, dancing happily. I've seen the flames of my energy before, but I didn't realize he hadn't until this moment.

"What are you, sweetheart?"

When I look up at his face, I see the reflection of my light in his eyes. He's looking at me like I'm the most beautiful woman in the world.

"Can you touch me?" I ask, holding my left hand out to him.

I hold my breath as he lifts his hand over mine. The flames soften their glow, the tendrils like wisps of smoke. He gasps as they wrap around his fingertips and slide over his skin. They look like glowing ribbons rippling over his hand.

"They like you," I say with a smile.

His smile is huge when he looks up from his left hand. "It's a part of you, Vale. That's why."

"This is what I give you when we're together. I didn't see them myself at first. I only felt them, but they've gotten stronger whenever we touched. They got so strong I could see it when I gave them to you."

"I feel them, but this is the first time I'm truly seeing them. They're beautiful, just like you."

Our hands lock, and I notch my fingers through his as the heat grows. The glow becomes brighter, and one tendril connects us, wrapping around our hands, pressing them closer together. It tightens around our fingers and wrists, the ribbon knotting. Suddenly it burns me and I wince. It must burn him as well because he hisses but doesn't let go. The tendrils flash and a small puff of smoke floats up and dissipates in the breeze.

His breath becomes shallow and quick as he stares at our joined hands with wide eyes. I try to pull away, but he doesn't let me. "Oliver, are you okay?" I ask, worried.

His eyes fill with darkness. "Vale," he gasps. "Don't move."

"Why? Are you alright? Am I hurting you?"

"Let it finish," he says, and he closes his eyes. His mouth opens as if he's freeing a silent moan.

I look at our joined hands, and that's when I see it. The marks. I've burned him. I've hurt him. My eyes go wide with fear. I should have known because he never closes his eyes like that. He sees everything and right now, he can't.

"Let me go," I cry out. "I'm hurting you, let me go!"

I jerk at my hand, but he holds it tighter. "No," he growls and the sounds slithers down my spine, making me shiver. He falls to his knees. I scream, so scared of what's happening.

"No! No! No!" I cry, tears spilling from my eyes. "Please let me go!"

Why? Why won't he let me go?

I fall to my knees in front of him, still tugging at my hand, trying to break us apart. The flames over my skin glow brighter. I shake my head as he bows his head, taking great gulps of air.

"Don't hurt him! Please! Please stop!"

Steam rises from his skin as it heats up. The skin across his chest and face turns a mottled red as the air around us sizzles. I'm afraid at any moment he's going to go up in flames, and I'll lose him forever. I don't want to lose him.

He's silent but for those quick breaths. His lips tremble around his open mouth. Then suddenly his jaws snap shut. Once again, he moans and it sounds so painful, it hurts my soul. *Please let him be okay.*

"Oliver, I love you. Please let me go. I'll never be able to forgive myself if I hurt you."

He doesn't let go. In fact, he reaches out and pulls me forward, wrapping his other arm around me tightly. "I'll never let you go," he groans, each word filled with pain.

"Then drink from me, maybe it'll heal you," I tell him. "Maybe it'll heal you like you healed me."

"I'm not hurt," he growls, finally opening his eyes. "Your magic is binding us, marking me. It's just—" He has to take a deep breath. "It's very strong, give me a minute."

I can't wait. I lift his head and kiss him. If I can nick my lips with his fangs, he'll be able to heal. I know it's hurting him. I can feel it deep in my gut. I close my eyes, and he thrusts his tongue into my mouth. I do the same, slicing my tongue against his fang. The moment blood flows, he moans into my mouth.

I'm lifted into the air, and we fall back onto the pallet made of blankets and pillows. Oliver presses me down into the blankets, but all he does is hold his weight against me, essentially stopping most of my movements.

I stare down at the top of his head, clutching his hand in mine as he shakes and groans. The music filters into my consciousness. I watch the candle flames dance and sputter. My heart calms a bit. I curl the fingers of my free hand in his hair, petting him, trying to calm the pain I've caused. Between sniffles, I hum with the music.

My flames calm, dimming, and eventually sinking back inside me.

He's still pressed against me, but his breaths are calming, his hand still holding mine. Finally, he lifts his head to look at me. He reaches up with his right hand and caresses my cheek.

"Vale, don't be scared. I'm alright. I promise."

"What happened?" I lean into his hand, comforted by his touch.

His left hand separates from mine. When he holds it up between us, there are dark, curled lines, woven into a band, almost like a tattoo, wrapping around his finger. "You put a ring on it," he says simply, and it takes me a moment to understand what he means.

"I did that," I gasp. "I hurt you. I burned you."

I start shaking and the tears keep coming as I stare, horrified, at the burn on his finger. I grab his hand gently, pulling it closer. I kiss it. When I press my lips to it I realize it's smooth skin, not burned at all. I pull back and turn his hand over. The black woven band wraps all the way around his finger. My brows knit together in confusion. I turn his hand back around. It really does look like a ring.

Oliver grabs my hand and lifts it to cover his. "Vale, look."

There's a ring around my finger as well. "Oh, shit." It's woven like knots, intertwining.

"See, I thought you'd be happier when you married me," he says, then chuckles like this is funny.

I turn my hand over, then back. It's still there. "What are you talking about? I don't understand."

I look up at Oliver, and I'm taken aback by his wide grin. "Oh, sweetheart, it's your magic. It bound us. It left a mark you understand, that you recognize, wedding rings."

"But I didn't," I whisper, shaking my head. "I didn't do that."

Oliver rolls over beside me, pulling me against him. "What were you thinking when you started glowing?"

It takes me a moment to remember. "I was grateful I found my soulmate. I was thinking about your love and how much I love you. I was thinking about how I wanted to spend . . . " I couldn't say it.

"Tell me, sweetheart," he whispers into my hair.

I cover my face with my hands, hiding, unable to look at him.

"How I want to spend the rest of my life with you. I'm so sorry. I didn't know I could do that to you."

"You think I'm mad?"

I shake my head. "I don't know what to think. I was only human and now it feels like I'm more. I didn't have any kind of magic before I met you. Much less some way to permanently mark you without your consent. I didn't mean to. I wouldn't blame you if you were mad at me."

"Funny enough, last night I imagined how you'd burn me. I wanted you to mark my skin so the whole world knew I belonged to you. Trust me when I say, I wanted it, this. I want the world to know I'm yours. If I didn't want to be bound to you, I could have fought it, but I didn't want to. Tell me you understand that I chose you," he explains, and my heart flutters like butterflies dancing around in my chest.

"I understand what you're saying, but I don't understand how I did it. I don't know what I am." As the words leave my lips, I know that's not true. His grandfather did something to me, but I'd promised I wouldn't tell Oliver. Maybe that's what caused this.

"You're exactly who you're supposed to be, Vale. You're my mate, my fate, and hopefully my wife when you're ready to be of course. I think you should know that a mate is more than a marriage license. When a bond is accepted, that's it, two halves of the same soul become one. I accepted your bond, your claim on me. You're it for me. I'm yours. But I understand that this is happening very fast. If it's too much, I get it."

"Do you really want to marry me?" I whisper, hiding my face in his chest.

"In my mind, I'm already yours. We don't need any kind of ceremony, but if you wanted to be married in front of your family, if you wanted Nick to walk you down the aisle, then I would be at the altar waiting for you. I'd be proud to be your husband, Vale. I'm proud to be your mate."

I roll onto my back and stare up at the sky. I take a deep breath. "Oliver, I'm eighteen."

"Trust me, I'm well aware," he says deadpan, like this is something he's thought about a lot. "I'm old enough to have fathered you over a hundred times. I admit it, it was difficult to overcome how old you are."

I hadn't thought about how he'd feel about my age because I only learned how old he was last night. I feel guilty for not having tried to place myself in his shoes. I should have asked him how he felt about it.

Oliver places his hand on my abdomen, the one with my ring on his finger. I did that. I claimed him. I married him, I think. I didn't know I was doing it, but it matters to him.

"I told Gramps I wouldn't get married young, like my mother. I told him I wouldn't give everything up to be a wife," I explain. "My mother was twenty when she married my father. I'm eighteen. He's going to murder us both."

Oliver chuckles. "Yeah, I'm not sure how we're going to explain this." He holds out his hand above me. He shows me his ring again and the smile that spreads across his face is genuine.

"Oh, God, I'm in so much trouble. How on earth am I going to explain that I fucked Silver Spring's newest, most eligible bachelor, and he liked it so much he let me force him into marriage?" I laugh as soon as the words leave my mouth.

Oliver jerks me closer. "Is that what happened?" he growls, and my core clenches.

"No, of course not. I hypnotized you. That's the only explanation," I say, then chuckle.

He sits up and slides his palms between my legs, pulling them apart, then sneaks between them. "I don't know, Vale. I don't believe the hypnosis angle."

I shrug my shoulders. "Well, that's what people are going to say. That's the only way people are going to believe I managed to snag a man like you. Or worse, they'll say you knocked me up."

One of Oliver's eyebrows quirk up. "I'm very familiar with the ins and outs of getting a female pregnant," he says with a smirk. "I want to learn how you'd hypnotize me though. You have to show me, or I'll never believe it."

I shake my head, lifting one foot and pressing it against his shoulder to push him back. He smirks at me, of course, and I spread my legs, bending the other at the knee, one foot flat on the floor. I bite my bottom lip when I notice how stiff his cock gets. "You're very sexy," I tell him, making him wait.

He starts to speak, but I wave my finger around to silence him. "Kiss my ankle," I demand, and it makes those cute dimples show up.

He grabs my calf and turns his head. He presses a soft kiss against the inside of my ankle, then he turns back to look at me, waiting for my next command. This could be so much fun. "Do you want to taste my skin, Oliver?"

"Yes," he says, the word spoken so softly I barely hear him.

"Trail your tongue up the inside of my leg till you get to my thigh. Be a good boy, and I might let you taste something else." The fact is he could break this hold at any moment and fuck me, and I wouldn't complain. I'd win either way.

Oliver grips my calf harder and leans in, breathing me in. His tongue peeks out and licks right above my ankle. I take in a deep breath as he gets farther north. His warm, wet tongue makes my leg shake.

"Now wait right there. I want to feel your teeth too. Focus the soft and the sharp. Tongue and teeth."

Oliver closes his eyes for a moment, his jaw going tense, then he opens his mouth wide and I see the edge of his fangs. He scrapes them against my skin, the movement driving me wild. I lose it. "Oh, God," I moan. "That feels so good. Why do I like that so much?"

He lifts his eyes up to meet mine as he licks over one sharp canine. My core spasms with the visual. Damn. I might scream. Why did I start this? I want him. I'm already wet for him.

He continues up until his teeth threaten on the inside of my thigh, right above my knee. "Did you know I can make you come from sinking my teeth into your flesh, right here?" he says, his voice a gravelly tease that makes my core clench again.

I don't hesitate. "Do it," I whisper.

That smirk is back, that devilish look making my panties wet. His long hair has fallen over his shoulders, teasing my skin where it hits.

My body is on edge, already scaled the wall and just waiting to plunge over the edge with one of these mind-altering orgasms that Oliver is so good at giving. I hold my breath for a moment just to get some control.

"Breathe through it," he growls, just like the monster did last night.

There's a moment when the music fades and the pounding throb between my thighs stops. It's like most of my senses are dulled with inactivity, like time stands still. Only when he leans in and sinks his teeth into my inner thigh does time suddenly speed back up. The pain is sharp, his teeth sinking deeper into my flesh than what I'm used to. It's so intense, it sears my flesh and I sit up screaming. I grab the back of his head, trying to pull him away, but he doesn't let me move him.

I heave air into my lungs, thankful when he pulls those sharp fangs out. His hot breath hits the wound, and I shiver at the feeling. Then he wrecks me. As Oliver takes the first pull of my blood, his eyes look up into mine. His mouth is suckling rhythmically, and I feel it everywhere. My core spasms involuntarily, and I explode.

I slam my hand down between his shoulder blades, digging my nails into his back. I try to cling to him so I don't float away, and he hisses against my thigh. I cry out as I come undone. I'm so dizzy with pleasure I worry I'm going to faint. One of my hands has slid into his hair, cradling his head. My other hand claws at his skin between his shoulders, holding on tight. I whimper as the muscles in my core spasm and squeeze tight.

He suctions down on the wound hard. *I love you,* I hear him gasp the words, but he isn't speaking. His words are inside me, filling up my pleasure-addled mind. *Oh, God, let me keep her forever.* His thoughts make me tighten my hold on him as I shiver with each draw of his lips. *Please, I'll do better*, he continues, desperate, as if he's praying. *Please, I can't lose her.*

"You won't lose me." I say and sit up straighter. His inner voice sounds so worried, so scared. He looks up at me, his green eyes wide with confusion. Then his mouth loses its suction, and my thigh twitches as I try to pull away.

"I heard you," I explain. "Sometimes . . . I hear you. It's never been that loud before."

Oliver sits up, all thoughts of pleasure forgotten as he licks a drop of blood from his lower lip. "What do you mean?"

"You tell me. I don't know what I'm hearing. It sounds like you're talking to me, but your mouth doesn't move. I don't hear it all the time. Were you praying? I heard you say, 'Oh God, let me keep her forever.'"

I'm watching his lips when his voice sounds in my head again, *What's happening to you?*

I shake my head. "I don't know. Please help me figure it out."

One eyebrow lifts in question. "Can you hear my thoughts? I hope not," I say, then laugh. "That'd be really embarrassing."

Oliver chuckles. "No, not usually. You're very hard to read. I heard you once, in the restaurant. You'd just asked me if I loved you. I thought you were praying when you said, 'Please, let Oliver love me.' I hope you know I wanted to tell you then."

Oliver looks back to the bite on my thigh that's pooling with blood. He lifts my knee and the blood drips in a slow line, making its way toward my panties.

"Are we still working on hypnosis?" I ask.

"That depends. Can I rip your clothes off?"

I drag the satin nightgown over my head and toss it behind him. "I like that too much for you to tear it, but you can tear my panties off."

My core clenches when he smirks. He pushes at my right thigh, spreading my legs farther apart. I sit back on my elbows as he longingly eyes that line of blood. Now it's only an inch from my panties. He bites his lip before he turns to my panties and his smirk gets bigger, those dimples showing when he sees how wet they are.

He grabs the gusset of my panties in a fist, then jerks at them once, and I almost lose my position. "So wet already, soaking these tiny panties." He doesn't sound like Oliver right now, he sounds like my monster with that reverberating growl.

"Yeah, I am," I admit as he squeezes his hand tighter around the gusset.

Oliver looks at my thigh, still waiting, then he glances back at my core. He slides his hand up and down the satin, his knuckles brushing softly against my slit, teasing my flesh.

I moan at the touch. "Do it, Oliver. Rip them off me. I know you want to."

"I want to do a lot of things, Vale," he says without looking at me, still studying the blood that's dripping down my thigh.

His knuckles slide over my slit again. It's not words this time, it's a vision of me screaming with his head between my legs, both his hands up on my breasts as if he's worshiping me on his knees. I gasp when I see it. "I want it," I cry, then the fabric rips and it's like an alarm going off.

That little bead of blood slides down to the crease separating my core and my thigh. The growl he releases is intimidating. He licks at the wound, healing the skin, then he follows that line of blood with his tongue. Two of his long fingers slide into me.

"So tight for me," he says as he licks the last bit of blood. "You grip me so well."

Oliver curls his fingers inside, making my eyes go wide and my hips lift. I know what he's going to do. I remember how intense it was. I remember how I screamed in the car as we watched the sun come up. "Oh, my God!" I scream. "Not again, baby. Please."

He chuckles as he pulls his fingers out. My mouth falls open as he takes my pleasure away. I take a deep breath, and he looks into my eyes. "Afraid of what I'll do with these fingers?" he asks, and now I know I'm losing him. I had control, but I don't anymore. He took it all. Hypnosis, my ass!

Oliver brings those fingers up to his lips and sucks them deep into his mouth with a groan that damn near makes me come again. His eyes close as he savors the taste of me. When he's done, he slides them right back in, curling them up inside me. He keeps them curled as he drags them back out. I clench my inner muscles. I feel my wetness slide out, and he thrusts his fingers back inside.

My head falls back. I'm lost when he does this. It doesn't take long for that pleasure to build and burn inside me. It feels like I'm going to explode as he finds that spot over and over again, tapping at it. All the muscles in my body tense and I sit up.

"Oliver, please," I cry as he drives those fingers back inside. He loves this, making me crazy. "Prick!" I yell, but he just smiles brightly. I shake my head, begging him. The slickness that's going to come flooding out, it's going to kill me.

"Doesn't it feel so good," he says with a sadistic smile, tap, tapping those fingers inside me. "Don't you want me to force the come out of you?" His laugh is maddening.

"I thought," I gasp. "I thought I was hypnotizing you. I thought you had to do what I told you to, like a good boy." I smile at him with challenge as he sinks those fingers deeper inside, the curl of his fingers making me slide my hips forward to chase them down. I have no control, this has gone on too long.

"I've never been a very good boy. Just look how panicked you are. Oh baby, don't worry, it'll feel good. I promise. I bet one day you'll actually want me to do this to you. One day I'll lay you down and keep doing it until you lose your mind and beg me to stop."

I lean forward and grab his wrist between my legs. I shake my head, panicked. "Don't!" I tell him. "Please don't!"

His hand halts. "Do you think you can stop me?" he says as my hold gets tighter. I claw at his wrist.

"I know I can't stop you," I tell him. I hold my mouth open and pant as he slides his fingers deeper, tapping again on the way out. If I'm completely honest, I don't want to stop him. This orgasm will be soul shattering. I've thought about it multiple times. I've wanted him to do it again, but I can't tell him that. Not right now while I'm trying to be strong.

I clench around his fingers, and he groans. "That's it, baby. I know you want to come for me." He pulls his fingers out and slams them back inside, getting rougher.

I fall back against the pillows. My hips lift and I scream. I feel so much wetness slide out, my cheeks heat in embarrassment. What he's doing makes me feel like I need to pee. The urge is so strong a part of me wishes I could, then it'd relieve this terrifying feeling.

Oliver doesn't stop. I come, screaming like a banshee, bucking my hips up. The pleasure is so intense it borders on pain. I can't take much more. He laughs as he leans down and sucks my clit in between his lips. My hips thrust against his mouth, needing more even though I'm currently mid-orgasm. All the while he continues to fuck me with those curled fingers.

I can't stop screaming as it intensifies. It's agony and ecstasy all at once. I feel him smile against my slit. I grab his head in my hands and hold him down against me as I lift my hips and grind over his mouth. I come so hard and for so long that eventually my body goes lax with the exhaustion of it, my head flying back into the pillows.

My hips still and I let him go even as the aftermath of that orgasm makes my body tremble and shake. I think this is it, I'm going to pass out. I felt like this the last time he did this.

His hand slides up over my stomach, then over my left breast as I shake from the sensation. He thumbs my nipple as he takes one last lick up through my wet folds. He pulls those talented fingers from inside me, and my slick glistens like honey on them. I can't look away. I'm fascinated at how he stares hungrily at those fingers.

Then he paints it across each breast. I shiver with each wet touch, and my nipples shine with my release as the breeze chills them. He looks up at me with hot, hooded eyes and slides those fingers past my lips. He's silent, watching me with devotion so strong it borders on obsession, as I suck his fingers in deeper, consuming every drop left. When he pulls them out, he smiles like a devil.

Oliver moves with such speed, licking up over my stomach, circling one breast before sucking a nipple into his mouth. He suctions so hard it stings, but then he soothes the ache by flicking his tongue over it. I arch my back, trying to get away. He lifts off with a popping sound and our eyes meet. His head tilts to the side, his long hair falling forward and tickling my stomach. His eyes are so dark they reflect the fire from the candles, and it's like he's lit up with an absolute primal need. He's more animal than man.

He licks a straight line across my chest. Each swipe of his tongue painting my skin in fire. Everything he does feels more than good, it's amazing. It feels like magic washing over me. He's right, there's no other word for these things. My Oliver, he's magical.

He lifts off my other nipple and studies me again. He tilts his head, those eyes lighting up. I'm in awe of him. "How is it possible that you're so beautiful?" I ask. "There's no creature, no human, no being more beautiful than you. How do you even exist?"

Oliver leans forward and holds himself up with a palm against the burgundy bedspread. He gets in my face. "I told you. I was made for you," he whispers. "Just like you're the most beautiful being I've ever seen."

My eyes fill with tears, but they don't spill over. I grab his face in both of my hands and nod my head. "Do you know what that means, Oliver? It's not your magic that keeps me drawn to you. It's just you." I wait for those words to hit home. He'd said he wanted it to be real between us, well, I don't think it could get anymore real.

His eyes shine, that unique green lifting the darkness from his eyes. Then he moves, shifting his pants lower on his hips and pulling his cock over the waistband. He's like a wave, crashing into me, sinking into my body so achingly slow. My mouth opens and I release a solitary rush of breath when he bottoms out inside my body. He tosses his head back and his jaw clenches. The moment his eyes close, his tears fall. I watch them slide over his cheeks.

I reach for him. "It's okay, baby. I'm here with you. Let it out. I love you."

He tilts his face down and those tears shine. I brush his hair to the side and tuck it behind his ear, then run a finger across his forehead and down his temple, over the top of his cheek, and down to that sharp jaw. I cup it in my palm.

"You feel like love," he gasps. "Being near you feels like love. Being inside you is love. Every single piece of you embodies love. I've never been loved, Vale. You're my first, my last."

I lift up and wrap my arms around him. We fall back against the blankets, and he kisses me desperately. I roll my hips back and wrap my legs around his waist, dragging him closer. I can never get close enough.

He grabs my hands and slides them above my head, our fingers intertwined. I cradle his body with my own as he stretches out above me. My back arches even as he holds me down. Our arms touch, our chests press against each other's. He's hard and thick inside me, stretching me open.

When he shifts his hips back, my core tightens around him. I don't want him to pull away, I'm aching again. But then he thrusts his hips forward, sinking his full length inside slowly, gently. He glides in so perfectly. It almost feels like too much, like he can't possibly get any deeper, yet he does. He sets an unhurried rhythm with his hips that fully captures my attention. How could this be any better? It always gets better though.

I feel him everywhere. His eyes are all I see, his body all I feel. He is my oxygen in that moment. The world outside of us ceases to exist. The song fades. The night fades. The stars in the sky, the moon, it's all of little consequence because we are one.

We get lost in one another's eyes like this moment could end at any second. Every single shared breath counts. It's love, strength, and absolute devotion. We're lost to the rhythm of each other. This isn't just lust, not just a desire for the ages. This is soul deep, a bond that can never be broken. I feel it all when we're like this.

Those long thrusts pierce through the shroud of my longing. My body quickens with every slow, drawn-out press into me. I tilt my head back and a desperate moan is freed from my lips. My energy builds, the flames licking out over my skin. I'm too overwhelmed by the feel of him to care when they shoot into his chest and his hips falter.

Something is about to happen, I can feel it. Oliver widens his eyes when he feels it too. There's a buzz of electricity in the air, stinging and poignant against our skin. It's as if every moment together has been leading to right here, right now. Our breathing kicks up, hearts beating faster, syncing. Tendrils of flames wrap us both up tightly, sinking into each other's hearts, tethering us further.

Oliver frees my arms. He pulls his knees up under him and lifts me up over his lap. I slide down his thick shaft and he bottoms out. The buzzing becomes louder, my flames growing with bright light.

He places one of my arms around his neck, then tears into his own wrist with his fangs. He slides it to my lips while his eyes grow darker, the shadows swirling with the glowing green. I don't suction my mouth onto the wound until he grabs my other arm and sinks his teeth into me.

We move on instinct. Our bodies sync up as we take the first taste together. We've shared blood before. We've shared our bodies. But this is something different. This is heavenly power that filters through us, bringing us together like a sudden lightning strike. There are no beings closer in this moment as my awareness flows through him and his through mine.

We float in that warm place, bodies sliding, sweat beading, pleasure flowing into each other. Time has no meaning. He's inside me just as much as I fill him. We throb, we ache, we come together, and I realize our souls really are one. This is what made it so. Our power, our hunger, our blood, our flames, our love had to be utilized at that exact moment.

It was fate.

His wound heals, and I toss my head back, crying out to the heavens, thanking God for his generous gift that is my mate. I'm so grateful for him. Oliver wraps his arms around me, pulling me closer. When I'm able to look into those eyes again, I see it. He feels it. We are one.

Our faces are barely an inch apart. We float along on waves of pleasure, of lovemaking. Our bodies shake with it. I can feel what he feels. I feel his cock tighten and swell. I feel the come rushing through it and spilling into my heat. I feel an orgasm, but it feels so much different from my own. We cry out as one. We sink into the devastating pleasure as one. We are a solitary being, one of complete love.

"Forever," we moan into each other's mouths.

52

ONE

OLIVER

The world around us melts away. Nothing else exists. I am her breath. I am her heartbeat. I am her love and her lust. I am her fire, her magic, her soul. But above all else, we are one, finally complete. We bonded through fire. We bonded with rings from the mortal world. We bonded with the blood of vampires and the lust of Lilu.

For the first time in my life, I feel whole. There's no emptiness anymore, no loneliness because she's there. I reach into her, sliding over her consciousness, sharing exactly how I feel as we come down and her fire cools. I hear her echoing words in my head, *I feel it too.*

We're fully bonded and neither of us could have stopped it. It was instinctual. It happened naturally without so much as a thought to urge it on. We became one there on the rooftop, under the stars and the moon she loves so much.

Our love is blessed.

"Say something else inside my head," I tell her as I smile in awe of this woman. She's everything.

Did the hypnosis work after all? she asks.

I laugh as I see my own face in her mind. The way she sees me, the fuzzy, golden light that shimmers around the edges of the vision, the way it makes her heart race. No one has ever seen me like this. She was right when she said it wasn't my magic. She just loves me, and this is real. It was always real, and that was why I couldn't get her out of my head.

Her truth triggers such happiness inside me. "I love you, Vale."

"I love you," she says and smiles up at me. "This is the best night of my life. We are one. I see the way you see me. I can feel your heartbeat. I can feel you breathing. I feel the hunger inside you. I can speak to you there now. It's easy. I didn't know this would happen. It's beautiful." She's in awe of the bond, as am I. It feels so easy, so simple when nothing has ever been simple. It seems we can have it all.

Tears wave over her aqua eyes, but I know for sure she isn't sad. I feel her absolute, blissful happiness in how we're bonded. Her head is tilted as she studies my face. She sees the same in me. Her hands lift to cup my cheeks, and she takes in a deep breath.

"I always knew you were the one for me. I may not have been able to feel that attraction for others, but I knew it when I felt it for you." Vale shows me her first memory of me. She plays it like a movie reel in my head. I feel how her body sung for the first time with attraction and desire. How fast her heart beat even as her lungs seized. I feel how hard it was for her to speak, to move. She'd been so overwhelmed by it she hadn't known what to do.

Then I show her what I saw. How I watched her from the shadows before I said hello. She was lit up, unlike anything else that surrounded her. She shone with life, with that energy. Vale takes a deep breath when she sees Nick and how different he looks from her, how muted his skin tone, his hair, and features are. It was hard to look at him when she stood there.

I show her the night I kissed her, how I felt when she shook in my hands, intimidated by what she felt for me. I show her what I saw when she sat on that stool and looked through her telescope. In every image she shone like gold while everything else was muted in color.

"That's how you see me? Why is everything else so dark?"

Memories of my life flash in quick succession in her mind. "Everything is muted compared to you," I explain. "I didn't live until I saw you. I've only been surviving. I lived in a state of changeless apathy, Vale. It was like living in black and white until you showed up. Then suddenly I was blessed with vivid color."

Vale sobs with a devastation so great as she feels the lonely state I was in for so long. It breaks her beautiful heart. "How did you survive?" she cries as she squeezes me in tight against her chest.

"The demon inside promised you'd come back. Hope hurts, but it's also a blessing. Have you not noticed how he thinks you were in this world before? He knew you were our mate from the beginning. It was only me who denied it. I'm sorry for that."

Our eyes meet and she seems a bit nervous. "He does know me, Oliver. I've known him most of my life."

Her bright memories flash in my head. *There's a little girl stuck in nightmares. She chokes on sobs as the darkness surrounds her. She feels like she's being suffocated by them. The darkness wraps around her throat like large hands as she screams and thrashes.*

The beast appears, looking around like he doesn't belong in this nightmare. It isn't one of ours. Then he sees the little girl, the only source of light in the dream. She glows in the shadows. She's afraid, scared of the new monster, but he smiles at her. He's gentler than I would have imagined him to be.

"My fiery Princess, would you like me to kill them for you?" he asks her with a huge grin, like he'd destroy anything for her.

"Help me!" the little flame-haired girl cries. "Please!" Her cries hurt my heart.

The monster beats back the shadows that try to trap her, try to hurt her, and choke her tiny neck. When he's finished and the sun rises over the dreamscape, she runs to him without a thought. She wraps her tiny arms around him and cries into his stomach where she hides her face.

He kneels before her. "I'll protect you, little one. I swear it."

Little Vale's cheeks are red, tears streaming as she watches him. "Are you a demon?"

"I am Ashmodai," he says proudly, a fist coming to his chest as if he speaks to a general and not a tiny girl. "And you, what's your name now, little one."

"I'm Vale Granger. I live in Atlanta, Georgia. I'm six years old," *she tells him, her tears slowly stopping. "Thank you for making them* *go away. I don't like them. They hurt me, Ashmodai."*

He picks her up in his arms. "Do you know who all monsters *fear?"*

"I don't. I'm afraid of monsters," she says sadly.

"They're afraid of the biggest, baddest monster of all," he says *with a smile.*

"The demon As-mo-de-us," she says slowly, with wide eyes while *she stares up at his face. It makes me laugh.*

"Oh no, little one. They're afraid of me."

"You're a beautiful monster, Ashmodai. Can I braid your pretty *hair?" she asks as if what he'd said meant nothing to her. She isn't* *afraid. She gives him her trust blindly, like any small child might a* *superhero.*

Vale speeds the dreams up, showing me all the pretty dreams they shared. She became a brave girl in her dreams, but if she was hurting, he always comforted her.

"My fiery Queen, he calls you. I never knew why. He didn't show me these dreams, but there have been times when he disappeared from my consciousness for long periods. It makes sense now that he was with you. I'm glad he comforted you, protected you from your nightmares."

"I can't wait to braid your pretty hair," she says with a silly grin.

"It all makes sense now. You like my unfashionably long hair because you loved him. Do I get a daisy chain as well?"

"I'll make you a daisy chain if you promise to fly our future chil-dren around, like you did with me." Her smile is so sweet, making me think of those children we would have one day. I hope they all look like her.

"I don't know how—" I never get the chance to finish. The change takes me and suddenly she's holding on tight to my neck. We lift on wings that seem to know what they're doing already. I hold her tightly to my chest as we hover about six feet off the ground. My heart is pounding. I shouldn't be doing this, someone could see us. I could get us both hurt.

"There's my beautiful monster." There's such love in her eyes when she looks at me. My mate is the most beautiful woman in all the world. I love her with all of my being, even the monster that stirs inside me.

"Always and forever," I tell her because I know we'll have it always, our forever, together, as one.

53

A LOVE LIKE THAT

ASMODEUS

I float inside the veil between worlds, just outside of their reality. I watch them. I spy on that precious, most beautiful explosion when two halves finally collide, becoming one. The power radiates out of them and across the cosmos. Such beautiful chaos.

Their love puts a smile on my face and brings tears to my eyes. I understand now why Lucifer coveted those souls so much. I understand why he yearned for that gift. My brother Lucy, ever the asshole, was one lucky angel. He was promised a soul, a happily-ever-after of sorts. The Light thought he was entitled to it. We weren't all promised such a glorious fate. Some of us held down the fort and held out hope that we'd be blessed as well.

Not me though. The woman I loved, she had no soul. I'd loved her before time existed. I held out hope that one day we would be mated, though it only happened to the soul blessed. I've waited for so long. I've loved her from the shadows. I've protected our offspring. I've given them everything, even though she hates me.

I take one last look at Vale and Ash, my light shining in both of them. I feel their connection in my heart, and it makes me so happy. I hope it's enough. I hope they're brave and strong in their love, so they can survive their future trials. For there will undoubtedly be many.

I regret nothing. I don't regret parting with a bit of my light for their happiness. I don't regret bringing her back. To see this beautiful match is worth every torture, every pain it's brought me. You see, my angelic brothers believe I'm mad. They believe I brought her back without care for them and their well-being. The Angel Killer, the balancing fire, the annihilator, the limb of Asherah.

There are only two beings who can unmake angels. The Light, which created them, and the wife Asherah, who was the embodiment of chaos. Before the goddess Asherah ceased to be, she created an immortal. They had within them the power of cleansing fire. A power so strong, so feared that the entire supernatural world had been afraid of them at one time. Now they were little more than legend, forgotten long ago.

Even though they were immortal, they often died very human deaths. Their magic was strong, but their bodies were not. If they weren't burned to ashes after death, they wouldn't be reborn. They were lost so long ago, hunted to extinction. Asherah was left to balance the scales, but she had no worshippers, and lost her strength, ceasing to exist like so many other gods. Her last gifts were to Lilith, the blood, creating the first vampire and the Angel Killers, her fire.

My grandson Ashmodai was fated to the last one, but she was gone with no memory of what she'd been. Her soul was floating in the veil, trapped and hidden there by someone or something. She was lost until I found her.

I searched for a vessel for her soul, and it was fortuitous when a human man, Phillip Granger, began to call my name, worshipping me as if I was some god. Honestly, it disgusts me how he drew these humans from the Light to worship someone he compared to a devil. His beliefs gained traction though, and he was able to form a cult. Then he married a pretty young premed student named Shannon Dalton from Silver Springs, Georgia.

Shannon was unique, she carried vampire genes, the blood of Asherah. Not enough to turn but enough that she could carry Vale to term and birth her back into the world.

I did all I could to bring her back for Ashmodai. I knew he'd find her in the end because that's how mates are. They find each other because they must. Still, I did all I could to steer them to each other. They must be complete, and he'd struggled for too long without her. The soul was never meant to be split. It was a punishment to all immortals, that came with such an amazing side effect, fated mates. Their curse became their salvation. The bond so strong when two beings shared one soul.

I left the veil, inspired by their new bond. I'll see my love. It's been a few weeks since I visited her, but her silence is painful to behold. "My beautiful Lilith, I've missed you," I speak into the darkness. I unveil the halo I try to keep hidden in the mortal world, and it lights up the large tomb.

"My love, your grandson is now bonded to his mate. I made sure of their union before coming here. I thought you would want to know. I hope this news gives you some happiness."

Lilith has slept for a thousand years. Her porcelain skin wraps tightly around her bones. She's starving herself, trying to find a peace the Light may never grant her. Her beautiful hair continues to grow, even in her self-imposed exile. It's so long it spills over the edge of her stone resting place. Once it had been as red as fresh blood, but now it's dull like dried straw.

I hold out my palm and call the dust around her. It's much easier to manifest from something, rather than nothing. I mold the matter, creating a hairbrush, then run it through the long strands, getting the tangles out. Afterward, I plait it for her again. I've done it many times. I do try to care for my Lilith's earthly body even when she will not. I call fresh water and a soft cloth and rinse the dust from her skin while tears fill my eyes.

"I think the first time I cried was when you birthed our son. Those months before his birth and after were the happiest of my existence. I miss the days when you allowed me to love you, Lilith. You know, I still love you. I wish you would come back to me."

I tell her of Tiberius and his granddaughter Lily, who was named after her. I tell her of Lais and all the beautiful grandchildren she bore.

I tell her how she'll be a great-grandmother again when Gabriella gives birth.

"I saw Ash and Vale unite. It made me long to be at your side. I don't need a soul to know that you're the only woman I'll ever love. One hundred thousand years could pass between us and I'd still live with the hope of belonging to you again. I'll always be here, waiting for you. I'll always watch over our children. I swear it."

I promised her, every time she slept for long periods, that I'd watch over them. I have done my best, hoping the choices I've made will be looked upon kindly by her when her eyes open again. I want her to look at me with love again.

It takes hours to cleanse her body of dust, but in truth I slow my actions purposely. Her hair braided and secured, I clip and file her nails. I run floral oils into her skin so it doesn't crack. With every touch my heart breaks. I press my ear to her chest, listening for a heartbeat to thunder to life. It still beats, but it's been so long since she's fed that I don't know when the thump will come. I've been here for hours now and not heard it beat, not even a shallow breath.

"I'm worried, for this body is much worse for wear than it has been in the past. How long must you do this?" I ask as I lean in over her face, watching and waiting for her to inhale.

My tears fall on her face, dripping down over the extreme angles of her emaciated cheekbones. They slide across her skin, all the way to her mouth, where they disappear through her barely parted lips. She drinks my pain.

"Will you feed on my tears, dearest Lilith?"

I press my lips against hers. I breathe deep, trying to pull her scent into my lungs, but her blood isn't flowing. It's only dust in her veins and no matter how I wish she'd awaken, she hasn't in so long. She's been asleep for much longer this time.

"When you come back, will you please love me again? Please love me," I cry over her, hoping my tears revive her. "Dammit, Lilith! I love you. Don't leave me. Please wake up."

I grab her head in my hands, watching. Once she woke up by my very presence alone because her hatred burned so brightly. I'd fucked everything up. She's hated me for so much longer than she'd ever loved me. But I wouldn't give up, I couldn't. She was as much a part of me as the Light.

"I need you in this world," I sigh.

I should leave her here. This is what she wanted. She wants to sleep. But conflict is coming and she has to open her eyes. I do the thing that will make her hate me even more than when she went to sleep. I tear into the meat of my hand with my teeth. I make it hurt as punishment for what I do now. I pry her lips apart with my thumb, just enough, and drip the golden ichor into her mouth. I watch as it spills between her lips. I'm desperate for her to wake. The world needs her. I need her.

Drastic changes happen over her body as the ichor fills each cell, healing all that'd been broken, all that'd been starved. Her cheeks already look much less hollow. I look down at her hips. Before they looked like jagged knives about to burst through her delicate skin. Now her flesh is filling with life.

By the time I look back up at her face, I notice the long braid is the color of blood once more. My beautiful Lilith will come back. Her face is no longer that of sunken death. Her plump lips fill with blood, her cheeks fill out and flush rosy. Every moment I watch she becomes more beautiful. She's the most exquisite female to ever be created, all pale in comparison to her.

Her stomach fills in, no longer concave under her ribs, and her thick hips flare, rounded and the perfect place for my hands to pull her over me, onto me. How I remember those nights with her, how I yearn to have them again.

Right now, the divine blood fills her. She looks the same as the first time I saw her in the Garden before Asherah's blood changed her forever. Tears fill my eyes for how she'd been cursed. If only she had wanted me. If only I could have protected her. Maybe we'd still be there now.

I climb onto the stone altar and kneel between her legs. My wings flare out behind me as I hover above her, imagining our life together. The Light allowed me to witness the creation of Lilith. I was nearly new myself at that time, but from the moment I saw her form take shape, I knew she was meant for me. The Light hadn't breathed life into her yet, but they knew what I felt. They were proud of me for the love I had in my heart. My maker was proud of me and my love's creation meant it was one of the best days of my life.

I lower myself against her cool skin, placing my ear on her chest and wait. The first beat of her heart isn't loud. In fact, it isn't a true beat at all. It sounds more like rushing water, but then, like magic, there's a soft pump as the muscles contract. It hasn't yet filled with blood, so I wait for another and another. Soon it beats so fast, every thump strong, furious. Lilith will be furious with me.

I hear her deep, crackling inhale, opening her airways wide. The blood flows and suddenly her scent floods the room around me. She smells of Eden, a place long lost to the both of us. She smells like astringent herbs mixed with honeysuckle and violets. The musk of her skin is earthy, woodsy with hints of sweet vanilla. But all that is nothing without the jasmine that wafts from her hair, mingling it all together, tempering the herbs, making her scent softer, sweeter. I breathe her in the way humans inhale drugs. My entire body awakens. Her scent is an aphrodisiac for my angelic body.

Lilith wouldn't like me hovering above her, so I grab her body and flip mine below hers, letting her arms and legs sprawl out around me. I make myself smaller, the size of a human male. Her head falls at my shoulder, and I wait some more. Why isn't she awake yet? She's healed. She's alive. She breathes. Her heart beats wildly, echoing in the tomb around me like a marching drum.

"I don't know if you listen while you sleep anymore, but I often come to speak with you, to tell you about our children and our grandchildren. Today, I witnessed a miraculous thing, my love. I saw Ashmodai bond with his mate. Her name's Vale. She's a beautiful Angel Killer who got lost between worlds. I brought her back for him, for his happiness. They're beautiful, so full of love." He smiles once more.

"I saw them, and I had to come. I've missed you so much, but our world . . . it needs you. Our children need you. Will you fight with me once more?"

I sit up on my elbows the moment I feel her limbs jerk awake. Her breathing picks up, her heart speeding up. I hold my breath as I watch her come back to life. Her body jerks as if she's having a seizure, but I know she's just stiff from being on her back for centuries. Her head swings back on her neck with an audible crack, and it's gruesome. I run my hands over her back, her arms, and the base of her neck. I try to comfort her because I know how much it hurts.

She screams into my chest, her vocal cords not yet able to speak. She cries in pain and tries to lift her head, but she can't. Her hissing breath is frequent against my chest. Her limbs flail against me, kicking and scratching at my skin. She's fighting so hard to come alive.

"Be still, my love, it will pass. I assure you, this pain will pass," I whisper as I continue to rub my hands over every muscle I can reach.

The agonizing cry that escapes from her lips is horrifying. I know what she thinks. I'm bringing her back to torture her once more, but that isn't my intention. We need her. She must know that we're destined to fight together or fail. If we fail, our children will die. All the beautiful immortal lives will die along with them. She had to have known.

I hold her for over an hour, massaging her skin as she twitches in spurts and fits on top of me. I wish I could take this pain away. I wish I could end the pain for her, but I can't. The Light cursed her for her unholy desires. She's the only immortal who can't truly die because she's not, and never has been, the same as any of us. She is wholly different, a unique being who could never be recreated, a failure in the Light's eyes.

Lilith's body is still, her breathing calm, her heart slowing. I sit up with her in my lap, holding on to her hips so she doesn't fall to the floor. I lean forward to see if she can hold her head up yet, but she presses her face into the crook of my neck, hiding.

"Will you not look at me, my love?" I ask and lean in to place a kiss at the juncture between her shoulder and neck. Lilith tenses at the touch of my lips and it feels like a knife to the heart. She hates me, I know she does. She's told me many times, but I wish so much that it wasn't like this between us.

"I—" Lilith gasps with a cough. She tries to clear her throat. "I cannot."

"Have you listened to me at all over these centuries when I've visited you? I've cared for our children. They're safe."

Lilith curls into herself, sinking lower to my sternum, her back bending as she tries to get smaller in my arms. Her stuttered breaths scare me. I don't want her to cry.

"Everything you say is a lie to prey upon my heart. You're worse than Lucifer," she growls as her shoulders tighten with rage. I should have known it wasn't her tears she'd offer me, but her hatred.

I grab her shoulders and lean her back. I lift her chin, seeing her gorgeous, healed face finally. Her eyes are still sealed shut. She's punishing me, rightly so. I deserve all her ire.

"I'm not like Lucy. If I were, I would have finished my task already. I would have been rewarded, but I haven't because I love only you. I want only you. No other being will do. You must listen to me, Lilith. Hear the truth in my words."

I see the tightening of her eyes right before she opens them. I can barely take in air for the beauty they behold. Those emerald eyes that glow with power, doom me every time. They're filled with such a painful desire that I can't fathom the hunger there.

I grip her face in my hands as she watches me warily. I lean in closer; I can't stop myself, I need to kiss my woman. She licks her lips as we stare each other down. I get closer with every second that passes. I lick at her sweet lips. "I love you, Lilith. I want you to belong to me, the way I'll always belong to you."

My beautiful Lilith, how sweet she tastes. I breathe her in as I lick at her lips. I watch as her eyelids close, but her lips don't move against mine. She doesn't touch me back. She sits there, and I can't take it.

My jaw tightens and my heart throbs painfully in my chest. "Will you never kiss me again?" It hurts so badly that she doesn't want me. I'm the embodiment of lust but there is nothing I can ever do to make her want me again.

I pull away. "I'm sorry. I shouldn't have kissed you." My shoulders slump in defeat.

"You should be sorry, Asmodeus, but your kiss is inconsequential. It matters not. You wake me to a world of pain, of hunger. You hurt me so by bringing me back. You promised you would not this time. You promised. I, who have only asked you for this, and yet you deny me with your broken promises and selfishness. You are a deceitful being who chooses yourself in all things," she says in a hateful tone as I shake my head in denial.

"Deny it all you want, but I know why you wake me now. It is not to fight at your side, to protect our child. It is for the lust you have at being denied my body for too long. You run out of mortals to play with and so you need me," she spits as if anything I want is so simple. I wish it were. I shake my head vehemently, and she laughs. She grabs my throat between her hands and squeezes. She's not trying to kill me, she can't, Asherah never gave her that fire.

"Our children!" I yell back. "The two children we have! Not just one. Tiberius isn't the only child we have, but they both need to be protected now. I swear that to you, Lilith. I won't deceive you about them."

The skin beside her lips twitches for a moment before she grins sadistically. "I do not know this other child. I do not know her. You took her from me! You stole Lais! You stole her from my womb! You deceitful creature!"

I don't deny it. I did it. I stole her from the womb. "I would not let his wrath pollute them both."

She laughs, letting my neck go. "Samael was kind, beautiful, and sweet. He loved me. He sacrificed his Light for me," she whispers, pained by the thought of him.

There it is. Even though I've sacrificed my light, pieces given to our offspring and their offspring. "You covet a being whose apathy was the same as his love. He left you. Samael was not built for love, he was built for death," I yell back. That's who she always wants. That's who she would love.

"Who has stayed in this world to protect our offspring, to watch over you, to fight for you even though you hate me? It wasn't him. He hasn't spent a solitary day being a father. He feels nothing but directive. I do! I have done everything for you. I understand, you'll never love me, but I will never give up. I will love you till this world ceases to exist and the Light starts over, a day which will come soon enough."

She slaps me across the face. "He gave up his light for me! How dare you? Everything you do is to serve yourself!"

I grab her face in my palms again. She doesn't struggle but anger flairs deep in her eyes. "You keep saying it, but that doesn't make it true, Lilith. I will only tell you this one more time. Samael never gave up his light for you. He's still celestial. He is death. I can't give up my light for you because it's what gives me the power to protect our children. It's how I could find our grandson's mate. The ichor is what brings you back. My light is the power to heal them, to save you. I cannot give it up."

I place my hand over her heart, where my crescent moon mark shimmers. It was a gift to her when she left, a promise of my love, but she's always deemed it a curse. Sometimes I wish I could go back to then and change things. If she loved me sooner, maybe we'd still be there now.

There's a single moment when she looks like she feels more than hatred for me. I wish I knew what it was. I wish I knew that emotion. I wish I could tease it out of her. I wish it was love.

Lilith forces me down to the table and though I could fight her, I don't. I give in to her anger. I allow her to manhandle me. The way her hips slide down my body is sexual and for a moment I believe she may finally believe me. If hope made things right, she would never have slept. She would be with me.

She grabs my hands in her own and draws them taut over my head. My halo flickers and reacts to Lilith. Her tits are near my face. I wish I could wrap my lips around them and suckle her. It makes me think of the old days and how often she used to come with my mouth on them.

"Still so pretty, Asmodeus. Some say Lucy is the most beautiful, but I never agreed. I think you are the finest, most handsome of all. The Light knew what lust should be and they gave you the most beautiful face, the most beautiful body with the greatest cock ever known, and it has been well known, hasn't it," she purrs, then slides down my waist, placing her sex over me.

I'm surprised by her wetness. I'm surprised she'll touch me at all after I said anything negative about Samael. "It was well loved by you for a while," I tell her. Once upon a time, I spent all my nights inside her.

Lilith smiles darkly. "That it was. Will you let me love it now?"

"I'm yours." I look up into her gorgeous green eyes that darken with lust. "Have me."

There's no foreplay, no loving distractions. I know what she's doing. She's going to torture me with her body. She'll take her pleasure, then leave me. I deserve this. I deserve the pain she'll leave me with because I have caused her pain. I give her my willful surrender anyway because I can't help myself. I am lust. I am hers.

Lilith raises her hips over mine, my cock standing straight up since her weight is no longer holding it down, then she sinks onto my tip. I hiss as her cool core envelopes and spasms around me.

"New jewelry?" she questions when she feels the first barbell sink inside her. Her back arches up as she lets my wrists go. She looks down between our bodies, where she slides onto me.

"One for every century you slept. You weren't here to punish me, so I had to do it myself. Do you like it?"

Lilith doesn't answer. She stays bent, watching herself take me. I'm not in my full angelic form because it's hard to hold it in this plane. I'm not small by any means. Even in a more human-sized form, I'm much larger than most of them. I'm lust, and I'm endowed with a very impressive cock. That's not me bragging, it's the truth.

"It's been so long, my love."

Lilith's head pops up, and I finally get to see myself entering her. Each ring gets tugged as it enters her, causing the slightest pain.

"Does it hurt?" she asks as she slides down my cock, sinking down over the next one. She tilts her head back and moans.

"Hurts so bad, Lilith. Hurt me some more," I beg, knowing how wet it always makes her for me to beg. Oh, how she loves to torture me.

She's only fallen down over six barbells, but she lifts up anyway to the very tip. Her head tilts forward, eyes wide, and she slams her body down hard, taking me to the root. She screams because it hurts her.

My jaw clenches, my breath coming painfully fast. Lilith's fingernails dig into the flesh of my chest as she lifts herself again and slams down. She closes her eyes, unable to look at me. She batters her body with mine, using my cock as the blade to hurt herself.

Tears fill my eyes. "It doesn't have to hurt," I tell her.

Just to prove me wrong, she slams down doubly hard and shakes with the pain of it. The next time she lifts up, I see her blood shimmer with ichor on my cock. I break loose from her thrall and grab her hips. I steady her, but I don't try to control her. No one controls Lilith.

"The act shouldn't hurt you, my love. It should never hurt."

Her body slides slowly down my shaft again. Bloody tears that shimmer with glitter fall over her cheeks when she looks at me. "My body or my heart, it always hurts. You do this to me, Asmodeus. You see this pain, but you wake me up anyway. You hurt me so much," she cries. "What did I ever do to you to deserve this? Why can't you let me go?"

Lilith shakes like a human who's freezing out in the elements. I wrap my arms around her, clinging to her. She doesn't hug me back, she would never, not anymore.

"I'm sorry. I'll beg the Light to forgive you, to free you. I'll release you. I'm sorry." My heart breaks as I say the words. I remove my arms from her body and try to pull away, but she stops me.

"You'll ask them for my end?" she asks with a hope in her eyes I despise. "You will gift me with my end."

I shake my head. "I can't, Lilith. Don't ask me to do that."

"Why?" she asks, confused. I don't understand how she doesn't get it.

"Lilith, I know you don't believe me, but I love you. Please remember that I loved you back then. I love you now. My love for you has never once wavered. I may have screwed up time and time again, but my love remains. I have loved you from the moment you were created, before you were given the breath of life. When I am gone, my love will still echo in the chaos. You may yet get a way out, but I will never be free of you."

Lilith rears back and slaps me across the face again. "Why do you still lie to me?"

"You and I both know I can't lie. I may be able to omit things, to circle the truth, but I'm no liar!"

"You are! You promised you would not wake me. You promised," she screams in my face, her cheeks turning red, her body heating up. "If you break a promise, it is a lie."

"I promised to only wake you if our children were in danger. I promised only if they needed you. I let you sleep for a thousand years. Even when your children suffered, I let you sleep, and I did what I could, but I can't fight what's coming alone. We need you. The Fata claims we must fight together, all of us, or we die."

Lilith snarls at me. "I hate you, Asmodeus! I hate you."

"You already know what my feelings are. I love you with my entire self. I love you infinitum. I'm truly sorry I hurt you. If I had a soul, it would belong to you, just as my heart belongs only to you."

Lilith slams her fist through my sternum, snapping bones and ripping organs. She could have gone up through my abdomen, but she chose the most painful path into my chest cavity. It won't kill me, but it's very painful nonetheless. I swallow the cry that wants to bellow from my lips.

"Take it. I told you it was yours. It belongs only to you," I tell her, through painful breaths that don't fully inflate my lungs.

I grab her head and yank her forward. I slam my lips against hers. Lilith opens for me and it's the most spectacular kiss. She fucks my mouth with her tongue as she holds my still beating heart in one of her cruel hands. She slides her thumb over the organ lovingly and I think Lilith might love me. There is hope!

The moment she yanks her body away from mine, she smiles like a devil. I smile back feeling like a winner. I have fought and won the greatest battle. Lilith still loves me!

"I love you, Lilith," I growl a second before she tears my heart out through cracked and splintered ribs.

I have only a few precious moments before my system shuts down entirely, entering a sort of stasis where my light can repair this body. I watch her twisted smile get bigger as she licks the golden ichor from the meat of my heart. There's a moment of awed rapture on her face before she tears into it, her body shivering with a sick kind of excitement. She doesn't look away, not once does her gaze falter, as she sucks my heart's blood into her mouth, using my torn aorta like a straw.

I use up the rest of my strength to grin at her. How I love her beautiful cruelty. I love this fucking woman.

THEY'LL BE BACK

Vale and Oliver will return in Queen of Fire, 2026.
Along with them,
Asmodeus.
Here's to the lady puddles!
Stay Hydrated.

ACKNOWLEDGMENTS

Thank you for reading *Prince of Lust*. I hope you enjoyed it and want to leave a review as it really does help indie authors. This story isn't finished yet. Vale and Oliver, Asmodeus, Lais, and even Gramps are coming back with a bang. Especially Asmodeus. Because that guy, damn, isn't he one hell of a man? He's at the heart of this series, always. From this book out, you'll hear a lot more from him. But I couldn't allow him to overshadow Vale and Oliver's story, because he's good at doing that kind of thing. He enjoys being the center of attention.

I want to say a big thanks to the people who, without them, this book wouldn't exist. To Riley L., you're an inspiration! Thank you so much. To Sarah McGuire from By the By Editing, I don't know what I would do without you. I'm grateful for our long Zooms and your knowledge and experience. I'm so sorry as well, Sarah. I should have warned you that I'm chaos incarnate. Thank you for being on the team and believing in my story even when I don't seem to understand the basics of the English language. You're the best.

To my ARC readers and street team, you're some of the most amazing people I've ever met. Emily Jenary, I'm glad I could teach you about vampires. Your early review was amazing. To my insane, soul sister Stevie (we must have been separated at birth), girl, I love you, you're my type of chaos. To MT Duke and Mel, I can't imagine a world without you two in it, and I'll be standing in line to buy your book. To Erika, Nicole, and Gina, your friendship through this has helped me hold myself together, thank you for your support. To

Brooke, thank you for your support. To Grace, for her truly kind and loving heart, who gives it her all to support indie authors, I'll always remember you. To Beatriz, who wrote a review that had me crying for hours, you're a fantastic human being. Thank you for just being you. To Sarah, my first friend on the socials, thank you for your kindness, for showing up, and being patient with this boomer. To Pedro, Raquel, and Betty, who are forever in my heart, you are brilliant, lovely people.

To the unbelievable amount of authors who have reached out to me to show support, thank you. To Cassie Alexander, who told me to appreciate the little things, you're so right. To Layla Fae, you're my hero, thank you. To Lu Langley, another soul sister, this hick loves her Brit. To Fenella J. Rookery, I really don't know what I'd do without our friendship. You get me! Thank you for being there.

This book, has been a journey which encompasses twelve years of my life. Twelve years when I'd given up on publishing, but I never gave up on the story. I kept writing. This series is my fight song. It's about overcoming some of the worst trauma with the healing power of love. That's what love is to me. It's a powerful thing that can bring out the best in ourselves, help us grow, and hold us when we need it the most. I wish you all to have that because it's real, and it does exist.

With that message, understand that this book is a love letter to my husband who urged me onward, to live out my dreams. The man who stood up and said, *You're worth taking this chance*. The person who said, *You can do this, Rho. I've got your back*. The person who didn't like romance novels, who said, genuinely, that he loved mine. The man who cheers me on when I'm so low and at my worst, thinking I'll never come out of the trauma spiral. I hope you know, wonderful husband, that your love shines within these pages, glowing brighter than the characters themselves and, without it, this story could never be told. You're the real hero in my story. You're my hero, always.

I hope you take from this book, this series, a knowledge that love lifts us higher, it doesn't tear one down. It makes us better. It makes us want to be better people. But if you have experienced the kind of love that breaks you, that tears you down, please know that there's help available. You never have to suffer in silence, the way I did. Please, get the support you need. If it breaks you, it's not really love, and you're deserving of real love. You are. And never let someone tell you different.

Sincerely,
Dame Rho

GLOSSARY

- **Draw-** Survival Adaptation. A Lilu's innate magic to draw in mortals, so they can feed. This adaptation makes Lilu undeniably attractive to mortals, but not necessarily immortals, it is a remnant of Asmodeus's power as the manifestation of Lust.
- **Lilu-** a male demon who feeds on the sexual energy of mortals, i.e. an Incubus. Used as a name for the entire species of incubi and succubi. Akkadian in origin.
- **Lilitu-** a female demon who feeds on the sexual energy of mortals, i.e. a succubus. Akkadian in origin.
- **Vampire-** a class of immortals who feed on blood. Can be born or made.
- **Angel-** soulless beings created by the light for specific purposes. They have one purpose above all and that is to love humanity. They have manifestation powers. They don't necessarily have a body, but they can create one temporarily. They don't have free will in the same context as one with a soul. There are three types: heavenly, fallen, and death. They're not allowed to interfere with mortals unless the Light tells them to do so.

- **Fallen**- Angel/Celestial being who was asked to work/rule in Hell. Once they fall, they have a body at any time, they don't have to create one. It isn't necessarily a consequence of judgment, though some celestials fall for other reasons, meaning that they're punished for something and the Light throws them out of their heavenly home for a while, but that's normally a short punishment.
- **Fata**- Latin in origin, meaning fate, destiny, or death. The fates. A witch who is given the power to see the past and the future, sometimes called an Oracle. They're coveted by other immortals, so they hide, protecting themselves, leaving their lives behind to serve their gift.
- **The Light**- the God over all that is on Earth, the heavens, and possibly other worlds. They are the God of Creation with such a strength that they give the power of manifestation to its angels. Souls are molded pieces of the Light. Every living thing has a soul, with the exception of Angels (Celestials) and Lilith, or the demon ghosts who escape Hell.

ABOUT THE AUTHOR

Dame Rho is a survivor.